"Diplomacy's End"
'The d'enchia Incident'

Part Three Of The

Ic'nichi - Human Chronicles

Concluding The

First History Of The Interstellar Concord

An Ic'nichi novel translated into human language

by,

Robert A. Boyd

ISBN: 978-0-9851547-8-3
English Trade Paperback Edition

Proceeds from the sale of this work go to support self-published and small press authorship. If you wish to aid this effort, please go to the publisher's website —

The-Written-Wyrd.org

—for further information.

Thank you.

§

*****

A Note From The Human Translator

Sadly, despite ongoing efforts over a period of years, improvements to the translation software have been stymied by the differences between the Ic'nichi and human languages. A number of Ic'nichi words and phrases remain indecipherable, and have, perforce, been given in phonetic form. As is becoming a tradition, an Addenda with possible meanings has been included in the back of this work. We hope this will prove helpful to the reader, since we are at a loss for any other solution.

"Oy, As The Humans Say"
(Related by Defender I'eiBida)

"I'eiBida?"

It was the Staff Herd Guide, which is *never* good news. What did *he* want now? I struggled to the surface of my 'to do' basket, and discreetly tipped my computer screen to one side so he couldn't see what I was reading. "Sir?"

"I have a job for you." He handed me a memo form.

"Sir?" As if I didn't have enough to do. "Not *earth* again?"

He gave me a jaundiced look. "No, thankfully. You're due for a physical." He gestured at the form already forgotten in my hand. "You need to get over to the Institute." He offered a dismissive ear twitch and stomped off to harass the next staffer in the circle.

Needless to say, that caught me completely off guard. I wasn't due for my annual physical for some time yet, and I *was* feeling pretty good lately. Tired of course, with the endless work here on the Staff and at the Academy. If there is any Universal truth besides one's Ancestors seeing every foolish thing one does, it's the paper stampede. The *ui'DmukNa*-shoveling never quits, but since we returned from our last misadventure on earth, I was *finally* getting caught up on my duties. So now all of a sudden they wanted me to have a physical? Why? And why at the Institute, of all places, when the staff physichs at the spaceport clinic could handle such a routine matter? I wasn't sure what to make of it, but it tasted off somehow. Curious, I started reading...

"A *psychological* exam?"

Now I was completely flummoxed. About the only time they give defenders a psych review is when we're recruits, to weed out the potentially violent ones. I went through that when I first joined the 'Green-And-Tans', and again when I transferred to the 'Grays', but aside from that, such things are unknown—unless they think there's something wrong with you.

I slumped on my belly cushion and stared at the wall, trying to grab tail on this. Why a psyche exam? Was I getting erratic from lack of sleep? Pity the junior staffer: the hours are long, the work deadly dull, the paper shuffling relentless, and the gratitude nonexistent. I *was* feeling better, coping with the stress a lot better lately, and the work was flowing faster and smoother than ever. Still, perhaps the load was getting to me and I hadn't noticed? Or was this a third time around because I was now a part of the 'Dark Grays'? Mysterious. I had a sudden premonition nothing good would come of it.

The subdued din of office equipment penetrated my distracted haze, drawing me back to the here-and-now. Our new Admin Circle was a single enormous room, with the Fleet Eldest's grotto in the center and the rest filled with concentric rings of work stations and busy people. We were still moving in here, and the place was already filled to overflowing. Despite the ventilation, the air was slightly stale with the oder of packed bodies and hot electronics, and my daily burden included a more or less permanent headache from the noise. My Worthy had the good sense to spend most of his time at the Academy; having, unlike me, the wit to gallop when our assignments came down. I hated him.

My desk was backed against the wall near one of the entry ways as far from the hub of power as could be, as befitting very junior elders, with our tiny herd, an unattached Fourth Degree, a worthy candidate, and four clericals in a sub-circle around me. You never get the recognition around here. My Worthy and I were our foremost experts on human military history, methods, and technology, which put us at the center of planning for our new stellar fleet. You'd think we at least deserved a few partitions, but they would impede the flow of paper, and we can't have *that*, can we? And now they wanted me to take a psych review? Well, it *was* recognition of a sort, and Ancestors knew I probably needed it. The Institute I was to report to did medical research on conditions in space for the 'Dark Grays', so I'd find out what this was about soon enough. It'd be a welcome break, anyway.

But first there was something I waited for for some time. My successor at the embassy on earth, the precious Third Degree L'datMparn of distasteful memory, was rotated home recently, and I had accessed his personnel file (which is what I hid from the Herd Guide). There was an old debt to settle, and it looked like someone got there ahead of me.

"...in my considered opinion, Defender L'datMparn performs his duties adequately, and is well suited to be assigned to duties on d'enchia in the future..."

My Ancestors *do* love me. Here I was debating whether to try twitching his fitness report, but it seemed Arbiter U'tdaPagrn shared my opinion of him, and his tail was a *lot* longer than mine. I never did like Third Degree L'datMparn, and as sure as the Ancestors are watching, I never trusted him. *'Performs his duties adequately'*; I loved it. In the mad stampede for promotion around here, such faint praise was worse than outright condemnation. And that last slap, *'duties on d'enchia'*, was beautiful for its subtlety. The only 'duties on d'enchia' for the 'Dark Grays' were on the Staff...or in Supply. And with the smell his activities on earth created around here, his chances of making Staff were nonexistent. The priceless L'datMparn and his attempt to politicize the defenders had hit a brick wall, which made me feel sooooo good.

"Account settled, Pierre," I muttered as I added an 'urgent priority' flag to the file so he would be reassigned directly without getting any rest release time. That settled a favor I owed Agent Roubidoux, the human APA's former embassy liaison. He wouldn't have to worry about being blackmailed into spying for us any more. Now all I had to do was get past this psych exam.

§

Getting out of the Circle this early in the morning was like being released from the Uttermost Darkness. Honestly, I was in no galloping hurry as I headed for the trolley station. The day was too nice, and the busy rumble of shuttles taking off from the spaceport was a refreshing reality check. One can only stare at paper for so long before the rest of the Universe starts to feel like a distant dream.

The 'Dark Grays' Circle was built conveniently close to the spaceport by tearing out a group of warehouses, including the one we used when preparing our first expedition to earth. (The Arbiters since moved to a much larger one.) The main runway's flight path passed directly overhead, and a steady stream of shuttles came drifting in as I walked. The place was still under construction, in fact, and the whole area was a building site as support facilities, power substations, an array of communication antennas, and a larger trolley station were being added.

We needed them. The fleet was hustling to repair battle damage from the recent Dreamsingers' War as well as pressing ahead on new construction. The shuttles were on the go day and night, and would be for another year or more. We were also busting tail to absorb all the recent graduates from the tech circles and the Academy, who, like all new tails, needed to be spoon fed their duties while they absorbed the difference between text books and real life. A lot of money and material was being poured into space, and where they got the paper to make the forms to account for it all was beyond me.

The day was clear and bracingly cool, which picked me right up and got the old metabolism pumping. Another shuttle passed overhead, climbing toward the scattered clouds with its turbines roaring. I paused to admire its size and power, and wished I could be on it. That was where the real action was, in orbit with the fleet. Mind you, I wasn't a trained spacer at the time, but surely I wasn't too old to learn. I was daydreaming as it vanished in the distance, remembering all the exotic things and places I'd seen on my few stellar journeys. Yes, those were good times (I couldn't help but gloss over the *bad* times; reflexive instinct, you know). I was pleased and a bit bemused with how my life had changed since that day nearly four years ago when I reported to the Assignment Circle three days early, and got tossed tail first into an adventure. It felt good to be alive and part of something this important, and even the mountain of paper I *knew* would be sitting on my desk when I returned didn't faze me.

I reached the station as the next express came rumbling in. I didn't look back as we rolled away.

§

It was midday when I reached the World Nest. The terminal was packed with travelers off the long distance trains, but I felt so good that I didn't mind the jostling herd. I paused when I noticed a *l'ni'ddi* stand on the concourse, and debated whether to grab a quick mid-meal. I *was* hungry, but it was still early, and C'traBenla and I had to stretch our limited resources, so I reluctantly passed. I would get this psyche *x'mnnb'* cleared up, then swing by our quarters for a quick bite and to see how she was doing.

The Institute was close enough that I decided to jog over there from the train station. I needed the exercise, anyway, and I got more than I anticipated. With the nice early season weather, road maintenance was out in force, so I wound up making a couple of detours. I stretched out to a rapid trot, and then a full gallop, chanting "excuse me", "pardon me", "coming through," to pedestrians I passed. I earned a couple angry squawks as I hurried down the boulevard, but right then I didn't care.

I finally reached the Institute, and after some not very diligent searching found the administration circle. Someone at an information kiosk directed me to a room at the far end of the campus. That figures. So on the trail again, fighting my way through a stampede of apprentices who, to a one, lacked the wit to allow someone to pass without delaying and obstructing.

I eventually found the right room...

...with an old antagonist from our last misadventure on earth, *T'virDoma, ab Clas'nch,* of distasteful memory, squatting at the desk. "Well, there you are at last," she condescended in her best get-under-one's-scales tone.

"I got here as soon as I received the order."

"If you're expecting a medallion, we're fresh out." She shoved a handful of forms at me and gestured at a row of seat cushions. "Squat, and fill those out. Maybe there's still time to save you."

"Do I get a pencil, or should I bite the end off my finger, and fill them out in blood?"

She gave me a chilly look, and tossed a pencil at me. "Here. *Perhaps* it'll keep you from fainting."

So I squatted, somewhat miffed at her, and tackled *yet* more paperwork as she went into the next room. I should have realized she was an ominous portent of how this day was going to play out, but right then I was simply annoyed. I needed *her* back in my life like I needed a lovely bow knot in my tail after putting up with her for a year on earth. Nor was I the only one: she and C'traBenla were bitter enemies, which was why I was glad she wasn't there.

8

There was nothing for it but to bear up, *as usual*, so I wrote it off and concentrated on those forms, which I soon recognized were the standard psychological profile test I'd taken in the past...

"You aren't done *yet?*" She'd come back in while I was preoccupied, and was glowering at me with her ears laid back in a fine gesture of contempt.

"I was waiting for you so I could dazzle you with my brilliance," I grumbled.

"Don't hurt yourself." She returned to her desk and glowered at me in silence while I went back to work.

I firmly put her out of mind and went back to the test, determined not to let her high-tailed attitude get under my scales. My resolve didn't help much: these standard psych tests are no joy. The questions prey on the mind, and I soon found myself going back and changing earlier answers. What was worse, it was deadly dull, so I had to constantly fight the temptation to check things off at random. Anyone who is serious about their career in the defenders takes these tests seriously, and this was on orders direct from the front of the herd. It was enough to make anyone nervous.

"There," I said when I finished. "Proof I can do simple tasks with minimal supervision."

"Remarkable." She snorted in contempt, and gestured to the inner door. "He's been waiting for you all morning, so you need to gallop so he can get you committed as soon as possible." I offered her the completed forms. "Take those with you. You might as well do *something* useful."

'May your egg be hard-boiled,' I thought as I headed for the inner sanctum. I was glad to be rid of her, and eager to find out who was in charge of this *hro'n'nad* stampede so I could...

"N'detLeda?"

He turned ponderously and studied me with a cool eye. "That's *Learnéd* N'detLeda. About time you showed up."

"Oooohh, well excuse me for existing." I should know better by now. "What's this all about?"

"It's about seeing if you're still fit for duty." He took the test forms from me, and gestured at a seat cushion surrounded with ominous-looking medical equipment. "Squat."

I examined the rig with no pleasure, wondering what he was up to. "Honestly, I've been feeling fine lately."

"Hmmm, it looks like we got to you just in time, if in fact we are in time." And on that optimistic note, he herded me onto the seat cushion, and set to work wiring me up to his contraptions while I sat there and fretted. By the time he finished dotting me with those self-adhesive electrodes, I *tentatively* decided he was twisting my tail.

T'virDoma came in while he was festooning me with lead wires. "Any signs of life?" she asked.

"Not as yet."

She took over the wiring while N'detLeda started fiddling with his machinery. "Ow!" I protested as she snapped the leads onto the sticky pads with careless force. "Easy there!"

"We're depending on *you* to save us from the humans?"

N'detLeda fired up his instruments, which produced an ominous chorus of beeping and humming noises. "Now get to work on these forms." He shoved a clipboard with a thick wad of paper at me.

"I'm sure I don't deserve all this attention," I sighed.

"You don't, but we have a job to do."

Mind you, I cope with paperwork all day every day, and you don't know the *meaning* of bureaucracy until you've struggled with defender paperwork, but this second test he wished off on me charted bold new horizons for meaningless *x'mnnb'*. Once I got past 'Name', 'Service Number', and 'Home Address' I was lost. And I'm not even sure I got the address right.

The questions were so much meaningless psycho-babble, and I was lost right from the start. For example, *'Describe the color 'red' as seen by human eyes'*: how am I supposed to describe something we even can't see, since their visible range is different than ours? For that matter, how do you describe *any* color? Or how about *'Analyze the psychological and physiometric effects of coffee on the human perception of upper range audio stimulation'*. After some thought, I wrote "Huh?", and considered it the height of witty repartee. The whole earless *thing* was like that!

"What is this?" I waved the forms at him impatiently. "This is all *hro'n'nad* nonsense.   Why do I need to bother with this *x'mnnb'*?"

"That's not just *any x'mnnb'*, it's a specially prepared psychological test to examine specific issues. Fill it out while I monitor your brain activity, and we'll see how thoroughly the rot has set in."

"This is *er'trxxda*," I grumbled. "But then that's your specialty, isn't it?"

"Curing it, anyway. I'll do my best, but I can't promise you anything."

That exam made everything in the past seem as simple as playing 'grab-my-tail'. If the first page was a nightmare, the further in I went, the worse it got. By time I reached the twelfth page, I was a nervous wreck, and it completely ceased to make any sense whatsoever.   That page was one long, rambling sentence of fourteen hundred and eighty-five words (I counted 'em) of absolute gibberish.   I tried working through it one word at a time, but couldn't keep track of the logic from one line to the next. I couldn't even figure out what it was about.   And all the while he and T'virDoma watched the instruments, and mused over the printouts, and made disparaging little noises.   Their instruments *must* have told them I was about ready to strangle both of them. To add insult to injury, down at the bottom was, *"Do you agree with the above? Yes___ No___."* I checked *"No___"* because I simply didn't care by then.

Fifty-five Ancestorless *pages* of *p'quas'tka!* I was agitated and wrung out by time I was done. "There." I shoved the completed form at him. "I hope you're satisfied."

"Oh, hardly, but the results ought to be...illuminating."   He glanced through it quickly, then handed it to T'virDoma, who threw the entire lot in the trash bin.   "Now what you're through the *preliminaries*, we'll give you the complete *extended* work-up." He threatened me with more forms.

"How much more of this is there?"

He gave me a superior ear twitch.   "You don't need to worry about being bored."

"I'm *worried* we might run out of paper."

"You can relax. The Ancients dedicated an entire forest to supply the pulp needed." He plopped the next lot of forms down in front of me. "And I even have a brand new pencil for you."

"Thank you, I guess."

"Be careful, it's sharp," T'virDoma snarked.

That pile of *ui'DmukNa* was even worse! I couldn't figure out what he was testing for, but if it was paranoia he'd have been in luck. It kept me going into the evening, and left me doubting my own sanity. The worst of it was this was official, coming down from the Chamber itself. Such things make any defender nervous, and not knowing *why* was unnerving.

And as if all that *p'quas'tka* testing wasn't enough, he followed up with a *complete* physical; threw odd, penetrating, often disturbing questions at me; made me take endless sensory tests, word association tests, reflex tests; gave me a full set of head scans; took a blood sample for laboratory analysis; and I finally revolted when he wanted to take a brain tissue sample.

N'detLeda was in his element, as self-righteous and overbearing as ever. Despite my asking repeatedly, he didn't offer a hint of what it was about. That worried me, and the longer this went on, the more worried I got. And all the while those blessed machines hummed and clicked and drew squiggly lines across their screens as they watched and made cryptic noises at each other.

"That will be all for now," he said at last. "And you certainly live down to expectations."

"Happy to oblige," I muttered as I stretched to get the kinks out of my back. "How's the book doing, by the way?"

That got a sullen glare from him. He wrote a huge textbook on human psychology after coming back from earth, and from what I heard, it made him a laughing-stock in the medical profession.

"Better than anything *you've* written!" she hissed.

"Whatever. I'm finished, and good riddance to you both."

"I hate to burst your happy delusions," N'detLeda said. "But there may be additional sessions after we study these results, so don't make any career plans until further notice."

"Oy," I grumbled, and headed for the door.

§

I was a bit surprised to find it was dark when I *finally* got out of there. The campus was largely deserted except for a last few figures headed for the main gate in the distance. Even the evening circles had let out, which didn't amuse me when I realized N'detLeda's tail-chasing ate up the entire day. There was nothing for it, so I headed down the walk with a sigh of frustration.

I could have taken the tram, but it was a pleasant evening with all three moons in view, so I decided to walk. I needed some time to sort out my head, and the exercise would help work off the tension of my little day.

The World Nest is a nonstop place, but the streets I took were mostly empty. The clubs and other late night attractions are over more toward the center of the nest. This area was devoted mostly to the Institute and various government offices, so it was pretty well deserted at this hour. The peace and quiet, and the mild night air helped soothe my jangled nerves, and I was able to indulge in fuming over N'detLeda's high-tailed arrogance. Just how *does* one define the color 'red', anyway? I could tell that was going to plague me for days to come. To the Uttermost Darkness with the priceless *Learnéd* N'detLeda and his tests.

At least when we were on earth, we knew what the dangers were; not like here where some *un'tdar* brain mechanic could worm his way into the darkest corners of your fears. I honestly hated N'detLeda more than ever right then, not only for his *ui'DmukNa* attitude, but for how he liked to twist peoples' tails. Why they ever made *him* as an aberrant psychologist is beyond me.

Dealing with those two was just like our time on earth, which was no joy, I can tell you. Mind you, there are some humans I liked, and was sorry to part company with them, but *humans* in general can be truly unsettling on good days. There was our run-ins with Inspector Dassault... And the time the Anti-Techs besieged the embassy... Not to mention how the third floor of the embassy collapsed... And the blizzards... And the heat... And their stellar bombs... And the Elvis Worshipers... And the riots— especially the riots... Earth is the Cosmic Tail Knot of the Universe, but life there was never dull. Thinking on it brought back the memories of when I was a simple-minded young

13

'v'thorble whose great ambition was to someday command my own echelon. Now look at me: high-tailed Staffer shuffling paper all day and trying to avoid the Herd Guide with his endless memos. It was all too easy to get killed on earth, but at least my greatest paperwork headache was filling out the daily report. In a way, I kind of missed it. Maybe I was *er'trxxda*.

§

It was nearly midnight by time I got back to our quarters at the Junior Elders circle. By then I was weary, starving, emotionally wrung out, and still worried about all that psych nonsense. The place wasn't much: junior elders don't rate luxury, but dingy and run down as it was, it was good to be home. I was thankful when I trudged up the often-patched walk to our little nest. Right then all I wanted was a hot meal and a quiet evening.

C'traBenla lay on our bed pad wrapped in a loose-fitting lounge robe when I came in. I could tell right off she was listless and down, and I wondered if her Possession Syndrome therapy went badly. I didn't need her pining for the egg we gave to the crèche last year. Come to think of it, it surely hatched by now, which must be what she was fretting over.

"How was your day, love?"

She sat up and looked at me. "Oh, it was about average, I suppose. You're late."

"It's been one of *those* days."

"You did well today?"

There was definitely something troubling her; I could feel it. "It was busy, but I got a lot done." I decided not to mention my psych exam, since there was no need to worry her further. "What's the matter, love?"

She eyed me uneasily, then got to her feet, came over, and cuddled close to me. "I...well...something came up today."

Like I should be surprised. She had settled down somewhat since we returned from our last misadventure on earth, and she was making good progress with her therapy, but she was still impulsive and hot tempered, and managed to get into some squabble or other fairly regularly. And here I was hoping for some quiet time with her.

14

"What's the matter, love?" I tried to sound reassuring; she needed it at the moment.

"I'm not in trouble or anything," she said, hastily. "It's nothing like last time."

She must have read my mind. *That* was a big relief, since we got the charges dropped only a few days back. "You haven't been arguing with the neighbors again, have you, love?"

"...no..."

"Well then, it can't be all that bad, can it?"

"...you'll be upset at me, I know."

"C'tra, it's all right." Not good: but not time to get paranoid, yet. "I understand you're a bit impulsive, and I know you don't mean any harm by it." I took her snout in one hand and caressed her ears with the other. "I won't be mad, I promise. Tell me, what's wrong?"

She hesitated, then, "...I'm...carrying..."

"Carrying what?"

She gave me *that* look, the one which implied my skull was full of lard. "An *egg*," she growled. "I'm carrying an egg. I'm pregnant."

*****

"A Tradition Of Bad Judgment"
(Related by Learnéd K'deiTai)

"More *V'liz?*" Eldest Arbiter G'cetGian's hands trembled as he poured without awaiting an answer. The one thing I *didn't* want was to be sitting here chatting with my nemesis over *V'liz* and sour rolls, but one does not refuse the hospitality of the Eldest. "I think you will like this new aromatic blend. I added some sort of plant from earth—mint, I believe it is called. Or was that Canopus?"

"I believe you mean cannabis, Eldest. Canopus is their name for a star." I sipped the mystery concoction cautiously: not mint, thank my Ancestors, although this was bad enough.

"Um, cannabis?"

"A psychoactive agent found in hemp. It's illegal in most parts of the humans' Alliance of Nations."

"Hemp?" Now he seemed befuddled, more than usual of late, which wasn't comforting. "What is hemp?"

"It's a plant. The humans use it to make rope."

"Rope? Illegal?" He eyed his bowl suspiciously. "Why would rope be illegal?"

"It's nothing, Eldest. A superstitious earth custom." I watched G'cetGian with concern as he puzzled over his bowl. He really was getting too old to herd the Arbiters Service, although who could succeed him was beyond me. I took another cautious sip; yes, cannabis, no doubt about it.

"But...what does rope have to do with *V'liz?*"

"Different worlds, different ways. Humans can be unfathomable at times; don't worry about it."

"I suppose so." He took another cautious sip. "Not mint, hmmm?" I got the distinct impression he didn't like the flavor. "Can you tell what it is, then?"

"I'm afraid I'm not all that familiar with earthly foods. Are you sure this is safe?"

"It is something new. I heard the environmental sciences Learnéds are examining it. One of the apprentices brought a sample back from earth, and I thought I would give it a try." He sniffed at his bowl suspiciously. "It has a nice aroma, anyway.

You know so much more about earthly customs than I do; what would you suggest?"

I couldn't share his enthusiasm for the 'aroma', either. "Try some lemon. It has a tart flavor and a flowery scent, and was popular when I was our Arbiter there." I admit I took a certain vindictive pleasure in not mentioning that the one time I unwittingly tried it at an embassy function on earth, I got passed-out drunk, which set off a diplomatic crisis. There are some parts of my 'distinguished' career I would rather forget, and it would be fitting justice.

"Yes, I shall have to do that." He set his bowl aside, and I took the opportunity to set mine aside as well, covering the act by reaching for one of the buns on the ornate serving tray. "It was so good of you to come," he said. "I imagine you are a bit skittish about being here by now."

"Do you suppose? Let me see: three and a half years on earth, enduring riots, revolutions, terrorists, media vultures, cult crazies —not to mention the odd interstellar war—you could say I am a *bit* nervous to be sitting here. And if you plan to send me back there, the answer is a resounding *'no'!*"

He chuckled. "I daresay your Aide would not be pleased with you if you did go back."

"He would never speak to me again, not that I'd blame him. I'd never speak to me again either!"

He offered a dismissive ear twitch. "Not to worry. Actually, I hope I might impose on you for a small favor. I need for you to go over to the spaceport and meet Arbiter U'tdaPagrn, who will arrive this afternoon."

"U'tdaPagrn? Here?" This was a surprise, and an unsettling one. "What's this about?"

"He has been recalled from earth."

"Recalled? Have our relations with the humans taken a downward turn? You don't intend to send me there to backstop him, do you?"

"Oh, no, not at all. I received those instructions from the Most Ancient himself. He did not tell me what it is about, except that it is important."

"The Most Ancient?" I admit I was fairly disconcerted by then.

"He called in person some time back, said it was urgent for U'tdaPagrn to come home at once."

I pondered this doubtfully, trying to grab tail on it. "You haven't heard any suggestion of trouble?"

"No." He seemed perplexed. "If anything, I understand the humans are more anxious than usual to avoid a conflict. I do not know what to make of it."

That was a relief. With the losses the 'Dark Grays' suffered in the Dreamsingers' War, our space fleet was practically back in its egg. We were in no shape to fight a war with anyone. Thankfully, neither were the humans.

"Well...I would be happy to see U'tdaPagrn again, but why do you need me? Couldn't one of the apprentices take care of it?"

"Oh, I suppose so. However, I want someone with your experience to meet him before he gets caught up in official circles. I hope you could sound him out about how things are on earth. Perhaps he can explain this mystery."

I mused on it, trying to put it all together, but it simply didn't make sense. Why recall U'tdaPagrn when he was right in the middle of critical, delicate negotiations? And why was the Most Ancient—who was pretty well back in *his* egg by all accounts—involved? The Most Ancient was, in fact, the most ancient member of the Chamber, having served for over forty years. His mental state was a topic of endless gossip, although he still managed his duties well enough. There was no denying, however, that he was getting on in years, had lost much of his former edge, and would retire sometime soon.

"I would love to help, but I'm afraid I can't." As curious as I was in spite of myself, I was desperately anxious to avoid getting caught up in this, since it could only mean I would wind up on a planet I'd regret. "My teaching schedule keeps me galloping, you know."

G'cetGian gave me a skeptical look. "But you found time to drop by here, eh?"

"I happened to be going by and dropped in to see what you wanted." Truth, I came half-way across the World Nest in response

18

to his e-mail, and for the life of me I couldn't imagine why. This was sheer folly, but I suppose I'd become conditioned to his manipulations, Ancestors help me.

"It was most kind of you to come by. Surely you could tweak your schedule, hmm? Take a bit of time out? It really is important."

"It's such short notice...I couldn't arrange a substitute instructor so quickly." Having foolishly stuck my tail in the wringer, my one desire right then was to get out of this mess.

"No doubt your Aide could cover you?"

"I *doubt* he will feel very cooperative. I'm afraid it's just not possible." And *this* time I would *not* let him manipulate me!

"But who knows *what* U'tdaPagrn may have uncovered? Surely with your experience, you could interpret some small detail he might overlook..."

§

If I were my Ancestors, I certainly would have given up on me by then. To my lasting mortification, and despite my sincerest resolve, G'cetGian backbeat me into running his 'little errand'. Why do I let that *M'mendoch* hustle me so? I should have been relieved that all he wanted was something so simple, but based on past experience I was pessimistic, convinced this would lead me to no end of grief. But then, anything involving G'cetGian made me nervous.

I trudged along the ornate walk in front of the Arbiters' Circle as it wound back and forth across the decorative landscape, and wondered why I have such a limp tail around him. I used to take pride in being an Arbiter, and felt I was doing valuable service for our people; the innocence of youth I suppose. Then we met the humans. Oy! He managed to toss me and my Aide in tail-first to set up an embassy on their world, and being cast into the Uttermost Darkness would have been kinder. Nor was that the only occasion. I can state without fear of contradiction that two tours on earth will cure the most optimistic soul of any misguided enthusiasm. But despite the bitter lessons, he *still* managed to backbeat me into some *er'trxxda* adventure. Maybe I was paranoid, but was he putting some sort of mind-altering drug in that *V'liz?*

19

Well, there was nothing for it. I needed to get this done and get back for my evening instruction circle. As I boarded the trolley, I decided to stop by the Institute and let my Aide know about this before he got a taste of it through the endless Institute gossip, or he might *not* speak to me again.

§

Our grotto at the Institute was more crowded than ever since it was mid-term, and many of our candidates were in for their program counseling sessions. The place was jammed with apprentices who jostled each other impatiently while the overflow spilled out into the hall. The air was thick as I struggled through the tangle of tails and elbows, and despite their earnest good manners, the undercurrent of whispered conversations and random noise made it hard to focus. Every bit of available space was taken; the furniture was disarrayed, someone knocked the large photo of the earth embassy loose from the wall, and my Mozart poster was torn.

"Well there you are!" was how my Aide greeted my arrival. "Where did you get off to? We have counseling reviews lined up for the rest of the day."

Great. He was in a bad mood, which wouldn't make this any easier. "Sorry. Actually, G'cetGian asked me to drop by..."

That set him off. "You let that *M'mendoch* hustle you into going to earth *again?*"

"I am *not* going to earth, honest! He asked me to go over to the spaceport to meet U'tdaPagrn, is all."

"This is *cc'v'renk!*" he yelled. "I thought you knew better by now!"

"You're over reacting..."

"Considering what happened the last *two* times you went to see him, you can't blame me!" A couple of the candidates watching this with wide-eyed dismay retreated discreetly out into the corridor, joining those peering through the open door.

"It's just a simple errand..."

"Not likely with *him*. Your sorry tail will wind up in Geneva, or worse! And when you do, *don't* expect me to be there to hold your hand!"

Several more candidates retreated outside, and those left withdrew to the far edges of the grotto.

"I am *not* going to earth! He simply asked me to meet U'tdaPagrn at the spaceport."

He glared at me for a long moment, breathing hard, then, "U'tdaPagrn is here? Why? Is he being recalled?"

"I don't know, nor does G'cetGian. The Most Ancient ordered it, and G'cetGian wants me to question U'tdaPagrn about it. That's all. Really."

He seemed a bit nonplussed by the news. "Even so, you'll get your ears clipped; you know it. I had *hoped* you would see through his games by now and steer clear of him, but that's asking too much, isn't it?"

"Sarcasm doesn't help!"

"It beats biting your tail!"

I knew he was right: my priority was with our Human Studies program now, but I had too much emotionally invested in earth, Ancestors save me, to simply ignore the matter. I should have given in to the voice of irate reason and stayed, but the mystery of U'tdaPagrn's recall was compelling and, sad to say, I never can take mysteries involving the humans lightly.

"I'm sorry you feel that way," I said at last. "And I'm sorry to leave you dangling like this, but I really need to get this done. I'll be back as soon as possible to help you."

"Give my regards to the humans' Chancellor," he grumbled. And on that positive note, I fled the scene.

No sooner was I out in the hall then, as luck would have it, I ran headlong into another person I sincerely did not want to see, the priceless T'virDoma, ab Clas'nch. "You again," I sighed in exasperation.

"Yes, me." She gave me an imperious flick of her tail. "This is your lucky day, isn't it?"

"If you consider bad luck, then yes, it is."

"So...I hear you're on your way to earth. Who will be taking over your Human Studies program?"

"I am *not* on my way to earth! And what do you care who teaches the program? You know it all, already."

"Hmmm, yes, I do. As much as you're offering, anyway." She may have been my brightest apprentice, and the most capable of the lot, but she was also why I regretted having to come to work each morning. "Actually I was sent to bring you a message. Learnéd N'detLeda wants you to come to his laboratory."

I have her a jaundiced, annoyed look. "Honestly, I'd rather go to earth than put up with that *un'tdar.*"

"My, such *r'vebbe.*" She expressed her opinion with a superior ear twitch. "Jealous, Learnéd?"

"Of him? Not hardly. What does he want, anyway?"

"It's something to do with the recent Dreamsingers' War."

That had me for a moment. N'detLeda and I were drafted into the liaison herd coordinating our joint war effort with the humans, and as if an interstellar war wasn't bad enough, he dragged her along just to make things interesting. It was a year-long nightmare I would prefer to forget, and I had no desire to revisit it *or* him. Still...anything involving the humans was not to be taken lightly, and I got the feeling this would involve the mysterious Dreamsingers as well. As much as I hated the prospect, I supposed I should go see what he wanted.

"Whatever. I'll drop by when I get the chance. Now if you'll excuse me, I have an errand to run."

"Give my regards to the humans' Chancellor."

As I headed for the station to catch a train to the spaceport I had another premonition that, as sure as my Ancestors were sighing in resignation, I would regret this day.

§

Since my suspicions were aroused and I was headed for the spaceport anyway, I decided to stop by the Interstellar Diplomatic Service's fancy new grotto to see if V'koBilen had some idea of what this was all about. I hadn't seen the place, and it was impressive. The warehouse was larger than the one we started out in only four years (*Ancestors, was it only four years?*) ago, and far busier as well. Our supply ship was in orbit, and people were galloping every which way shifting pallet-loads of food, furnishings, and supplies bound for earth into a rank of trucks at the dock doors. Beyond the warehouse, the admin area was a sea of clerical workstations with Ancestors know *how* many busy paper shufflers hard at it. I was a bit dismayed at the scene, and bemused by how much it changed since those early days when we had to steal truckloads of supplies because there simply wasn't time to fight our way through the bureaucracy. I wondered idly if they ever got it all straightened out.

V'koBilen's administrative grotto was tastefully decorated with a mix of exotic earth decor and his Aide's woven hangings. Unlike the pandemonium outside, the place was restful, with subdued lighting, warm pastels, and a lovely small fountain; necessary in view of V'koBilen's heart condition. For a wonder, V'koBilen and his Aide were both there, relaxing on plush seat cushions over a light mid-meal. Finding him there was unusual considering the state of his health.

"What? *He* has his hooks into you *again?*" was how he expressed his pleasure at seeing me.

"Love you too," I grumbled.

"You're not headed for *earth*, are you?"

"Not hardly. *He* wants me to meet U'tdaPagrn."

That confused them both. "U'tdaPagrn is here?"

"In orbit. His shuttle is due in shortly."

He and his Aide both sat up in alarm. "He was recalled? Has something happened?"

"I was hoping you could give me a trail to sniff out." Their obvious surprise was a bit disturbing.

They sagged on their seat cushions and pondered me uneasily. "Actually, relations are a bit tense right now," his Aide said. "Their fleet is a shambles after the Dreamsingers' War, and they seem to be concerned we might take advantage of them."

"I don't see how. Our fleet suffered every bit as badly."

"If not worse," V'koBilen said. "It was reported in a recent classified briefing we attended that it will take a year or more to get back to normal."

"What passes for normal around here," she added. "We're not capable of attacking anyone, and from what we hear that has some of the Ancients worried."

"Some? Z'keBalf and his hard-liners, you mean."

"You know Z'keBalf is not to be taken lightly," he said. "Nor can we entirely rule out the idea that something might happen. The humans pose no threat right now, but you know common sense is hardly their strong point."

"Or our strong point when dealing with them," she added.

"Oy, *that's* the truth! So what do you make of this? Are relations deteriorating?"

"If you were on your way to earth, I'd be worried," V'koBilen said. "But as is, I'd say tensions are up some, but not critically."

"Then why recall U'tdaPagrn when he should be busily polishing their scales?"

"I haven't the faintest. This is the first we've heard of it."

"The thing which bothers me is no one seems to know anything about it," she said. "Surely the gossip would be flying thick and fast by now."

V'koBilen pondered that. "Unless it's a secret?"

"G'cetGian said this was ordered by the Most Ancient in person."

"That *n'bna'nmn?* Ancestors, I hope this isn't some random nonsense cooked up in his feeble mind."

"I wonder if this has to do with N'detLeda?" she mused.

"What?"

"He called a little while ago asking for you. He said he needs to see you urgently."

"His urgency is *not* my urgency!" I grumbled. "I'll get around to seeing him when I feel like it."

She reacted with an amused ear twitch. "Well if you get to feeling like that, then you'll probably *need* a psychiatrist!"

"Oy."

§

The spaceport is the largest air terminal on d'enchia, and was busier than ever. Aside from planet-bound aviation, no less than three liners and the embassy supply ship were in orbit; according to the boarding notices one was a colony ship heading to the inward frontier. The boarding zones and food concessions were packed, and the main aisles were busy with travelers and well-wishers. Like terminals everywhere, the cavernous dome echoed with the muted roar of voices, the steady rumble of baggage conveyers and utility carts, and occasional squawks from the announcement system. There was major construction under way. My luck being what it is, they redid the concourse since I was here last, so I soon got lost in the thundering herd.

After wandering around at random for some time, I finally got the bright idea to ask directions. After that, footsore and fed up, I reached the interstellar wing which was even busier than the planet-bound section if possible. There were an uncommon number of 'Dark Grays' uniforms in sight, since repairs to the fleet were in full gallop. I noticed a small party of humans towering over the herd in the distance, new arrivals for their embassy no doubt. I paused to study them curiously, but didn't recognize any of them at this distance.

U'tdaPagrn was in one of the passenger waiting areas near Customs, squatting on his travel kit fiddling with something when I arrived. "K'deiTai?" He was surprised to see me, and I was surprised by how *old* he looked. "It's good to see you again."

"Likewise, I hope." Then I noticed what he was fiddling with. "Are you *still* fooling with that thing?"

He paused at twisting the little multi-colored plastic cube back and forth, and gave me a guilty look. "I can't help it." He seemed embarrassed and distraught. "It's addictive."

"You know they're likely to ban those things. I'm surprised they didn't confiscate that one."

"They must! It's driving me *er'trxxda,* and my wrists are killing me. I wish I'd never discovered it."

"Um...did you ever solve it?"

"No!" A cry of anguish. "The most I've ever done was to get three sides aligned, and that was sheer dumb luck!" He pondered the little cube ruefully. "And to think it's just a common toy on earth. These humans are beyond understanding. So much of their culture simply doesn't make sense."

"Whatever gave you the idea that earth service is supposed to make sense?"

He tucked the offending toy into his pouch with a sigh and a weary head shake. "You're right; foolish of me."

"Honestly, you don't look so good. I can see the stress is getting to you. You look like you need a vacation." From my own experience on earth, I knew all too well what the stress was like.

"I suppose I do. Well, since I'm here, I might as well seek some psychiatric counseling; work-related injury, you know."

"You may be in luck. N'detLeda is at the Institute now, and he has plenty of experience with the conditions of earth service."

He gave me a chilly look. "He is the *last* person I would seek psychiatric help from!"

"Sorry. Just a thought."

We secured a baggage cart, loaded his travel kit and several lesser items, and headed for the trolley terminal.

"So...what brings you here?" he asked as we pushed our way through the traffic. "You aren't heading to earth, are you?"

"Why does everyone assume I'm headed for earth!"

"I was just wondering."

"Sorry. I'm a bit paranoid about that place. G'cetGian sent me me to meet you."

"Did he?" He gave me a suspicious look, and I could tell he was perplexed and a bit alarmed. "Is there some crisis? Is that why I was recalled?"

"That was what he wanted me to ask you. I stopped by the home grotto, but V'koBilen had nothing on it either."

He offered a perplexed ear twitch. "I haven't the faintest. All I know is that we received an urgent dispatch signed by the Most Ancient himself ordering me to return at once. I was instructed to offer my regrets to the human Chancellor, and to assure them this was a 'routine internal matter'—whatever that *x'mnnb'* means—and that the negotiations would resume presently. Beyond that, you probably know more than I do."

"And your Aide remained on earth?"

He gave me an unhappy ear twitch. "Yes. It doesn't make sense: if the mission is being recalled, or we're to be replaced, why did he remain with orders to carry on with routine matters?"

"I have long since given up trying to make sense of anything involving the humans," I sighed.

§

26

"It is good to see you again," G'cetGian said when we arrived at his grotto. "How are things on earth?"

U'tdaPagrn's snout creased in a tense expression, and his ears laid back. "About the same as always." He collapsed with a groan on one of the plush seat cushions and stared morosely at the fountain. "Why was I recalled?"

"I was hoping you could tell us. All I know is that the Most Ancient ordered this in person."

U'tdaPagrn gave him a vexed ear twitch. "Have you considered that he may have finally gone back to his egg altogether? I don't see any sensible reason for this."

"Well, if so, there is nothing we can do for it. I suppose we shall find out soon enough. Would you care for some *V'liz?*" G'cetGian was already reaching for the ornate pot and some bowls. "You look like you could use it."

U'tdaPagrn lifted his head. "I could at that."

"I took K'deiTai's advice," G'cetGian said as he poured. "I called over to the human embassy, and they are sending over some lemon concentrate. We should have lemon-*V'liz* tomorrow. I am rather looking forward to trying it." U'tdaPagrn gave me a suspicious look, but said nothing.

"And you can relax, K'deiTai," he said as he handed me a bowl. "I left the cannabis out of this pot." U'tdaPagrn gave *him* a suspicious look, but still said nothing.

"So what do you make of this mystery?" G'cetGian asked once we were settled again. "Could it have something to do with our relations with the humans?"

"I have no idea," U'tdaPagrn said. "The Third Accord negotiations are proceeding well, and I hope to have them wrapped up by the end of the year. As to this turn of events, this is the first I heard of it, so I can offer nothing."

I could tell G'cetGian was relieved to hear about the negotiations. "That is good news. You seem to have an uncanny knack for relating to the humans, more than many here suspected."

U'tdaPagrn gave me another suspicious look.

"I have followed your progress closely, and this new treaty will do much to improve relations."

"It...doesn't resolve the underlying issue of trust between the two races, but it will help. They can be so alarming at times. Building a lasting peace with the humans will take many years, and until then we still need to tread warily with them."

"Oh, no doubt. Still, every step forward is to the good. You are doing some solid work there. I just wish we understood what this present mystery is about..."

...U'tdaPagrn absent-mindedly reached into his pouch, pulled out that human hand game, and began fiddling with it. Acting on impulse, I snatched it out of his hand. "Hey!" He lunged for it, but I held it firmly out of his reach. "Give it back! That's mine!"

"You know this is for your own good."

"I'll decide what's for my own good!" He lunged at it again, and we tussled over it briefly.

"What *is* that thing?" G'cetGian was clearly alarmed at this sudden outbreak.

We separated and stood glaring at each other. "Something mere mortals were not meant to fool with," I said. U'tdaPagrn lunged for it once more, but I kept it away. "You know you have to give this up, so don't fight it," I added to him.

"This is...most irregular." G'cetGian was vexed and a bit dismayed by our squabbling. "Is this really necessary?"

"You tell him," I said to U'tdaPagrn. He stared at me for a long moment, trembling and breathing hard, then nodded and slumped on his seat cushion with a defeated sigh.

"Thank you. I *trust* we will not have any further displays of this nature?"

"My apology, Eldest; a regrettable necessity." I tucked the offending cube safely out of sight where *I* wouldn't be tempted to fool with it.

"Forgiven, forgotten." His beatific smile was back. "What is a little disagreement between fellow professionals, eh?" He eyed the spot where I hid the little cube curiously, but said nothing further.

"It's...earth," U'tdaPagrn muttered. "It gets to you after a while."

"Then perhaps it is a good thing you are here. You look like you could use a vacation."

"I could at that."

G'cetGian considered him anxiously. "Perhaps you should take the day and get some rest. You must be weary from your long journey, and you will want to be fresh for whatever they have in mind. We can meet tomorrow for an informal debriefing."

"*Ancestors*, I do need a rest."

That was my cue. "Well, if you will excuse us, Eldest, I'll get U'tdaPagrn settled into transient quarters, and then I have to get back to the Institute."

"Thank you, K'deiTai. Oh...and Learnéd N'detLeda called a while ago. He said he needs to see you as soon as possible, and he wants to see U'tdaPagrn as well."

That set my ears twitching with a sudden premonition of danger. What could he *possibly* want with me, to say nothing of U'tdaPagrn? And how did it tie in with this mystery? Whatever he wanted, it couldn't be good. "Ah...yes...so I understand. I'll look him up as soon as I can."

"I suppose," U'tdaPagrn mumbled.

"Excellent. Nothing like a get-together of the old herd, eh? Celebrate the past over a drink or two?"

"I'm looking forward to it," I sighed.

"And do please drop by tomorrow for lemon-*V'liz*." He offered one of his beatific smiles and a twinkle in his eye which always make me nervous. "I promise not to send you to earth if you do."

"Ah...thank you, Eldest. I'll see if I can get free." I collected U'tdaPagrn and got out of there while I still had my tail, and made sure to leave that accursed toy where G'cetGian would find it.

*****

"Patches On The Patches"
(Extract of testimony)

"Are you a figment of my imagination? Or am I one of yours?" Admiral MacKenna growled.

Minister Jacek Hogarthy was just sitting his briefcase on the Admiral's desk, and gave him an angry glare. "Really, MacKenna, that was uncalled for. I see no reason for these personal insults."

"I'm sure you don't, but they feel so damned *good!"*

Hogarthy fumed for a bit, locked in a bitter eye-to-eye battle with the Admiral. "I suppose they do," he ground out at last. "Just one more indication that you are no longer suited for this job."

"Well if you meant that as a threat, then you can take this job and shove it up your personality!" Right then MacKenna was fighting a nervous headache, which the Defense Minister's unwelcome arrival wasn't helping. It made him more combative and short-tempered than usual, which for him was something.

"You should be ashamed of your unprofessional behavior," Hogarthy lectured him. "I come all the way out here to Singapore to help put the fleet back in order after that disaster you got us into, and this is how you greet me? I would think you..."

Mac lost it, and pounded his fist on the desk. "I don't give a flying purple DAMN what you think!"

"That will be enough..."

"If I may, Minister," Captain Rostokovich interrupted. "Please excuse Admiral's temper. He is under much strain, and is still not recovered from his injuries."

MacKenna bridled at that, but kept his peace. Ivan was right: he needed to dial it down, no matter the provocation. In fact he wasn't *fully recovered from what happened at the Battle Of The Dreamsingers' World—he died, horribly, from the effects of the Black Sphere's death-wish projector —nor did it seem likely he ever would. The alien J J Ballas revived him and wiped away most of the memories, but something like that marks a man, regardless.*

Hogarthy hesitated, and the temper in the room cooled a bit. "I suppose so," he said at last. "Still, it goes to show that the Admiral has outlasted his usefulness. The fleet is a shambles by all accounts, and I have come here to put things back in working order."

MacKenna bit down on his temper, which took some doing, but allowed himself one last zinger. "Yeah? Well good luck with not disappearing up your own arse."

That was greeted by a silent wave of approval, which one hardly needed to be telepathic to feel, from the Admiral's staff assembled in his office. Hogarthy was hardly here for their benefit, and everyone knew it. His many sins of omission became so painfully obvious during the war that his political position was in jeopardy. In fact, the stock joke making the rounds right then was that he would be transferred to the Ministry of Sanitation and put in charge of the Alliance's sewage treatment plants; to which the stock reply (depending on party affiliation) was either "Is that a threat?" or "Is that a promise?" Despite his many failings—or perhaps because of them—he knew when it was time to Cover Thy Posterior, so he was in Singapore on a rare 'fact-finding' junket, complete with a retinue of flunkies and yes-men, and journalists to immortalize him on the evening news as he plagued the long-suffering Admiral and reduced fleet operations to a finer, purer havoc.

Hogarthy huffed up as much as his short, rotund figure would allow. "Your insubordinate, to say nothing of rude, behavior does not cover up your dereliction, Admiral!" He ignored the ugly murmur from the Admiral's staff, and launched into another of his lectures. "I know all about your excuse that wartime expenditures are heavy, but that clearly is due to all the waste and inefficiency in your supply system. Right now we are going through no end of legal hassles terminating all those huge defense contracts you got us into. Your belief that the war would be long and expensive was obviously *wrong! What's more, your disposition records show no* end *of needless expense for 'expedited' this and 'emergency' that, as if the Alliance gave you a personal blank cheque..."*

"What-ever!" MacKenna pounded his desk again; it was enough to bring Hogarthy to a halt. They glared at each other for a long moment, then Mac sighed, and turned to his Aide, Hythe-Morrison. "Leftenant, take the Minister over to the Squirrel Cage and get him settled in."

"Squirrel cage...?"

He ignored Hogarthy's latest squawk, and added to the rest of his staff, "We'll have a general briefing for him this afternoon, after which we will no doubt learn the worst. Planetary defense takes second place to procedure, it seems, so all departments drop everything and get your paperwork in order NINS."

Hogarthy took exception to his tone. "Really Admiral, your attitude is a discredit to the Fleet. The lack of proper ceremonial when I arrived does not reflect well either."

MacKenna favored him with a weary glare. "And there will be a general short-arm inspection when the Minister returns to Geneva."

"Better, I suppose." Hogarthy nodded in satisfaction at his imagined one-up as the staffers suppressed their snickering.

"Gawd," Mac muttered once Hogarthy was hull down on the horizon bound for the VIP quarters at the other end of the base. "Some days it's not even worth chewing through the restraints."

"It could be worse, sir," Captain Rostokovich offered. He and Lieutenant Night Eagle, commander of the Marine security company, had remained to offer their support for the old man.

MacKenna rubbed his eyes wearily. "How?"

"Fleet headquarters could be in Geneva."

"Yeah...I guess you're right."

32

"You are not well, sir?" The Admiral ignored Ivan, and stared at the door. "Is the mind powers again, da?"

MacKenna nodded. "They're getting stronger by the day. It's like being in a crowd...all the time...can't sleep, can't think...hard to concentrate."

The two junior officers watched in dismay, worried about the old man's health. He'd been through far too much for far too long. Both knew their share of combat from before joining Space Fleet, but could hardly imagine what MacKenna's lifetime of service had done to him. And these empathic powers...

These strange phenomena first appeared during the late war, and had grown stronger for months. A half-dozen humans showed the symptoms at first, but now most of the ships' crews were affected to some degree. The fleet medical and scientific wings had an all-out effort going to understand what was happening, but they were making precious little headway. The best guess was that the mysterious Dreamsingers were telepathic; they had a hard time connecting with human or Ic'nichi minds, and it was beginning to look like they changed them somehow to make communication easier. The side effects of that were interesting—and disturbing.

"Do you need anything, sir?" Night Eagle asked softly.

MacKenna settled back in his chair and sighed. "Nothing you'll find this side of Heaven, Lieutenant."

§

Life went on despite Hogarthy. A few days later, Captain—brevet Commodore—Morgan came to report on the state of the 'Marco Polo', fresh from a major refit and due out on a mission she was barely fit for.

"We patched all the holes and reconnected all the wires, sir, so she's about as ready as we can hope," she said as she stood stiffly in front of his desk.

"Which means she's not quite a decrepit hulk?"

"She has a few miles left in her," Morgan said, sullenly. Then she added, "Thank you for not scrapping her."

33

MacKenna sighed. "She's given us many good years, more than she was designed for." The 'Marco Polo' was mankind's first starship, now fifteen years old with far too many miles and far too many battles on her. "Maybe...once we're past this mess, we can turn her into a museum piece."

"That would be fitting, sir."

Back to matters at hand. "You've been back on line five days now; what about your run to New Patagonia?"

"We only received our supply allotment this morning, sir, and getting a shuttle assigned to us was a nightmare. The last of our cargo is being loaded now."

"Yeah, sorry about that. Our priceless overlord has the place in an uproar with his new 'Procedures and Protocols'. I don't know if we can survive being any more efficient."

She sighed in exasperation. "Is that pompous pain-in-the-ass still here?"

MacKenna shorted in contempt. "That's Minister Pompous Pain-In-The-Ass, Captain."

"He is indeed, sir." That aged bon-motte gave them both a much-needed chuckle.

"How do you feel?" he asked, gently.

Morgan sighed, and rubbed her eyes. "Like hell." She stared at the distance for a bit, then, "But we have to go out. New Patagonia needs those supplies, and we have to maintain what little operational proficiency we have left, no matter how drained we all are."

"The Ic'nichi aren't going to try anything."

"I know, sir. But we need some sense of normalcy to maintain morale."

The Dreamsingers' War was a disaster for the tiny human fleet. Aside from the 'Zulu', lost with all hands, the 'Conestoga' was a wreck, and 'Comanche' and 'Tartar' were down for major repairs. Even the 'Marco Polo', never intended for battle and getting so rickety that MacKenna debated whether to scrap her, was fresh out of dock after major damage was restored. As long as she could jump, they had to use her.

They were as bad off for manpower, as their ranks were depleted by casualties. Most of those were psyche cases: victims of the Black Sphere's devastating death-wish projector. The least damaged were returning to limited duty one by one, but until the newly graduated class of recruits could be absorbed, the fleet could barely man five of their eight ships. Right then Space Fleet needed a sense of normalcy like a sinner needs salvation.

MacKenna gestured to a chair by his desk. "Sit down, Loraine." She eyed him uncertainly, then settled in the chair. "I've been meaning to get your thoughts on repair priorities." He dug up a folder with a list of their ships and the repairs they needed. There were too few names, and far too many notes. "Now that 'Marco Polo' is operational, who should be next?"

She stared at nothing for a bit as she tried to collect her thoughts, then focussed on the list in front of her. "From what I saw in orbit, the 'Comanche' should be our first priority since they're in the best shape, followed by the 'Conestoga' so we can get supplies moving to the colonies more effectively..." She was tapping the list with a pencil she wasn't holding a second before; they both faltered at the sight.

"God, that gives me the creeps," MacKenna muttered at last.

"I don't know how it..." The pencil vanished. "Um...I...don't know how I do that, sir." She looked a bit shaken, as she usually did when these strange events happened. "Yes, I feel fine. In fact, I feel...I've never felt better."

That shook MacKenna a bit in turn, since she'd answered a question he was about to ask. "What did the Dreamsingers do to us?"

"I'm sure they had good intentions, sir. I don't think they're hostile."

"Yeah, I know." They stared at each other for a moment, disconcerted by their growing powers, which were *stronger than anyone else in the fleet. "I'll ream the science pukes again to see what progress they've made." He gave her a searching look. "Are you fit for duty, Captain?" But he didn't need to be psychic to know what she would say.*

"Yes, sir. We have to get those supplies out there."

"Well...all right. But take it easy. This is a simple out and back supply run; don't strain yourself or your ship needlessly."

"Yes, sir." She stared at nothing for a bit, then paused as she headed for the door. "Actually, I do feel good. Whatever J J did, it really helps. I washed away the exhaustion just now by thinking about it."

"Handy trick, that," MacKenna sighed. "No word from him lately?"

"Not since right after the war, sir."

J J Ballas was their Dreamsinger contact, who used the Captain's memory of an elderly Blues musician she knew as a child to reach out to them. Even then, their connections were brief and sporadic. As ominous as their alienness was, the Admiral would have welcomed a visit from that hulking old black man with his aura of warmth and good cheer right then.

"Oh, sir, do you have the updated fleet transit list?" That was the master schedule of all ship movements for the next several months: essential in case a ship became overdue, or they had to rendezvous for some emergency.

"Oh." MacKenna winced in embarrassment. "Sorry; it slipped my mind completely. I'll get after Operations about it, and have them send it to you NINS."

"New Patagonia must be in a bad way. I really shouldn't wait until a courier can deliver it, sir."

MacKenna mused on that while nursing his headache. Their outpost on New Patagonia hadn't received a supply run for months; they were probably out of fuel, and dangerously low on rations. Why they bothered with that frozen hell-hole was beyond understanding, even if it was one of only two inhabitable worlds the humans knew of.

Still, since they were there, they needed the supplies, urgently. The rhyme and reason of it was more than MacKenna could bother with just then.

"The war pretty well killed off the notion that the Ic'nichi are hostile. I'll have them transmit it in code."

"Thank you, sir."

He sat for a long time after she left staring at the pen set in front of him without really seeing it. "God, I'm too old for this," he muttered at last. Ninety years old; coming up ninety-one, and that after a lifetime of combat during the Collapse. The thought of it left him bemused.

Something Captain Morgan said earlier came back to him as he stared at the wall: 'I washed away the exhaustion just now by thinking about it.'

He toyed with the notion for a while, and wondered if there was something to it. He was feeling every one of his ninety years just then: the aches and pains and bone-weariness of a lifetime of duty. One man shouldn't have to carry so great a burden. A lifetime of war and self-sacrifice...a lifetime spent guarding humanity against its inner demons...a life he lost in the recent war...and was given back by J J Ballas. A man gets Godawful weary carrying a burden like that. Anything which could help ease the strain would be all to the good.

"Hell," he mumbled at last. "Can't hurt to try." He sagged in his chair, resting on his elbows, and closed his eyes...

§

...his blood pressure was high; dangerously high; he not so much felt it as knew it. *'You'll have a stroke, you keep that up,'* he thought as he marveled at his new self-awareness. There was no sound, no sight, only a strange other-worldly *presence.* He seemed to be lost in a gray fog which parted here and there to give him faint glimpses of a surreal landscape. His mind and body spread around him like an intricate mosaic which he could

37

only get vague, fleeting glimpses of. He turned his mind outward, his thought roaming through that fog, sensing the tension in his shoulders, and the ache in the pit of his stomach. It was utterly alien, yet fascinating.

But he had no time to unscrew the inscrutable, and he was here for a reason. He focussed on the stress, trying to grab hold of it and tamp it down. It wasn't easy, or simple. Grasping the fabric of his psychic being took effort. But he slowly did it, willing it to gradually relax a bit here and a bit there. It was difficult at first, but as he learned how to manipulate the unseen presence in that fog, he had more sweeping results... He touched something in the darkness, evoking a burst of revulsion...

§

...and was jolted back to the here and now. He opened his eyes: the headache was gone, and he could tell his blood pressure was much lower. He was still old and weary, but his energy was up, the tension in his shoulders was gone, and he felt better than he had in a long time.

"Damn," he muttered. "Ain't that something?"

§

'Marco Polo' left orbit four hours later after receiving the coded transmission. They weren't the only ones to note it. The next morning, the Ic'nichi courier ship requested permission to leave orbit for d'enchia. No one thought much about it, since the couriers were busy with the aftermath of the Dreamsingers' War. Permission was granted in a routine way, and shortly thereafter they headed for deep space.

*****

"Learning To Live With A Knotted Tail"
(Related by Defender I'eiBida)

"I'eiBida?" It was the Herd Guide again, with another memo to saddle on me. "You're wanted over at the Institute to follow up on that psych exam from the other day."

"Sir? That's unusual, isn't it?" All of a sudden I was worried. Did they find something?

"Do I look like a psychiatrist?" he grumbled. "For that matter, what do you consider 'unusual' around here?"

I glanced over the memo quickly. "Um...perhaps that these orders come direct from the Most Ancient, sir?" *That* was decidedly ominous, now I thought about it.

He frowned, and offered a perplexed ear twitch. "Yes, that would qualify. What do you make of it?"

"No idea, sir. All I know is they knotted my tail in grand fashion. They gave me every test known to medical science, and then made up new ones. Whatever it is, they must be looking for something huge."

He pondered for a bit, and I could tell he was not happy. "You worry me. Could this be something aimed at us?" A lot of us in the 'Dark Grays' were a bit paranoid about our reputation with the other services, and the Herd Guide caught every whisper and gripe thrown our way.

"I haven't the faintest taste, sir."

He gave me a disgruntled look. "Perhaps it has to do with some of our wilder characters. They may be questioning our recruiting standards."

"We do seem to draw an *individualistic* herd, sir." Aside from training, part of my duties included reviewing the Service Warden arrest reports, which made an *entertaining* read at times; only to be expected with a brand new Service notable for the *'v'thorbles* it attracts.

"Exactly. We should be more worried about all the 'normal' ones in *this* place."

I offered a wry ear twitch. "Then perhaps it's good that I'm ahead of the stampede, sir; a new kind of 'seniority', no doubt."

"No doubt. And it gets better: they want to see your bondmate, too."

"C'traBenla?"

He eyed me severely. "What? You have another bondmate?" He gestured at the memo. "Pick her up and get over to the Institute, at the gallop." With that, he stomped off to work his charms on the next victim.

§

When I arrived home, I was dismayed to discover our quarters were a disaster area. It seemed C'traBenla spent the morning rearranging the furniture, then scrubbed every pot, dish, and utensil we owned, and now was busily folding all our freshly washed clothes with mathematical precision. All the cabinets were emptied, their contents lined up neatly awaiting new shelf liners, and there were mops and sponges and buckets of water everywhere. This wasn't good.

"You're nesting again, love."

She eyed me uneasily, probably thinking I would yell at her or something, although I was more disturbed than anything else. "I'm just tidying up a bit, I'ei."

"And you did a great job of it." (They taught me how to handle these crisis as part of her possession syndrome therapy.) "But perhaps you should take a break. You don't want to strain yourself while carrying."

Once, when she was carrying our first egg, she went for two days and nights despite my pleading with her until she all but dropped from exhaustion. Right then, she looked weary and frazzled and a bit frantic. I was afraid this would happen, and I was worried about her health.

"Well, I guess you're right." She left off and slumped wearily on the sleeping pad.

"Are you feeling tired?"

"I know it's awfully soon after having our first, but you know how strong I am..."

"C'tra, don't worry about it."

"You're not mad at me?"

"No, love, but I am concerned about you."

40

Truth, I was still a bit stunned and not sure how I felt about her pregnancy. My mal ego was pleased, of course, but my big worry was her emotional health. Last time, she gyrated back and forth between insecurity and near hysteria with flashes of temper thrown in for variety, which made life *interesting* to say the least. It looked like she was shaping up for the same this time, which was enough to unsettle anyone.

She gave me a defensive look. "I know I'm temperamental, but I can't help it. I don't mean any harm by it, honest."

That was an *odd* thing for her to say; what brought that on? "I know, love. It's all right."

She smiled tentatively. "You are *so* patient with me; that's why I love you *so* much. I love carrying your eggs."

On second thought, my big worry was that it might be like this forever: one egg after another after another... Oy, as the humans say.

She must have felt how concerned I was, because she gave me another defensive look. "I'm sure we can afford the crèche fees. We'll have to pinch, but we can do it."

Another odd comment on something I hadn't even thought about. I decided I'd better go through our budget right away, although I knew there was no way we could afford the extra expense.

"Um..." She eyed me warily. "So what brings you home now, love?"

"Oh...ah, the Herd Guide told me to come get you and go over to the Institute." I dug the memo out of my pouch and offered it. "They want to run some medical tests."

She took the memo, looked at me uncertainly, and began reading...

"A psychological exam?" That set her off. "I'eiBida, fan D'chr, if you think I've gone *er'trxxda...*"

"No...love...this has nothing to do with your therapy..."

"Well then, *what?*"

"I don't know. It's something the Herd Guide dumped on me. I was over there the day before yesterday, and they want me to come back and bring you. I have no idea why."

That set her off again. "You were there before? Why didn't you tell me?"

"I didn't think it was important, and I was a little preoccupied by the news you gave me that evening."

That mollified her somewhat, although I could tell she was still miffed at me. "I suppose you would be." She clambered to her feet and started dressing. "Well if we're going, we better go," she said, coolly. "You're under orders, so we need to gallop."

I let it go at that. She can be touchy at the best of times, and is especially temperamental when she's carrying. Her chilly tone was a small price to pay, and she'd get over it soon enough.

As I expected, by the time she was ready, her mood had improved. "All set, love." She gave me a sensuous come-hither flick of her tail. "How do I look?"

She looked good in fact, but then she always does. I gave her a suggestive ear twitch in return. "Mmmmm, perhaps it's best we have to hurry." It never fails: as temperamental as she can be, she always bounces back.

She smiled. "You are a naughty *'v'thorble*. Why I put up with you is beyond me."

"You put up with me because I *am* a naughty *'v'thorble*. That's why you fell tail-over-ears for me."

She offered a mock-exasperated sigh. "I never did have standards, I guess."

"Then you won't be embarrassed to be seen with me. Shall we?"

"So, will we see Learnéd X'venMbaa?" she asked as we headed out the door. X'venMbaa was handling her possession syndrome therapy.

"Um..." That brought me up short as I realized belatedly I was walking into trouble. This was going to be delicate. Probably best to get it over with, rather than spring it on her when we reached the Institute. "...no. We'll be seeing...Learnéd N'detLeda."

"N'detLeda?" One can but try. I'm sure the only reason the neighbors didn't call the Peace Wardens was because they were well familiar with her temper.

§

42

Her mood was still chilly when we reached the Institute, but at least she seemed to be over her mad. I could only hope N'detLeda wouldn't do anything to set her off. He knew her temper of old, and as arrogant as he was, he was no *n'bna'nmn,* so maybe we would get through this after all.

We ran into Fleet Elder H'rhAtor and his Worthy on our way through the campus. "I'eiBida?" He gave us a curious look. "So you're caught up in this tail chasing too?"

"Yes, sir. Do you have any idea what this is about, sir?"

"Not the faintest taste." I could tell he was seriously annoyed by this mystery. "A senseless waste of time, likely. As if we don't have enough to do."

"So how fares the fleet, sir?"

"Don't you people read the reports?" he snapped. Then he gave me a pained look. "Sorry. I haven't been sleeping well lately." He was silent and withdrawn for a bit, and I could tell his nerves were frazzled by worry and exhaustion. "We're making progress," he said at last. "But I'd say the fleet is marginal at best." He sighed in exasperation. "I *wish* I could get a decent night's sleep. I need some release time; lately I spend all day fretting over details a common rating should attend to."

"We all need some time off," his Worthy grumbled. "Even I'eiBida, here."

H'rhAtor glanced at me again. "Oy. Maybe we should just declare a holiday."

I winced at the thought. "Please don't, sir! You have no *idea* how much paperwork that will generate!"

He sighed. "We can't win, can we?"

§

We also ran into K'deiTai and Learnéd M'tinDegan outside N'detLeda's circle. "Learnéd!" C'tra's mood picked right up at the sight of M'tinDegan. "It's good to see you!"

"Delighted. How have you been?"

"Well, we have some good news." She smiled and offered a shy tail flick. "We're expecting again."

"You're carrying? Congratulations." He gave me a pitying glance. "So...are you feeling all right?"

She practically beamed with pleasure. "I feel fine! It's still early, and you know how strong I am."

K'deiTai was his usual grumpy self, and greeted us with a weary, frustrated look. "What is this about, anyway?" he asked me.

"No idea. I was here a couple days ago, and N'detLeda put me through a huge mental tail chase."

He nodded at that. "I was here several days back, and I've never seen the like. Did His-High-And-Mightiness say anything to give you a clue?"

"You know how close-tongued he is when sniffing the trail for mental cases."

M'tinDegan nodded morosely in agreement. "Even that assistant of his kept her ears down. This must be serious."

K'deiTai ear-twitched his exasperation. "That's saying a lot, with her. Well, I hope it's something important. My Aide will be impossible if this is just more mindless tail chasing."

"It was organized by the Most Ancient, I understand," H'rhAtor said. "So it must be for a good reason."

K'deiTai gave him a sour look. "'Important' and 'good reason' are two different things."

Just then, as luck would have it, N'detLeda came wandering by with T'virDoma trailing. C'tra hissed at him, and her ears laid back to which N'detLeda gave her his patented Superior Look. "Ah, charming as always. Your presence brightens the day, I'm sure."

"Like old times on earth," T'virDoma snarked. "Only now we don't even have meaningless make-work for you to do."

"I can keep busy mopping the floor with you!"

"Enough!" N'detLeda grumbled impatiently. "There are important matters to attend to. After our meeting, I need for you and H'rhAtor and his Worthy to remain for an evaluation." The look C'tra gave him was pure poison, but she kept quiet.

"So what is this all about?" H'rhAtor demanded. "This better be something serious. I have neither the time nor the patience for your tail-chasing!"

"This is about seeing whether you are a danger to our species, or just to yourselves," N'detLeda snapped. "And since you are

44

here under orders from the Most Ancient, you have all the time, *and patience*, you'll need!"

"The fleet is in no shape for this! There's too much to do."

"If you hadn't sloughed my repeated requests off, you could already be through with it. But since you are so concerned about the fleet, you can be relieved of duty and a replacement appointed until you comply!"

"That serious?" H'rhAtor eyed him uneasily, but offered no more objections.

N'detLeda turned to C'traBenla. "And as for you, this is medically necessary, so one *hopes* you can contain your temper until this unpleasantness is finished."

"One might find one's tail knotted around one's neck!" she snapped at him.

I needed to step in before he set her off again. "I don't want you to over-exert her. She's carrying right now."

"An egg?" He eyed her suspiciously. "How long have you..."

"It's been ten days," she muttered.

He pondered her for a moment, no doubt wondering if he could get a tissue sample from the egg, but thought better of it. He knew her temper.

§

Pleasantries past, N'detLeda herded us into the inner room where I went through his tail-chasing the other day. His equipment was still there, but several seat cushions had been moved in, so the place was a bit cramped. It looked like we were in for a lecture. We all made it in, and settled uneasily.

U'tdaPagrn was already there, squatting on one of the seat cushions, and gave K'deiTai a sour look. "You should be ashamed of yourself! The Eldest went on an epic binge last night because of your lemon-*V'liz!*"

"Serves him right," K'deiTai grumbled. "It's about time *he* endured a little immersion in human culture."

"A *little*..." U'tdaPagrn was apoplectic. "You should have seen him! I had no idea he was such an *er'trxxda* drunk! It took four Peace Wardens to corral him, and he was just released from the clinic this morning."

"That lemon concentrate must be something." K'deiTai was completely unapologetic, even grimly smug.

"They called in a hazardous spill unit to remove it. The stuff is *TiHiuta* in paste form! Have you no shame?"

"None."

U'tdaPagrn shut up and flopped on his seat cushion in a fine mood while we wondered what *that* was all about. An ominous silence descended.

§

N'detLeda finally took center stage and waited impatiently until he held our undivided attention before he began.

"The reason you have all been called here is because you have all been exposed to mental contact by the alien the humans call J J Ballas," he told us. "We have reason to believe this has resulted in changes to your mental processes, and we need to know what sort of changes and how extensive."

That produced a stir among us. J J Ballas was the image of an old human blues musician which was projected into our minds by the Dreamsingers; the mysterious, empathic beings of a gas giant world.   He—they—reached out to us in our minds, first to communicate with us, and later to draw us all into a psychic neverland after we saved them from extermination. They depend on psi like we do on speech and hearing, and as benevolent as they seemed, none of us doubted they were formidable.

"What evidence do you have thus far?" M'tinDegan asked after an awkward moment.

"The preliminary tests show marked increases in empathy, precognitive skills, and some indications of latent telepathy. Some of you are beginning to show low level telekinetic skills as well."

"Precognition?" K'deiTai wondered. "Telepathy? What does it mean?"

"That...would be consistent with the Dreamsingers trying to communicate with us," H'rhAtor said, doubtfully. "Their telepathic link might have affected us somehow."

"Yes," M'tinDegan added.   "I suspect you're looking at some sort of realigning of the neural synapses, which would make it easier for them to link with us." I could tell he was fascinated by

46

this development. "However, I'm not sure this is such a bad thing. Many of us rely on high levels of empathy in our professions; this would simply be an improvement on latent skills."

"Perhaps," N'detLeda grumbled.

"I can say it certainly is helping me," U'tdaPagrn said. "I've had a much easier time understanding the humans lately, which has the Third Accord negotiations galloping right along."

"Charming." I could tell N'detLeda was not amused to have his lecture getting out of control. Maybe there was something to this?

"That's the same with me and my apprentices," K'deiTai said. "Our grade curve is up sharply, and I've received a number of compliments on my instruction lately."

"How nice."

"And now I think of it, I've been doing much better at the Staff lately," I said. "The stress is a lot less, the work is going smoother, and personal frictions are lower." I didn't add how that last was between C'traBenla and me.

"How proud I am for you," N'detLeda said, impatiently. "The fact remains this phenomenon is an unknown quality. We don't know what is happening to you, or how extensive the changes will be, or how they will affect you. And since most of you hold sensitive diplomatic or military positions, interference with your minds is not something we can take lightly. As such, I have asked for you all to be detached for the moment so we can study this closely."

"But this will disrupt the negotiations!" U'tdaPagrn objected. "The Third Accord is essential."

"I understand the Most Ancient has sent a personal message to the humans saying the talks will have to be suspended for the moment due to your illness."

"But I am not ill!"

"According to the leading medical authorities, (we knew who that meant) you are."

"They may well misinterpret this as a diplomatic setback. Relations are still in a delicate state."

"There's nothing for it. Relations will have to limp along as best they can." Then he turned on the rest of us. "And since I am certain each of you has compelling arguments, complete with signed affidavits from your Ancestors for why you can't take time off, the Most Ancient has given this top priority. You're all going to have a little vacation, and you'll just have to cope."

§

Needless to say, we were all a bit shaken by this turn of events. But what really set things off was when N'detLeda announced we would all be transferred to a prominent clinic—for observation and monitoring, he claimed—to warehouse the lot of us, we were sure.

"This is *x'mnnb'*!" H'rhAtor snapped. "It isn't bad enough for you to take us off duty in these critical times, you have no reason to lock us up, too!"

"We aren't showing any adverse symptoms," M'tinDegan said, reasonably. "We will be far more comfortable in our own homes, and since most of us live nearby, we can be reached easily for further testing."

N'detLeda huffed and gave him his stern 'physich-knows-best' glare. "I hardly need to remind *you* that *I* am the medical authority here, and in my *considered* opinion, observation is essential!"

It was plain that try as they would, and they argued long and loud about it, they weren't going to make any headway with him. But I *sincerely* didn't want to spend my time as his lab specimen, so I waited until the others gave up in disgust, then got him off to one side and hit him where it would hurt the most. "Are you *really* sure you want her under foot all the time?" I asked, confidentially. "She gets broody when she's carrying, and you know how she is when she's upset. Do you want to risk it?"

He fumed for a bit, then eyed her uncertainly. Despite his bluster, I could tell he was more afraid of her than he let on. Nice stuff, this empathy.

"She's rather upset right now," I added to dig the needle in. "All this talk of mental problems...while she's carrying..." (I could tell that worried him.) "She's concerned about her egg..." (He was wavering.) "Anything she perceives as a threat...even unspoken thoughts...she might panic..." (Which sent a chill through him.) "And to be honest, you two don't hit it off..."

"Ah...perhaps some accommodations can be made..."

48

"She'll be more stable in a familiar environment...less prone to lose control..."

I could tell when he caved in. "All right. You can remain at home, but you are off duty for the time being, and I want both of you to stay close to home and avoid any untoward excitement."

"Thank you." I turned to go, then had a thought. "Ah, that would mean the others can go home as well?" I said aloud. "Unless you don't mind showing favoritism?"

"All right, curse your Ancestors!" Love this empathy. I got while the getting was good, as did the rest of us.

§

We gathered outside to try to make sense of this unexpected turn of events. We stood looking at each other for an awkward moment, then H'rhAtor turned to M'tinDegan and said, "So what does this mean?"

M'tinDegan shook his head doubtfully. "Ancestors alone know. There are reports of individuals with psychic abilities going back to our earliest history, but nothing I know of could be considered scientifically credible."

"This is preposterous!" K'deiTai shook his head in dismay.

"I'm not so sure about that. I've had some *strange* experiences lately. I guess they can be traced to these psychic abilities."

"And it might explain our recent problems," H'rhAtor said. "Lately I've been fretting over minor details, things ordinary ratings would worry about." He gave M'tinDegan a pained look. "Are we picking up the thoughts of everyone in the fleet?"

"That does sound like it, at first glance." M'tinDegan pondered for a long moment, then, "This might possibly be an advantage in combat, if you can relay orders instantly throughout the fleet."

"If we all don't go *er'trxxda* from all the noise!"

"Hmmm...perhaps so." M'tinDegan pondered a bit more. "Has anyone else felt anything unusual?" After comparing notes, it turned out we all experienced recent bouts of unusual empathy or precognition or hints of telepathy, which was a bit unsettling.

"There may be something to this." M'tinDegan seemed intrigued by the prospect, but then he *would* be. "It will be a fascinating sociological experiment, to be sure."

"You're no comfort!" K'deiTai muttered.

"I'ei...this isn't going to affect my egg? Is it?" I didn't need telepathy to see how worried C'tra was.

I took her hand to comfort her. "I'm sure it'll be all right, love."

"That's assuming anything passes on to your hatchling," M'tinDegan added, earnestly. "If anything, verifiable psychic powers could be an asset." He glanced at me. "For example, you handled N'detLeda like a professional back there."

"Well...I just persuaded him, is all."

"But you knew *how* to persuade him, which isn't easy for someone with his skills. I'd say someone with your *limited* background manipulating a sharp operator like him proves the point."

"Thank you, I guess."

"What*ever!*" U'tdaPagrn was not amused. "This will make a fine mess of our diplomatic effort. Things are still in a delicate state, the humans are more paranoid than ever with the shape their fleet is in, and I don't doubt my being recalled is sending all the wrong ear twitches to Geneva."

"Nothing for it, I'm afraid," M'tinDegan offered. "We just have to hope for the best."

U'tdaPagrn contented himself with a weary sigh and an off-color ear twitch. "Well since I have you all here, I have gifts for you; some little souvenirs from earth." He fished around in his file satchel, pulled something out, glanced at it, and handed it to K'deiTai, who examined it suspiciously.

"It's...lovely. What is it?"

"It's you."

It was a little plush figurine about two hands long, shaped like one of us and dressed in miniature clothes. K'deiTai puzzled over it, then glanced suspiciously at U'tdaPagrn. "Me? I don't understand."

"They're the latest thing on earth, and a smashing success for their year-end gift giving." U'tdaPagrn dug in his satchel and produced figurines for M'tinDegan, C'traBenla, and me. "They made these for all the major members of the original diplomatic mission."

We all studied our figurines curiously. Mine was recognizable, if rather crudely made, but the uniform was a vague mish-mash of dress and utility with far more insignia and medallions than I deserved. It looked like whoever made these got hold of *Ranks and Decorations*, and went at it with more enthusiasm than common sense.

"I'ei, is that the Honorable Order around your neck?"

"Huh?" I glanced at C'tra in confusion, then examined my figurine again. "Um...it's just a dab of paint; no idea what it's for."

"Still, it looks like the Honorable Order."

I was nonplussed. "It... Wonderful!" She was right. "Like I don't have enough problems without offending *them!*" The Honorable Order is the highest award a defender can receive. Membership is by invitation and comes with vast prestige, and they guard their perks jealously. I looked askance at U'tdaPagrn. "They only made a few of these, I hope?"

"They're turning them out by the carload. The shops are full of them." I winced, and my ears sagged in alarm.

C'tra gave that a dismissive snort. "Oh, really, I'ei, you are *such* a worrier." She went back to her figurine, then hesitated, and looked at it more closely. "Does my red sequin gown *really* show that much tail?" Oh, *now* she was appalled. "It makes me look like a *tra'taj!*"

"It's just a cheap figurine, love," I said, acidly.

"I wore that gown to the Chamber reception! I'ei, does my red gown make me look like a *tra'taj?*"

I winced again, and tried to cover my panicky reaction. "No! Ah... No, dearest, it makes you look lovely."

"Are you sure?" She studied the figurine in dismay. "I *do* look like a *tra'taj!* Ancestors, just *think* of the gossip! I must be the biggest sensation since...since ever!"

As if my little day wasn't happy enough, N'detLeda came by on his way out just then, accompanied by T'virDoma. He nodded to us in passing, then spotted the figurines and halted in surprise. "What are those things?"

T'virDoma eyed C'tra's figurine with a malicious set to her ears. "Perhaps they're taking up that human voodoo?"

"I won't be sticking pins in a little doll!" C'tra snarled.

"They're the latest gifting item from earth," U'tdaPagrn said. "They made these for all the major members of the original diplomatic mission."

"Indeed?" N'detLeda examined K'deiTai's figurine curiously. "There's no accounting for taste, I suppose."

"It's an interesting example of cultural differentiation." M'tinDegan examined his figurine curiously. "I doubt we would have thought to do something like it."

"Yes, quite." N'detLeda turned to U'tdaPagrn. "So...I presume you brought one for me?"

"Um..." U'tdaPagrn seemed embarrassed. "...they were...out of stock at the moment."

"Hmph!" N'detLeda was obviously disappointed, although he tried not to show it. So much for cultural differentiation. "Perhaps the humans have some redeeming qualities after all."

He and T'virDoma went on their merry way, and K'deiTai gave U'tdaPagrn a jaundiced look. "Out of stock, eh?"

"The humans must be using them for voodoo!" C'tra complained.

"Or target practice," I grumbled.

§

As soon as we got back to our quarters, I called the Herd Guide, who confirmed I was temporarily detached for medical release on orders direct from the Most Ancient. "Some people have all the luck." He was not happy, but then he never is. "We just lost H'rhAtor and his Worthy, too. Be thankful you're not here to deal with the paperwork."

That was an opportunity for a snarky cheap-shot, but I was too preoccupied with worry. "I guess it depends on how you define 'luck', sir."

"No doubt. Enjoy it while it lasts."

I debated with myself for as long as it took to hang up the phone, then decided to follow orders: I spent the next morning shamelessly sleeping in.

*****

"Futility As A Career Option"
(Related by Defender I'eiBida)

"I'eiBida?" It was the Herd Guide on the phone two days later, waking me out of a much-deserved sound sleep. "I have amended orders for you."

"Sir? More psyche testing?"

"You could probably use it. You're to report to the Chamber-Of-Ancients, at the gallop."

"But...I thought I was on medical release, sir."

"People once thought the stars were silver lanterns; they were wrong too. Get your tail straight and gallop over there, and be sure to make a good impression! We don't need to look slovenly in front of the Chamber!"

I mumbled, "Yes, sir", hung up, and heaved myself out of bed with a groan as C'tra came bustling in from the kitchen.

"So what did the Herd Guide want?"

I nodded wearily, being too groggy to catch that she knew who called. "He wants me to go over to the Chamber for some circular tail chasing."

"Well you could probably use the gallop. All this sleeping in is making you soft." She gave me an impish ear twitch as she turned and headed back to the kitchen. "I'll fix you something while you dress."

I was fiddling with my best uniform, trying to get the collar tabs straight, when there was a knock at the door. "What?" I wondered peevishly as I went to answer it. Perhaps the Chamber Wardens sent a car to pick me up...

...It wasn't a car from the Chamber; it was the last thing I would have expected. "*Pierre?*" I was flabbergasted to see the tall, spindly human standing at our doorstep with two Diplomatic Security types hovering in the background. "What are *you* doing here?"

He gave me a broad smile. "I am assigned to the embassy. I just arrived, and came to look up old friends."

"Um...come in. It's good to see you!" He had to bend over to fit through the door. "C'tra! It's Pierre Roubidoux, from earth."

She came trotting out of the kitchen, her snout lit up with pleasure. "Pierre? This is wonderful! So good to see you!"

"Je t'en prie, madamoiselle." He offered a small bow from his already cramped posture. *"Il est bon de voir de vieux amis."*

"Please sit down! I'm sorry we have nothing to offer you."

He settled on the floor and leaned against the wall. "It is no matter. Your company is refreshing enough."

"Pierre!" she giggled like a hatchling. "You haven't lost your touch with the fems!"

He smiled. "One can but hope. Speaking of which, I am honored to report that my lovely Jeanette came with me. We are to be married in a few weeks."

C'tra perked up even more, if possible. "We *must* have a party! We'll get the old herd together to celebrate."

That should have been fair warning, but I was still half asleep, and didn't realize at the time that that simple statement would alter the course of galactic history. "Um...Jeanette came with you?" Which shows how quick I was then. "Are they allowing non-essential personnel at the embassy now?"

"Did you not know? Jeanette works for the Education Ministry, and is a certified school administrator. She will be organizing a school for dependents here. There are a few children among the staff already, and more on the way."

I gave that a bemused ear twitch. "Things have changed, haven't they?"

He nodded. *"Oui.* It is not like the old days when the embassies were not thought to be safe for children."

C'tra and I exchanged glances, recalling our own misadventures in parenting on earth. "It's good to see that relations are starting to improve."

"Oh, there are still issues; we are not out of the woods yet by any means. We were told relations are delicate, but our Ambassador is confident things will improve in time. Jeanette proposed her school as an act of good faith to your leaders, which is why they agreed for her to come here."

"Well it has my support, for sure. I didn't realize there were that many of your young on d'enchia."

"Not many as yet, but as you know, aside from official duties, time lays heavily upon us all. I suppose they could make do with a few tutors for now, but showing our commitment to the diplomatic mission should make a positive impression, no?"

"One can but hope. In any case it's good to have you here. The more of us who have worked together, the better."

"We should get together on occasion," C'tra added. "I'm sure you could discover some insights into our culture which will improve our image on earth."

"*Oui*. I wish to learn more your cuisine in particular, now that we have the chance. We French have a national passion for *haute cuisine*, and I should like to explore your restaurants."

"That will be grand! Oh, but you will have to be careful of what you eat."

"*Oui*. We are as susceptible to your meat proteans as you are to ours, sad to say."

"Not to worry. I know a nice little *s'ff'v'bGkb'eed'b'B'g'bndd F'd'd'dcdreg'ngN* shop in the center nest." Pierre's expression fell, and I could see his confusion. "It's vegetarian; I'm sure you'll love it."

"Ah...*oui*, I look forward to the experience." There was a moment of awkward silence. "There is also an...informal matter I wanted to speak with you about," he said to me, somberly. "I was chosen for this assignment for my experience with your people at the embassy..." He hesitated, then said, "And because my close relationship with many of your military and diplomatic leaders will allow me to act as an *unofficial* conduit between our two peoples. The Admiral wishes to keep the lines as open as possible."

This was news, and I was thrilled to hear it even though it made me a bit uncomfortable, having just straightened out L'datMparn's blackmail effort. "Indeed? I'm sure Eldest H'rhAtor will be pleased."

He nodded solemnly. "Do send him my respects."

"Eeep! That reminds me, I was summoned to the Chamber of Ancients."

"Then by all means, you must go."

§

Pierre remained to chat with C'traBenla, which I knew would keep them both occupied for the rest of the day. I was already late (one is *always* late when summoned to the Chamber, no matter how fast one moves), so I *galloped* to the nearest trolley stop. It took two connections to reach the Chamber Of Ancients; not that it achieved a lot. The Chamber is spread out over such a huge area that it has no less than five trolley stations around its outskirts. My last connection dumped me at the head of the ceremonial avenue leading to the main entrance, which left me with a lengthy gallop to get anywhere—assuming I knew where to go. Typically, those *Urgent* orders neglected to give me a specific destination in an area which would make a sizable Nest in its own right.

I stood at the head of the broad plaza and studied the landscape, trying to decide what to do next. The Chamber dome rose like a low hill in the background, with the scenic plaza cutting a broad open swath through the endless warren of grottos, admin circles and support facilities all linked with a maze of passageways which had grown like some bizarre fungus for the last two hundred-plus years. There are legends of people being lost in there never to be seen again save for random sightings and frantic phone calls as they wandered eternally. Someone once joked that our vision of the Uttermost Darkness was based on this place: I believe it. Actually...the lack of a specific destination in those orders was understandable, since maps of the place were outdated almost before they could be printed. It made me wonder whether this was another of N'detLeda's *l'cc'vn* psychological tests.

The worst of it was I had no idea who wanted me there in such a hurry, or why. Despite being our resident human expert, I was still very junior; enough so that the Ancients wouldn't normally take notice of me. Some people seem to think attention from the front of the herd is a good thing; those of us who have been there know better. Getting noticed can mean plump assignments and rapid promotion, or it could get one sent to earth, or worse. Better to toil in obscurity and work one's way up by the knots in our tails. What worried me was my Worthy and I *were* the leading human experts, the only reason why anyone would notice me, so needless to say I was not thrilled by this unexpected call to adventure.

But it was an adventure which wouldn't get off the ground unless I could find my through this maze. I finally gave up and did the only thing I could think of: I hunted up the nearest Chamber Warden and asked *him*. That one took me to their watch station near the main entrance, where they made some phone calls, and in due order one Q'brnVen, from his name tag, arrived.

"You're one of *them*, eh?" He gave me a jaundiced ear twitch. "I only hope whatever you're doing is worth all the fuss we put up with these last few days."

"One of them what?"

"You don't know either?" He offered me a disgruntled look. "Why am I not surprised? I suppose we'll find out soon enough."

On *such* an optimistic note, he lead me *way* back into the labyrinth of grottos surrounding the Chamber proper to deliver me to a certain room deep in the darkest bowels of bureaucracy. If this was N'detLeda's game, I guess I passed the test.

§

"Here's another one," Q'brnVen announced when we arrived, but H'rhAtor was the only one there to greet me.

"Ah, I'eiBida, you're trapped in this maze too, eh?" From the set of his ears, he was clearly annoyed by whatever dragged us here. "I hope you brought something to read since we don't seem equipped for much else."

Our grotto was brand new; it even smelled faintly of paint. It was like the thousands of its kind which housed the Chamber staff; circular, a hundred paces across, with windows all round except for the short passage to the main corridor. The place was still bare but for a single telephone on one desk, a few seat cushions, and a stack of unassembled furniture and office equipment still in their packages. The view was an unimpressive landscape of similar structures crowded around us with a few forlorn plants in the narrow spaces between us and the neighbors. The floor was tiled, the walls painted a depressing institutional pale green, and the overhead was studded with light fixtures. They literally stamp these things out by the thousands as pre-fab kits which can go up in a day, but the fact that they even went to this much trouble said someone expected something from us.

"So what's this all about, sir? Why are we here?"

"It seems things are trotting with the Chamber for some reason.   The Ancients want a liaison circle, and since we're *officially* detached at the moment, this appears to be our tail knot."

"Um...yes, sir." I wasn't thrilled, since if the Chamber felt it necessary to set up an expedited communication channel, things must be getting tense. "I thought we were on medical release, sir?"

"One would suppose.   To hear it said, we shouldn't even be here. But that would make sense, wouldn't it?"

I surveyed the bare room with some foreboding. The place had the uncomfortable atmosphere of a hole where one's career could all too easily be buried. "But why us? You're too important to be propping up a telephone, and I have no experience in Chamber politics.   Couldn't they find someone better suited for this?"

He offered a vexed ear twitch. "I suspect the real reason is because we're caught up in this mind-thing. They want to keep an eye on us, I guess."

"Oh." That made uncomfortable sense. "What are our duties, sir?"

"For the moment?   Salute anything that moves and collect dust, I suppose." I didn't need to be telepathic to see he was put out by all this. "They're sending over some communications and clerical ratings to get things up and galloping, but Ancestors know *when* they'll arrive.   After that, we wait around until we go *er'trxxda*, or we're told to go home."

Knowing the bureaucracy as I did, this wasn't promising. "Ah...what do we do with all this, sir?" I gestured at the mountain of crates and cardboard boxes.

"There was a herd from Chamber Services here earlier. They just left for mid-meal; once they get back, they should get this sorted out fairly soon."

"Um...you say so, sir." I sized the place up with no favor: it looked like the reception desk would be opposite the door, with our semi-grotto to one side of the restroom, and the clerical herd in the larger other half—assuming things got that far.

"Any idea how soon our people will be here, sir?"

58

He gave me a jaundiced look, then sighed. "From Replacement Circle? I may retire from here first. Perhaps we can bring in some hammocks; at least we can be comfortable."

"Wonderful. My Worthy is not amused to be stuck handling our Academy duties all by his lonesome; he'll have some choice comments when he hears *this* one."

There was a discreet tap on the door, and Chamber Warden Q'brnVen returned with Learnéd M'tinDegan.

"I don't suppose you've heard any gossip on what this is about?" H'rhAtor said to Q'brnVen.

Q'brnVen had nothing to offer but a bemused ear twitch. "I don't think you have the time for all the speculation, sir."

"Or the nerve, either." H'rhAtor dismissed him, and turned his attention to M'tinDegan. "Welcome, and condolences on being dragged into this collective tail knot."

M'tinDegan eyed the scene uneasily. "I am happy to help, especially since we academics don't draw full pay while on rest release." He offered a nervous ear twitch. "So what is the situation?"

"It seems N'detLeda's research is knotting tails in the Chamber. We've been ordered to set up an expedited communications link to the fleet and to the Arbiters."

"Our conditions hardly seem like cause for alarm," he said, doubtfully. "We can all be replaced if need be."

"And I don't see how this would raise the risk from the humans, if they are even aware of it, sir," I added.

"Well your minds must have been altered indeed if you think this Universe is supposed to make sense," H'rhAtor grumbled. "I see this sort of thing all the time. I'm sure they'll get over it presently, and we can go back to being invalids. In the mean time, we polish our buttons and keep busy so we don't go any more *er'trxxda* than we already are."

"Sounds like a plan?" M'tinDegan muttered.

"Oh, Pierre Roubidoux came by our place this morning," I said to him. "He just arrived from earth to work at their embassy."

"He did?" M'tinDegan was pleased. "I shall look him up. It'll be nice to chat about the old days."

Which reminded me... "Um, sir? Pierre said he was assigned here specifically as an informal line of communication with the Alliance."

H'rhAtor pondered that. "He's the tall, thin one?"

"Yes, sir."

"Works in diplomatic intelligence?"

"Yes, sir."

"Does he have MacKenna's ear?"

"I presume so, sir."

"Good! We shall make a point of cultivating him."

I wasn't happy about it, and I could tell M'tinDegan wasn't either. Pierre only just managed to get out of being forced to spy for us, and I didn't want to see him caught up in that again.

H'rhAtor gave me a hard look, having felt my reservations. "Something?"

"Ah...no, sir." I struggled to conceal my thoughts. "I'm just concerned about him being in the middle, is all."

He considered me, then nodded, although I could tell he was still skeptical. He was about to speak when the door opened again, and the regrettable L'datMparn came in. H'rhAtor gave him a chilly look. "Something I can do for you?"

"You can tell me what my specific duties are, sir," he said, sullenly. "I've been assigned here."

"Charming," I grumbled. Then I noticed he was wearing a Second Degree brassard as well as a Chamber collar tab. "What? You're working for the Ancients now?"

"That's right." He gave me a chilly look. "I have been seconded as a service liaison."

"*And* they made you a Second Degree?" I was dismayed when I realized my flagging his file must have set him up for this assignment; *Deja Vu*, as the humans say. "They're giving brassards away now!"

"It seems not everyone at Staff Circle shares your low opinion of me."

"Not everyone at Staff Circle knows you!"

"All right you two," H'rhAtor growled. "Swallow your tails!"

§

I'll say this for the Chamber: whatever failings the bureaucracy has—and they are legendary—the Chamber's tech support *moves*. Much to our surprise, the herd of technicians turned up promptly after mid-meal, and turned to in a manner which impressed even H'rhAtor. The stacks of boxes vanished as furnishings, computers, equipment and supplies were unpacked and assembled in a well-oiled effort. Our expected herd of rankers arrived from fleet by mid afternoon, for a wonder, and found a complete communications suite installed and running, along with work stations, security passes for all, and a lounge in one corner.

"Ancestors," H'rhAtor grumbled as the last of the tech support vanished out the door, leaving not one scrap of trash behind. "We could conquer the Universe if we all moved like that."

"True, but *think* of the bureaucracy we'd need then," M'tinDegan said.

H'rhAtor winced, and gave him an icy glare. "If you're going to talk like that, you can leave!"

Having nothing to do at the moment, M'tinDegan and I did: setting out to locate the nearest food source. It proved to be a good fifteen minutes' gallop away, but our Chamber passes got us in for free, and the *bv'nunma* was excellent.

"So what do you make of all this?" M'tinDegan asked over his *uf'thoka*.

"Soft duty for once," I mumbled as I dug into my *l'ni'ddi*. "Nothing to do but polish buttons and look important; a pleasant change from my usual work, I can tell you."

"You hope. Suppose something does go wrong?"

"What can go wrong?" I gave him an exasperated ear twitch. "The Ancients are chasing their own tails. N'detLeda will figure out this mind-thing presently, we'll all take a pill, and go back to our regular duties. In the mean time we have a nice vacation with pay, and the feeding is first finger all round."

He shook his head skeptically. "I hope you're right."

I didn't need to be psychic to see he was worried. "So what can go wrong, hmmm?"

"Probably nothing. But anything which could involve the humans should be taken seriously."

"I suppose you're right. Still, it's hard to imagine anything worse happening than this mental problem. You know the humans want good relations; we just need to get past all the mutual suspicion and distrust, is all."

He sighed. "You're right. I should know better, but I can't help but feel something will go wrong. It always seems to with the humans, you know."

"Ah...there is that." I wondered idly if we were having a premonition with our supposed mental powers. "Look: don't worry about it; it's not our problem any more."

"One can but hope." We ate in silence for a bit, losing ourselves in the excellent food and the tasteful decor of the Chamber cafeteria system. It's easy to forget one's woes when pampered with first finger service. Honestly, by time we finished, I was starting to like the idea of Chamber duty. Perhaps it wouldn't be so bad if N'detLeda didn't make much progress after all.

"Um...about L'datMparn," M'tinDegan said as we headed back to our grotto. "Perhaps it will be best if we keep as much to ourselves as possible. He must be a spy for Z'keBalf's faction. We don't want him passing anything damaging along."

"Good point," I grumbled as I recalled Pierre's news of that morning. "I'll match ears with H'rhAtor as soon as I can."

§

There was another interesting development waiting for us when we returned from mid-meal; K'deiTai, looking grumpier and more sorely vexed than usual. "Are you a part of this too?" I asked.

He was *not* amused. "I never would have imagined a Learnéd could be pressed into military duty," he grumbled. "What is this world coming to?"

"He was added to our menagerie by the Most Ancient himself," H'rhAtor said, somewhat bemused. "It seems our little show is drawing more interest than I imagined."

"The Institute Elders sold me out, is what happened!" K'deiTai snapped. "They caved in to political pressure!"

"Well you *are* caught up in this mental matter," M'tinDegan said to soothe him. "I'm sure they are concerned for our well-being, and want to keep close touch on us."

Not that it helped. "What? The *Chamber* is going to cure us? We're doomed! I must be *er'trxxda* to put up with this!" There was another knock, and U'tdaPagrn was let in. K'deiTai looked askance at him. "Ancestors, you too?"

"I suppose so," U'tdaPagrn said, doubtfully. "What's this all about, anyway?" Between the four of us, we managed to bring him loosely up to speed. "Will wonders never cease?" he muttered. "How long will this *x'mnnb'* last, do you suppose?"

"Impossible to say," H'rhAtor said. "But knowing our luck, we could be stranded here for a very long time."

"This is going to wreck havoc with our diplomacy," he sighed. He pondered the silent room and the ranks of clerical types at their desks watching us for want of anything better to do. "So what do we do for laughs around here?"

"Stare at the walls, mostly," M'tinDegan said.

"And take naps," H'rhAtor grumbled.

"And there is mid-meal," I added. "Wild and abandoned, us."

"So it seems." U'tdaPagrn offered a resigned ear twitch, plopped on an unused seat cushion, and after reflecting a bit, pulled a familiar plastic cube out of his pouch and began absently fiddling with it. After a bit, he noticed K'deiTai staring at him. "Yes, I got it back." He gave K'deiTai a hostile look and an irritated ear twitch. "You could be charged with treason for that, you know."

H'rhAtor and I exchanged confused looks, M'tinDegan eyed the ominous cube as U'tdaPagrn fiddled with it, while K'deiTai threw up his hands and walked away.

§

All in all, despite L'datMparn, it was a good day...until I got home, whereupon things started unraveling. C'tra was waiting eagerly for me, practically bouncing with curiosity. "So what was all that about?"

I sagged on the bed pad and pulled my footsocks off with a weary sigh. "I've been assigned to temporary duty. The Chamber set up a special liaison grotto, and H'rhAtor and I were bonged since we've nothing better to do."

"But aren't you supposed to be on medical release?"

63

"It's nothing but make-work. Our greatest effort will be galloping back and forth to the cafeteria. Anything interesting happen today?"

That vexed her. "Your Worthy called; he was *most* rude! You need to get his tail straight if he wants to be welcome around here!"

"Wonderful." I knew what that was about: he was miffed at me for slack-tailing while he carried the load for both of us. "I'll have a talk with him."

"You should! His language was atrocious!"

She *hates* people dumping on her, so I decided I better call him right away and apply the old scale polish. That took some doing since he could be at any of a hand's worth of places, but I finally caught up with him at the Academy.

"I'm sorry I can't help right now," I said, earnestly, only to be greeted with a fair sample of his 'atrocious language'. "It's not like I went off at random; I'm under orders."

"So why don't I ever get orders like that? I thought we were supposed to be a team, and I could use a little down time with all the work you left me to do!"

"Just be thankful you weren't on earth with us, and were never exposed to J J Ballas," I lectured him. "These psychic powers are getting to be a real nuisance!"

He climbed down a bit. "How bad is it?"

"Not too bad yet; hard to focus at times. But it's getting worse steadily. Truth, I'm not fit for duty right now." His answer was an exasperated sigh, and he hung up. Ancestors, the things I do for a little domestic peace!

By then C'traBenla had late-meal ready, and we settled in for what I *hoped* sincerely would be a quiet evening. "So how was your day?" she asked as she served up some *V'liz* stew. "Are they keeping you busy?"

"Not hardly. There's really nothing to do, so we sit around all day."

"You will receive orders soon, won't you? It must be something important; they wouldn't go to all the trouble for nothing."

I hastily washed some wilted *uf'thoka* down. "Actually, H'rhAtor made several phone calls, but couldn't learn anything. It looks like we've been warehoused for the time being."

She eyed me curiously, and I could tell she was suspicious of that story. "But why does the Chamber want a liaison circle?"

"Something to do with this mind-thing. My guess is someone's got a knot in their tail over it, and they're concerned about the humans getting involved."

Bad move on my part. Her ears shot up, and I could *feel* her wave of excitement. "That's wonderful, love. I'll be happy to pitch in, of course."

I backtracked hastily, although it was already too late. "There's nothing going on there. We don't even have any paperwork."

"But if there is a risk from the humans, I can be a real help. Don't forget my experience at the embassy!"

I well remembered how 'helpful' she was on our two tours there, and while she could get seemingly impossible results, I shuddered at the thought of her trying her games in the Chamber. And how did the idea of a conflict with the humans come up, anyway? "Honestly, we sit around all day staring at each other...

"But, love, you can never tell what might happen, and I could do a lot through unofficial channels..." At least she knew shouting and temperament didn't work with me, but she kept pleading and negotiating and wheedling well into the night so it was way late when exhaustion took its due, and I finally fell asleep...

§

...until early the next morning, when she picked up her campaign from last night.

"I'ei, love," she said, plaintively. "You can't ask me to sit at home all alone while you're off preventing a war with the humans." She cuddled next to me and caressed my neck, which can be *l'cc'vn* distracting and she knew it. "I want to help, and I have plenty of experience with the humans. I'm sure I can do something useful."

War with the humans, eh? Oy. I could tell this was a losing battle; she could wear down a stone statue. "I'm not preventing a war," I protested feebly. "This is just make-work, and deadly dull. There's nothing to do, and with your present state..."

"My 'state' is fine, thank you! I'm not due for a long time yet, and you know how strong I am. I'll manage." She snuggled closer and nuzzled my ear. "Please, love?"

Sometimes one simply gets too weary to continue the fight. "Well...it's not for me to say, anyway. H'rhAtor would have to approve it, at a minimum."

"Then we'll ask him."

Good enough. One learns to choose one's battles over time, and to accept a victory no matter how tiny. If she was ready to pass the responsibility for rejecting her to H'rhAtor, then far be it from me to argue. At least there would be fewer recriminations that way. I felt a bit guilty about passing my domestic problems off on him, but that's what we have senior elders for.

§

K'deiTai was there when we arrived at the liaison grotto, and gave C'traBenla a suspicious look. "Why are you here?" he asked as introductions were being made all round.

She offered a diffident ear twitch. "I came to join the effort. I want to help out."

He sighed. "Why do my Ancestors hate me so?"

Her diffidence vanished like someone—K'deiTai—threw a switch. "You're being *hro'n'nad!*" she snapped at him.

"Whatever." He threw up his hands in despair and slumped on a seat cushion in our small lounge as far from her as practical.

"Why does he always have to be so grouchy?" she demanded. "I only want to help."

"Don't fret over it, love."

H'rhAtor arrived a short while later, and sagged visibly at the sight of her. One didn't need to be psychic to tell that his little day was getting off to a bad start. "What can I do for you?" he asked, with an ominous glance in my direction.

"I'm here to help," she said.

K'deiTai had the wit to stay quiet and not get involved.

H'rhAtor contemplated the scene with no enthusiasm. "Surely I'eiBida told you there's nothing much happening here." He waved vaguely at the clericals, who were lounging listlessly at their desks or playing video games. "We have more help than we need."

66

"I'm sure there is something I can do," she insisted.

"Honestly..." H'rhAtor didn't want to be in the middle of this; his tough luck. "...from all the signs, things won't change. This is a make-work detail, and with your present condition..."

"My condition is fine! I'm a strong, healthy fem, and I'm still a long way from delivery. Surely I can do something useful around here."

H'rhAtor considered our clerical staff, some of whom were napping or reading popular magazines for want of any useful work. "We're hurting for something to do as is; I wouldn't want you to strain yourself with anything more physical anyway."

"This is my third egg. Honest, it isn't a strain at all. And who knows what may come up that I could help with?"

"I'm afraid we can't. We don't have security clearance for you, to start."

"I'm sure you can arrange clearance."

H'rhAtor was not amused to have his arguments shot down one by one. "I know you want to help, and I do appreciate your interest, but I'm afraid it simply won't work."

"I won't be a problem, I promise."

"Honestly, there's nothing to do here," M'tinDegan said.

"It really is boring," U'tdaPagrn added. "You'll get tired of it in a hurry."

K'deiTai kept his ears down and stayed out of it.

C'traBenla was ear-fallen. "*Please* let me stay," she pleaded with H'rhAtor.

"I'm afraid it's really not practical..." For a moment it looked like she would accept defeat, for a miracle, but then the door opened, and L'datMparn came in. "Oh, and you know Second Degree L'datMparn..."

She turned to him...he looked at her...and her wave of anger hit me almost as hard as her tail swipe which bounced him off the wall and laid him in a heap on the floor. *"Don't you DARE think that again!"* she yelled.

"C'tra!" I was appalled.

"Did you *hear* what he thought about me?" She rounded on him in a rage. "I'll stuff your tail down your throat!"

I managed to get between them and held her back. "Love! What are you doing?"

"Are you just going to *stand* there and let him *think* like that? What kind of mal are you?"

I finally got it through my thick skull that he said—thought—something which really offended her. "Dearest...you can't kill someone for thinking..."

"*p'quas'tka* I can't! That...*un'tdar!*...thought I'm a common..." That'd do it. She lunged at him again, and I earned a couple bruises saving him from her temper. "I'll have your ears!" she screamed at him.

By now all four of us were trying to contain her while the rankers hovered nervously in the background and K'deiTai scuttled to the far side of the room. "You shouldn't be like this, love." I implored her. "Not while you're carrying. It'll have a bad influence on our hatchling!" Yes, I know that made no sense whatsoever, but I was improvising desperately to stave off disaster.

Whatever; it was enough to bring her down from a raging volcano to an ominous simmer. She shook me off, and glared at him with murder in her eyes. "This is your lucky day," she snarled. "Make the most of it!"

Needless to say he did, to everyone's relief; favoring one leg as he beat a hasty retreat. Warden Q'brnVen was right outside when he ran out, and demanded, "What's going on in there?" But L'datMparn ignored him, and vanished down the hall.

"We *have* to get rid of her!" M'tinDegan hissed to me as we watched nervously from one side.

"Later," I whispered. "Not while she's like this..."

"Perhaps she should stay," H'rhAtor said.

"Sir?"

He mused over her glaring at L'datMparn as he scuttled down the hall in ill-concealed panic. "She might prove useful after all."

*****

"A Plot Is Hatched"
(Extract Of Testimony)

There are never *any routine requests from Ancient Z'keBalf. L'datMparn sensed right from the first, with the instinct of all good lackeys, that when Z'keBalf summoned him to his grotto, he meant 'instanter'. That instinct paid off over time: he was a Second Degree now, and still had his ears. He also knew better than to be caught slacking off, so when his patron called, he came galloping.*

The Chamber Wardens escorted him to Ancient Z'keBalf's grotto, which he entered with some trepidation. The room's decor held a certain severe reserve, yet was somehow luxurious, as befit its occupant. A broad marble desk sat opposite the door, with a back desk holding office equipment. The desk was bare, polished to a fine glow. The rest was lost in the glare of the spotlight illuminating the spot directly in front of it.

L'datMparn halted directly under the spotlight, and gave his patron his sharpest tail wave. "Reporting, Ancient."

Ancient Z'keBalf was elderly and heavyset, but hard from his disciplined daily routine. He wore a plain, almost severe business suit unadorned but for his gold-embossed Chamber pass. His ears were notched, a remnant of a fringe fashion popular thirty years ago, and the icy calculation in his eyes intimidated most everyone.

"I summoned you here to fill you in on the details of your new assignment," he said. "No doubt you've been wondering about the Liaison Grotto, and your role in it."

"I presumed you have good reasons for setting that up, sir." In truth, this was the first he'd heard of Z'keBalf being behind that x'mnnb', and it worried him, like a lot of what Z'keBalf did.

The set of Z'keBalf's ears clearly showed his opinion of his scale polishing. "I am concerned that Eldest H'rhAtor and company may have given away too many of our secrets

69

during the joint defense effort in the recent war. From rumors I hear, he compromised us most alarmingly."

That touched a raw nerve. "I'm afraid I can't help you there, Ancient," L'datMparn said, heatedly. "I was kept out of the war planning, even though it would have been part of my embassy duties. U'tdaPagrn brought in my predecessor, Second Degree I'eiBida, to supersede me."

Z'keBalf frowned. "So I understand; a matter we will attend to in due order. It appears to be part of a greater pattern in fleet and diplomatic circles of underestimating — or even dismissing—the human threat."

L'datMparn spoke carefully. "I sincerely hope those shortcoming can be corrected, Ancient. It won't do to have human sympathizers in our most sensitive military and diplomatic positions." Z'keBalf had shown him his fitness report, and he wanted bitterly to score U'tdaPagrn and I'eiBida.

"Indeed. Which is partly why I arranged for them to be sequestered in that so-called 'communications grotto' and why you are assigned there."

"I...see." L'datMparn could hear the wheels turning, and knew someone was about to be ground under. But while he relished the thought, he wouldn't want to be there to witness it if it meant his precious tail being caught in the grinder. "Actually...I was wondering if I might be of more use to you in some other capacity. It seems there is some...personal friction between me and that...fem."

Z'keBalf chuckled at his discomfiture. "She is riv'Agna, there's no doubt about it. I understand you've already run afoul of her temper."

His ears wilted in embarrassment. "I...survived..."

"A remarkable fem," Z'keBalf mused. "One wonders how that I'eiBida manages to keep her in check? No matter. You are right where I need you, and greatness is often measured by the knots in one's tail. Keep your ears up—and your head down—and report anything of interest, no matter how trivial."

L'datMparn was not thrilled to be tossed back into her reach again. "I'll do the best I can, Ancient."

Z'keBalf gave him a chilly look. "You have served me well in the past. Your promotion, and the resolution of some recent complaints show how I appreciate your efforts. Continue in that, and there will be further appreciation."

From experience L'datMparn knew those weren't just empty promises. From what he had heard of others who failed Z'keBalf, he knew the unspoken reverse wasn't just an empty threat, either.

*****

"Crisis As A Conversation Starter"
(Related by Learnéd M'tinDegan)

"I swear I will go *er'trxxda* If I have to spend one more day standing on my tail," H'rhAtor grumbled for the umpteenth time. "Nothing is going to happen, so why doesn't the Chamber get over their *r'vebbe*, and let us get back to work?"

"As you pointed out, Eldest, nothing is going to happen," I offered, reasonably. "I'm sure the fleet has plenty of routine matters to keep them occupied, so they can manage without you for a while."

"Plus, to hear it said, we're already *er'trxxda*, sir," I'eiBida added with a wry ear twitch. "No need to *go* anywhere, so we might as well relax and enjoy a bit of paid down time."

H'rhAtor sighed. "I guess so."

What little novelty our liaison grotto offered in the beginning had long since faded as time went by. We sat here at our desks day after day while the Chamber debated, and aside from occasional visits to N'detLeda's laboratory for further testing, the highlight of our little day was mid-meal. What was worse, N'detLeda's concerns were proving well founded. We all showed signs of psychic abilities by then, and as the days crawled past, our powers grew steadily until we wallowed in an invisible mental fog of random emotions. There were even times, when things were especially stressful, that we could hear each other's thoughts. I, for one, saw it as the start of our becoming true empaths; a fascinating concept, but something none of us looked forward to.

Time dragged on, and frustration soon turned to desperation. We played video games, and schmoozed the internet, and read magazines, and held long 'meaningful' conversations, but those wells of inspiration, shallow as they were, soon ran dry. Imaginations exhausted, we stared at each other while the psychic atmosphere grew thicker and thicker.

'Ancestors! What a mess!' We all caught H'rhAtor's burst of psychic angst.

'Calm,' I thought to him. *'Focus inward and calm your thoughts.'* He looked at me, confused, then sighed.

We were beginning to be distracted by random bits of thoughts, not only from ourselves, but from those in the fleet who were at the battle of the Dreamsingers' world and thus exposed to J J Ballas. It was like being in a crowded room overhearing countless whispered conversations: annoying for what you overheard, frustrating for not being able to catch what was said, and it never ended.

H'rhAtor slipped out of his seat cushion, and began pacing back and forth in frustration. We all felt the same, and our collective mood often caused a feedback which drove us to despair. In a way, I think we envied U'tdaPagrn, who had his little cube puzzle to keep him occupied amid a steady stream of muttered obscenities. Even the clerical staff had nothing to do, which will give you some idea of how deadly dull things were.

"*How* long will it take the physichs to figure this out?" H'rhAtor complained. "I can't squat here forever, and I hate to think of what conditions are up there in orbit." What he didn't say, but we could all feel, was his fear that we might all go back to the egg from this psychic interference and wind up in an institution.

"Your fretting only makes it worse," K'deiTai grumbled. "They haven't forgotten about us. They'll call as soon as they figure out what to do."

"I've never been one for standing on my *l'cc'vn* tail when there is urgent work to be done!" He paced back and forth, radiating his angst like a sticky oder. "It's not like the fleet is in good shape!"

"They're managing by all accounts, sir. We can be thankful we're not needed right now."

H'rhAtor paused, and looked at I'eiBida with a weary sigh. "I suppose. Still, I wish *something* would happen."

Our Ancestors must think us amusing indeed: no sooner did he say that, when the phone buzzed. There was a scramble to reach it; H'rhAtor won. "Liaison Grotto!" He listened for a second, then his ears wilted. "A *banquet* hall?" More silence. We could feel his aura of frustration changing to confusion. Then he covered the mouthpiece and turned to us. "Did we requisition a banquet hall?"

"Ah...not that I know of," I said. I'eiBida shook his head, K'deiTai looked confused, U'tdaPagrn stopped fiddling with his plastic cube.

H'rhAtor gave us a doubtful ear twitch, then went back to the phone. "Ah...there must be some misunderstanding. We didn't requisition a banquet hall... *Chamber Priority?!*" He turned to us in dismay. "The requisition was authorized by the Chamber!"

"For something *we're* supposed to do?" The aura of confusion and panic was thick enough to see by then. I turned to I'eiBida. "Were we supposed to put on a reception? Fleet leaders, perhaps?"

"Ancestors! I don't recall anything!"

"It might have slipped your mind?"

"If it did, the Ki-Eldest will have my ears!"

"Figure it out, fast!" H'rhAtor was back on the phone. "We...ah...seem to have misplaced the paperwork on it."

But of course pandemonium is a game for all, and the more players, the more fun for everyone. There was a knock on the door. I went to answer it, and Chamber Warden Q'brnVen handed me an interoffice memo with a bemused look. "What has she done now?" he asked uneasily, having had his share in her misadventures lately.

"I'm afraid to know."

He left it at that, and withdrew with a resigned ear twitch. Curious, I studied the memo:

Grotto Of
Ancient Y'veNipbr, che Ae'Kigin
Chamber Of Ancients
The World Nest

To: C'traBenla, rani D'enta
Chamber Of Ancients Special Liaison Grotto

Dearest C'tra,
All the arrangements are complete. I will be delighted to attend your party, and to meet your guest from earth. From what you described, he sounds like someone well worth knowing. My best to you,

Y'veN

"We are in big trouble." I showed the note to I'eiBida.

He glanced at it, did a double-take, and his tail wilted. "She's at it again!"

K'deiTai snatched the memo, and his eyes bulged in dismay. "I knew this would happen! I warned you! All of you!"

U'tdaPagrn snatched it next. "What? I don't understand."

H'rhAtor snatched the memo in turn, and went through it with growing dismay. "Ancestors! What has she done?"

"Someone?"

"That fem is a walking disaster!"

H'rhAtor shrugged K'deiTai's near-hysteria off, and turned on I'eiBida. "I want explanations, mister!"

"Honest, sir, I have no idea what she's been up to!"

"She's your bondmate! Are you really that *hro'n'nad?*"

I'eiBida was shaking by then. "This is the first *any* of us heard of it! I never imagined she'd go this far!"

"Not good enough! This is a Righteous First-Finger tail knot, mister, and she has a lot of explaining to do!"

"Um...seeing as this memo is addressed to 'Dearest C'tra' from 'Y'veN', you might want to approach the matter circumspectly," I cautioned.

H'rhAtor did a double-take in turn, and studied the memo closely. "Y'veN?" he muttered, then turned on I'eiBida. "She's on intimate terms with *Ancient Y'veNipbr?* What has she been up to?"

"Honest, sir, I have no idea!"

"She always was comfortable in political circles," I said. "She must have decided to cultivate some of the Ancients as part of working with this grotto."

"Great!" H'rhAtor was appalled. "Y'veNipbr is not someone to trifle with!" He pondered the note again. "And who is this guest from earth, anyway? And why a party, *especially* when the Ancients are involved?"

"I'm afraid I have no idea," I said. I'eiBida shook his head, K'deiTai looked dismayed, U'tdaPagrn stuffed his plastic cube in his pouch. To say confusion reigned supreme in our grotto would be an understatement. We were all so mentally off-balance by then that none of us had the faintest clue.

"Where is she?" H'rhAtor demanded of I'eiBida.

"No idea, sir!" Unlike most of us, C'traBenla came and went as she pleased, and rarely mentioned where she was going or where she'd been. Up until then it hadn't mattered.

"I want her! We need to find out what she's been up to before the Ancients clip all our tails!"

§

Nice sentiment; easier said than done. C'traBenla didn't return until mid-afternoon, by which time we had received confirmations for the buffet, the guest list (which wilted our collective tails when we went through it), and reservations for a special train to bring fleet personnel from the spaceport. For once our clericals were busy figuring the cost of all this frivolity: the numbers were appalling.

And the *reason* for it? "I'm making arrangements for Pierre and Jeanette's wedding," C'traBenla told us when we confronted her.

"A *wedding?*" H'rhAtor was appalled. "You invited *Ancient Y'veNipbr* to an ordinary life-bonding? And why, in the Ancestors' name, did you put on this...this...this...*ceremony!* The bureaucracy will have our ears! *How* are we going to justify all these expenses?"

C'traBenla wasn't fazed in the least by *his* near-hysteria. "Pierre is an unofficial contact with the Alliance and their Admiral, and Ancient Y'veNipbr is the Herd Guide of the pro-earth faction in the Chamber. It's only natural that they should meet. Plus she used her influence to get priority for the hall, and arranged the entertainment, too."

"...entertainment?"

"The Chamber's Choral Herd."

"The...Choral Herd...?" They were one of the finest musical ensembles on the planet, and much in demand for the most high-toned affairs. One pretty much needs Chamber sponsorship to *see* them, to say nothing of having them perform at a function.

"They've been practicing some traditional human music," C'traBenla explained. "I understand they have a pretty good Elvis impersonator."

"But... But... But..." But by then H'rhAtor was reduced to speechless dismay.

"I know you mean well, love," I'eiBida implored her. "But *why* make such a huge fuss when you could simply have introduced Pierre to Y'veNipbr?"

She looked askance at him. "I'ei, we haven't been to a party since we came back from earth."

"But...the Chamber reception... We were the honored guests..."

"Oh, that's *politics!* And it was *so* long ago. This will be a special day for Pierre and Jeanette, and it's a chance for us to relax and have a little fun!"

"Love, any event the Ancients come to is hardly 'fun'. Ancient Y'veNipbr will be there for purely political reasons."

"And she won't be the only one," H'rhAtor added, grimly. "Fleet will be there; so will Intel. And I'll wager the tip of my tail Z'keBalf and his faction will be there too."

If anything, her aura of excitement grew stronger, to where it began to affect our judgment. "Good! With all those tail-shakers around, this is your chance for some serious scale-polishing, love!"

"If it doesn't blow up in our snouts!" We didn't need to feel I'eiBida's dismay to know this could be a disaster to all our careers if it turned out badly.

"Really, love, you need to be more optimistic. The Ancients are just ordinary people like anyone else. Now if you will excuse me, I need to review the arrangements for the humans' buffet."

"Just ordinary people?" H'rhAtor grumbled after she left. "Honestly, I don't know *what* we can do with her."

"We could put her in charge of the fleet, and tell her there's a huge party on earth," I'eiBida muttered. "We'd stampede right over them."

H'rhAtor replied with a rueful chuckle, and shook his head in dismay. "That would be *too* cruel!"

"Why do I get the impression I'd be safer on earth?" U'tdaPagrn mumbled.

"Because you probably would be."

*****

"Into The Fray"
(Related by Learnéd M'tinDegan)

It seemed Chamber Services understood the consequences of an officially sponsored event far better than we did. The preparations for C'traBenla's party went on for *days*, and even Chamber Services was hard pressed to keep up as truckloads of furnishings, food, and supplies poured in. The news media soon caught on, and our clerical staff were all of a sudden complaining about the work load as the demand for press releases and publicity handouts grew out of control. Where grim silence reigned before, now there was the constant buzzing of telephones and the hurried comings and goings of messengers. The accountants were swamped, and our days grew longer and longer. Needless to say, the more it went on, the more dismayed we became.

"Ancestors," H'rhAtor grumbled as we watched the banquet preparations from a safe spot. "If we could harness this energy, we could conquer the Universe."

"Yes, but who would put on official functions then?" I wondered.

Truth, Chamber Services moved smartly and with little wasted effort, which was only to be expected. We watched for some time, bemused at this unaccustomed spectacle. "I just hope this doesn't blow up in our snouts," H'rhAtor said at last.

"Well if it does, the explosion will be so big we won't feel a thing." K'deiTai was in one of his perpetual sour moods.

"You are no comfort!"

"I wasn't trying to be."

The much put-upon Warden Q'brnVen came by just then, and gave us a sour ear twitch. "What a mess! This is all your fault. Our Wardens work until they're ready to drop, and what thanks do we get? Nothing!"

"This wasn't our idea," H'rhAtor said, curtly.

"You could at least keep better tabs on that marauding fem! Can't you lock her up somewhere? Every time we turn around, she's adding some new detail which we have to oversee. I don't know how we'll get all of it ready in time."

"Trust me: we feel your pain," I said. C'traBenla was hard at it, in fact, ordering herds of Chamber staffers about, who tried to be polite while ignoring her and going ahead with what they were doing anyway.

"And forget about keeping her in check," K'deiTai grumbled. "It'd be easier to wrestle a typhoon."

Q'brnVen shook his head in despair. "And then there's the paperwork, Ancestors save me." He wandered off, shaking his head and muttering to himself, "It's not like we have nothing to do around here..."

§

Finally, despite C'traBenla's help, everything was set. The enormous hall was beautifully decorated, and the buffet was a wonder to behold. A small orchestra was retained to provide live music, and Q'brnVen was there, put out as ever, along with plenty of attentive tails to help out and keep order.

"I want you all to watch your step," H'rhAtor lectured us when we met for a final briefing before the event started. "The most powerful tail-shakers will be there, and the place is infested with media. Any embarrassment will get all our ears clipped."

"Indeed. And we should use the opportunity to keep our ears up," I said. "With this many long tails in one spot, who knows what we might overhear?"

"You two are such *hro'n'nad*," C'traBenla lectured them. "Why don't you simply relax and have a good time?" She was dressed to kill in a new maternity frock she made from some mottled green and brown fabric she brought back from earth. "It's not every day we have a party like this!"

"Thankfully!" K'deiTai sighed.

"Still, everyone guard your tongues." H'rhAtor gave her a stern look. "This herd could make or break all of us."

§

Speaking of which, the guest list was a sparkling galaxy of the most prominent tail-shakers, drawn no doubt by the prospect of some major political maneuvering. The special train brought a stampede of senior 'Dark Grays' led by the Ki-Eldest himself, and there were almost as many Ancients and top level bureaucrats as

79

there were media journalists. The Chamber Wardens had their hands full since everyone who was anyone clamored to get in, and the herd around the main entrance threatened to stampede.

Not to be outdone, the humans came in force; their Ambassador leading a herd of diplomatic, trade, intelligence, and protocol representatives girded for battle with their counterparts here. They were backed up in turn by every human news vulture on the planet to cover *the* social event of the year.

Needless to say, Pierre and Jeanette were overwhelmed by all the attention. "*Mon Dieu!* What have you done, my friends?" Pierre sputtered. "We intended no more than a simple ceremony."

"I'm sorry, Pierre," I said. "This was C'traBenla's doing. You know how she is at times."

"*Oui*, how could I forget? As much as I admire her, she is a walking diplomatic crisis."

"Oy, that's the truth," I'eiBida groaned. "So how are your people reacting to this?"

Pierre gave him a vexed look. "The Ambassador raised Cain with me over it. This puts our delegation in a most sensitive position as none of us expected a social gathering of such magnitude. We hardly have any positions prepared, to say nothing of negotiating strategies. And we could hardly fail to come to an event on such a scale, so we shall have to tread warily."

"You could simply relax and enjoy the festivities," I suggested.

Pierre smiled ruefully. "Alas, such is not the way of our diplomacy."

"*She* is having a good time, at least." Jeanette nodded toward C'traBenla, who was making a nuisance of herself at the buffet. "My, what an unusual dress!"

"Camouflage?" Pierre was bemused at the sight. "One wonders what the Peacekeepers would think of her adaptation? Still, it suits her somehow."

"I hope she doesn't strain herself in her condition." C'traBenla's egg was fully developed by then, but she was in her element bouncing back and forth trying the patience of the Chamber staff as she fussed over details they already had down to perfection.

"Ancestors," I'eiBida muttered in dismay as she fiddled with the place settings. "She's nesting again." If her 'condition' slowed her down, one would need scientific instruments to tell the difference.

"I believe this an historic 'first'," I mused as we watched her go. "Nesting syndrome disrupting a Chamber function. We live to see strange portents indeed."

Pierre chuckled. "Pray she does not have twins!"

"Ancestors forbid!" I'eiBida said, fervently.

"Still, it is a huge fuss to make over such a simple affair. I only hope some good comes of it. Her enthusiasm has made my position with the embassy rather *delicate*."

"Get them all drunk enough, and they'll solve all the Universe's problems," K'deiTai mumbled.

"I passed along your message about acting as an unofficial conduit to the Alliance," I'eiBida said, softly. "She intended this partly as a chance for you to meet some of the tail-shakers, Ancient Y'veNipbr in particular."

Pierre was a bit nonplussed, not that I blame him. "I do appreciate her thought, but we are supposed to conduct our activities discreetly."

I'eiBida gave him an annoyed ear twitch. "When was the last time she did *anything* 'discreetly'?"

§

In fact, Ancient Y'veNipbr made a point of meeting the happy couple as soon as she arrived with a contingent of her faction in tow. All of them were eager to meet a genuine human, many of them for the first time, and the somewhat bewildered happy couple were soon surrounded by a churning sea of attentive bronze ears.

"I am please to know you," Y'veNipbr greeted them. "I learn your language? My human talk is so good per...haps?"

"Your Swiss is excellent, Madame," Pierre assured her. "And we are honored that you would go to all this effort for us."

"I have help of one who was on your world. She tell much of your people."

Pierre grinned awkwardly. "Ah...*oui*, I know of whom you speak. She has some *interesting* stories to relate of those times."

"Darling, you are being diplomatic," Jeanette said with an unabashed grin.

Y'veNipbr considered him closely, rearing back to look him in the eyes. "That one tell me you are good to know. We concern for peace with the humans, and I wel...come someone to talk."

"*Oui.* Our fondest wish is for good relations between our peoples. I am happy to aid such a noble cause."

"Good. Then we under...stand together." She gave him a stern look and a warm set to her ears; it was a thinly veiled hint that she intended to use Pierre's 'unofficial conduit' with the Alliance to the fullest.

Pierre offered her a small bow. "Your servant, Madame."

Y'veNipbr dropped down again, and glanced at C'traBenla, who was driving the buffet staff to distraction. "What a curious gown," she said, bemused. "That one did make good...image on your world?"

"She was a popular figure in diplomatic circles," Pierre assured her. "She will not soon be forgotten."

"And she certainly knows how to liven up a party," Jeanette added. I was thankful they left it at that.

§

Speaking of which, the party was soon in full stampede. As large as the hall was, it was packed. The noise level was such that we could hardly hear the orchestra, and the staffers were busy supplying the buffet with both solid and liquid refreshments.

The happy couple, admittedly rather unsettled at the moment, were the center of attention. Pierre was impeccably dressed in a traditional black costume, while Jeanette was an etherial vision in flowing white. The two towered over the guests, a matched set of slender, pale figures surrounded by a churning sea of scaly bronze.

Pierre was soon swept up in an endless round of discussions with various factions from both the human and Ic'nichi camps; frequently with one or more embassy personnel, sometimes privately. His role as unofficial facilitator was common knowledge by then, and most of his supposed 'blessed day' was spent in a whirlwind of discreet conversations with this or that group hoping to improve their position *vis-a-vis* earth.

While Jeanette was largely ignored in the official stampede, she was not lacking for attention. The society columnists and lesser lights, particularly fems, descended on her. Our curiosity about the humans and their strange customs was fanned to a red heat, and everyone wanted to gossip about human bonding and mating customs. She gave no end of interviews through several translators, some of which made the evening news broadcasts, and there was boundless speculation about whether she was carrying, and how many hatchlings they might have. She seemed a bit overwhelmed by all the attention at times, but carried it off with flawless grace. If any good came out of the whole affair, at least the gossip improved the humans' public image.

§

Two familiar snouts turned up around mid-day. "It seems like old times," Learnéd W'kiLap greeted us. "The old herd together again, humans under foot, diplomatic crisis..."

"...C'traBenla running rampant," T'apiDien added. "Yes, I'd say the ceiling will collapse any moment now."

"What diplomatic crisis?" U'tdaPagrn demanded. "Have you heard something?"

"We heard she is involved in a major diplomatic social; based on her history, disaster should strike at any time."

"Not funny," U'tdaPagrn muttered.

"And she's carrying, too." W'kiLap gave her a jaundiced look, then turned to I'eiBida. "My, my; how do you keep her in check, one wonders?"

"I gave up on that long ago," I'eiBida grumbled. "We plan to cancel the stellar bomb program, and turn her loose instead."

"So how did you two manage to get in here, anyway?" K'deiTai asked. "I know she invited you, but how did you get past the Chamber Prefects?"

"Rank hath its privileges, you know," W'kiLap said, smugly. "But connections are what really matter."

"And speaking of rank privilege..." T'apiDien nodded toward the main entrance, where Ancient Z'keBalf was making a theatrical entrance with a retinue of his faction, followed by N'detLeda and T'virDoma hovering in the background.

"Wonderful," K'deiTai sighed. "They let just anyone in here, don't they?"

"No accounting for taste, I suppose," I'eiBida said.

"But what accounts for the lack of it?"

"Indeed. One wonders how will C'traBenla react?" I asked.

"Hmmm, I better give her an ears-up." I'eiBida excused himself, and moved off to intercept her with Pierre and Jeanette.

"Do you suppose a discreet ear in their conversations might reveal something interesting?" W'kiLap mused.

"What are you thinking?" K'deiTai demanded.

"Oh, nothing. I was just thinking they must have some *revealing* discussions in chambers."

"If you think you can tap the Ancients' telephones, you are badly mistaken!"

"Chamber security has been massively upgraded in the last year," H'rhAtor said.

"We know." T'apiDien gave him an amused ear twitch. "We designed the human-specific upgrades."

"Well be that as it may, *don't* try it!"

"You are *such* a spoil-sport."

I discreetly took H'rhAtor to one side and asked, "Are you sure we shouldn't? I don't trust that *un'tdar*, and it might not be a bad idea to keep tabs on him."

H'rhAtor hesitated. "...no. You may be right, but there are limits to what is acceptable, and I am in no position to condone such a thing."

"I suppose." I let it go at that, although as events turned out, I would come to regret the decision.

§

A short time later N'detLeda came around with T'virDoma in tow. "Well, I see you managed to create a sensation, as usual," he said. "I trust you are all mindful of my instruction not to strain yourselves in your present condition?"

"It's no strain at all," C'traBenla snarled. "The experts make it look easy."

"Yes, pandemonium is your natural skill, isn't it?" T'virDoma snarked.

N'detLeda interrupted, which probably saved T'virDoma's ears. "Let's not delve into personalities; proper scientific detachment, always."

"My apology, Learnéd." T'virDoma was not the least contrite. "I should remember to treat *specimens* impartially."

"Yes, quite." N'detLeda gave us all his Superior Physich Look. "Still, I think we shall have another round of reviews in the next few days to see how you are progressing." With that he trundled off with her in tow.

"I'll show her how this *specimen* is progressing!" C'traBenla fumed.

"They're doing that to goad you, love. Don't let them get to you." She fumed for a moment before I'eiBida's words soaked in, then stomped off in the other direction. I was impressed by how deftly he defused her anger.

§

Pierre finally managed to escape by mid-afternoon, and retreated into the restrooms for a breather. He emerged sometime later, and after a cautious look around, made his way to the buffet, where I happened to be grazing.

"Such a day," he sighed. "My Jeanette and I will long remember this time."

"So will everyone else, I daresay. How are you two managing?"

"Better than I might have expected. My Jeanette makes me proud." She was surrounded by an excited herd of news personnel, keeping three translators busy in a lively give-and-take.

"A remarkable fem," I said in admiration. "You made a fine choice."

"*Oui.* I am fortunate indeed." He turned his attention to me. "Are you still working with the Arbiters?"

"No. Actually I am on medical release at the moment."

He eyed me skeptically. "Nothing too serious, I hope."

"It's just a precaution; something N'detLeda has a knot in his tail over. Right now I'm with a special liaison grotto for the Chamber, along with U'tdaPagrn and K'deiTai."

"But if you are ill..."

85

It was then I made what I only realized later was a serious mistake. My only defense is that, as a Learnéd, I am more in the habit of sharing information than concealing it. "I feel fine. It's just an annoying little gift from your friend J J Ballas."

He hesitated, and looked at me in alarm. "You are having that too?" It wasn't until later I realized what he let slip.

"Yes, all of us including H'rhAtor."

"How bad is it?" he asked, cautiously.

"It's getting to be a nuisance, I can tell you. We're all experiencing precognition, high-level empathy, and even bouts of telepathy. It clogs the mind with all manner of random emotions and stray thoughts. Hard to concentrate at times."

"What about telekinesis?"

"Nothing as yet." That was a curious thing for him to say, and I began to wonder if the humans were experiencing the same phenomena.

"So...how are the symptoms? Are they getting stronger?"

That set my ears twitching. "Yes, steadily. I'm sure whatever the Dreamsingers did, they meant well, but it creates more confusion than anything else. Have your people experienced similar problems?"

"I cannot say I have felt anything." I got the distinct impression he was hiding something, and I wondered if he might have been affected by whatever J J did to us. "*Oui*, I met J J Ballas once, when he first appeared at the Defense Ministry, but it seems not to have affected me."

That was even more suspicious, as he had answered my reservations without my asking. Moreover, I could tell that was a carefully crafted non-answer by someone who was skilled at the art. I was rather bemused by how easily my heightened empathy allowed me to read his hidden thoughts and emotions. On reflection, I decided rather belatedly to guard my speech.

"Well hopefully it won't be too much of a bother," I said, carefully. "Are many of your people affected by this?" There was no telling how many other humans were changed by contact with the Dreamsingers, but if our experience was any example, it had to be extensive.

"A few. I am uncertain how many." I could tell he was pulling back as well, and his answer seriously understated the facts.

"We really need to have a long talk with J J about it."

"Um...indeed, you should."

He made his excuses rather awkwardly, and slipped away to join his bride. As he left, I noticed L'datMparn listening nearby, but didn't think anything of it.

§

We eventually found ourselves in an informal pattern of circulating around the event, then meeting periodically to compare notes on the latest gossip. So it chanced that we met near the buffet in the mid-afternoon.

"The humans are the topic of the hour," U'tdaPagrn reported. "Mostly about their social customs."

"Same here," I'eiBida said. "A lot of the gossip is about their mating customs; some of it rather lurid."

"I heard a bit about economic matters, especially possible trade," K'deiTai said.

"The closest I heard to anything critical was some speculation on long term defense issues," I said. "But that was just talk about defense contracts."

"The mood seems remarkably light," H'rhAtor added.

K'deiTai nodded. "So, all is right with the Universe, for once. Imagine my surprise."

"Oops...hate to disappoint you; storms on the horizon." H'rhAtor nodded toward Ancient Z'keBalf, who was sauntering our way. N'detLeda and T'virDoma followed right behind, with L'datMparn hovering in the background.

"What does *he* want?" I'eiBida grumbled. From their eager expressions, we could tell trouble was brewing.

"Well, well, it's good to see you again, Pretty-tail," Z'keBalf said when he arrived. C'traBenla hissed at him, and her ears laid back; not surprising with that insult. He gave her a chilling, superior look. "Ah, I see you have fond memories of me. The years have been kind to you, considering."

"I've done well enough after I *manipulated* you into sending me to earth," she said, coldly.

87

I caught just a hint of surprise, although his demeanor remained arrogant and remote. "Yes, that was amusing, wasn't it?" He gave I'eiBida a calculating once-over. "I see you've finally been domesticated. Bonded way down, hmmm? A shame; you used to be the life of any party. Still, I'm sure it's more comfortable for you than the fringes of high society."

I'eiBida was watching him intently. He didn't say anything, but I could tell he was fighting to restrain himself from saying—or worse, *doing*—something regrettable. I focussed on sending him a mental warning to restrain his temper. He twitched nervously, and threw a sidelong glance at me, but remained silent.

"I'm not ashamed of the company I keep *now*," she snarled.

"That's good. You used to make quite a splash in certain circles." He studied I'eiBida with theatrical distaste. "It's good to see you have adapted to a life of mediocre self-denial. Not like the high times on earth, eh?"

The rest of us watched uneasily as they sparred with each other. I knew she detested Z'keBalf, but her hate radiated such that I was afraid they would come to blows. I'eiBida must have felt it too; he closed up by her side. "She was a hard-working member of the herd on both our tours there, *sir!* She did her share and more, and it all helped a lot."

Z'keBalf eyed him coldly. "Oh, no doubt, although her 'share' produced more problems than it solved, by all accounts."

'He's goading you,' I thought. *'He wants you to do something he can use against you.'*

'I know.' I'eiBida's thought came back clearly, which showed how tense we were. We could tell Z'keBalf had it in for those two, and probably all of us. "I wouldn't know about accounts, *sir,*" he said, coldly. "I have better things to do with my time than listening to self-serving gossip!"

Ancient Y'veNipbr came rumbling in just then, and from the set of her ears, she was cleared for battle. "C'tra darling, how are you doing? You look a bit stressed; you aren't straining yourself in your delicate state, are you?"

"Not at all, Y'veN," she said, coolly, as she glared at Z'keBalf. "We were just discussing our last visit to earth."

"Indeed." Z'keBalf eyed the two, no doubt wondering at their show of familiarity. "From all accounts she has much to relate, such as how she all but burned down the human Defense Ministry."

"Indeed?" Y'veNipbr gave them a chilly look. "It seems the *accounts* disagree: *I* heard there was a minor fire which was quickly put out. It's quite a leap from that to accuse her of arson!" She glared at N'detLeda, which I could tell worried him. "Gossip gets *so* overblown! You don't imagine the human Admiral would tolerate such a thing for an *instant*, do you?"

Z'keBalf hesitated and eyed her warily. I could sense his uncertainty at Y'veNipbr's sudden attack. "I can hardly claim to know what the human Admiral might think..."

"So all your war-mongering is mere speculation, I see."

"The fact remains there was a fire, and she was involved! She was preparing *V'liz* stew..."

"What? A little cooking spill? Hardly worth noting, and to the best of *my* knowledge, *V'liz* is not flammable."

"But..."

"Surely the humans would have deported her on the spot for such a blunder, wouldn't they? They deported people for less, *from all accounts*. So I think we can dismiss *that* as a rumor."

N'detLeda winced; I got the distinct impression *their* deportation was a delicate point between him and Z'keBalf. H'rhAtor looked at C'traBenla in surprise. She cocked an ear at him while maintaining a murderous glare at Z'keBalf.

"Well be that as it may, there are bigger issues!" Z'keBalf was starting to lose his temper at her interference. "These two have hardly been an asset to our diplomacy, by all accounts."

"Actually, *by all accounts*, both she and Defender I'eiBida did outstanding work on the joint defense liaison herd, especially in dealing with the human news media. You *must* have heard how *excitable* they can be? My sources said Defender I'eiBida did a lot to counter the wild rumors circulated in their media." T'virDoma winced in turn as Y'veNipbr shot a pointed glance at her.

I could feel I'eiBida's surprise at that one. *'You told her everything?'* he thought to C'traBenla.

Her aura changed from anger to embarrassment. *'She already knew!'*

"And I understand the human Admiral complimented her contribution to the joint war effort." She turned to me. "What did he say about her again?"

"Ah...that he wished he had ten like her, Ancient."

"Still..." Z'keBalf seemed disconcerted by all this. "...there were reports of mismanagement...brawling...personal frictions...hardly professional. And she's no diplomat by any means! She's a former Sliv-dancer, you know."

C'traBenla managed to keep her temper in check. I'eiBida simply looked dismayed.

"Of course she isn't!" Y'veNipbr drilled Z'keBalf with a hard look like a predator targeting her prey. "She volunteered her services to provide hot meals for our people. Do you *really* think the Inner Policy Circle would select incompetents to represent them...unless there was *inappropriate* pressure brought to bear? *Imagine* the scandal if *that* ever leaked out!"

N'detLeda and T'virDoma both winced. Z'keBalf seemed decidedly uncomfortable.

Y'veNipbr gave C'traBenla a comforting smile. "In fact, speaking of diplomacy, she was instrumental in gaining the support of the Dominions of Versailles, and in persuading the human Chancellor to back the war effort—all informally, of course." Z'keBalf's ears rolled forward in surprise as she turned on U'tdaPagrn. "As I recall, the Alliance was reluctant to get involved in the war, weren't they?"

"Ah...yes, Ancient," he mumbled. "The Chancellor was going to shut the effort down...but she...had a little chat with him, and he...ah...changed his mind."

"You see? *From all accounts* she and Defender I'eiBida were instrumental in saving the joint war effort. Who can argue with that?" Y'veNipbr gave Z'keBalf an icy glare. "By rights, since they did such *outstanding* work on earth, they should both have their names read into the Chamber minutes. Don't you agree?"

Z'keBalf was nonplussed for once, and gave N'detLeda and T'virDoma a chilly look. "Indeed. This puts a new light on things.

We must take *all* these matters under consideration." He left abruptly, with N'detLeda and T'virDoma scuttling to keep up. L'datMparn had long since faded into the background.

"Arrogant *un'tdar*," Y'veNipbr grumbled. Then she turned on I'eiBida. "It seems you two had a few misadventures on earth, or more than a few, by *all accounts*."

"It was nothing, Ancient, honestly..."

She met that with a cynical smile. "You don't *really* think you can hide anything from the Ancients, do you, youngling?"

"It wasn't like it sounds! I can explain..."

"Not to worry!" She silenced him with a peremptory ear twitch. "You got the job done, and if there were a few missteps along the way, well, as the earthers say, 'we're only human'." She gave C'traBenla a knowing look. "Now if you will excuse me, it seems the happy couple could use some rescuing." She gave us all a courteous nod, and headed across the hall to where Pierre and Jeanette were besieged by the media.

H'rhAtor watched her go with a blank expression, then turned to C'traBenla. "You set fire to the *Defense Ministry?*"

"It was an accident." She actually cringed under his bemused expression. "I didn't mean to."

He gave I'eiBida a pointed look. "So what *did* she say to the Chancellor that changed his mind, anyway?"

I'eiBida cringed in turn. "We...ah...blackmailed him, sir...threatened to expose his corruption."

He pondered for a long moment, then sighed. "Do I *really* want to know everything that went on there?"

"No, you don't," K'deiTai told him, pointedly.

§

The climax of the event came in the late afternoon when the actual 'wedding' took place. The human mystic from the embassy conducted what was the most underplayed part of the whole affair with I'eiBida and C'traBenla pressed into service as the unlikely 'best man' and 'bride's maid'. With that, by unspoken agreement, the politicking ended and the real party began. According to human tradition, Pierre and Jeanette had the 'first dance', and put on a stately performance for the television cameras. After that, those of both races inclined to dance did so, while the rest descended on the buffet for some industrial strength grazing and drinking. The media gossiped and interviewed, the Ancients and other long tails maneuvered, and the rest of us kept busy dealing with minor headaches. The Choral Herd provided a good show (I can't say about their Elvis impersonator, but Jeanette was delighted), the buffet was utterly destroyed, and the last guests didn't depart until twilight.

§

Despite everything, the event was a success. Ancient Y'veNipbr came by as we last few gathered to wish the new couple well. "This is a day we shall long remember, thanks, I understand, to your kindness," Pierre said to her.

"Is well worth for good feeling with earth," she told him. "We say much with humans this day."

"Indeed." Pierre offered a rueful smile. "The Ambassador made it clear he wishes everything prepared and on his desk by Monday...two days from now." He took Jeanette's hand and gave her a gentle mouth-press, which is how they show affection. "It would seem our honeymoon will have to be put off for a while."

"Don't worry, love. We'll have it all sorted out in no time."

Y'veNipbr turned to Jeanette. "I see you have work at you embassy." She considered C'traBenla's state, then asked, "Per...haps you go home to make hatchlings?"

"Actually..." Jeanette's snout turned pink, and she laid a hand on her midsection.

C'tra's ears shot up. "You will soon lay an egg? We *must* have a party!"

"You *know* how long it takes humans to bear offspring, dearest," I'eiBida implored her.

And on that happy note, the newly-bonded left with a herd of their human friends.

"Well," Y'veNipbr said once they were gone. "This has been a most productive day. The diplomatic exchanges have been instructive, to say the least. We managed to 'unofficially' air a number of issues, and get their viewpoints in turn, all of which will do some good."

"Yes, well, for our part no *end* of intelligence data was gathered, and we sent out a number of feelers," the Ki-Eldest said.

"I even managed to get in a personal message to their Admiral," H'rhAtor added.

"It should keep Pierre busy for days sorting it all out," I'eiBida said.

"You should all be ashamed of yourselves!" C'traBenla reproved us. "They should be spending this time together, not passing secret messages back and forth."

Y'veNipbr gave her a sardonic ear twitch. "This was your idea, you know."

C'traBenla's ears wilted, and we could feel her embarrassment. "I didn't think of that."

"Not to worry, dear. They'll survive." Y'veNipbr gave her a brief hug, something unknown from her. "You made this a memorable day for them, which will give us plenty of influence at their embassy. And all the information he received will likely do some good when it reaches the right ears."

"If the poor *n'bna'nmn* can just remember it all," K'deiTai grumbled.

*****

"Up To Our Ears And Sinking Fast"
(Related by Learnéd K'deiTai)

"We were lucky that didn't blow up in our snouts," H'rhAtor lectured us when we met in our grotto for a party post-mortem the next morning.

"It was a smashing success!" C'traBenla said, defiantly. "The Chamber Services know what they're doing."

"It's not *them* I'm worried about!"

"And Ancient Y'veNipbr authorized it, so it's all paid for and has the Chamber's blessing, so I don't see why you have *your* tail in a knot!"

"You were playing with fire." H'rhAtor was carefully curbing his temper, which took some doing around her. "If it went bad, we all would have suffered."

"I would *think* you'd put a little more faith in Ancient Y'veNipbr! It was my idea, but she approved it. And she saved our tails from Z'keBalf. That should mean something!"

"There's another thing: the defenders have a time-honored tradition of keeping our snouts out of politics. As much as I appreciate Ancient Y'veNipbr coming to our rescue, courting her patronage is stepping into a quagmire."

"We more or less need her if Z'keBalf is after our ears," M'tinDegan said, diffidently.

H'rhAtor paused and considered him for a moment. "Even so, I am uncomfortable with this. She and Z'keBalf are practically at war with each other, and we run the risk of being caught in the middle. Getting dragged into a *ui'DmukNa*-fight in the Chamber could ruin us all."

"She may have simply blocked Z'keBalf on general principle, sir," I'eiBida said, hopefully. "You're too important for anyone to try manipulating you, and what good can we be for her?"

H'rhAtor sighed. "Maybe. I hope so. Still, we can't afford any more adventures." He gave C'traBenla a stern look. "I know you meant well, but you're in way over your ears here. One false step could ruin us all. In the future *please* check with us first before starting something."

C'traBenla eyed him uneasily, sensing our grim mood. "I...guess you're right. I won't do anything unless you agree to it."

"Thank you." We were all relieved that she was being sensible for once, although how long her good intentions would last was problematical. "I suppose we should..."

The telephone buzzed just then, interrupting our little therapy session. The duty clerical answered, then handed it to H'rhAtor. "Of course, Ancient," he said after a moment as his ears wilted. "We'll be there right away." He hung up and looked at I'eiBida and C'traBenla with obvious misgivings. "That was Ancient Y'veNipbr; we're all to come to the Chamber at once."

"Wonderful," I muttered.

§

We were intercepted at the Ceremonial Entrance by the Chamber Prefects and Y'veNipbr's Aide, and which of them was more officious was hard to say. Her Aide fussed over the delay while the Prefects lectured us on proper Chamber behavior, and went over our appearances with hard eyes.

"We need to hurry," the Aide kept insisting.

"We can hardly receive them looking like *this*." The leading Prefect waved disdainfully at H'rhAtor's spotless uniform. "We have standards, and proper decorum demands..."

"His uniform is fine. In any event, they were summoned, so they'll have to do."

"Even so, what about these others?" The Prefect took us all in with a dismissive gesture. "Casual dress simply isn't proper!"

"They can go home and change if you prefer," the Aide snapped at him. "But that could take the rest of the morning, and the Ancients *do not* like to be kept waiting!"

"But they need to be properly introduced..."

"Do you *really* want to disrupt the debates to announce the arrival of a herd of nobodies?"

"Well..." The leading Prefect conceded the point, and after fussing over us a bit more, let us in.

"*hro'n'nad* bureaucrats," the Aide grumbled as he hustled us along. "I swear if the human fleet showed up, they'd insist they straighten their collars before storming the Chamber."

Despite our preoccupation, the Chamber was an awesome sight which filled me with wonder and no small degree of trepidation. This was the center of power on d'enchia—in a very real sense the center of our civilization. Standing in this hallowed place was disconcerting enough; being summoned here was especially unnerving.

The Chamber dome is the largest free-span structure on d'enchia, large enough to seat all eighteen-hundred-plus Ancients and their retinues in concentric rings around the central rostrum. The furnishings were made of polished hardwoods inlaid with fine scrollwork in an archaic tradition popular some three hundred years ago. The tile floor was set in an intricate pattern representing the world as our primitive forbearers envisioned it. The walls were covered with heavy tapestries as part of the acoustics, and the lighting was tastefully subdued, with discreet foot lights to illuminate the walkways, and a faint blue background glow overall. The whole place had a solemn *gravitas* befitting the greatest—one of the greatest—deliberative bodies of the Universe.

The central rostrum held the high seat cushion of the Most Ancient, with the thirty-member Inner Policy Circle seated around the rostrum's edge. Z'keBalf and Y'veNipbr stood before them on the rostrum as we entered, addressing the assembled delegates. The glare of spotlights illuminated them clearly, leaving the rest of the Chamber in shadow. Y'veNipbr was speaking; the small candle showing how much time she had left burned on the pedestal next to her. The semi-darkness was picked out with countless small lights, some blue, some yellow, one for each Ancient at their places in the gallery. As she spoke, a light would change color here and there, or come on, or go dark, as opinion shifted back and forth.

"...the fact remains that our fleet has suffered substantial losses which will take time to replace. So right now the real need is to complete repairs, train new candidates, and drill the crews to a proper state of readiness. Our defense funds should be put to this purpose, rather than building more ships we cannot properly use."

At that point, the little candle guttered and went out, and the Most Ancient bestirred himself. "Well spoken, both of you," he mumbled. "You have given us much to ponder. Right now we need to move on to other issues, so we shall table this discussion until tomorrow."

Z'keBalf turned and headed back to his dais.   Y'veNipbr glanced at us, then said, "I have one more minor defense matter which needs attention." Z'keBalf halted in mid-step and looked at her warily.

"Eh?" The Most Ancient bestirred himself again, and gazed at her uncertainly. "We have nothing more in the minutes...do we?"

"This will only take a moment, and I ask the Chamber's indulgence."

The Most Ancient pondered for a bit, then gestured to the Prefect and went back to sleep. The Prefect stuck another candle in the holder and lit it as Z'keBalf stepped back to his place on the rostrum and eyed her warily.

"I summon H'rhAtor, tem dre Fradash, I'eiBida, fan D'chr, K'deiTai, sen V'ran, U'tdaPagrn, dro Mev'menk, M'tinDegan, cro V'menba, and C'traBenla, rani D'enta," she announced.

"*p'quas'tka*," H'rhAtor muttered. "What is she up to?"

"Whatever it is, it can't be good," M'tinDegan said.

There was nothing for it, so we trooped reluctantly onto the Chamber floor and up on the rostrum, forming a semi-circle around her while Z'keBalf glared at us.

"I call the Chamber's attention to the recent Dreamsingers' War, and our diplomatic efforts with the humans in general," she announced.   "You have all seen the official reports, but *official* reports often fail to discuss minor but important details which shaped the greater effort. This is especially the case here. There were many undercurrents which are not readily seen, and these people played important, I daresay vital roles in those undercurrents, and in the outcome of the crisis."

Z'keBalf said nothing, but watched her warily.

"For example, C'traBenla and defender I'eiBida were instrumental in quelling a planet-wide panic when our war plans were leaked to the human news media by an incompetent underling." She gave Z'keBalf an icy, triumphant glare before going on. "That underling was summarily deported, and rightly so, by the humans."

"Where did she get *that?*" M'tinDegan whispered to me. The barrage of revelations about our misadventures on earth, both at the party and now here, was disconcerting.

"What else does she know?" I whispered back.

"And defender I'eiBida worked closely with the human APA's 5th Office, their intelligence apparatus, to trap the notorious Anti-tech terrorists," Ancient Y'veNipbr went on. "Their organization was largely wrecked through his unofficial aid."

"*Ancestors!* This is going out *live* to the whole planet!" Indeed, the Chamber televideo system was locked firmly on us.

"And while the *official* reports say C'traBenla influenced the human Chancellor to agree to the war effort, what *isn't* known is how she cultivated the support of the Dominions of Versailles, a powerful faction in the human Parliament, and used it to blackmail the Chancellor by threatening to expose his corruption!"

That produced a collective gasp from the Chamber, and a scattering of applause. All of us winced, and stood there in woebegone dismay, except for C'traBenla, who preened at the attention she was getting.

'She knows everything!' I clearly heard I'eiBida's dismayed thought.

'They'll arrest us all!' The strength of U'tdaPagrn's thought showed how much stress we were under.

'If they don't tear us apart!' I thought in turn.

But Y'veNipbr went on to reveal even more dirt. "Then she twisted the tail of the human defense minister to get him to approve the deployment of their stellar bomb arsenal, which proved vital to the victory. Without their efforts, the combined war effort would never have gotten off the ground!"

And so it went. Y'veNipbr outlined a damning case against each of us, from H'rhAtor's confidential revealing our lack of stellar weaponry to the human Admiral which shaped the war effort, to my and U'tdaPagrn's behind the scenes diplomatic tail-twisting, to the sweeping campaign of disinformation, confusion, and obstruction we all engaged in to counter political interference from home and keep the original diplomatic mission and the later war from collapsing.

Finally, after what seemed a lifetime in the Uttermost Darkness, the candle guttered and went out. The Most Ancient stirred, but Y'veNipbr overrode him and went on, speaking out of turn to a Chamber so rapt that no one, not even Z'keBalf, raised an objection. We stood there in utter dismay as the catalog of our dubious actions rolled on, and I for one tried to keep a running tab on how many years we would spend in a penal community.

After an eternity, our shame was laid before all, by which point the video monitors showed the broadcast was being watched by an epic viewer share. "As you can see, the *official* reports clearly do *not* tell the *whole story* of their contributions to interstellar peace, which I have only touched on." Y'veNipbr gave Z'keBalf another hard look. "That *whole story* can reveal a lot which was unspoken, and deserves attention which sometimes gets overlooked. In light of this, I move their names be read into the Chamber minutes in recognition. Do you agree, Ancient?"

Z'keBalf was clearly put out by her maneuver, and for a moment I wondered if he would denounce us for the tail-knotted *hro'n'nad n'bna'nmn* we were.

"In light of the *whole story* you discovered," he ground out at last, "I *have* to agree."

The Most Ancient bestirred himself again, and after giving her a cautious look, gazed around the Chamber. "Well: a most interesting development, I must say." He paused to gape at us for a bit. "Most interesting, indeed. The resolution is offered and affirmed. Let us vote."

With Z'keBalf's and Y'veNipbr's factions in rare agreement, it was a foregone conclusion. The dimly lit Chamber around us blazed with a galaxy of tiny yellow lights while it was all I could do to keep from fainting. "Well, that will put an end to his scheming as far as you all are concerned," Y'veNipbr said when we returned to her dais.

"Thank you, Y'veNipbr!" C'traBenla was thrilled that she could put (Chamber) behind her name from now on.

"Think nothing of it, dear. Now you all need to leave; we have plenty of work to do."

§

99

We met out in the main corridor to try to absorb what just happened, and we were a bit overwhelmed, to say the least. "She twisted his tail so hard it almost came off," H'rhAtor said in dismay. "It will be hard for Z'keBalf to move against any of us after being publicly lauded by the Chamber."

"Including by his own faction," U'tdaPagrn noted. "If I'm not mistaken, there are no dirty little secrets he can exploit any more."

"Yes," M'tinDegan said. "More than that, many of those incidents she alluded to can be traced back to his influence, the *whole story* as she put it. She was telling him publicly that if he moves against us, she'll make sure he goes down as well."

"The whole world knows everything now." H'rhAtor gave C'traBenla a stern look. "You had to spill everything, didn't you?"

"I did not! I don't know *where* she got it all!"

"Well, at least we're safe from Z'keBalf," U'tdaPagrn said, morosely. "His reputation for making and breaking is well deserved. Being on his bad side would have finished us all."

"We went to great lengths to avoid getting tangled up in Chamber politics when we came back from earth the first time," I'eiBida complained. "My Worthy will not be thrilled when I tell him this."

"What are you whining about?" I snapped. "My Aide will bite my tail off at the stump!"

"What dismays me is how our embassy on earth must be rotten with political spies," U'tdaPagrn said, mournfully. "How can we conduct proper diplomacy when we're caught up in Chamber tail-biting?"

"What are you all complaining about?" C'traBenla demanded. "She saved our ears! Doesn't that count for something?"

"Make no mistake about it," H'rhAtor said. "She didn't do it out of any misguided sense of charity. Nothing is free in politics; she owns all of us now, and she'll collect. Like it or not, we're allied to her faction."

C'traBenla was thrilled, which was to be expected. "That's wonderful, love!" she gushed to I'eiBida. "It's *good* to have friends in high places!"

"Oy! I suppose it is, love."

L'datMparn came wandering by just then, and paused to glower at us until our collective stares made him feel uncomfortable, and he turned away. As he did, a flower pot hit him squarely in the back of his head, knocking him into the wall. He staggered to his feet, threw a panicked glance at C'traBenla, and bolted.

"That must have hurt," H'rhAtor mumbled.

We all turned to her in surprise, but she looked dismayed rather than angry. "*C'tra!*"

"...I didn't, I'ei...honest..."

"She didn't throw it," U'tdaPagrn said. "It just jumped at him!"

We all looked at each other in dismay as we absorbed that bit of news. "Telekinesis!" M'tinDegan said at last. "It's started."

"As if we don't have enough problems," H'rhAtor grumbled.

"No doubt he'll run straight to Z'keBalf with this," I said, morosely. "The one thing we *don't* need is to give him any more ammunition."

"But we have Ancient Y'veNipbr to protect us," C'traBenla insisted. "Being allied to her faction will do some good after all."

"No doubt," H'rhAtor said. "Still, I hate to be caught up in anyone's politics."

I'eiBida sighed. "Well, better her than Z'keBalf, I guess."

§

If we ever got the notion that our problems were over, we were sadly deluded. The media besieged us for interviews about the sensational revelations in the Chamber, and they were as aggressive at their human news vulture counterparts. After talking it over urgently, we decided to close herd and reveal no more details, since if the human embassy *somehow* missed the Chamber broadcast, we didn't want to push our luck.

Not that it helped. The story became the hottest news item of the season, building on itself until it spilled over from the news broadcasts into commentary programs and even to specials. They even preempted the All-Nests *b'Ven'gtt'* finals, which must have peeved sports fans no end. They kept after us until we were forced to give interviews to counter all the wild speculation rocking the networks, but even that did nothing to quell the uproar.

101

Much to our dismay, C'traBenla soon became the media darling, and her spicy prattle about life on earth had the channels buzzing. "*How* did we get into this mess?" H'rhAtor grumbled as we watched her latest coverage in our grotto. "Space exploration *used* to be fun, until we met the humans." He glared at I'eiBida. "Until *she* came along!"

"What can I say, sir?"

"You could say you're sorry!"

"I'm sorry, sir."

"You're just saying that!"

"At least she's taking most of the interest away from us," M'tinDegan said. "The media can't expect her to reveal anything critical."

"She can open her mouth!"

"Hmmm, yes. So we're not safe yet."

We fretted over her interviews for some time, afraid she would say something which would start a war, until we realized she was giving them nothing of importance. As much as I hate to admit it, she had complete media presence, and gave them endless empty air while they lapped it up and begged for more. But then, most of the interviewers were mals, so perhaps it wasn't so surprising.

Someone—Z'keBalf, no doubt—tried to counter her popularity by leaking the sordid details of her past, but it just made her more popular, and she never showed a hint of her formidable temper and her contempt for him. It was quite some time before the interest died down, and all the while she was in her element, basking in the attention.

§

Needless to say, when C'traBenla is involved, there is plenty of trouble to share. The Chamber Wardens were not amused by all the extra fuss they were inundated with. "It wasn't bad enough before," Q'brnVen grumbled to me at one point. "Now we have to give you First Finger security, *and* we have no end of tourists wanting to visit your grotto."

"This is you're here for," I snapped at him.

"Think of it as job security," M'tinDegan added, which didn't sooth our frazzled Warden in the least.

"Job security? We already have far more than we can handle around here with all the Ancients demanding we run errands and do favors for them. Fetching their mid-meals is what staffers are for! Now we have you making a huge fuss all over the media, and everyone wants to come gape at you. Some of those people get really irate when we can't let them in, and they don't care about Chamber policy. They dump on us, the poor, downtrodden Chamber Wardens!"

"Well if you're tired of this, I can give you a letter of recommendation," I told him, acidly. "You could transfer to embassy security on earth."

"There's no need to get vulgar!"

"And it's not nice to threaten, K'deiTai," M'tinDegan admonished me, then added, "We're sorry for all the trouble we cause your Wardens. I'm afraid it can't be helped."

"*You're* sorry? *We're* the ones with our tails in the wringer." He threw up his hands in despair and stomped off.

"He really needs to learn how to relax," I noted.

§

We had our own major scare in the meanwhile when Pierre Roubidoux called and asked us to meet him for mid-meal. "It is most urgent, my friends," he insisted.

"This doesn't sound good," U'tdaPagrn said, woefully. "He must be calling in his unofficial capacity. What can be the matter?"

"Only one way to find out," H'rhAtor said. "I'll hold things down here; the three of you go see what he wants."

It was a lovely, rather warm day. We met in a local restaurant which was becoming popular with both us and the humans partly for its vegetarian fare, and partly for its relaxed, open air verandah which reminded them of the Mediterranean. However, Pierre was anything but relaxed as we settled in over drinks and pastry.

"We monitor the transmissions of the Chamber," he announced somberly. "And when I saw all of you on the rostrum, I ordered a priority translation of the broadcast." He gave us a solemn, wary look. "That translation was just completed, and we were stunned by your activities on earth, to say the least."

"But you already knew of these things," I protested. "You will recall your Admiral confronted us about it shortly before we returned home."

Pierre stirred uneasily. "*Oui*, your efforts to hide your actions left, shall we say, something to desire. But we did not know all the details of what transpired, nor was the story widely known. I must tell you our Ambassador was incensed when he heard the facts."

That was not good news. "What will he do?" I asked.

"He was prepared to send a detailed report back to earth, and to make formal protests to your government."

To say I was alarmed was an understatement. "He must know the consequences of making this official. This could trigger a major crisis!"

Pierre nodded. "I spoke with him most urgently, as did my counterpart, the Military Attache; we had to invoke the Admiral's name to get him to calm down."

"If the Admiral is already involved, won't that do?" M'tinDegan said. "Your Ambassador knows how wary we are of provoking an incident."

"Our Ambassador is of the Old School; he is mortally offended by what he sees as improper tampering. I promised to question you for explanations while the Attache sends an urgent request for clarification to the Admiral, but it buys you a little time, nothing more. I hope you can give me something to satisfy him."

This was our worst fears laid before us: Ancient Y'veNipbr's exposé could trigger a crisis. "What she revealed is nothing more than what usually goes on in Alliance politics," M'tinDegan protested. "And it saved all of us from potential disaster."

"The problem is not our politics, as regrettable as they are. It is your meddling in our affairs which raises such offense."

"Then tell your Ambassador those actions were a regrettable necessity which we have been thoroughly taken to task over by your Admiral, and were not official policy by the Chamber."

Pierre hesitated. "I already assured him of these things."

"Surely he knows this will blow over in time, then."

"But how can it now? Why did she have to reveal it all?" Pierre cried. "Now it is out in the open where we cannot pretend to

ignore it! The entire staff knows! Rumors will spread! Have your Ancients no discretion?"

"Ancient Z'keBalf was using it to support his anti-human stance," I'eiBida said, grimly. "She did that to thwart him, and to protect us, your friends and allies here on d'enchia."

M'tinDegan grabbed that crumb and ran with it. "She nullified Z'keBalf's move, and a few indiscretions on earth must surely be outweighed by having us here as military and diplomatic leverage."

"All true, but I am not sure he sees it just now."

"Then tell him the situation in the Chamber is very delicate, and she had to keep the lid on."

"And give him our official regrets," I added.

He brooded on that for a bit, staring off into the distance without noticing the curious passers-by. "It...will have to do," he muttered at last. Then he came back to the here-and-now. "I only hope the Admiral will speak up as well for our 'friends and allies'." He finished his coffee at a gulp, then took his leave. "But tread warily, my friends! This is very delicate. My best to you all."

"Their friends and allies here on d'enchia?" I grumbled once he left. "So now we've been sold to the humans as well, I see."

"What could I say?" I'eiBida snapped. "He needed a life-line, and I gave him all we had."

"Hopefully it will defuse a blow-up," M'tinDegan added, morosely.

I sighed in resignation. "I hope it works. We're running out of factions to ally to."

§

"I suppose it doesn't matter," H'rhAtor grumbled when we reported back to him. "We're in so deep already, we can't even find enough time to panic over it all."

"Well I *wish* you thought to include me in your little adventure!" C'traBenla berated us. "You know I can sweet-talk Pierre, and through him their Ambassador."

"It concerns an official matter, something of the highest gravity," H'rhAtor said, sternly. "Some things can't be 'sweet-talked' away."

"You, of *all* people, should know human politics is all about personalities, and human mals are *so* easy to manipulate! Since most of the incidents they are upset over were my doing, I could go to their Ambassador if need be, and confess. Toss in a little ear wagging, and I could have him eating out of my hand. They can't blame the rest of you for something you had no control over."

"True enough," I muttered.

"Absolutely not!" H'rhAtor was adamant. "The diplomatic situation is already delicate. Leave these things to the diplomats for once!"

"Really!" she huffed. "If that's how you feel, then you know how to reach me when it all falls apart!" She gave him an angry tail flick, and stomped out.

"I'll give her this," H'rhAtor grumbled once she left. "She has an answer for everything."

"Uncanny," M'tinDegan mused. "You know...if she could become the Supreme Ruler of the Universe, all our problems would be solved."

H'rhAtor gave him a chilly look. "Yes, we'd all be too busy partying."

"Or recovering from our hangovers," I muttered.

"I'm *pretty* sure Pierre can talk their Ambassador down," M'tinDegan assured him.

"The Admiral will back our claim, sir," I'eiBida said.

"Ancestors, I hope so." He gave I'eiBida a pointed glare. "Let's just *hope* nothing more happens until this mess dies down."

"Yes, sir. I'll do what I can, sir."

H'rhAtor sighed. "Still...things could grow worse. The tensions between us and the humans are bad enough. If Geneva gets a taste of this, who knows *what* they'll do. I *wish* Ancient Y'veNipbr had ordered the video cameras turned off."

"A confidential Chamber session on last moment defense matters would have stirred public unrest," M'tinDegan said. "She may have felt public exposure was necessary to thwart Z'keBalf."

"Or she didn't realize how the humans would react. This only stirs things up, and tensions are high already. We sincerely *do not* need an incident now."

"The fleet is already maintaining a low profile these days, sir. As for the diplomatic end, we need to give Ancient Y'veNipbr an ears-up."

"G'cetGian too," I added. "The Arbiters need to prep for possible damage control."

H'rhAtor looked askance at me. "I could have been an accountant. We *all* could have been accountants."

"Too late."

*****

"Some Days It Just Doesn't Pay To Worry"
(Related by Learnéd M'tinDegan)

The next day *started out* more or less normally...

"Are you sure you want to be here, love?" I'eiBida asked as C'traBenla settled awkwardly on a seat cushion. "It's as boring as ever, and with you getting so close to delivery..." She arrived in mid-morning after a medical appointment, and he was understandably concerned for her.

She smiled, and gave him a happy ear twitch. "I feel fine, love! The physichs said I'm doing well, and I'm still a long way from due. Besides, my next interview isn't until late this afternoon, and I might as well be here as anywhere."

"Well, I guess, if you feel all right." He fetched a steaming bowl of *V'liz* for her as she settled in, which she accepted with a radiant smile and the happy aura she exhibited whenever she was the center of attention.

"You are in a fine mood this morning," I offered.

"Am I that obvious?" Her aura of pleasure took on a faintly embarrassed tone. She was a fount of happiness over her endless interviews and news programs since our appearance in the Chamber, and her aura helped lighten the psychic atmosphere.

"Yes, you are," H'rhAtor said. "It's good to see *someone* is happy to be here."

"You've all been so grumpy lately," she lectured us. "I swear it's enough to put a fem off." Not that anything could penetrate her blissful mood, it seemed.

"Honestly, I believe you have the the strongest and most advanced powers among us," I said. "I would think I'eiBida would be the strongest since he had so much exposure to the Dreamsingers."

"If I'm not mistaken, he comes in a close second," K'deiTai said. Our growing empathic powers were an obsession among us, and a lively topic of discussion was always welcome.

That tickled her no end. "What a breeding pair we make! Just *think* of the powers our hatchling will have! We should have more; they'll be the wave of the future."

I'eiBida flinched, which she, fortunately, didn't notice.

"Imagine it: a genuine second generation empath. She'll redefine our entire species. I'ei, this is *wonderful!*"

He eyed her doubtfully. "Well, for one thing, you don't know it's a 'she'...do you?"

She hesitated. "No..."

"So it could be a 'he', and who knows what powers, if any, might pass on to the next generation?"

"You are *so* negative," she scolded him. "Have a little faith. This is our hatchling! He, or she, will make history!"

"Well, he, or she, will have to be approved first..." Even as I'eiBida started ticking off points on his fingers, her mood shifted abruptly.

"...and we'll have no *end* of medical bills..." An icy psychic blast seemed to fill the room as she stared wide-eyed at him.

"...and there's the crèche fees, which I don't know *where* we'll..." He faltered as the building started to shake with a chorus of ominous creaking and groaning...

"Now you've done it," H'rhAtor mumbled.

"...ah...well, actually I meant..."

Then the building started trembling...

"...love...I didn't mean anything!" I'eiBida cried in alarm.

"I'ei?"

"C'tra!!!!"

"You can't let them hurt my egg!"

A pile of books on someone's desk toppled onto the floor...

"Don't let your Possession Syndrome get to you!"

"*p'quas'tka*," U'tdaPagrn muttered as he dropped his little plastic cube and dove under his desk...

A shrill wind came up out of nowhere, blowing papers around like leaves as our staff cowered under their desks...

"They can't hurt my *hatchling!*"

"C'TRA! Get ahold of yourself!"

A window shattered. I felt my desk move, then all its drawers shot out across the room. The staff, as one, scrambled as far from her as they could amid a growing blizzard of papers and small items, cowering against the wall and behind filing cabinets.

"C'TRA!" I'eiBida tried to comfort her, but was knocked off his feet by a flying seat cushion.

"I'm sure the Egg Testers...have no protocols about...psychic abilities," I cried. "If anything..." I ducked a flying trash can. "...I'm sure they would..." A filing cabinet sailed over my head, collapsing in on itself as it bounced off the wall. "...they would rate them positively!"

A light fixture shattered...then another...

I looked to H'rhAtor, who was clinging to his desk. *'Say something before she explodes!'* I thought to him. We had a living stellar bomb ticking in our midst.

"An empath would...be priceless for the space program!" C'traBenla's head jerked around to focus on him, her eyes wide in panic. I realized she was feeding on the general alarm we all felt, trapping us all in a devastating psychic typhoon. "She'd be...she'd help com...munications..." H'rhAtor cringed as his desk flipped bodily upside down...

"A-and an empath would help the Arbiters!" K'deiTai cried. "Don't hurt meeee!!!!"

But by then she was in full-blown panic mode, beyond reason as per Possession Syndrome took over, her telekinetic powers feeding back on our alarm to wreck havoc.

"It's all right, C'tra!" I'eiBida bellowed over the rising storm. "Don't..." He ducked as a section of wall panel ripped away and went flying. "...get ahold of yourself!"

L'datMparn stuck his snout through the door just then, took one frightened look, and vanished as a section of the ceiling came crashing down. Two of our clerical staff bolted in panic, following him out the door.

"C'TRA!" I'eiBida tried to comfort her, but was smashed against the wall by some unseen force. One of the clericals dove head-first out a window, while another was knocked off his feet by flying debris.

"*Why* do my Ancestors do this to me?" K'deiTai moaned.

"C'TRA!!!" Another light fixture shattered, then the windows exploded. We all cowered under what cover we could find as the grotto was shredded around us.

110

Then J J Ballas was there, standing tall and solid amid the typhoon of flying wreckage. "Lawdy Baby-Chile!" he cried. "What's wrong wit yo?" He waded through the storm and laid both hands on the sides of her head. "Calm yo-self, chile!"

As suddenly as the storm erupted, it vanished amid a thunderous clatter as what was left of our furnishings and office equipment skidded to a halt.

"We're alive?" U'tdaPagrn gasped, then twitched anxiously as the building creaked around us.

"Now you calm down, Baby-Chile," J J said, sternly. "Yo' powers are too strong fo' you t' lose control like this."

"But...my egg..." C'traBenla seemed under control for the moment, but then I realized J J was holding her in check by main force. "...t-the egg testerrsss..." She slipped loose from his control enough to start bawling.

"Baby-Chile, there ain't nothin' you can do 'bout that by losing control this way. You—all-a you—need t' learn self control."

C'traBenla was a shivering wreck by that point. I'eiBida staggered to his feet and moved to comfort her. J J gingerly took his hands away, ready to grab her again if she lost it. She started sobbing, but managed not to panic as I'eiBida took her in his arms.

"Thas better. You really got to work on yo' self control, Baby-Chile." J J turned to us. "As fo' the rest of you, these powers ain't nothin' t' take lightly. You-all need t' learn self discipline."

"Ah...we're trying, J J," I said, uneasily.

"Well yo' need t' try harder! This-heah is th' sort of thing our young-uns do. You-all are grown-ups, you should know better!" And with that, he vanished.

H'rhAtor was the first to recover his wits, poked his head up reluctantly and looked around. "Anyone hurt?"

Before anyone could answer, the door burst open, and Q'brnVen and two other Chamber Wardens charged in, with a medical team right behind. They ground to a halt, and took in the scene in dismay. "What happened?" Q'brnVen asked at last.

I'eiBida paused in comforting C'traBenla. "It...was nothing." He considered the shattered ruins in dismay. "Don't worry about it. We'll clean up the mess."

"*Don't worry about it?!*" Our office equipment and furnishings were mangled, our carefully filed records scattered and shredded, there were large pieces of wall material torn loose, and we could see daylight through a rent in the ceiling. "It looks like a stellar bomb went off in here!"

"Closer than you think," K'deiTai muttered. I made frantic hushing gestures at him, and he checked himself. "It was just a little misunderstanding, is all. It's over now."

"A little mis..." Q'brnVen was incredulous; understandable since the room looked like it was run through a trash compactor. "This hardly seems like a *little* misunderstanding!"

I made frantic hushing gestures at him. "It's all right. She's under control now."

"What? She...?"

"It was just a...well...she had a panic attack."

"A panic attack?" He stared at me blankly, then eyed C'traBenla with growing alarm.

H'rhAtor staggered to his feet and herded the Chamber Wardens out into the hall before Q'brnVen said something to set her off again. "Don't worry, we'll take care of it. Everything is under control for now."

"*How* am I going to write *this* one up?"

"You'll think of something; I have complete confidence in you." He forced the door shut, which took some doing, before Q'brnVen could protest.

By then, C'traBenla was sobbing and trembling. "I'm sorry, I'ei!"

"It's all right, love."

Actually it wasn't. The place was trashed, the building was about ready to collapse, a spray of water came from a broken pipe in the restroom, and several of us suffered minor injuries.

"Look, I'm going to go next door and call Chamber Services, then I'll take you home."

"You're not mad at me?"

"No, love, of course not!" He caressed her cheek, and nibbled one ear tenderly. "You couldn't help it."

"I don't know why you put up with me."

"Love conquers all, I guess." He took her hand and nibbled her ear again. "It'll be all right."

As he went out, the medical staffers made a cautious entrance, clambering over the piled wreckage, and soon had their hands full dealing with any number of sprains and lacerations. Fortunately none of the casualties were severe, although a couple were taken to a nearby clinical station for further treatment. At that we were lucky.

I'eiBida returned shortly after they left. "Chamber Services are on their way, and I don't know *how* we can explain this." He turned to C'traBenla, who was still trembling. "We're pretty much out of business here while they make repairs, so let's go home."

"But...my interview..." Trust her to think of getting attention at a moment like this.

"Call in sick; they've had enough of your time, and you're in no shape for it now." He nibbled her ear tenderly. "We'll have a hot meal and spend a quiet evening together."

She sniffed, and gave him a grateful look. "You're always thinking of me."

"Well, yes. I love you." He nibbled her ear again. "I'll go call the interviewers, then we'll go home." He headed for the door again, then hesitated and twitched all over as we all felt a sudden rush of pleasure. *'C'tra!'* he thought to her. *'Not in public, dearest!'* Her only response was an innocent ear twitch and a sense of smug satisfaction as they left.

"She always bounces back," I mused. "Remarkable."

"Like their young-uns, hmmm?" H'rhAtor said once they were gone. "This telekinesis is *dangerous!* We have to do something about these powers, fast."

"Yes. We obviously can't put things off any longer, especially with her."

"Any ideas?"

"Evidently, J J's people train their 'young-uns' in mental self discipline, so we need to develop some sort of program."

"Hmmm, yes."

"I don't know about you, but I wouldn't care to have J J spank me," K'deiTai sighed.

L'datMparn *would* choose that moment to stick his snout through the door. "Um...what happened?" he asked, hesitantly.

H'rhAtor gave him a chilly look. "Someone mentioned your name."

He shuddered, and surveyed the wreckage in dismay. "That fem is dangerous!"

"Not to us; just to people who get on her bad side." L'datMparn flinched. "Since we're out of business until this gets cleaned up, you are dismissed for now."

"Thank you, sir!" He offered a hasty tail wave, and vanished.

§

I stayed around long enough to get an initial estimate of the repairs from Chamber Services. Once they got over their shock, and stated that it would take some time to put things in order, I decided to drop in on T'aPidien and W'kiLap.

"She *what?*" W'kiLap asked in dismay when I recounted the events to them.

"She had a panic attack, and her telekinetic powers almost leveled our grotto."

"My! Talk about a temper!" T'aPidien said.

Like a lot of small software concerns these days, their 'business' was little more than a corner of their luxurious nest which held an impressive array of computers and equipment. Business dress code was lounging robes printed in the wild hula style which was becoming popular with *certain* elements of society just then, and the room was dotted with impressionistic human art and faux 'Navajo' rugs. It was all quite colorful in a *disturbing* way, and it seemed to fit them. But I wasn't there as an art critic; I had an urgent problem to deal with.

"Thing is, L'datMparn saw what happened, and no doubt ran straight to Z'keBalf. We need to know what he'll do, so can you tap his phone?"

"*Of course* we can," W'kiLap said in mock-indignation. "We're the experts, you know."

"So—I see you appreciate our skills after all," T'aPidien said.

"It's more likely he's homesick," W'kiLap snorted. "Miss the good times on earth, do we?"

"Sneakery and spookery..."

"...connivery and treachery..."

"...spying and plotting..."

"...manipulating and infiltrating..."

"...next thing you know, he'll sponsor Inspector Dassault to immigrate!"

"*That* would be an event to ponder," I admitted. "Seriously, can you tap Z'keBalf's phones?"

"Well, yes. Still, it'll be a neat trick," T'apiDien said, somberly. "The humans have an ongoing effort to penetrate Chamber communications; security has been tightened up like never before."

"They have?" That was an uncomfortable surprise. "How did you learn that?"

"By penetrating *their* embassy's communications, of course."

"Oy, what a stampede," I grumbled.

"Wheels within wheels, as the humans say. They love this sort of thing." He leaned on his plush seat cushion and gave me a cynical look. "So...you want to make a career change, hmmm? Academia getting a little too dull, and you want to switch to Intelligence work?"

"We could make some connections for you, if you like," W'kiLap added.

"Ah...no, thank you. We have a problem, and I'm hoping you can help us with a little informal favor, is all."

"By spying on one of the most powerful members of the Chamber? I'd hate to see what you consider a *big* favor!"

There was another thought to ponder. I admit, reflecting on it now, that my life was going in the *oddest* directions. As recently as four years ago, I never would have considered such violations of academic detachment, to say nothing of prying into the inner recesses of the Chamber Of Ancients. It knots the tail of every standard of normal behavior, not to mention being near-suicidally hazardous.

"I *do not* believe I'm doing this," I complained.

But then, normal standards don't apply on earth, or when dealing with the humans, or with Ancient Z'keBalf. I should write a paper on it some day.

"You understand we can't be seen as involved in this. You'll be on your own if you get caught."

"Not to worry." W'kiLap dismissed my concern with a contemptuous ear twitch. "We have connections."

"Connections who would be interested in what Z'keBalf is up to as well," T'apiDien added. "So, you see, we're covered."

I must be getting dense in my old age; the light suddenly dawned. "You two! You told Ancient Y'veNipbr about what happened on earth!"

"Of *course* we did!" They both laughed at my dismay. "Z'keBalf was after the lot of you, so we knotted his tail *and* moved you right up-herd where you can do some good."

"So how do you like adding (Chamber) to your signature?" W'kiLap snarked.

"That was completely unethical."

"The best moves always are."

"If you're going to dabble in Intelligence work, you need to start thinking like the humans..."

"...devious and treacherous..."

"...cunning and calculating..."

"...wary and slippery..."

"All right you two." Having had enough of them for the moment, I headed for the door. "Please let us know if you find anything."

§

My next thought was to call Pierre Roubidoux and arrange an urgent meeting with him at the restaurant.

"Has something happened?" He was thoroughly agitated when I arrived. "Have the revelations in the Chamber created a crisis?"

"It's not a diplomatic crisis," I assured him. "I suppose you might call it a personal matter."

He gave me a jaundiced look. "You dragged me away from my desk for personal matter?"

"It's these psychic powers; they're getting out of hand. We need to set up some sort of mental discipline program, so I hope you could help us by connecting us with a Zen instructor."

He was thoroughly confused by then. "A...Zen instructor?"

116

"There was an incident this morning. It has us seriously worried."

"We heard something... So this 'incident' worries you enough to seek help from us?" He frowned, and I could tell he was concerned. "I am afraid we have no Zen followers among the staff, other than a very young secretary who would probably be of little use to you."

I hesitated for a long moment, then took the plunge. "Could you arrange for someone to come from earth?"

"This *is* serious!"

"Very," I admitted.

He mused on that for a bit. "I *suppose* we could arrange for a Zen master to come here...but my superiors will view this with alarm, and they will wonder why they should go to such expense."

"Your people have the same problem. We need to work together to find a solution. We will share our findings, of course."

"Perhaps so. Very well, I shall send the request, although I am not sure how Geneva will react."

"Please tell them to expedite. This is urgent."

"I was afraid Ancient Y'veNipbr's speech had set off an interstellar incident," he said as we parted. "Something critical, perhaps desperate."

"I wish it was so simple."

§

My final stop, as reluctant as I was, was to visit Learnéd N'detLeda. As little as I trusted him, he *was* one of the leading aberrant psychologists, not to mention well familiar with the situation already.

"I heard there was some sort of commotion in your grotto," N'detLeda said when I related the matter to him.

"Well for once the gossip doesn't exaggerate," I said, somberly. "Her psychic powers wrecked havoc. Our grotto is shut down while Chamber Services makes repairs."

He twitched an ear disdainfully, although I could feel his dismay. "Her temper is a threat to public safety at the best of times. I was afraid this might happen. We may have to institutionalize the entire lot, her especially."

That was the *last* thing I wanted from him, so I moved immediately to talk him down. "Well, you *are* the psychologist, but I wonder how she will react. It ought to make an interesting scientific paper."

(Uncertainty.) "Her temper tantrums hardly seem worthy of scientific review."

"Actually, it wasn't her temper. She had a panic attack."

(Doubt, tinged with nervousness.) "A panic attack?"

"Yes. And seeing how she nearly leveled the grotto, I'd hate to be the one who panicked her."

(Rising alarm.) "Leveled...?"

"It looks like a typhoon hit it. Chamber Services said they'll have to tear down what's left, and completely rebuild."

He blinked at me in unabashed dismay. "How powerful is she, anyway?"

"For now? Enough to level a building, especially if her egg is threatened. You know how possessive she is. But she keeps getting stronger all the time, so I can't say how powerful she will ultimately be."

I felt a chill run through him.

"Of course, once she got over her panic, there's her temper..." I gave him a nervous ear twitch, which sent him nearly into a panic himself. "But you *are* the psychologist, so if you feel she needs to be institutionalized..."

"Ah...on second thought, that may not be necessary."

"I suppose. Locking her up will hardly contain her psychic powers, anyway. The only thing which will is to find a cure, you know."

He seemed vexed. "Honestly, I've made precious little headway so far. The issue seems to be physical, rather than psychological. I am consulting with a leading herd of neurologists, but we haven't been able to define any gross tissue abnormalities or distorted neural patterns as yet. This is genuinely frustrating."

I didn't like the sound of that, or his evident frustration. "Well I, for one, would not recommend radical neurosurgery to her in any case."

He shuddered openly. "Yes, quite. But what else can we do?"

"J J Ballas said we were like untrained hatchlings. I thought to ask the humans to send a Zen instructor to help develop a self-discipline program."

That caught his interest. "One wonders how they can grasp our mental processes when they have so little self-control as they do. Pity we've never developed a need for Zen or something like it. As for J J Ballas, perhaps he can help; I don't see much hope otherwise."

"I'll ask J J to contact you so you can..."

"*NO!*" He spasmed all over in panic. "Ah...no...I have to maintain clinical detachment."

"Hmmm, suit yourself." I was inwardly pleased by how thoroughly I could manipulate him; completely unprofessional, of course, but it felt so *l'cc'vn* good.

The door flew open just then, and T'virDoma came bouncing in. "I have the results of the latest reviews completed, Learnéd." She shoved a thick file folder at him, and looked me over like I was something rather unsavory. "I still say we need brain tissue samples if we're to look for a physical source of their problems."

"Thank you," N'detLeda said, curtly, as he took the file. "We will wait until the genetic analysis comes back before going any further."

"Suit yourself. So, are you through with *him*, Learnéd?"

"Not as yet." She offered an indelicate ear twitch, and left. N'detLeda sighed in annoyance.

"You might think about keeping her away from C'traBenla, while you are at it," I suggested. "She can be a bit irritating at times."

"She is a thorough *un'tdar*," he grumbled. "Brilliant; but thoroughly *un'tdar*."

"Oh, I don't know; she might become a first finger aberrant psychologist someday."

I could tell that thought disturbed him. "Yes, I suppose she may, although I how effective she'll be with her abrasive personality."

"Actually, I understand she wants to work in diplomatic intelligence..."

He shuddered again, and I caught a fleeting montage of images from their experience on earth. "Ancestors forbid!"

§

"Perhaps we should set ourselves up a separate civilization, or even a separate species," U'tdaPagrn bellyached when I caught up with the herd who were killing time in the Chamber cafeteria. "We have our own intelligence service, our own military, an intellectual class, a diplomatic herd; perhaps we could strike out on our own on some new world. It's the only way I see how to get through this mess!"

"It may come to that if all the *ui'DmukNa* we're wading through surfaces." H'rhAtor was equally put out by this latest revelation, and turned his angst on me. "I would think you, of all people, would know better than this!"

"We more or less have to," I said, stoutly. "As you said some time ago, we're caught up in politics now, so we need to cover our tails, especially against Z'keBalf!"

H'rhAtor brooded on that, then shook his head wearily. "What a mess. Can those two be trusted to keep quiet?"

"Ah...to a degree," U'tdaPagrn said. "They're a couple of free spirits, decidedly Monrovian, as the humans say."

"Bohemian," K'deiTai muttered to him. "Still, they have enough experience with the humans to know how volatile they are. I *think* we can depend on them to be discrete."

"It's not the humans I'm worried about! Going after Z'keBalf could sink us all if he finds out!"

"Yes, well, we need to know what Z'keBalf is up to, so we'll have to hope for the best."

H'rhAtor gave him a vexed look. "What scares me is what 'best' could amount to."

*****

"Direct Action"
(Extract Of Testimony)

It was raining, and Second Degree L'datMparn fretted over it vaguely, worried that his soaked uniform would make a poor impression. He would have gone to the Junior Elders Quarters for his overtunic, but the phone call was explicit: report at once to his patron at the Chamber Of Ancients. It wasn't bad enough that Z'keBalf tracked him down to the local 'Grays' Elders' Club where he spent as much time as possible avoiding that homicidal tra'taj, *but as luck would have it, the steady drizzle turned into a genuine downpour as he left the trolley station. Nothing for it, so he arrived in the Chamber Complex soaked to the scales and silently cursing his ill-fortune.*

The Chamber Wardens escorted him to Ancient Z'keBalf's grotto, which he entered with some trepidation. Z'keBalf was reading something as he entered, and spared him no more than a quick glance, His science advisor, Learnéd N'detLeda, squatted on a comfortable seat cushion to one side. Neither one gave any hint of what they wanted or his current standing with his patron, which made him nervous. If Z'keBalf knew he was shirking...

He halted directly under the spotlight, and gave his patron his sharpest tail wave. "Reporting, Ancient."

"Well, L'datMparn." Z'keBalf set his reading aside and looked him over. "Still raining, I see." His tone was dismissive, but the set of his ears said he liked what he saw. He settled on his chin rest, and studied him for an uncomfortable moment. "What is your opinion of the humans, having worked among them?"

L'datMparn wondered what this was about, and why Z'keBalf would ask that now rather than when he returned from earth. He tried to pick his words with care. "I would say they are all er'trxxda, *Ancient. Every last one of them."*

Z'keBalf pondered him for another moment. "Indeed. Do they pose a threat, in your opinion?"

121

That put L'datMparn on alert: someone as powerful and as connected as Z'keBalf hardly needed his opinion on the human threat. Something was going on; past experience told him it meant a new assignment, and it could be a challenge. Being Z'keBalf's creature had definite advantages, but there was always a price.

"If we can maintain good relations with them, then the risk is fairly low," he said, carefully. "The problem is understanding them; they can be so confusing at times. When I was stationed at our embassy, I was concerned that Arbiter U'tdaPagrn may not grasp all their eccentricities." Like all good toadies, he never failed to blacken a potential threat when given the chance, and he still had a score to settle. "If relations deteriorate for any reason, then the humans pose a serious threat."

"Indeed." Z'keBalf mused over him briefly. "Yet by all accounts, the humans are so erratic that 'deterioration', as you put it, is highly likely, if not inevitable."

There was another uncomfortable silence as Z'keBalf pondered him. L'datMparn knew his patron was weighing him, deciding whether he would be of use for what he had in mind. That scrutiny was not comforting.

"What is your opinion of the human Captain Morgan, of their Space Fleet?"

"I've...not met her, Ancient."

"She played a major role in the recent war. You must have developed some impression of her."

That knotted L'datMparn's tail. "I regret that I can't give you much about her due to my being excluded in the war planning."

"Yes, U'tdaPagrn and company have much to account for. Unfortunately, they are out of reach for the moment due to Ancient Y'veNipbr's interference; not that we shall forget them." Z'keBalf slapped his hand on the desk to emphasize his impatience. "Still, you must have formed some opinion on Captain Morgan, and I would like your assessment, Second!"

There it was again: Z'keBalf took a very real interest in the human. Something was up, and it couldn't be good. L'datMparn answered cautiously.

"Based on the intelligence we have on her, I would say she is more er'trxxda than most of them. She suffers severe psychological problems which I believe Learnéd N'detLeda is better qualified to speak on, Ancient."

He and N'detLeda exchanged brief looks. "As a matter of fact, we have discussed that, at length." Z'keBalf eyed him closely. "Have you ever been contacted by the alien the humans call J J Ballas?"

"Um...no, sir."

Z'keBalf nodded. "Good. We have just been discussing an interesting new development, which he can fill you in on the specifics."

N'detLeda picked up the thread. "The conversation you overheard recently led us to discover that the humans contacted by the Dreamsingers have had their minds altered..."

"How bad is it, sir?" His very real alarm overrode good manners.

"As we have learned, all those exposed have developed an array of psychic abilities, including telepathy, and recent evidence of telekinesis."

This confirmed what he suspected for some time, and it put L'datMparn on high alert. "So that's why all those people in the liaison grotto are on medical release. They were exposed too..."

"Indeed," Z'keBalf said. "And why I had them assigned there, and included you to keep an eye on them."

"I...hope I am being useful, Ancient. I have found little to report."

"More than you might expect; most particularly the conversation you overheard at that ridiculous 'bonding ceremony'."

L'datMparn struggled to recall what Z'keBalf referred to, but drew a blank.

"I told my sources at Fleet Intelligence to follow up on your lead, and they came up with some curious notes," Z'keBalf went on. "It appears the humans have suffered the same result from these contacts; most particularly Captain Morgan, who has had the most frequent and prolonged exposure. We would like your expert opinion on the impact these powers will have on Captain Morgan in particular."

"Ah...how extensive are these powers, sir?"

"Limited as yet," N'detLeda said. "But the test subjects here are gaining strength steadily, and we can only assume the same is true for the humans."

"Your opinion, Second?" Z'keBalf snapped.

"Ah...it's hard to say, Ancient. But if she has the ability to read our thoughts...and even to act directly at a distance, she could be even more formidable than she is now."

"Especially as she is next in line to command Space Fleet," N'detLeda said. "Their Admiral is too old and sickly to be around much longer. She is next in line of command, and her ability to telepathically control their fleet will give them a decided advantage."

"Which I'm sure you find disturbing in view of how militaristic and unstable she is?" Z'keBalf asked.

"Yes, Ancient."

Z'keBalf nodded. "We cannot allow such an advantage to alter the balance of power."

"Um... I heard we are making significant progress on developing stellar bombs, Ancient. From what I've read about the humans' fear of those weapons, they will improve our strategic position substantially."

"Indeed?" Z'keBalf frowned. "One wonders how you heard about that, as it is our most closely guarded program." He drilled L'datMparn with an icy look. "No matter; we are still years away from an operational weapon, but there are other recent developments which will serve."

"I...find it hard to imagine anything comparable to a stellar bomb, sir."

"Stellar bombs are a blunt instrument, ideal for smashing nests and laying waste to whole regions, but lacking in finesse." Z'keBalf drilled him with a sharp look. "Have you read the works of a human named Sun Tsu?"

"No, Ancient."

"You should. A remarkable fellow," Z'kebalf mused. "According to Sun Tsu, every enemy has a weak spot, and the secret of military success is to find and exploit that weakness. While we lack the destructive abilities of the humans, we are more than capable of taking advantage of their weaknesses—most notably a certain carelessness on their part." Z'keBalf handed him the document he was reading. "Here is some recent intelligence from earth. It seems the humans trust Eldest H'rhAtor more than is wise, and transmitted this rather than hand delivering it."

L'datMparn's ears shot up as he read the translated fleet rendezvous schedule, and moreso when he got to the page of specifications for the new missiles...

"We will take advantage of this error to nullify one of the most critical threats the humans pose. You are to assume command of a ship I have arranged for. You will intercept the humans' 'Marco Polo', and make sure the problem is resolved."

"Sir? But I'm..."

"You are on detached assignment as my liaison, so no one will miss you for a while." Z'keBalf gave him a stern look. "I am confident that you will be successful in this critical mission." He didn't need to say what would happen if L'datMparn refused. Or failed.

§

Two days later, Fleet Traffic Control cleared one of the newest cruisers, ship 189, to leave orbit on a vaguely specified 'training mission'.

*****

"Frustration As A Lifestyle"
(Related by Learnéd K'deiTai)

It took Chamber Services several hands of days to clear away the wreckage of our grotto and build a new one, which they turned over to us with much grumbling and surly ear twitching. However, our new grotto turned out to be pretty much useless, since Chamber Services expressed their pique by 'losing' the paperwork to reequip the place. H'rhAtor stormed at them with the rare quality one learns on earth, but they shrugged him off with the usual platitudes about waiting patiently for the paperwork to go through, and left him standing there seething in frustration. There was nothing for it, so H'rhAtor tasked I'eiBida to draw up a supplemental appropriation, which he did with much grumbling of his own. The preliminary ten page form resulted in a cart-load of *thick* books labeled:

Equipping And Procurement

General Office - Category 334.4.0072.112
Standards, Practices, Policies, Philosophy and Regulations
with notated addenda and updates

(277 Common 5th Nmi'fru'tr, Rev. 26 edition)

Including therewith the eighty-five page procurement form, to be filed in octuplicate.

"Ancestors!" M'tinDegan said as we pawed through it. "I thought academia was bad!"

"That's private sector," I'eiBida said, glumly. "Now you know how I live."

"How are we going to get this filled out without our staff?"

Absenteeism among the few staff we had left was rife as anyone who could found excuses to take time off for 'duty related matters' or otherwise; not to mention we had no office equipment to prepare the form on.

"Well..." H'rhAtor thumbed through the huge form with a grim aura. "...I guess we'll have to do it ourselves."

So we had no choice but to take a collective deep breath, and pitch in. That took several more days of frustration and arguments which increased the psychic tension, strained friendships no end, and all but drove us *er'trxxda*. What was worse, aside from M'tinDegan, none of us were good with typing, and he had the only typewriter among us. We rented further typewriters and bought supplies out of our own pockets, and with much angst and dark mutterings about the eternally *cc'v'renk* bureaucracy, we finished all eighty-five pages (with attached documents) and off it went with our fervent blessings.

"*Ancestors*, I hope we got it all right," I'eiBida grumbled once we were rid of it. "For once, I wish L'datMparn was here; he *deserves* to be stuck with this!"

"Don't count on miracles," M'tinDegan told him. "I don't see how *anyone* could shovel through those regulations!"

"Including the bureaucracy," I added. "Pray for a miracle; maybe the bureaucrats will give up trying to understand it all, and pass it, for once."

"That *would* be a miracle!"

Until it could rumble its way through the machinery of state, we lacked communications gear, and furnishings, and our records thus far were history, but we were back in business after a fashion. Knowing how long we would have to wait for action, we dug into our own pockets again and came up with an odd assortment of hammocks, camping gear, defender surplus and thrift store finds, so at least we had something to squat on. The *Equipping And Procedures* books, stacked on the floor, made a convenient table.

Not that the lack of equipage made much difference. We were pretty much alone in our cozy little nest-away-from-the-nest thanks to C'traBenla. Our staffers were notoriously skittish around her, vanishing whenever she turned up, and a few didn't even bother with excuses, but simply deserted, terrified by her psychic powers. H'rhAtor understood their nervousness, and didn't report them. They weren't missed, since we still had no office equipment for them to use to go with having no reason for them to use it. L'datMparn was the worst at that, having disappeared into thin air. He wasn't missed either.

Nor were they the only ones. Solemn purpose notwithstanding, most of us took time off to manage our personal lives or simply to escape the claustrophobic atmosphere of the grotto. About the only exceptions were H'rhAtor and I'eiBida, who were visible enough so they had precious little leeway. C'traBenla stayed close out of loyalty to I'eiBida, but she was frustrated and snippish, which made our trial that much greater. The rest of us took turns in the Chamber Visitors' Gallery to keep up to date on their deliberations, since a Chamber monitor was something else we lacked. When we weren't doing that, we would drift out when the boredom got to be too great.

Time went on; a seemingly endless daily drudge while we stared at each other and grew ever more desperate for something to do. For want of anything better, H'rhAtor made a constant nuisance of himself grousing at the bureaucracy to get our furnishing requisitions approved. As to be expected, his only reward was our paperwork sent back with the dreaded 'Under Consideration', with correction highlights, stamped all over it.

"I swear our species is hopeless," he grumbled after the latest rebuke. "I don't know *why* the humans consider us a threat. It's not like we ever get anything done."

"There's nothing for it, sir; trust me," I'eiBida said. "We go through the same thing at Fleet Circle every day."

H'rhAtor gave him a pitying look. "I'll see if I can get you transferred to combat duty."

"Thank you, sir." He stared absently at the wall for a bit, lost in thought. "Maybe we can do like we did when we outfitted the original expedition to earth."

"Well if you plan to steal everything, you can forget it!" I said, sharply. "We don't need to tempt fate again."

H'rhAtor gave me a jaundiced look. "I heard rumors about that..."

"Trust me, they don't *begin* to tell the story!"

"No doubt." H'rhAtor sighed and picked up the phone again. "Well, I guess the only thing to do is kick it up-herd, and see if we can get someone in charge to act."

"Good luck on that."

He did so; hope is such fleeting joy. "Hello? Yes, this is Eldest H'rhAtor. I need to... Hello? He hung up on me!"

§

H'rhAtor was still arguing with them several days later, with much swearing and angst, but no luck. Our clerical staff were down to four steadfast holdouts who found his gyrations most entertaining. They whiled away the time with a running game of cutthroat *V'wit'mo'nop*, thus showing more common sense than the rest of us, perhaps. U'tdaPagrn continued fussing with his hand game, another source of venomous comment and staff amusement, while the rest of us made do as best we could.

H'rhAtor had just been rebuffed by the sixth level of bureaucracy when the even tenor of our little day was interrupted by C'traBenla arriving after a mid-morning visit to her physich. "You look a bit wrung out, love," I'eiBida said to her. "Are you all right?"

"I'm fine, love. Carrying an egg is a bit tiring, is all."

"Let me get you something." I'eiBida headed for the *V'liz* maker propped up on our improvised table.

"Don't bother, love. I have it."

I'eiBida paused and looked at her in confusion. She was holding a steaming bowl. "How did you get that?"

"I just thought about it, and it appeared." We recognized the bowl as one of those from the Chamber cafeteria. "I seem to be able to do that lately."

"Your telekinesis...?" It was just like her to develop some new arcane power, and not bother to mention it.

"I suppose. It comes in handy." She sipped her *V'liz*. "We really should keep some pastries here, too." She held out her other hand, and a large roll appeared. "It's easy, once you get the knack for it."

Sure enough, our last loyal handful of clericals were absent the next day.

§

H'rhAtor's hopeless battle went on as days passed and spring turned into summer, and as much as we sympathized, he at least provided us with a bit of comic relief. His protests reached all the

129

way up to the Chamber Service First before he was finally shot down. He spent most of the morning on the telephone (bought out of his own pocket) in an increasingly irate and desperate argument through the upper echelons. His lack of success taught us several useful Truths: notably pulling rank on herd-front bureaucrats gains one absolutely nothing. Still, he tried; I'll give him credit for that.

"This grotto was set up by express order of the Ancients," he explained with grim patience. "Without equipment, we can't do our duty... *What do you mean we sent the wrong form?* It said 'Requisition Form' right at the top!" He listened in growing dismay for a moment. "Long form?" He glanced at us with a look of panic in his eyes. "He says we used the Short Form by mistake!" I'eiBida blanched. M'tinDegan excused himself and slipped out. "Are you sure about that?"

A moment's silence...

"Your people could have told us this from the beginning!" More silence...

"Fill out the form? *To get the form we need?*" Grim silence...

"Three...hundred pages...?" His ears and tail wilted. "Yes," he mumbled. "We'll send someone to get it right away." He hung up and fumed for a bit, then glanced at I'eiBida. "They don't give the Martyred Order for ulcers, do they?"

"Um, no, sir. In any case, I have seniority on that. Maybe if we throw in nervous breakdowns..."

H'rhAtor sighed in all too evident frustration. "We should get hazard duty pay at least."

'Put in a requisition for it', I thought.

H'rhAtor gave me a venomous look. *'I'll make* you *fill it out!'* We were at a point where we could hear each others' thoughts clearly with a little effort. It could be awkward at times.

"Sorry."

§

Thankfully the requisition form for the requisition form was *not* three hundred pages long, but a mere twenty-five. The correct 'Long Form', all eight copies, arrived in a *heavy* cardboard box twelve days later.

"I do not *believe* this," H'rhAtor muttered as he struggled to move it to our improvised table. "Where do they get all the paper?"

"Admit it," I said to him. "This is the real reason why we have a stellar empire; to supply enough wood pulp!"

H'rhAtor offered a disgusted ear twitch. "No comment."

§

U'tdaPagrn was out that morning to consult with G'cetGian on the latest dispatch from his Aide who held down what was left of our diplomatic effort in Geneva. There was some speculation that he might smuggle himself aboard the courier in desperation (one *has* to be desperate to want to go to earth), and a few small wagers were made about whether we'd see him again any time soon. Nonetheless, to our mild surprise, he turned up right before mid-meal. After pondering the 'Long Form' with no joy, he filled us in on how the real Universe was managing in our absence.

"The latest word is that things are well on earth, and my Aide has cleared two minor negotiating points with the humans. At this rate, the Third Accord will be finished within the year. So it looks like relations are going smoothly."

"You mean as of twenty days ago," I grumbled. "A lot can go wrong in the time it takes the courier to get here."

"No doubt. But at least things *look* good for now, and there's no particular reason to think otherwise," H'rhAtor said.

"Other than our requisitioning," M'tinDegan groused. He was digging through the enormous 'Long Form' and taking copious notes for a scientific paper.

"Other than our requisitioning," H'rhAtor allowed.

"I also stopped by the human embassy to follow up with Pierre Roubidoux on the Zen instructor you asked for, M'tinDegan. Pierre said he put in the request, and it's scheduled out on the next courier in a few days."

'He can't get here any too soon.' H'rhAtor's thought came clearly to us.

'Indeed,' U'tdaPagrn thought as he glanced at the 'Long Form' again. *'Now if you will excuse me, I have an appointment with my physich.'* He left, rubbing his badly swollen wrists.

I'eiBida turned to me once he was gone, and stuck his hand out. "Pay up."

"Hmmm?"

"He came back, so pay up."

"He's more of a *n'bna'nmn* than I thought," I grumbled as I handed over our wager.

"Speaking of *n'bna'nmn*..." M'tinDegan started handing out copies of the 'Long Form', which we tackled reluctantly.

§

U'tdaPagrn coined a new catchphrase somewhere amid our struggles: "Martyrdom is filling out the 'Long Form'!" It soon became our mantra.

"I can't believe I wish I was back at Fleet Circle," I'eiBida grumbled as he massaged his writers' cramp.

"Think of it this way," M'tinDegan offered. "If we get this done, our Ancestors can't help but accept us into the Ancestral Herd."

I'eiBida sighed in frustration. "I wonder if they have paperwork in the Uttermost Darkness...?"

"Don't even *think* about it!" I cried.

C'traBenla walked in during our little conversation. "Still at it?" she asked.

H'rhAtor looked askance at her. "Just imagine my response; I'm too tired right now."

"My, such language!" She offered an amused ear twitch. "You all need to take some time off. It's a lovely day outside."

"*Is* there an outside?" M'tinDegan asked, plaintively.

"Yes, there is, and you need a break."

H'rhAtor rubbed his snout wearily. "I guess we do. She's right; let's take the rest of the day off."

We shut down the grotto forthwith, and headed our separate ways. The feeling of freedom was heady. It *was* a fine day outside, and I for one had several small errands to run. I luxuriated in the simple joy of doing as I pleased at first, but after a while the unfinished paperwork began nagging me, so I wound up back there by mid afternoon. The rest of them were already back at work.

§

Our return from mid-meal the next day was interrupted by a string of equipment carts blocking the aisle and a veritable stampede of Chamber Services hustling familiar-looking packages into our grotto while Q'brnVen and a couple of his Chamber Wardens did traffic control. "What's all this?" H'rhAtor demanded.

"They're reequipping your grotto," Q'brnVen said, sullenly. "It seems someone up-herd did some righteous tail knotting."

"Well it's about time," I'eiBida muttered.

"So, complaining works after all," H'rhAtor said, bemused. "Who would believe it?"

Q'brnVen didn't share our optimism at this development. "Ancestors alone know what will become of it. There's sure to be more trouble for the poor, downtrodden Chamber Wardens."

"Aren't you being a bit paranoid, sir?" one of the junior Wardens asked.

Q'brnVen shook his head in dismay. "Trust me: paranoia can be a *good* thing around this herd!"

§

If we thought Chamber Services moved fast before, they bemused us by their new standard for alacrity. Not only were we completely reequipped, but the furnishings we received were premium quality, the sort reserved for the Ancients. We watched in amazement as they installed plush carpeting, comfortable indirect lighting, a service bar with microwave and ornate *V'liz* maker, and a really lovely fountain.

"It's a miracle," H'rhAtor muttered once they left. "My Ancestors *do* love me." Our grotto was completely equipped, in style, between mid-meal and day's end; everyone at a dead gallop, all the furnishings assembled, all the equipment up and running. If our staff hadn't fled in terror, they could have started doing nothing right away.

"Let's not get too comfortable," I said as we admired our good fortune. "This is obviously some bureaucratic foul-up. They're likely to catch it at any moment, and come to take all this stuff back."

H'rhAtor gave me a jaundiced look. "Allow me my cherished delusions, please."

C'traBenla made her usual grand entrance just then, and paused to glance around the room. "Good, they got off their tails and did their job for once."

That aroused H'rhAtor's suspicions. "You had something to do with this, didn't you?"

"Of course." She gave him a smug ear twitch. "I mentioned it to Ancient Y'veNipbr, and she scorched a few tails to get them to move." She plopped comfortably on the best seat cushion, and gave him a triumphant look. "Since we're beholden to Ancient Y'veNipbr's faction, as you said, we might as well get some benefit from it."

H'rhAtor shook his head in resignation. "I give up."

"Well! I don't see what *your* tail is knotted over!"

"She has a point," I said, reluctantly. "Being beholden to Y'veNipbr has its advantages. We're completely reequipped, and Z'keBalf has been conspicuous by his absence lately."

"The diplomatic effort with the humans seems to be going well, too," U'tdaPagrn said.

"And to all appearances, the ground opened up and swallowed L'datMparn, sir," I'eiBida added.

H'rhAtor gave him a sour look. "One can but hope."

"You know...actually...as strange as it sounds, everything seems to be right with the Universe, for once," M'tinDegan said.

"*Now* you're starting to worry me."

*****

"The Quick And The Dead"
(Extract Of Testimony)

The 'Marco Polo' came out of hyper-C with more than the usual creaking and groaning, and the bridge crew waited anxiously until the overstrain gauges on the engineering panel settled down. "She's going to break up some day," Ensign Ling, the trainee Duty Officer muttered.

"She has a few miles left in her," Captain Morgan snapped. "Our position?"

Ling turned to the navigation scope, embarrassed by the Captain's rebuke, and wondering what 'miles' were. "We are..." he hesitated while adjusting the binocular calipers which would give them a quick rough range and bearing on the planet ahead. "...Roughly 240,000 klicks from the planet, on a bearing of minus thirty-five degrees on the planet's ecliptic, Captain."

Morgan studied the image of New Patagonia in the navigator's screen. "Hmph! Nice arrival, Mister Ling."

"Thank you, Captain." Ling was pleased by her praise, which was rare enough to be notable, although he was vaguely annoyed to come out of hyper-C so far out. He excelled in navigation plotting at the Academy, and thought he could have done better for his first deep space mission. He nodded to the sensors rating—they only had three commissioned officers on board, what with transfers to fill gaps in the fleet—who activated his radar to get a more accurate fix and start the approach plot.

"What's your ballpark arrival time?" Morgan demanded. She was aware of his inner grumbling, and zinged him partly to keep him on focus, and partly to clear him out of her mind.

Ling did some quick estimates in his head while wondering what a 'ballpark' was; the Captain was a fount of obscure jargon from the lost past. "I estimate about fifty hours, sir."

"Uh-huh. I want the first load ready to go the moment we make orbit. Those people must be freezing down there."

Ling nodded morosely. Aside from standing one duty watch in three, he was the ship's Loadmaster, second hat, and as soon as he got off watch he would have to start loading their borrowed shuttle. His annoyed thought monologue was a constant hassle to Morgan, which vexed her in turn. Her psychic sensitivity had grown to the point where she was hard put to concentrate with all the random thoughts and emotions around her. Most of the deck watch were busy with their duties, their thoughts a steady murmur in the background. Ling was the exception, and she was getting heartily sick of him. Their cargo was heavy drums of heating oil, which he felt would be a challenge for his under-strength deck section even in zero G. The scientific outpost on New Patagonia received mostly rations last trip, and despite being built into a cave near the equator, they must be miserable. Why Fleet thought the human race would ever colonize that frigid hell-hole was beyond him...

...his brooding was interrupted by a beep from the communications panel. "We've been painted by a laser, Captain," the comm rating said in surprise.

"Capture it." Morgan's distraction with Ling's grumbling was replaced by a faint sense of unease: this happened once before, nearly seven years ago...

There was another beep. "Got it." The comm rating examined her instruments. "It's an Ic'nichi long range tracking laser, sir."

"The Ic'nichi? What are they doing here?" Morgan's sense of unease increased, just like seven years ago... "Lock on with the telescope. Get the main radar on them."

Ling hurriedly shifted the navigation scope to a new bearing to the system north. It took a little hunting, but he finally locked onto a faint heat signature. "It's black...camouflaged?...a warship?" He adjusted his instruments with finicky care; the nav scope wasn't the most accurate at long range, especially tracking the heat *signature of a blackened ship. "I estimate their range at about one point four million klicks, sir."*

A few seconds later, the faint, fuzzy echo of the radar came back, confirming the range and bearing. "They're in stealth mode, Captain," Communications reported.

"Jamming?" Morgan's unease was turning to alarm. "What are they up to? Contact them, ask why they're here."

§

"This is the human ship 'Marco Polo' to unidentified Ic'nichi ship. You have entered Alliance space. Please identify yourself, and state your purpose."

"Standard inter-lingua transmission, sir," the Comm rating said. "Shall I respond?"

"No." L'datMparn turned to the Weapons rating. "Arm the missile." Things seemed to be going to plan. The fact that they were sending one of the prerecorded inter-species messages suggested they weren't alarmed as yet.

"Missile armed and ready, sir." Weapons was no more thrilled about this than Communications, or the rest of them; not that their opinion mattered. He glanced at the Ship's Eldest watching morosely nearby, who frowned and offered an unhappy ear twitch, but kept his peace. They had their orders.

L'datMparn studied the situation for another moment, wondering if anything could go wrong. They'd been waiting here for several nerve-wracking days, and the predicted arrival of the alien ship only heightened the tension. Even he had his reservations about this, primarily for the consequences to him if it went bad somehow. The fact that it could trigger a war with the humans was secondary: that was Z'keBalf's lookout.

"They've locked onto us with their scanner, sir," Weapons reported.

Time to get it done. "Right. Launch the missile."

§

"They've launched something, Captain." Navigation *studied the radar screen in confusion. Whatever it was, it lacked stealth technology, and was clearly visible on their scope. "A missile?"*

By now alarms were going off in Morgan's mind. "It can't be. We're way out of range..." She was interrupted when the faint blip on their screen suddenly accelerated. "...what the hell...?"

"This doesn't make sense," Ensign Ling muttered. "Some new technology?" The missile was gaining speed and closing rapidly. It should have run out of fuel by now at that rate. Then Ling paled. "A mass polarizer!" He turned to Morgan in near panic. "Captain! That missile must have a mass polarizer!"

"If it does, it will have plenty of range to reach us," Communications added. "And they wouldn't have fired otherwise."

Morgan's voice cracked like a whip. "Helm! Get us out of here! Best speed!" She hit the intercom. "All hands to battle stations! Prepare for missile impact! This is not a drill!"

"We can't outrun it, Captain." Navigation had to raise his voice over the warning klaxon as he feverishly worked his calculator. "Best guess, it'll reach us in under three minutes, and it'll be moving ten times our speed."

"Capacitor?"

"Seven percent charge, Captain," Power Board said. "I'm pouring that and the reactor's power directly into the polarizer."

"That will get us nowhere," Ling muttered. The alarm cut off just then, and he glanced at the Captain in embarrassment.

Morgan was busy studying the faint white dot of the approaching missile in the view screen, and missed his comment. Not that he was wrong; there was no chance of losing that missile, and by time it got into range, there would be no chance of the gatling gun hitting it. They were all dead...but then inspiration came to her when she needed it most. "Take charge, Mister Ling!" she snapped. "Take any and all defensive measures at your discretion." She grabbed the metal ladder running the length of the ship, and began climbing up into the navigation blister. "Until I come back down, I am not to be disturbed for any reason whatsoever!"

Ling watched incredulously as the Captain disappeared into the cramped navigation dome, and the hatch slammed shut. Then he shrugged her odd behavior off and focussed on saving their lives.

§

Once the hatch was shut, she braced herself against the navigation telescope as the ship swayed beneath her, and tried desperately to reach out with her mind. "J J! J J Ballas! I need your help."

'Ah hear you, child,' the voice came to her from some fathomless distance as a vague sensation of the large, elderly Blues musician filled her mind. 'What's wrong, Honey Lamb?'

"We're under attack! The Ic'nichi fired a missile at us. Please help me!"

'Lawd, that ain't supposed t' be!' She could feel the wave of dismay which radiated through the Dreamsingers, and realized she was touching their collective mind directly as they rallied to help her. 'What can we do, Honey Lamb?'

She hesitated for a second, realizing that there was probably nothing J J could do to save them, and their chances of surviving the attack were nil. That left her only one course of action; she fought down her despair and focussed on her duty. "I need to warn the Admiral. I need to connect with him."

'We gave you that power, Honey Lamb. Yo' jus' got to reach out fo' him.'

"I don't know how!"

'Calm yo'self, child.' A wave of serenity flowed through her, damping down her panic. 'Make yo' mind smooth.

139

Think yo'self round. You can do it.' *She fought down her alarm by main force, drawing on J J's strength.* 'Thas' better. Now, think 'bout the Admiral; think what he looks like.'

§

MacKenna was at his desk in Singapore at the moment, laboring through the quarterly supply report and longing to chuck it all and retire. "God-damned paperwork," *he muttered for the umpteenth time. So much for the Heroic life of a military legend. Most of his career had been spent in one war or another, and most of* that *went to wrestling with logistics, which was his proverbial fingernails on a chalkboard. The eternally blessed Hogarthy wasn't helping either: his new 'Procedures and Protocols' were rapidly tying Space Fleet admin in knots.* "Gawd," *he grumbled.* "Who thinks these forms up, anyway?" *Right then he would gladly offer his soul for a really good Master Chief Storekeeper...*

'Admiral!'

MacKenna looked up from the paperwork on his desk and searched the room in surprise. There was no one there, and the only sound was the faint noise of a passing truck.

'Admiral, can you hear me?' *The voice was distant, fading in and out, barely audible; but he recognized it as Captain Morgan, and she sounded scared.*

"Loraine?"

§

"Admiral, we're under attack! We're at New Patagonia, and an Ic'nichi cruiser fired some new kind of missile with a mass polarizer at us."

'Thas' the way, Honey Lamb. You got it. You reachin' to him now.'

She ignored J J's unseen presence, and focussed on MacKenna's image in her mind. "The missile is closing rapidly. Range is at least one and a half million klicks, and it's going far too fast for our defenses."

§

140

Without thinking, MacKenna hit the intercom button to his Aide in the outer office. "Issue a general planetary defense alert! And call a staff meeting! My office, five minutes!" *He didn't wait for a reply.*

§

'I hear you, Loraine,' *the thought came to her faintly.* 'Do whatever you have to.' *She knew that meant she was weapons-free, not that they had any means of striking back at the Ic'nichi.* 'Good luck.' *The Admiral's presence faded as her concentration was broken. That was duty attended to; now to focus on saving their own lives.*

"J J, can you stop that missile? Can you use your powers to deflect it, or destroy it?"

'Ah suppose we could if we were closer, but we can't rightly hit it from so far away.' *There was a sensation of deep brooding, then,* 'Maybe you can reach inta' their minds an' get 'em to stop this.'

"But... I don't know who they are. How do I visualize them?"

'It ain't that hard. You can do it, Honey Lamb. Jus' calm yo'self and focus. Turn yo' thought outward; you'll find 'em.'

She fought down her panic, and reached out with her mind, trying to envision the distant faint dot on their radar scan as an alien starship full of alien minds. She felt the emptiness of space around them, and was faintly aware of the mass of the planet nearby, and sensed a vague presence in the void...

'Thas' the way, Honey Lamb. Feel his thoughts in yo' mind. It'll draw you to him.'

Somewhere in the distance, she should feel the rumble of the ship's engine, and the faint vibration as the aged hull trembled under the strain. She forced herself to blank that out and focus into the outer emptiness. Her thought roamed the void, trying to touch that faint, distant presence...

§

"Two minutes to impact," Navigation said.

Ensign Ling studied the radar image, then turned to the navigation rating. "How fast will it be going when it gets here?"

Navigation gnawed his lip as he fiddled with his calculator. "Rough guess, point forty-two C, sir."

"We'll never hit it at that speed, sir." Weapons was tracking the missile carefully with their gatling gun, which they all knew was a futile gesture. "What is the Captain up to?"

"You just focus on your board!"

§

...She listened carefully, trying to recapture...there it was. She brushed over a consciousness, then another, still more as she narrowed her search.

'You gettin' it, Honey Lamb.'

She tried to center herself in the strongest awareness...felt herself blending into it...perceived sounds and smells and sensations...and found herself watching a strange scene. She was in a small, circular room...the bridge of the Ic'nichi ship...almost identical to their human counterparts due to engineering and tradition. A group of Ic'nichi in dark gray fatigues focussed on their instrument panels while one floated in the center and watched. She felt a faint aura of contempt and distrust focussed on the center alien...

§

"One minute to impact."

The 'Marco Polo' was making her best speed, all of a solid 1/8th G without the aid of the capacitor, but it was hopeless. Ling studied the radar track and feverishly tried to come up with ideas. Perhaps they could change course to loop around behind the planet...but that would take far too long. No, unless they had a freakin' miracle, they would be destroyed in less than a minute. He was surprisingly fatalistic about it.

§

142

...She focussed on the Ic'nichi in the center, the one who evoked such distrust, and willed herself toward him. There was a brief disorientation...and she was watching the same scene through different eyes.

"Missile closing fast, sir." The Weapons rating's words were clearly translated through her host's mind.

That one didn't respond, but she felt a wave of vindictive pleasure. She could tell he was the key, the motivator of this attack. She looked closer, sensing his thoughts...his weakness...his was a mediocre mind...too lazy, too undisciplined for his ambition...he craved the power and prestige of rank without the bother of deserving it...thankfully he could ride the tail of his powerful patron...

'A toady,' she thought in disgust.

He cringed at that, and his mental barriers of self-avoidance threatened to sever the connection. She quickly focussed on the Weapons operator in front of him...

...That one was watching his screen carefully, following the data trace as the missile closed on the distant target. She could tell he was not happy. They had no call to do this...the humans were not to be trifled with...the whole thing was l'cc'vn *irregular...the orders didn't come from Fleet, but from that* un'tdar...*the Ship's Eldest was seriously unhappy about it... Something caught her eye because he kept glancing at it: a bright yellow button under a clear plastic shield. The* n'In'c *squiggles translated as 'Missile Self Destruct'...*

§

"This is an impossible shot," the Weapons tech muttered as he watched the missile closing rapidly. The gatling gun would have a tiny fraction of a second to score before the missile hit. Even then, the shrapnel would probably impact the ship, and that alone could wreck them.

§

...the temptation was there, tormenting him. This was wrong...he should push that button...defy this staff un'tdar...*he was a political hack, to hear the buzz...that*

143

bright yellow button...an earless political sell-out...the missile was closing fast...

She prodded him carefully, urging him to give in to impulse, to do what he knew was right. He wrestled with his conscience...started to reach for the access key stuck in the panel...but hesitated. He was too disciplined to defy orders, and too junior to dare the wrath of that 'v'thorble's patron in the Chamber... She could see he wouldn't be swayed; she needed to take a top-down approach.

She slid back to the unpopular one, and found herself watching the missile track over Weapons' shoulder. ...the humans were bad enough...this psychic power was too great a threat...too unnatural...he was pleased to strike out like this, at no real risk to his own priceless tail...it would earn him much favor with the hard-liners...

'Arm the detonator,' she thought...

..."Arm the detonator."

She slid quickly over to Weapons, and tried to project an impression that he misread the order...that unpopular one actually said, "Arm the self destruct."

That impression played all too well with his feelings. He turned the key on his panel without thinking, and opened the plastic cover. "Armed, sir. Missile is..."

She slid quickly back to the unpopular one. "...is closing fast, sir."

'Now,' she thought. 'The range is perfect. Do it now.'

He reacted instinctively too. "Fire..."

§

...The missile exploded just as the 'Marco Polo's gatling fired. "That was sheer dumb..." the Weapons tech muttered in disbelief before they were struck by several bits of debris. The ship reverberated from the hits, alarms were ringing, and their ears popped as the air pressure fell.

"We're breached!" Ling yelled. "Suits, everyone!"

The crew forgot the battle as they struggled to close up their crash suits, secure their helmets which often were floating around the bridge, and plug into the ship's

144

emergency oxygen system. Ling got his suit closed, and looked frantically around the bridge. Several panels were dark, their electrical lines severed, and the damage board showed swift decompression in the central column and the engineering space aft. Shrapnel must have cut some of the electrical conduits in the shaft, but the strain gauges were quiet, which meant no structural damage. It could have been worse.

The hatch to the navigation blister flew open, and the Captain came tumbling down head first. "Mister Ling! Shut everything down!" she snapped as she struggled with her crash suit. "Go to complete silence and play dead. And dump the shuttle, and the garbage and anything you have in the air lock, equipment included."

"Ah...yes, Captain."

The bridge crew hurriedly shut down the radars and radios while Ling helped the Captain into her suit. "What's the damage?" she demanded as she fought with the zippers.

"Light hits mostly in the shaft and engineering, sir. No word on casualties yet."

"They got the navigation dome too," Morgan wheezed as she snapped her helmet on, plugged into the nearest oxygen outlet, and gasped for breath...

§

..."Nothing, sir." Weapons adjusted his instruments with finicky care, trying to pierce the distant cloud of debris. "We're too far away for a good laser scan."

"What about your other systems?"

Weapons consulted the rest of his sensor suite, none of which were as good as the tracking laser at these ranges. "I have a heat signature...but that's residual. No radiation...no transmissions. "They must be dead, sir." He was not happy about what they did, orders or no. Nor was he happy about hitting the self destruct; he wondered why he did that, and if this staff un'tdar noticed. He shivered with the reaction: his Ancestors must have touched him...

"What about their course plot?"

145

Weapons shook off his dismay and consulted the course projection. "No heat bloom. Engines have stopped. No evidence of maneuvering, sir." Sad to say, it seemed his intervention came too late. "They should impact the planet in about five days..."

§

...Captain Morgan stared fixedly at the telescope screen, ignoring the chaos around her, and focussed on her mental connection with the unpopular Ic'nichi who fomented the attack. They weren't out of this yet...

§

...L'datMparn pondered the blurry images on their scopes while a thought, 'they're dead,' *stirred in the back of his mind. It* looked *like they were destroyed...but he wasn't sure. Perhaps they should move closer for a better scan...* 'The colony might spot us,' *the thought came to him.* 'No need to risk it. They're dead.'

"All right," he said at last. He turned to the Ship's Eldest. "Mission accomplished. Take us home." Then as a final dig, he added, "Remember, this action is under the Chamber's seal: you are not to reveal it to anyone."

The Ship's Eldest gave him a disgusted ear twitch, but didn't answer.

§

"Their laser is secured, Captain," Communications reported. The ranging laser locked onto them had abruptly shut down. She consulted her other instruments. "I'm picking up a heat bloom...and hard radiation. They're getting under way, Captain."

"We fooled them," Ling sighed as the bridge crew relaxed.

"So it seems." Morgan studied the faint telescope image until it was obvious the Ic'nichi ship was moving. "Maintain silence until you pick up their X-ray burst. We'll wait until the intruder jumps into hyper-C before making a run for it."

"Yes, Captain," Ling said, hollowly.

146

The crisis was over. Morgan sagged against the ladder and tried to relax, with little success. "Thank you, J J." *she muttered.*

'Happy t' help, Honey Lamb.' *As the presence faded, one more thought came to her.* 'This must be some kind-a mistake.   You-all try t' patch things up with them, you hear?'

*****

"Chaos Can Be *Most* Entertaining"
(Related by Learnéd M'tinDegan)

Once our grotto was up and running, H'rhAtor faced a new crisis when *all* of our staff refused to return to duty, risking charges rather than face C'traBenla's powers again. A few of them actually deserted, but most put in requests for transfer, which H'rhAtor reluctantly signed partly because he couldn't fault them, and partly because we had no one to fill out the disciplinary paperwork. He then put in an urgent request for new clerical staff, and was told they would be sent promptly—before winter for sure. There was nothing for it, so we settled into our plush new grotto to wait in less than perfect resignation.

"If this isn't the Ultimate Cosmic Tail Knot, I can't imagine what would be!" H'rhAtor was thoroughly put out by this latest delay, and paced back and forth in frustration as he grumbled about the unfortunate facts of life. "Can't they get *anything* right? What good is a fully equipped grotto when there's no one here to staff it?"

"Ancestors alone know, sir," I'eiBida said, morosely.

"I'd hate to see the forms we'd have to fill out to get *them* to answer! *How* does our society function at all?"

"By the orderly process of paperwork and oversight, to hear it told," I said to soothe him. "I know it's a burden, but we have to be patient. Imagine the chaos if all the paper were to disappear."

I'eiBida sighed longingly. "Wouldn't it be wonderful? All those clericals put to some useful work..."

"As if *that* would ever happen!" H'rhAtor grabbed the nearest telephone. "At least I can pull rank with Fleet, even if I couldn't with Chamber Services!"

"You already went through this once," I cautioned him. "Do you *really* want to confront them again?"

"Bureaucrats are the same, sir, whether in uniform or not."

That gave H'rhAtor pause, then he hung up the phone. "I don't suppose I should seem ungracious, I guess." He pondered for a bit, then glanced at I'eiBida. "You're our resident Staff paper-shoveler, so you take care of it."

148

"What did I do to you?" I'eiBida grumbled.

"It's called 'delegation'. If you ever achieve senior rate, you'll appreciate how valuable it is."

"It's called *something*," I'eiBida muttered as he reached for the phone.

§

One advantage (I suppose) of our current plight was that we had plenty of free time for contemplation, and the single most important topic of discussion continued to be our ever-growing psychic powers. After C'traBenla's panic attack, we all began experimenting (*cautiously!*) to see what we could do. The results were mixed, but on the whole impressive.

H'rhAtor and I'eiBida were already able to summon bowls of *V'liz*, but turned more cautious after I'eiBida summoned a sour roll and part of the cafeteria serving counter came with it. We went to ground for the next several days thereafter until the panic and investigations in the cafeteria died down.

After much effort, K'deiTai finally managed to teleport, but gave it up when he received a steaming hot bowl of *V'liz*—minus the bowl. He spent his time thereafter nursing his burnt hand and griping. U'tdaPagrn had the least success, probably because of his ongoing fixation with his human hand game.

As for myself, I soon was able to move small objects around, but forbore summoning food and drinks, since I was not optimistic about my abilities nor comfortable dabbling in something none of us understood. Instead I spent much of my time observing the others and taking copious notes for a future scientific paper on our experiences.

And so we went, frittering our lives away in our deluxe grotto, bored out of our minds except for U'tdaPagrn wrestling with his human hand game, and I'eiBida, whose battles over the phone with Fleet staff were no less frustrating.

"Look...I'm a paper-shoveler myself, seconded here from Fleet Staff." He was trying the reasonable approach at the moment since his efforts to date accomplished nothing but to raise his blood pressure. "I know how important procedure is, but can't you expedite at least a few temporary clericals?"

A lengthy silence.

"Well, yes, this *is* an emergency. We're a special liaison office for the Chamber, and we're non-functional without staff..."

More silence.

"It depends on how you define an emergency? I'd define it as when the Ancients become annoyed with rear-echelon *ui'DmukNa*. Can't you...the fleet *b'Ven'gtt' herd!?* We answer to the *Chamber*, for Ancestors' sake! Don't we get priority over the sports herd?"

His ears wilted.

"Can't you make some allowance?"

More silence, then he hung up.

"No luck, I take it?" H'rhAtor asked.

"They say they'll get to 'the preliminary qualifications screening' as soon as they finish restaffing the athletics office!"

H'rhAtor threw up his arms in despair. "There goes our summer!"

"What?" I asked. "Fleet sports is more critical than us?"

"We're a 'non-central function'," H'rhAtor said. "The fleet has priority, and extras like us are handled when they get around to it."

I'eiBida nodded morosely. "*And* the Athletics Office got there first. They estimate they will send the first candidates for preliminary interviews some time in *znm'brVrv*. Even then it'll be winter before the first staffers clear the Qualifications, Seniority and Aptitude Reviews, and get their security clearances."

"For clerical help?" K'deiTai asked in dismay.

H'rhAtor sighed. "And then there's the transfer paperwork. It never ends." He shook his head in despair, then turned to I'eiBida. "I had no idea it was so bad for you back-herd types."

"You have it soft out there confronting dangerous aliens, *sir*." I'eiBida picked up the phone again. "Might as well keep trying. It's not like there's anything else to do around here."

Thus our days: stupefyingly dull and bitterly frustrating, with moments of excitement when our psychic experiments went amiss; the worse of which was a blown out window. We bought a piece of glass and replaced it ourselves rather then incur the wrath of Chamber Services again.

§

Eventually the stink over the Chamber revelations died down and life returned to normal, which was no comfort. In a way, I think we missed the publicity since it kept C'traBenla occupied. Even then, since her pregnancy was well advanced, she stayed close to home, for which we were secretly thankful. Our daily routine went on, sitting around our grotto waiting for the Universe to end, wallowing in an invisible fog of angst and frustration which kept us all on edge and made tempers flare. And as the days crawled by, it got worse and worse until it was hard to tell whose thoughts were whose. The high summer settled in, and we had all the windows open to trap what little breeze we could. The muggy warmth dulled our minds, making us sleepy, which helped a little.

It all seemed to blend into a gray blur, so it was hard to say just when things came to a head. U'tdaPagrn was fiddling with his little plastic hand game, as usual, and gave vent to a storm of mental angst when he actually got four of the side colors aligned, but lost them again trying for the fifth.

I'eiBida recoiled from the psychic sewage and hung up the phone. "Will you *please* get rid of that thing?" he grumbled. "You're getting on our nerves."

"This...*thing*...is monstrous!" U'tdaPagrn hurled it across the room, making us duck as it ricochetted around the grotto. "It's more than enough to go to war with the humans!" He collapsed on his seat cushion, sobbing and rubbing his swollen wrists.

"You need to get hold of yourself," I told him, gently. "That thing will leave you a nervous wreck if you keep it up."

"I...know," he sobbed. "I can't help it. It's addictive!" He sagged on his seat cushion, whimpering in frustration as the rest of us shared a feeling of pity and concern for him. And to think that *thing* was only a harmless (to them) human toy. The intercultural implications were disturbing, to say the least.

L'datMparn *would* turn up just then after his lengthy absence, which was an unwelcome change in our little day. "And where have you been off to?" H'rhAtor demanded. "I was about to report you for desertion, you've been gone so long."

L'datMparn gave him a surly look and a barely subordinate tail wave. "I was given a temporary assignment, sir."

151

"Doing what?"

"With every respect, sir, my duties are to serve as liaison to Ancient Z'keBalf. I am seconded to this office, but I still report to him. He had me take care of something which I am not at liberty to discuss."

"So you admit to being Z'keBalf's creature, then? He stuck you in here to spy on us, did he?"

"I am simply doing my duties as assigned, and I would not *presume* to speculate on *Ancient* Z'keBalf's actions, *sir*."

"It's nice of you to grace us with your presence after all this time, at least. Is this some special occasion?"

L'datMparn gave him a chilly ear twitch. "I simply came in to pick up my messages, and to see if there was anything scandalous to pass along, *sir*."

"Well you know where your messages are, and as for anything juicy to report, I'm sorry to disappoint you."

L'datMparn left it at that and collected his memos from their box. As he headed for the door, he spotted U'tdaPagrn's hand game on the floor and paused to pick it up. It was still unbroken despite its many ballistic adventures. He considered it for a bit, then offered a sarcastic ear twitch and set it in front of U'tdaPagrn, who was still shivering and moaning.

'He's been up to no good, sir.' The strength of I'eiBida's thought showed clearly how tense we all were around L'datMparn.

'This surprises you?'

'No, sir. But where has he been? What was he up to?'

'I'm not sure I want to know.'

L'datMparn favored U'tdaPagrn with a contemptuous snort, and headed for the door.

'I get a bad feeling about this, sir.'

H'rhAtor studied L'datMparn with no favor as he left, then glanced at I'eiBida. *'You're not the only one.'*

He wasn't, in fact. L'datMparn's aura had my intuition ringing alarm bells as well.

§

L'datMparn's reappearance was disturbing enough that it reminded me of certain inquiries undertaken earlier. I excused

152

myself and headed over to see W'kiLap and T'apiDien to learn what progress they made in tapping Z'keBalf's phones.

"So, L'datMparn has you worried, hmmm?" W'kiLap said after I brought them up to a gallop on our situation. "That sounds like a personal problem to me."

"L'datMparn does have them, doesn't he?" T'apiDien added. "Flawed and failing..."

"...inadequate and imperfect..."

"...deficient and delinquent..."

"...perverse and pertinacious..."

"Seriously," I interrupted. "He as much as admitted he's Z'keBalf's creature. We all get a bad aura from him."

"*That's* hardly news," T'apiDien said.

"He disappeared for some time, and was decidedly secretive about it when he came back. They may have some sort of dirty business going on, and it might be wise to know what they're up to. Have you had any luck with Z'keBalf's phone?"

T'apiDien gave me a jaundiced look. "It's hardly a matter of 'luck'! We are the experts, after all, and we know what we're doing."

"Better than some of us," I muttered. "So what have you learned?"

"Nothing. We haven't been able to link in yet."

"And you're the experts?"

"We're not the *only* experts! Chamber security is as tight as an egg, and Z'keBalf has been adding his own security overlays on top of what Chamber Services installed."

"We're digging away, but it isn't like it was on earth. We have real computers and real network security on this world."

"So...how long do you think it will take?"

T'apiDien's frustration was starting to show. "That depends on how much risk we're willing to take. The Chamber network is a quagmire of intruder traps, reroute patches and security lock points. It's been overhauled and rebuilt and restructured who knows *how* many times over the last two hundred years. It's almost as complicated as the physical building itself."

"How it functions at all is beyond us," W'kiLap added.

153

"Navigating it is tricky at best. Navigating it without being spotted is all but impossible."

"Designed by bureaucrats, of course," I grumbled.

"Of course. No *sensible* person could conceive such a maze."

"So the question is, how urgent is this?" T'apiDien asked.

That put me in a quandary; this *was* merely an informal thing after all, and the consequences of being caught would be severe. But we were talking about Ancient Z'keBalf; all of us had a compelling interest, both personal and professional, in what he might be up to. I certainly had no authority to encourage their snooping, but sometimes, I decided, one has to break herd for the greater good.

"It's pretty urgent. We need to keep tabs on what Z'keBalf is up to, so please do whatever you can."

W'kiLap offered a pleased ear twitch. "We thought you'd say that."

§

I could tell H'rhAtor was in a foul mood when I returned to our grotto. *'He's been on the phone,'* I'eiBida thought to me. *'The bureaucrats have been after him all morning.'*

"Well, I hope you had a pleasant little walk," H'rhAtor grumbled at me.

"I gather your day hasn't been so enjoyable?"

"You could say that. The Fleet Eldest is knotting my tail about the lack of progress reports, the Chamber bureaucracy is after my ears because we haven't kept our records up to date, and I can't even get Assignment Circle to return my calls."

"But they know we don't have any staff. Can't they make allowances for that?"

"Obviously not!" H'rhAtor fumed, then offered an apologetic ear twitch. "It doesn't make your head explode, but it's very bad."

"Well don't despair; we're sure to have a good day sometime."

"Ancestors, I hope not!" I'eiBida said, fervently.

"Why?"

"Then we would have to file a *'Miscellaneous Unusual Incident'* report. That's twenty-four pages worth, plus signed affidavits from each of us."

"You're joking, of course?" H'rhAtor asked.

"I wish I was, sir."

"That...doesn't sound so bad," I offered, dubiously.

"Except we don't have the form, and I'm not sure what number it is."

"I'm sure the bureaucracy would tell us."

I'eiBida shook his head. "They won't take the responsibility. We would have to look it up in the *'Master List Of Forms, Instructions, And Related Documents'* catalog, which is *supposed* to come with a set of office equipment."

This was utterly ludicrous, but I was fascinated by the ever-convoluted depths of the bureaucracy. "So where is it?"

"They didn't include it." I'eiBida made a sweeping gesture taking in our deluxe surroundings. "This is an executive setup. The Master List only goes to the common herd."

"Then I suppose we would have to order a catalog?"

"Except we would need to fill out a forty page requisition form, plus the sixty-five page document explaining what happened to our issue catalog, why we should be issued a new one, and who should pay for the lost one."

"But if they didn't send it..."

"Then we're not authorized to have it. We'd have to file an eighty-eight page *'Exemption Issue Under Extraordinary Circumstances'* form and hope they'll cut us some slack."

"This is *er'trxxda!*" K'deiTai grumbled. "Isn't there *anything* they *don't* have a form for?"

I'eiBida shook his head. "That's covered by the *'Unclassifiable, Extraneous, Unexpected, and Inexplicable Event Or Matter Reporting'* form."

"Um...how many pages is that?

"One hundred and forty-seven, last I heard."

"*What*, in the Ancestors' name, can they put in *that?*"

"Ah...its mostly blank paper after you get beyond the Routing And Filing data on the title page."

"And I suppose we'd have to fill out every last page?"

"In detail. And in octuplicate."

"This is *er'trxxda!*"

"So let's be thankful we're having a miserable day, as always," H'rhAtor concluded.

For once, K'deiTai got in the last word. "With our luck, they probably have a form for that, too."

§

As if my day wasn't joyous enough, I received a call a bit later from Learnéd N'detLeda, who demanded I return to his office at the Institute for more testing. "Haven't you figured this out yet?" I griped at him when I arrived. "These psychic powers are getting to be a real nuisance."

That earned me a chilly glare. "I will gladly trade them for the nuisance of dealing with *some* of your fellow test subjects!"

I could tell he was angry and frustrated, which wasn't promising. "I take it you've made little progress?"

He gave me a sour look. "Nothing. All the psyche tests come back as normal—for *that* herd. It appears the issue is physical, rather than psychological."

"So, we're back to neurosurgery again, I see?"

That sent a chill through him. "We must not be premature in our diagnosis. We still must define what part of the brain controls these functions, and from there determine its mechanism."

"And only then can you start devising a treatment. This is not promising."

He grumbled for a while, then asked, "So, how advanced *are* your powers?"

I hesitated to answer, knowing whatever I said would soon reach Z'keBalf, but I couldn't see how it could be used against us, plus we faced an increasingly urgent need to find a cure. "We're seeing new manifestations all the time. C'traBenla recently demonstrated the ability to teleport; several of us have since developed the same skill."

That got his attention. "Teleport? How large an object?"

"We're pretty much limited to summoning bowls of *V'liz* thus far, and our abilities vary. I've only been able to move small objects like pencils."

That clearly surprised him. He offered a pencil and said, "Show me."

156

I wasn't thrilled, but I couldn't see any harm in it, so I laid the pencil on the table next to us. I still wasn't that good with this, so I cleared my mind and focussed carefully. Nothing happened at first, but then the pencil quivered, rose an arm's length into the air and hovered unsteadily.

"Indeed?" N'detLeda was transfixed by the sight. "Remarkable! Can you do more?"

"This...is about all thus far," I said carefully, trying not to lose my focus. "Some of the others can do better, but I haven't risked anything ambitious until we understand this phenomenon."

"A wise choice." He studied the pencil closely, and I could tell he was impressed. "No doubt you intend to write a paper on this; I would like to see it when you have it done."

T'virDoma came crashing in just then, and spotted the floating pencil as my concentration broke and it clattered onto the table. "How cute," she snarked. "You've taken up doing magic tricks?"

"It *appears* our test group is exhibiting telekinetic skills," N'detLeda said, shortly. "Learnéd M'tinDegan was offering a small demonstration, which you *interrupted!*" That wasn't my only skill; I could tell he was put out by her attitude.

She looked me over like I was some sort of dubious specimen. "Wasting time on *fuzzy* science, I see?"

"I am happy to help with any *legitimate* scientific study."

"A Learnéd of Flying Pencils; will wonders never cease? Or is this all you can do?"

"It's all I am willing to risk until we understand this better."

"Hmph! Tail too short for the challenge?"

"He is following *proper* scientific protocol, which you would do well to show a bit more *respect* for!"

"His Ancestors must have smiled on him to stick him in *that* herd." She offered me a dismissive ear twitch. "I suppose you're gathering all *sorts* of dirt on those *n'bna'nmn*? *er'trxxda*, the lot of them. Planning to write a book, are you?"

"Actually..."

"I thought as much." She turned on N'detLeda. "I don't know why we bother with those *people*; it's not like anyone needs them. We should grab tail on this, and start biopsy sampling."

157

"We will follow *proper* scientific protocol, as always!" N'detLeda snapped. "We will continue the genetic testing and scans until we can be sure we have all the data obtainable."

"Why? It's not getting us anywhere. We should go ahead and get those brain tissue samples, or even autopsy the lot."

N'detLeda was fuming by then. "*I* will decide the proper course of action!"

"Well *you* need to get on it, since all your paper tests don't produce anything." She waggled an ear at me. "And of course *he's* no better. I don't see why *he* gets any special treatment, or how anything *he* writes about it can be looked on as unbiased..."

I admit I lost my temper then. *"GO AWAY!"* I yelled at her. T'virDoma vanished into thin air, followed by a panic-stricken squawk from the next room.

N'detLeda was utterly flabbergasted, and stared stupidly at the spot she occupied for a long moment before turning to me in amazement. "Can you teach me how to do that?"

"It..." I was shaken by what happened. "It...seems I don't know my own strength."

§

"You teleported her into the next room?" H'rhAtor and the others were incredulous when I related the incident to them later.

"Yes, to my amazement."

"In one piece?"

"Yes, thankfully! They took her to the Institute clinic, but she appears to have come through it all right."

"Such a waste," K'deiTai grumbled. "You could have at least shortened her tail while you were at it."

"You don't seriously *mean* that?"

"These psychic powers are more dangerous than we thought," I'eiBida said. "I see what J J Ballas meant about self discipline."

"Especially as the incident seems to have been triggered by a flash of temper," I added. "We must give N'detLeda's research our full cooperation."

"But what do we do until he finds a cure?" K'deiTai asked.

"Well, for one thing, we avoid any stressful situations..." The others were looking askance at me. "...um...never mind."

"Ancestors, what a mess!" H'rhAtor complained. "What more could go wrong?" C'traBenla came in just then for the first time since our grotto was reequipped. H'rhAtor look one look at her, and slumped on his seat cushion in despair.

"Speaking of stressful situations," K'deiTai muttered.

"Hello, love." I'eiBida caught H'rhAtor's funk, and moved to head her off. "How are you feeling?"

"I'm fine, love. I'm a bit tired, but the physichs say I'm doing well." She gave H'rhAtor an irritated ear twitch, which for her can say volumes. "But all these sour attitudes are enough to put a fem off her mood. You all really need to lighten up."

"Sorry. We've been having a difficult time lately."

"So I see." She looked around the grotto. "Still no staff?"

"That's the problem. We're bogged down in bureaucracy again."

She gave H'rhAtor a peeved look. "Well it's no reason to get all tail-knotted with innocent bystanders."

"True enough, love. So what did the physichs say?"

That distracted her; she practically radiated pleasure at the thought of her hatchling. "We're getting close. I can feel the egg hardening. They increased my calcium supplement, so it won't be much longer."

"That's wonderful, love. You don't want to over extend yourself so close to delivery, so perhaps you should stay at home for now."

She gave him a skeptical look. "Well, I suppose. Still, you all need to improve your attitudes." She made the rounds among us briefly, then departed. We all breathed a sigh of relief.

§

The next day, like all our days, was no better. We began our morning routine as always: visiting briefly to wish each other a good day and catch the latest gossip (nothing important going on), reviewed the morning news broadcasts (nothing important going on), checked through the post and messages (nothing important going on), and briefly scanned the transcripts of yesterday's Chamber minutes (nothing important going on, as always.) After that, we had no choice but to get down to work.

"Well, time to gallop at shadows," I'eiBida muttered as he picked up the phone.

"It could be worse," I tried to reassure him. "You could be facing a major battle with the humans."

"*That* would be a relief!" I'eiBida sighed, and punched the number. After a moment, he looked at the handset curiously. "Out of order." He dug through the phone list, and tried again. "That's out of order too." A third try. "Still no luck. What's going on?"

"Is something wrong?" H'rhAtor asked.

"I can't get through, sir." He tried another number. "No luck there either." Another number. "That one too, sir."

"Something's wrong. Check with Chamber Services."

"Yes, sir." He dug up the internal system directory and punched again. "Hello? We are trying to call the Fleet Assignment Circle, but none of our calls are going through. Is there a problem with the telephones?" He listened for a long moment. "They did?" More silence. "?" More silence. "!"

"Well?" H'rhAtor demanded.

I'eiBida covered the mouthpiece and turned to him. "They've blocked their lines so we can't call them, sir."

"Can they do that?" I asked.

"Can they do that?" he repeated to the phone. "Services says they can to block nuisance calls."

"They must get those all the time," K'deiTai grumbled.

"So what do we do if we have to contact them in an emergency?" I'eiBida asked the phone. "*Don't* call Chamber Services? What...hello? They hung up on me!"

"I don't suppose we were popular with them to begin with," I said, philosophically.

"This is *cc'v'renk*! Enough of this *x'mnnb'*!" H'rhAtor was outraged. "It's bad enough those *un'tdars* won't do their jobs, but I won't have them ignore us too. I'm going down to Fleet and straighten them out *personally!*"

"Good luck, sir."

H'rhAtor paused at the door and gave him a smoldering glare. "And *you're* coming with me!"

§

160

It was late afternoon by time they returned to the grotto, and I could tell they were pretty well fed up, not that our little day was any better. U'tdaPagrn was working his human hand game relentlessly; his angst and frustration filling the grotto like a choking fog. I was so depressed by the atmosphere that I wasn't even taking notes. K'deiTai was half-collapsed in despair over the Arbiter's desk, and greeted them as if they brought Salvation on a golden platter. "Well? Did you have any luck?"

"Of course not!" H'rhAtor snapped. "What makes you think we're supposed to have any *luck* in this tail-knotted Universe?"

"We went all day, from one office to the next, until we finally wound up back where we started," I'eiBida added. "I should have spotted the old run-around earlier."

"You should have." H'rhAtor gave him a surly ear twitch. "It would have saved us from a day wasted chasing our own tails."

"Sorry, sir."

"It's frustrating, I know," I offered to cool the tempers.

"On top of which, they ordered their security to throw us out. The Fleet bureaucracy threw *me*, the Fleet Elder, out! Can you believe it?"

"When it comes to bureaucracy, I'll believe anything at this point," K'deiTai groaned.

H'rhAtor's ears drooped in despair. "This has been one of *those* days, and I've had enough. Let's give up and go home."

"We might as well, since we can't do much here, sir," I'eiBida grumbled.

By unspoken consensus, we wrote the day off as another loss and packed it in. After all what good could we do? "How long will this go on, sir?" I'eiBida asked as H'rhAtor was locking up.

"You mean until we get new staff, or until someone finds a cure for this psychic mess, or until we all go *er'trxxda*?"

"Yes, sir."

H'rhAtor sighed in exasperation. "I *knew* accepting a promotion was a mistake. I could be out on some comfortable supply run to the far end of our space." He brooded for a bit, then, "I have no idea, to all your questions. Things are as confused as ever, but on a higher level and about more important things."

"So we're making progress of a sort, at least," I said.

We were interrupted by three hands' worth of clerical ratings coming down the hall in a herd, escorted by an unhappy Warden Q'brnVen. "Here they are," he said to the foremost one. "Good luck." He gave I'eiBida a nervous glance and beat a hasty retreat.

H'rhAtor pondered them, then asked, "Something I can do for you?"

"Yes, sir." The junior Worthy in charge offered a sharp tail wave and a package of forms. "We're reporting for duty."

"What? Now?" H'rhAtor was bemused by their sudden appearance. "What came over the Assignment Circle?"

"I...couldn't say, sir," he replied cautiously. "But from what I heard, someone collected a whole lot of ears to get us expedited."

"Indeed? They might have told us this while we were there!" H'rhAtor leafed through the packet of transfer forms briefly, then glanced at me. "I think we know who is behind this."

"Indeed. She must have gone to Ancient Y'veNipbr again. Why didn't we think of that?"

"Because it would be too easy. We *never* do things the easy, sensible way; that'd be unnatural."

"We're not accustomed to thinking outside the herd," I'eiBida explained.

"It must be wonderful having an Ancient at one's beck and call," H'rhAtor lamented.

"We should try to keep C'traBenla at home for the time being," K'deiTai said. "We don't want her scaring this lot off."

"Good luck with that," I'eiBida said, irritably.

"Actually we should put her in charge of procurement all round," I suggested. "Her connections are all we have going for us."

H'rhAtor sighed again. "Oy. Bureaucracy will be the downfall of our civilization. You'll see."

"No, it won't. They'd never get the paperwork finished."

*****

"Meeting The Challenge"
(Extract Of Testimony)

By time the 'Marco Polo' came limping home, the human Space Fleet was on full alert. The damage from the missile strike was extensive, but mostly repaired by time they arrived. The crew were less fortunate: two dead from hypoxia, and two more injured. The survivors were shaken and boiling mad, ready to lash out at the Ic'nichi. The mood of the rest of the fleet differed only in degree: no one knew exactly what happened or why, but they weren't prepared to stand still for it. Orbit Dock wasted no time in servicing the ship for immediate departure while Captain Morgan made a hasty shuttle trip groundside to report to the Admiral.

"I do not see why they do this, sir," Captain Rostokovich said after Captain Morgan recounted the incident at a hastily called staff meeting. "Tensions are still there, but Eldest H'rhAtor is not one for such treachery. Is senseless."

MacKenna gave him a jaundiced look. "It made sense to them. What we need to do is figure out their reasoning: it will give us a strategic insight into what they want."

"I was able to read the mind of their leader," Morgan said. "A few brief thoughts, anyway. They're afraid of us— of those who have been mind-altered by the Dreamsingers. They think we pose a special threat."

"Likely you in particular," Rostokovich said to the Captain. "You are next senior to Admiral, and have strongest powers."

"And so they arranged a mysterious 'accident' for you." MacKenna nodded grimly. "Makes sense: eliminate the greatest danger, and break our line of succession all in one swell foop." He turned to Rostokovich. "Restructure the shipping schedule, and arrange a priority rendezvous chain to spread the new list to the fleet."

"Da, Admiral."

"The transit list?" Morgan asked.

"My fault." MacKenna sighed at his own stupidity. "I put too much faith in H'rhAtor, I guess. I should never have transmitted that schedule."

"You could not anticipate this, sir," Rostokovich said.

MacKenna sighed again. "Probably not. I'm getting too damned old for this."

"This doesn't add up, sir," Morgan said. "The one who lead the attack was a political flunky. Perhaps they thought H'rhAtor was too sympathetic to us, and he's been removed from command?"

MacKenna brooded on that, then shook his head. "No, their command structure is too thin to toss him on a whim, and we would have heard something." He gave Rostokovich a pointed look.

"Latest word from contact at embassy is he is on sick list, sir," Ivan said.

"Putting someone on the sick list is an old trick, sir," Hythe-Morrison said. "But as I understand, H'rhAtor has enough support in the Chamber that there would be a big fuss we would surely hear about."

That got a rise out of Ivan. "Our contact has been reporting on hard-line faction in Chamber Of Ancients, sir. Perhaps H'rhAtor really is sick, and this is their act?"

MacKenna nodded. "Taking advantage of a momentary power vacuum in their leadership? It's not like we've never seen that before, eh?" Then he gave Hythe-Morrison a sharp look. "If that hash on your sleeve is affecting your judgment, Leftenant, I can find a cure!"

Hythe-Morrison hesitated, disconcerted that his thought had been overheard, and concerned at MacKenna's increasingly short fuse. "I meant no disrespect, Admiral."

MacKenna sagged on his arms, and rubbed his eyes with a weary sigh. "Sorry. I just wish we could settle matters with the Ic'nichi so I could retire." Finally he turned to Captain Morgan. "Did J J say anything about what their objective is at the time?"

She hesitated, with a vexed expression. "...no. We should ask him."

"Yeah, but how? Linking with them nearly killed you last time."

Captain Morgan's revulsion at the memory of their desperate attempt to reach the Dreamsingers through a drug-induced state set all of them on edge. "We have to risk it, sir," she said, more calmly than her mental state warranted. "Should I make a quick trip to their world? We need to speak with him."

And there he was, as large as life, gazing around at them with the weary, benevolent expression they had all come to know. "Ah hear you, Honey Lamb. How can ah help?"

It took them a moment to get over their surprise. "Ah...J J, did you learn anything about why the Ic'nichi attacked the 'Marco Polo'?" MacKenna asked.

J J furrowed his brow in thought. "Ah can't rightly say. It's so hard fo' us t' understand how you-all think at times."

"You're not the only one."

J J pondered for a moment with a far-away look. "The ones you know, the ones that was in the war wit yo', they didn't have nothin' t' do with it. They don' seem t' know anythin' 'bout it. Ah can't rightly tell about all the rest."

"Is there any way they could find out?" Morgan asked.

J J gave her a crooked smile and tapped his temple knowingly. "Tha's an in-verse cognitive function, Honey Lamb." Then he vanished.

"J J..."

"Dammit," MacKenna muttered.

"What did he mean by that?" Morgan wondered.

"I just wish they'd be more plain. Can you make sense of that last, Captain?"

"Um...no, sir."

"Well...at least we know H'rhAtor's not involved, but that nullifies any confidence we had in his good intentions. So we're back to square one with the Ic'nichi." MacKenna *brooded as the tense silence stretched out. "We have to assume the worst," he said at last. "This must be a move authorized by the Chamber Of Ancients; their fleet wouldn't defy them and H'rhAtor otherwise."*

"But can we be sure, sir?" the Chief Of Staff asked. "It's hard to say just who's in charge, whether H'rhAtor has been superseded or bypassed, or if this is a policy shift or the act of a faction."

"That's the hell of it: you never can be sure what the other guy's thinking. There are too many options in this case, and with the lack of communication..."

"We must take our best guess, sir," Ivan said.

Mac eyed him, then nodded. "That's why I get the big bucks: to take the heartache."

There was another tense silence as he brooded over what he would have to do. He sensed the emotions of those around him: alarm, agitation, dismay, grim resignation. He felt those same emotions all too often in his career. There was nothing to do but what had to be done.

"Whether it's their decided policy, or the act of a faction doesn't really matter. I hate the whole idea, but we have no choice." He looked up at his retinue of senior staffers. "Prepare for Operation Triphammer. I will contact the Minister."

§

MacKenna drove over to the 'Squirrel Cage' a short time later to confront Minister Hogarthy. As much as he despised the little man, he was thankful Hogarthy was still there making a nuisance of himself. Word from Geneva was that a Parliamentary committee was investigating defense matters in general, so Hogarthy was camped out in Singapore where he couldn't be called to testify, sending a steady stream of glowing reports back home while his supporters in Geneva, few as they were, ran interference. It played right into MacKenna's hands, since he could brow-beat Hogarthy a lot easier in person than over the phone.

166

"Nuclear weapons?" Hogarthy was appalled at the thought of war with the Ic'nichi. "What are you going to use the nuclear stockpile for?"

"What they're usually used for: to blow stuff up."

"But... Do we have to?"

"We have no alternative," MacKenna said, somberly. "The Ic'nichi are afraid of us. They attacked Captain Morgan's ship already, and we have every reason to believe they will continue to do so unless we stop them."

"But..."

"We can't survive a full-blown war against them. A preemptive strike is our only chance to prevent a disaster."

Hogarthy seemed to shrink into himself. He sagged onto the couch and stared at the ocean view beyond the patio window without seeing it. The 'Squirrel Gage', VIP quarters, was luxurious by Singapore standards since visiting high muckety-mucks liked their comfort. In fact this particular quarter would have been MacKenna's except he spurned such indulgences for a room in the Senior Officer's Barracks. Hogarthy was all too pleased to enjoy such perks of office; now he was faced with paying the rent. "They'll crucify me," he muttered at last. "My party—all the factions—they'll hang me out to dry."

"At least they'll still be alive to do so."

Hogarthy have him a bleak glare. "Oh, you'll be safe enough: you have sound reasons for acting, and I don't suppose you care to stay in this job much longer. But me..."

"Hell, I never wanted this job to start with. If they want my hide, they can have it, and welcome. But right now we have a threat to deal with, so you need to quit worrying about your position, and start worrying about our survival."

Hogarthy ignored him, staring at nothing as he seemed to shrink into himself from the weight of his responsibilities. MacKenna watched patiently, and his heightened empathy showed him how Hogarthy's whole sense of self was tied to his position as Defense Minister. He was a tragic figure,

MacKenna realized, ill-fitted for such monumental authority. Now he faced a decision which would ruin him, but which he knew he couldn't avoid. It was more than professional suicide: it would destroy him from within as well. In a way, he felt sorry for the little man.

"I need release of nuclear weapons," he said, softly. "You must give me the key code."

After a long moment, Hogarthy nodded.

*****

"Ominous Portents"
(Related by Defender I'eiBida)

..."They've launched something, Captain." Navigation studied the radar screen in confusion. Whatever it was, it lacked stealth technology, and was clearly visible on the scope. "A missile?"...

Something was dreadfully wrong. I looked around in dismay at the packed humans, trying to understand where I was and what was going on.

...By now alarms were going off in my mind. "It can't be. We're way out of range..." I was interrupted when the faint blip on the screen suddenly accelerated. "...what the hell...?"

My hearts were racing. I recognized the scene as the bridge of the 'Marco Polo'.

..."This doesn't make sense," Ensign Ling muttered. "Some new technology?" The missile was gaining speed and closing rapidly. It should have run out of fuel by now at that rate. Then Ling paled. "A mass polarizer!" He turned to me in near panic. "Captain! That missile must have a mass polarizer!"...

What was all this? How did I get here? I watched in confusion as I looked around frantically, snapped an order to Ensign Ling, then climbed the ladder into the astrogation dome...

...'What's wrong, Honey Lamb?'
"We're under attack! The Ic'nichi fired a missile at us. Please help me!"
'Lawd, that ain't supposed t' be!'...

...I finally realized I was experiencing whatever was happening from Captain Morgan's perspective...

...."Admiral, we're under attack! We're at New Patagonia, and an Ic'nichi cruiser fired some new kind of missile with a mass polarizer at us."

'Thas' the way, Honey Lamb. You reachin' to him now'...

...There was an alarm ringing somewhere...

§

"...Wake up, you lazy lump." C'traBenla was nudging my side impatiently. "Time to get up."

I managed somehow to open one eye and glare at her. The alarm clock next to our bed pad was having second stage hysterics, and the early light was streaming in through the window. I'd been having a bad dream. "*Ancestors,*" I groaned as I crawled to my feet and managed to fumble the clock off without knocking it against the wall. "This is going to be one of *those* days."

I stared at nothing for a moment trying to pull my jangled nerves together before I noticed C'tra seemed withdrawn. Now that I thought about it, I could feel her tension and fugue. "Are you all right, love?"

"Yes," she mumbled. "It's nothing; a bad dream is all."

"You too, hmmm?" Her in a cranky mood was *just* what I needed before first-meal. Her pregnancy was fully advanced by then, and she was more broody than ever...

"You don't understand what I go through for you!" she snapped. "You think carrying an egg is easy?"

"Sorry, love!" I backtracked hastily, remembering too late how we could read each other's emotions. "I'm just kind of wrung out, is all."

She gave me an apologetic look, then nodded. "Would you like something to eat?"

"Um...not hungry." Truth, I was too weary and wrung out to eat. "I better have some *V'liz* I guess, if I'm not to get lost on my way. I'll get something at the grotto."

170

I crawled through my morning routine while she puttered in the kitchen, all the while wondering if this was an omen of how the day would go. It wasn't promising. "This whole psychic thing is getting to us," I mumbled when she brought me a steaming bowl. "I don't know how much more of this we can take."

She twitched a concerned ear. "We're going through a rough phase, love. It happens."

"And you make it all possible...that is, you make it all worth while."

She gave me a chilly look she didn't really mean. "I *better* make it worth while! You won't hear the end of it otherwise!"

"I know it!" I nuzzled her ear, and noticed the time. "Got to gallop. Aren't you coming?"

"I have my physich's appointment. I'll meet you later. You have your security pass?" She started fidgeting with my collar, trying to get the Staff medallions more perfectly aligned.

"Yes, love." I was still half asleep, waiting patiently for that bowl of *V'liz* to kick in, and wasn't entirely following her.

"And your travel case?"

"Yes, love." It was in my hand as I started drifting off again.

"And remember you need to meet with your Worthy today."

"Yes, love." He called last evening to remind me about some long overdue paperwork. Such fun.

"And don't forget we're to meet with Pierre and Jeanette for mid-meal."

"Um? Oh, yes."

"Now you be there!"

"I will, promise."

§

I was more or less awake when I reached our liaison grotto, but I made a point of hitting the *V'liz* maker for a steaming bowl anyway. I added a pastry, and headed to the duty desk where M'tinDegan was digging through a bowl of *l'ni'ddi*.

"It's a bit early for mid-meal, isn't it?"

He glanced at my pastry, examined his bowl doubtfully, then shoved it aside. "Nervous habit; I had a bad night. I'm just frustrated, I guess."

171

"Aren't we all?"

H'rhAtor came in then, looking as dragged out as I felt. "'morning," he said as he headed for the *V'liz* maker. "Anything new and exciting in our lives?"

"Aside from our putting on weight, nothing," M'tinDegan said.

"You seem a bit frazzled, sir."

H'rhAtor gave me a bleary-eyed look. "I didn't sleep well last night." He paused for a yawn and a weary sigh. "I had the most disturbing dream: that one of our ships attacked a human ship."

That shook me more than a bit. "I had that same dream, sir!"

"So did I!" M'tinDegan added.

"You did?" H'rhAtor turned to him in alarm. "What do you make of it?"

"Ah...I'm not a psychiatrist..." M'tinDegan pondered this development. "It must have something to do with our telepathy; one of us had that dream, and the others picked up on it, perhaps."

That seemed to still H'rhAtor's alarm somewhat. "Ancestors, I hope so," he muttered. "I'd hate to think any of us could be that stupid."

U'tdaPagrn turned up a little later, and headed straight to the Arbiters' desk where he plopped on his seat cushion and hauled out his human hand game.

"Well good morning to you, too," M'tinDegan said after we exchanged bemused looks.

"I suppose," he muttered as he twisted the cube back and forth. I could feel the tension rising as his frustration grew with each passing turn, but I also felt an underlying angst which seemed more than what he usually showed.

"How was your night?" I asked.

He paused and looked at me, puzzled. "What does that have to do with anything?"

"I don't mean to pry," I assured him. "It's important."

He pondered for a moment. "Not good," he sighed at last. "I suffered a most disturbing nightmare..."

"...that one of our ships attacked a human ship?" H'rhAtor demanded.

That startled U'tdaPagrn. "Yes, exactly. How did you know?"

172

"It seems we all had the same dream," I told him. "We think— we hope—it was a random dream which spread to all of us telepathically."

"Ancestors, I hope so! *Think* of the paperwork something like that would generate!" He sighed, and went back to twisting his hand game back and forth, still trying to line up the colored panels.

"You're going to hurt yourself if you keep it up," M'tinDegan said at last.

"I have three sides of this *p'quas'tka* thing done!" He paused to glance at M'tinDegan. "I can't quit now!"

"Can you quit at all?"

U'tdaPagrn hesitated. "Um...yes...certainly I can." He set the cube at arms length, and sat massaging his wrists. "It's just a stupid human hand game, after all."

I daresay we all had our doubts, so none of us said anything when he picked the thing up a few minutes later, and started fiddling with it again.

§

I was denied the wild pleasures of monitoring the Chamber feed or amusing myself as best I could when I received an irate call from the Herd Guide demanding I report to him at the Admin Circle *at once*. That did *not* sound good; junior elders lose their ears when he gets in the mood, so I made tall promises and *galloped* for the trolley.

The place was as chaotic and noisy as ever, and by time I tracked him down my semi-permanent headache was back, helped along by my nervous fugue. Our psychic powers didn't help either, since I was still tuned in to the collective frustration and boredom, especially with U'tdaPagrn's rising angst and all the brooding over that frightening shared dream.

"So—are you having fun in the Chamber Of Ancients?" he growled when I caught up with him.

"I swear I should put in for hazard duty pay, sir."

"You might deserve it if your paperwork was in order. I haven't seen your daily reports since late *B'matapur*, and who knows *what* state your Academy program is in? I sure don't! I thought you understood your duties better than this by now."

173

"I'm sorry, sir! Things are really hectic over at the Chamber."

"What? They aren't hectic here?" Obviously I wasn't going to find much sympathy in these parts, not that I ever did. "The Eldest is knotting *my* tail about the Academy program, and your Worthy has been bombarding me with requests for extensions and exceptions, which you know I can't allow!"

"I'm sorry, sir! I'll get on it right away!"

"One hopes so! *How* are we to provide an adequate defense if the paperwork isn't in order? Your Worthy is being overwhelmed, so you need to get over to the Academy right away."

In all the flying *ui'DmukNa*, I'd completely forgotten him. "Yes, sir. He called me last night in fact, and I'm on my way over there to take care of it."

"See that you do, mister."

§

The Academy grounds were busier than ever, with apprentices galloping in all directions. I about wore my tail out responding to all the salutes, which only ground on my nerves even more. My Worthy was busily grading test papers when I arrived, and his welcome was an annoyed ear twitch. "So—are you having fun in the Chamber Of Ancients?" he growled.

"I don't know *where* I get the strength," I said, curtly. It knotted my tail that *he* rated a comfortable grotto here at the Academy, complete with no less than *twenty* clerical assistants, while I made do with a desk shoved against the wall at Fleet Circle. "So how are things out here in the hinterlands?"

He gave me another chilly ear twitch, which can say wonders. "Worthy T'revNend is shaping up nicely handling the apprentice elders classes. I recommended him for promotion, in fact. At this rate, we may wind up not needing you at all."

T'revNend was originally assigned as an assistant for the two of us, since we were spread thin with our Human Studies programs.   My Worthy *would* assign him to handling the apprentice elders while he dealt with the apprentice worthies, which said something of his opinion right then.

"Well, if you feel he deserves a promotion, I'll sign the forms." He did deserve it, in fact.

"It was already approved. He got his bar back when the new course started."

"What? Don't I...?"

"You were on medical release *and* detached service, so I cleared it on the Academy Elder's approval." Trust him to know the regulations. He dug up the progress sheets and handed them to me. "T'revNend is doing a good job with his apprentices; our grade curve is above average, and we have one I'm looking at to go directly to the Command course."

"Poor *n'bna'nmn*," I muttered. "That's what you get for hard work around here." The grade curve *was* looking good, in fact, and his star apprentice was easy to spot from the statistical blip he caused. I could see his point; they might *not* need me after all. This is what I get for self-sacrifice and devotion to duty. "It was nice of you to let me know, anyway."

"You need to clear this up. Strictly speaking, you can't be both sick and on active duty; it snarls up the paperwork something terrible and makes a fine tail knot for some poor paper-shoveling *hro'n'nad* back at Fleet Circle."

"I'm so ashamed," I grumbled. "So did you just call me here to knot my tail?"

"Bad day, hmmm?"

"You have no idea." I paused to rub my eyes in frustration. "I've been having one of *those* days, you know?"

"Haven't we all?"

"Not like mine." I was beginning to feel my fatigue, fed by our collective psychic aura and fretting over that dream, on top of being tail-knotted by the Herd Guide *and* a long train ride to the spaceport just to receive some forms which should have been mailed to me. One of *those* days, indeed. "Chamber duty doesn't have *nearly* the ears most people think it does. Ancestors, some times I wish I was still on earth!"

He gave a snort of contempt. "You *are* sick if you feel like that!" He dug in a drawer, and came up with a *massive* file folder. "You may miss earth by time you're through with these."

"What? You called me all the way up here to handle a little routine paperwork?"

"Oh, that's not all." He dug up a second folder, then a third, then a fourth; each bulging. "These all need your signature plus your daily report forms since whenever. They've been piling up for far too long." He offered me a pen. "You, of all people, should know we have to keep the paperwork moving."

"I thought I was on medical release." The sad story of my life.

"People once thought the stars were silver lanterns; they were wrong too. Get your tail straight and get it done before the Herd Guide collects both our ears."

I hefted the four folders, which took some effort. "I could have been an accountant," I sighed. "Ancestors, I *am* an accountant!"

"Yes, well, whimpering doesn't count toward your productive quota, so squat and have at it."

Then I noticed the time. "Eeepp! I'm late!" My Worthy gave me a cynical look as I tucked the folders in my travel case and edged toward the door. "I...ah...urgent business in the World Nest. Got to gallop."

"Give her my best," he grumbled.

§

I was so preoccupied that I almost forgot our mid-meal appointment, and here it was almost midday. The restaurant was conveniently between the Chamber complex and the human embassy, but quite a gallop from the Academy by the spaceport, so I stampeded to catch the next train.

Pierre, Jeanette and C'traBenla were already there, embroiled in the latest gossip when I came trotting in. Jeanette's pregnancy was starting to show, matching C'tra's increasingly round figure, and they were at the fem-chatter hard and heavy. C'tra gave me a pointed look and an admonishing ear twitch when I arrived. "Well, I was beginning to think you'd forgotten."

"Sorry. Staring at the walls takes a lot of effort."

"So—are you having fun in the Chamber Of Ancients?" Pierre asked when we were seated on the veranda well away from other human tourists. This was a popular spot for them, so our meeting wouldn't stand out like a broken tail.

"Oh, I am happily going *er'trxxda*," I grumbled. "It's exactly the fate I would wish on my worst enemies."

Pierre chuckled at my discomfiture. "I have some good news which may cheer you up. Our latest courier brought a reply from Admiral MacKenna concerning your misadventures in the late war. He stood up for you most firmly, and demanded the Ambassador let his report of your actions disappear."

That was something, anyway. "What will your Ambassador do?"

"He is still very ill-disposed in the matter, but has agreed to bury the report."

"Well *that's* good news! We don't need any further provocations."

"*Oui.* We do not need to stir the pot with another incident, no? We can feel confident that unless something happened within the last twenty days, peace is upon us."

That brought back the memory of our disturbing dream. "Let's hope you are correct. I swear militaristic fools on both sides will be the end of us."

Pierre chuckled. "But stupidity provides our employment, as it does for so many of both races. One should not speak ill of fools, my friend. If common sense were ever to break out, I daresay both our economies would collapse."

I grinned in spite of myself at his jibe. "No danger there, my friend!"

With that bit of good news to lighten the atmosphere, we settled into a pleasant mid-meal. Vegetarian fare isn't my favorite, but it was impossible to be in an ill mood with the lovely day and the humans' cautious experimenting. Jeanette in particular had the *oddest* tastes, and her reaction to otherwise fine food was amusing, to say the least.

"Good heavens!" She huffed and fanned her mouth in alarm after a bite of *uf'thoka*. "That was hot!" She swilled the last of her coffee, then followed with the glass of water, practically gargling with it.

"Are you all right, love?"

She gasped for air, and her face was turning purple. "That...I like spicy food, but that was...incredible!"

"I warned you, love."

C'tra sampled her *uf'thoka,* and offered a dismissive ear twitch. "That's bland, actually. If you come over for dinner some time, I'll show you what *hot uf'thoka* is like."

Jeanette looked askance at her through her tears. "You people are more dangerous than we thought!" Which brought a round of laughter from us all as she turned to Pierre. "Their cookbooks are a greater threat than their fleet, love!"

"No doubt." Pierre mused for a moment, then turned to me. "We must enter into most delicate negotiations to ban dangerous ethnic cuisine."

"Indeed? If you feel that way, then we can start with your citrus fruits."

Pierre *tisk-tisked.* "*Oui*, K'deiTai's experience in the early days was most alarming. I can see why you want them restricted. We shall concede citrus fruits, but insist that *uf'thoka* be limited to no more than five on the Richter scale."

"Including the pineapple. You *must* include pineapple!"

"Very well, the pineapple. Do you agree?"

"Only if you agree to limit your peppermint to no more than gale force strength."

"Typhoon strength, for which we will limit *uf'thoka* to Richter scale six."

"Fair enough. Then there your dairy products."

Pierre nodded solemnly. "Lactose intolerance: our ultimate weapon. We shall agree to ban *crepes suzettes* and chocolate shakes in return for a ban on *bv'nunma.*"

"Well...I don't know about that..." I pretended to muse over the thought. "Good *bv'nunma* is hard to find, and expensive. We'll need further concessions."

"You two are impossible!" Jeanette was grinning as tears rolled down her snout.

"That's what mals are for, dear!" C'traBenla told her. "They keep us entertained."

C'tra and Jeanette soon got off into maternal gossip, leaving Pierre and me to fend for ourselves. "May I ask you something in confidence, my friend?" he asked at last.

"I'll answer if I can," I said cautiously.

"I understand."   He glanced about to see if anyone was listening.   "We are hearing persistent rumors about a hard line faction in the Chamber who supposedly agitate for a more strident position against earth," he said softly.   "Can you tell me what the opinion is there?"

There was that dream again, dashing our good mood.   I hesitated for a moment, then decided it was best to be honest. "There is some truth to your rumors.   Ancient Z'keBalf has been banging the war gongs for years, and he has a fairly large part of the Chamber behind him.   However, Ancient Y'veNipbr is leading the pro-earth faction, and has equal support.   Right now I would say there is no immediate danger, but we must all be wary of any incidents."

Pierre nodded thoughtfully.   "*Oui*. That is as we interpret our findings as well. But can she contain him?"

"They are practically at war with each other, and I wouldn't care to tangle with her."

"Indeed?" He brooded for a bit. "May I ask, how do the 'Dark Grays' feel about it?"

"I can't say what the fleet thinks in general, but I know our leadership is not eager to fight. We will if we must, of course, but we are not as warlike as you. If given the chance, we would prefer good relations."

Pierre sighed. "As would all of good will. But sometimes one is thrust into battle all unwittingly."

Which brought our shared nightmare to mind again.   "True enough. Ah...so how are things on earth these days? Any strategic crises we need to worry about?"

"No. In fact, according to the latest dispatches, things go well at home. I understand some small progress has been made in the treaty negotiations even though the Arbiter is here."

"That's good news!"

"Mind you, our latest dispatches are nearly a month old, so who can say what the current situation is?"

There was the echo of that dream again. "We can only hope we have enough warning to give us time to defuse any crisis which comes up."

Pierre shook his head sadly. "*Oui.* It is hard to imagine relations deteriorating too fast for word to reach here in time. Still, there is so *much* folly in this Universe we can never be entirely confident of the peace. I pray no one will do anything rash, but knowing my people, one can never be complacent."

"Um...well..." I hesitated, wondering if I should reveal this latest secret. No, no reason to stir the pot when we didn't know what was going on. Still, I felt uncomfortable enough to offer a reassurance. "I can say this: Eldest H'rhAtor and Admiral MacKenna reached an *informal* understanding back during the war. I think it would take a lot to break that understanding."

Pierre's eye ridges crept up. "This we did not know! It is good to hear *someone* talking common sense these days."

"Quite a change, isn't it?"

"OH!" Jeanette was at it again. She all but heaved right there in public, and grabbed her mug of coffee to rinse her mouth. "Good Lord, what is in this?"

"Um...that was the centerpiece bouquet."

§

But all good things must come to an end. Even though I made a hasty mid-meal, gave C'tra a quick ear nibble, and galloped, it was mid afternoon before I returned to our grotto. I was mentally rehearsing my excuses about 'delicate negotiations' with Pierre (if H'rhAtor even bothered to ask) when I ran into Chamber Warden Q'brnVen.

"You again," he grumbled. "We received a message for you."

"So why didn't you send it to our grotto?"

"I understand they did, but your people didn't know where you went, so this Learnéd N'detLeda twisted *our* tails."

"N'detLeda, hmmm?" So much for my good mood. "I know what *that's* about."

"Who is this Learnéd N'detLeda, anyway? He's been all over the place around here lately."

"He's one of Ancient Z'keBalf's creatures."

"That one? Wonderful. So what's his story?"

"N'detLeda?" I was too preoccupied wondering what he wanted to bother with it. "He's a leading Aberrant Psychologist."

I could tell Q'brnVen was worried. "So what does Z'keBalf need with a psychologist, anyway?"

"He has us all under treatment right now..."

"*Treatment?* For what?"

That pulled me out of my distraction. "Do you *really* want to know?" I asked with a sinister ear twitch.

Q'brnVen shook his head emphatically as he backed away. "No! I really don't want to know! Just...please don't go *er'trxxda* on my watch! I have enough tail knots from my superiors already. They don't believe half of what goes into my incident reports."

"Half? You're doing better than we are."

§

My return to our grotto was not triumphant; they scarcely noticed me, in fact. H'rhAtor was over at the spaceport dealing with some minor crisis, and the rest of them hardly acknowledged my return. Pity; those were some fine excuses I cooked up.

Sure enough, there were no less than three memos waiting for me, each demanding I haul my tail over to the Institute with greater urgency. "It never quits," I sighed.

"At least you aren't shoveling paper all day," M'tinDegan offered. "You can thank your Ancestors for that crumb."

Instead of answering, I dug the folders I received at the Academy out of my case, and dropped them on his desk with a resounding thud.

"Oh. Um...never mind."

"And I hoped I was starting to get ahead on this day." I glanced at the clock: I wouldn't see home any time soon, but there was nothing for it. "Got to gallop."

§

"Well you took your own sweet time getting here," N'detLeda groused when I arrived. "If you expect me to cure you of this telepathic problem, I will need better cooperation."

My whole life was turning into this: nightmares followed by bureaucratic hassles followed by N'detLeda, and my little day wasn't over yet. The one thing I *didn't* need right then was his attitude. "Sorry it took so long," I said, sharply. "I had important matters to attend to."

He gave me a dismissive ear twitch. "What could be more urgent than my research?"

"Mid-meal with my bondmate. If you prefer, I'll bring her along next time."

He covered his alarm admirably, although I could sense it. "That won't be necessary. Right now I need to put you through your regular test cycle." He gestured me to the seat cushion with its array of instruments.

"And to think they pay me to do this," I grumbled as I plopped on the seat cushion.

"A waste of public moneys," he muttered as he started wiring me up to his instruments.

"How perceptive. It's a gift. It must be."

"Common sense is *not* a gift, it's a punishment because I have to deal with everyone who doesn't have it." For a moment I wondered why he seemed more grouchy than usual; did he tune in on our communal nightmare too? Or were the Ancients—one Ancient in particular—knotting his tail over his lack of progress? It seemed we weren't the only ones catching heat from the Chamber, and I almost—*almost*—felt sorry for him. He finished the last few connections and shoved the first wad of test forms in front of me. "Get to it. You might as well earn your pay, for once."

My luck, T'virDoma came in from the front office to make my little day complete. "Hmph!" She glanced at the monitors. "At least you aren't flat-lined."

"I didn't mean to startle you."

"I'm more amazed than anything else." She turned to N'detLeda and offered a file. "We're in luck: the DNA report just came back on him."

"It took them long enough." N'detLeda leafed through the thick file as I squatted there wondering what was in it. "Hmmm...ranges are typical...markers average..."

"Anything interesting?" I asked.

He looked up from his reading. "It seems you are boringly normal. I'll have to go over this, but at first glance you appear to be the picture of genetic health."

"C'traBenla will be pleased to hear that." She would be, in fact, seeing how she fretted over our egg.

"I can't *wait* to see *her* DNA report," T'virDoma snarked.

I struggled to contain my annoyance by imagining what C'tra would do to her. "I'll provide you some coloring pencils."

"Enough of this half-witticism for now," N'detLeda snapped. "You get back out there and expedite the rest of those DNA reports!" T'virDoma exited in a huff. "And *you* get to work on those tests."

"Oh, I don't know; I rather enjoy being *er'trxxda*, actually. Perhaps we shouldn't bother."

"Finally, someone who knows his own mind." He shoved a pencil at me. "Get to it before your brains turn totally to mush."

"Ancestors," I sighed as I leafed through the thick forms. "I am not worthy."

"No, but it'll keep you occupied while I arrange for your padded cell."

§

It was early evening before I got back to our grotto, by which point I was completely wrung out from a long day at a pounding gallop and doubting my own sanity. The Chamber already adjourned for the day and the last of the staffers had shut their work stations off and beat an unseemly retreat, leaving me alone in our grotto. There was still no sign of H'rhAtor, so it fell to me to call the Herd Guide at our spaceport circle with the daily update of Chamber activities.

"They're still at it, eh?" was his only comment.

"Yes, sir, and there doesn't seem to be any sign it will end any time soon."

"No wars or disasters to report?"

"No, sir. They spent most of the day debating economic policy." Talk about deadly dull; monitoring the Chamber feed could put anyone to sleep.

"Oy," he grumbled. "Better them then us, I suppose."

"Yes, sir. Is there anything else, sir?"

"Oh, yes. Tell Eldest H'rhAtor all recent fleet activities are accounted for, except for one movement authorized by the

183

Chamber. We haven't been able to learn anything about it since it's under Chamber seal."

It struck me as odd and vaguely disturbing that H'rhAtor would investigate that dream. "Ah...which ship, sir?"

"Number 189, one of the new cruisers. They went out on what was billed as an exercise, and expended one of the mass polarizer equipped missiles."

"And the mission was sealed?" Odd, to say the least.

"It was." The Herd Guide was put out, as he always was by civilian interference. "It's not like we having nothing to do around here but indulge the whims of the Ancients!"

This had an ominous ring to it. "Yes, sir. I'll pass it along to him."

I sagged on my belly cushion and tried to collect my thoughts, which wasn't easy after a long, wearing day. A training exercise? Why keep a training exercise classified? Was Z'keBalf mixed up in this? Ancestors knew the fleet needed all the training they could get, but why would Z'keBalf take an interest in such routine matters? He held a low opinion of the fleet, and it wouldn't be any surprise if he decided to take readiness matters into his own hands, but micromanaging didn't seem like his style. But then I wasn't aware of any *other* Ancient who might order such a move. And those new missiles were *l'cc'vn* expensive, and few and far between; enough so that the fleet used simulators to train with. So what was he up to? I'd bet the tip of my tail this was some game of his, and with his anti-human stance, anything secretive was not to be taken lightly. This needed looking into. I pondered whether to call H'rhAtor, but by then I was so weary and disgusted with life that I decided to put it off until tomorrow.

*****

"Charging Down The Slippery Slope"
(Extract Of Testimony)

*"I swear I'm getting too old to be a Senior Citizen,"
Admiral MacKenna grumbled. He paused to rub his eyes
with one hand, then glanced at his watch, and was not
surprised to see that it was past midnight.*

*"God...it never ends." He wearily brushed the jumble
of fleet readiness reports aside, and rested his head in his
hands, too fed up for the moment to care about the sorry
condition of his command. He had been in some ugly
predicaments in his life—far too many—but this one was a
doozey. All their efforts to date only managed to improve
Space Fleet from 'hopeless' to 'damned desperate'. They
were scheduled to leave for their mission to d'enchia in
only two weeks, and how they'd do it was beyond him.
Space Fleet had no business breaking orbit, much less
going on a deep space raid. He toyed for the hundredth
time with delaying the mission or canceling 'Triphammer'
altogether, but he knew he couldn't. There was no telling
what the Ic'nichi might do next, and Minister Hogarthy was
in trouble back in Geneva; if he was replaced, their access
to the nuclear arsenal would go right out the window. No,
they had to go soon. Ready or not.*

*He wanted a cup of coffee in the worst way, but the
outer office was long deserted. Some things in life are
simply beyond reach. He rested on his hands, trying to
ignore his headache and the distant rumble of countless
voices like a white noise in the back of his mind. The
psychic powers originally revealed by Captain Morgan
were sprouting up everywhere now, and it was obvious that
everyone who was at the battle of the Dreamsingers' world,
and later drawn into their psychic neverland, was affected
by whatever the Dreamsingers did. One more worry in his
world of hurt. Singapore Space Port was hopping even at
this hour, and the telepathic presence of all those minds
was a constant distraction.*

He fought off a jaw-breaking yawn, and stared morosely at the papers on his desk. Repair reports, damage assessments, parts requests, shortages, delays... If only he wasn't so damned tired all the time. He turned ninety-one just last week, too old to be saddled with these burdens. His focus drifted to the far wall, and he thought longingly of Savannah. Maybe he should take some leave once this crisis was past? No, he couldn't. Even if 'Triphammer' worked—iffy at best—Space Fleet was a self-fulfilling disaster in progress. The only possible way he could retire was when they could turn their backs on the Ic'nichi, and good intentions by Eldest H'rhAtor notwithstanding, they were a long way from that.

A random thought crossed his mind, something Captain Morgan told him some time ago: 'Whatever J J did, it really helps. I washed away the exhaustion just now by thinking about it'.

Maybe... He hesitated at the temptation, wondering if he would only make things worse playing with powers not of this earth and poorly understood. It worked once before...

"Oh, what the hell," *he muttered. He settled back in his chair, closed his eyes, and turned his thought inward...*

§

...he was standing in a bleak, windswept landscape. It wasn't like last time; the image was clear, if vague and out of focus in spots. He looked around, bemused, at what seemed like a vast desert with rocks and trees and gullies and distant hills— but wasn't. It was as if someone made a desert landscape out of noodles and lumps of clay and bits of...stuff...something...an abstract artwork which chilled him to the bone with some unseen menace.

He scanned the horizon, vague and out of focus. That might be a line of low hills in the distance, but he couldn't make out any detail. The sky above was a flawless artificial blue, like a ceiling painted with cheap latex paint. There were no clouds, and no sun. No shadows. No movement. No nothing.

At first he was afraid, and longed to retreat back to reality if he could. It took him a bit to remember that this was *his* mind. He shouldn't be here, but if *anyone* had the right to trespass here, it was him. His back hurt and his exhaustion was getting to him, so he decided to sit down and think this over. He looked around for a place to sit...perhaps that rock...it was a rock? For some reason he was loathe to sit on it...

"You don't want t' touch that, Boss." He looked up in surprise, and saw J J Ballas standing nearby. "All this here," J J waved at the surreal landscape. "It's all yo' inner self. They's some parts you don't want t' fool with til ya can tell what's what."

"Um...yeah." After some indecision, Mac tried willing a chair into existence: sure enough, a folding camp chair materialized. He glanced at J J, then imagined a second chair, which appeared next to it.

J J nodded thoughtfully. "Tha's good. Yo gettin' the hang of this," he said as he settled on the chair.

"Um...what can I do for you, J J?"

"Oh, nothin' much." A battered steel guitar appeared, and he plucked a few chords of a Blues number Mac remembered from his youth. "Ah jus' happened t' see you was about to do somethin' un- wise, so ah stopped in t' caution you."

That rock...there was something *spooky* about it; Mac wondered what it could be. "Um, thanks, J J."

"No biggy." The music continued; a soft, lonely melody which went with the surreal landscape. Mac's gaze drifted again, trying to fathom this unreal scene; his inner self; his soul, laid out around them like a landscape by Hieronymus Bosch. There was something *painful* in that scenery; something that cried like a lost child; those terrain features must be the scars of a lifetime of slaughter. It filled him with revulsion.

"J J...this mission to d'enchia...am I doing the right thing?"

The music stopped. "You doin' what you has to, Boss." J J regarded him with sad eyes, eyes which saw the horrors of the Dreamsingers' War and the torment in his soul. "We don't rightly understand the way you folks do things, what with yo' machines and all, but you got a job t' do." He shook his head sadly. "Ah just hope this don' turn inta somethin' unthinkable."

"You and me both."

The music picked up again. There was something chilling about it. That rock caught Mac's attention, he stared at it morosely, wondering what it was that disturbed him so.

"You still learnin' yo' way." J J must have felt his revulsion. "It'll come to you in time."

"I guess." His gaze drifted over the bizarre landscape. "J J? What did you teach Captain Morgan?" He turned to the alien. "She said you showed her how to heal her emotions. What did you tell her?"

The music stopped, and J J pointed off to their left. "You see them lines?" Mac caught a vague impression of low ridges like plowed furrows in the distance. "They's yo' emotions, at least how they look in a way you can understand. See how they all tangled up?"

"Ah...not clearly."

"Think on 'em. They'll come inta focus."

He did, and the image cleared enough for him to see the furrows lapping back and forth over each other as if plowed by a drunken mule team. As he watched, the scene came into focus bit by bit.

188

"Tha's right. Now think 'em straight. Use yo' reason t' control yo' emotions."

He did. Nothing happened at first, but then some low dust came up, and he could see the lines shifting.

"Tha's right. You got a good imagination. It'll hep ya t' do this."

It took a lot of effort. The lines kept slipping out of his grasp, and he had to imagine corralling them one by one, wrestling with them like so many giant pythons. After a while he had them laid out in rough order.

"Good. You gettin' the hang of it. You keep on like that, an' yo' be able t' cure much of the troubles what ails you."

Mac pondered the distant furrows. They were everywhere, a vast prairie of tangled emotions and memories. He had a lot of work ahead of him.

"J J, these powers; how far is this going to go?"

J J mulled that over for a bit. "Ah can't rightly tell you. You folks ain't got th' words fo' this." He set his guitar aside, which vanished, and hunched in his chair, meeting him eye to eye. "It's so hard fo' us t' figure how you-all think, you not bein' connected and all. But as you get better, you'll understand."

There was a sudden gust of wind, and they both noticed the surreal sky was turning dark. "Well, I guess I'd best be movin' on," J J said as he stood. "My bein' here can still stir things up."

"J J, what will it take to achieve final peace with the Ic'nichi?"

J J paused and gave him a wry grin. "Well Boss, for that there you'll need an in-verse cognitive function, don'ja know?" He vanished before MacKenna could protest...

§

...He opened his eyes, and stared listlessly at the far wall for a moment, trying to collect his thoughts. "What the hell is an 'inverse cognitive function'?" he muttered at last. He couldn't make heads or tails of it, so finally resigned himself with the thought that aliens are the strangest people.

At least he felt better, reflecting on it. As infuriatingly remote as he was, Mac couldn't help but like J J; his advice made it a whole lot easier to grasp his inner self. His headache was gone, the pain in his shoulders was remote, and he was calmer and more awake than before.

He still wanted a cup of coffee in the worst way, though, not that he was likely to get one at this hour. Some things in life are simply beyond reach. But then it occurred to him that with J J's advice and his improved skills...

He relaxed and focussed on his desktop, willing a steaming mug of coffee to appear. After a long moment, a faint image faded into view: a coffee mug. He focussed on it, putting all his considerable willpower into that mug, and it gradually solidified. "Well how about that?" A real mug of coffee, steaming hot and fragrant. "Un-fuckin'-believable." He hefted the mug, bemused, and took a sip, then winced. "Damn. Needs salt."

*****

"Conspiracy Can Become Addictive"
(Related by Learnéd M'tinDegan)

"Ship 189?" H'rhAtor was not pleased when I'eiBida reported the Herd Guide's news to him first thing in the morning. "What do you make of this?"

"I suspect it's something Ancient Z'keBalf is up to, sir."

H'rhAtor was not amused, and gave I'eiBida a hard ear twitch. "Not good. You should have called me last night."

I'eiBida winced at his tone, and his aura radiated embarrassment. "I'm sorry, sir. It didn't seem to be that urgent at the time."

"*Anything* having to do with Z'keBalf is urgent! You should know by now we have to keep ears-up with him."

"Now you just lighten up!" C'traBenla snarled. She'd been irritable the last few days, and ready to snap at anyone who annoyed her. "I won't have you backbeating him over something so minor!"

That took H'rhAtor aback. "I wasn't backbeating him..."

"Well you don't need to knot his tail over every little thing!"

"Love...it's all right," I'eiBida implored her.

"No, it's not all right!" She rounded on H'rhAtor, her temper clearly slipping. "You should be ashamed of yourself for twisting his tail just because you can!"

"I am only exercising proper military discipline..."

"Whatever you call it, it isn't fair!" As luck would have it, L'datMparn showed up just then. "And don't you start!" she yelled at him.

"What? What did I do?"

"What *haven't* you done?"

"I just came in to see if I was needed for anything," he protested. "Sir, this is uncalled for!"

"Perhaps it is." H'rhAtor was quick to rein in his angst. "This doesn't apply to you anyway."

C'traBenla wasn't so forbearing. "There's more than enough reason to knot *your* tail!"

"What? I'm sorry if I offended you somehow."

I realized I could faintly catch his emotional state even through the storm of C'traBenla's temper: although he was careful not to show it, he was terrified of her. That was when I realized she was unconsciously feeding off his fear! She had a strong predatory instinct, which is what got her as far as she had in life, and his fear, amplified by her heightened empathic powers, was goading her into a killing rage. This was more than a little disturbing: her aggressive posture toward other fems made sense now. She instinctively protected her turf with I'eiBida, and the intimidation she caused in her supposed rivals made her even more aggressive. This was an unexpected twist on our empathic powers, and not comforting. I watched their confrontation with growing fascination while thinking what a *marvelous* sociological paper this would produce.

But right then, it looked like she was about to explode, and I'm sure the others felt it as well. "There is nothing we need you for right now, mister," H'rhAtor growled. I could tell he was worried about her temper, and was trying to get L'datMparn out of there. "Do you need anything else?"

L'datMparn eyed C'traBenla uneasily. "No, sir. If you will excuse me, I have other matters to attend to."

"You are excused."

L'datMparn was reaching for the door handle when a large book hit him in the back of his head, knocking him flat. He staggered to his feet, threw a panicked glance at C'traBenla, and bolted out the door.

"That's becoming a habit," K'deiTai mumbled.

"*C'tra!*" I'eiBida was appalled. "You need to control your temper!"

"Well it served him right!" C'traBenla snapped. "That *p'quas'tka* is a disgrace to the uniform."

"Love...your language..."

She rounded on I'eiBida. "I'll use whatever language I please! And that *un'tdar* deserved what he got!"

"No doubt," H'rhAtor said. "But mayhem with blunt objects is not the solution."

'Don't bet on it,' K'deiTai thought.

Mercifully, she didn't catch that. "Well?" she demanded. "Why do we have to put up with him? You're the head of the fleet; can't you get him transferred to some place nasty, like earth?"

H'rhAtor tried to reason with her, which only made her madder. "I'm not the Eldest, and he is protected by Z'keBalf, so there isn't much we can do about him..."

"Z'keBalf! It's always Z'keBalf with you people! Why don't you grow a tail, and..."

"What's th' matter, Sweet-Chile?" We looked around in surprise, and found J J Ballas standing there looking concerned. "Is carryin' yo' young-un upsetting you?"

C'traBenla snapped out of her rant, and looked embarrassed. "It...was nothing, J J. We were having a little discussion, is all."

"Um..." I'eiBida glanced back and forth between the two of them. "...we've all been under a lot of strain lately. I guess tempers are a bit short." C'traBenla considered him for a moment, then nodded.

"Well, ah hate t' see you-all snappin' at each other, what with all yo' other problems."

"True enough," H'rhAtor said. "We have plenty to worry about these days between our hassles with the bureaucracy and getting caught up in Chamber politics."

"Yeah. There's that run-in between your ship an' that human one, too. It sho' does worry us. It ain't right you-all goin' shootin' at each other."

"Then it really happened!"

"Yeah. Cap'n Morgan asked fo' help, an' we helped her get out of the attack."

"Thank you for that! So you sent the dream to warn us?"

"Well, no. Ah was wonderin' what you-all were up to, so ah made a little *in*-quiry. Ah'm sorry if it alarmed you. Ah didn't mean t' cause you no upset."

"Um...that's all right, J J," I said. "We needed to know about it anyway."

"Glad t' help. It seems none of you had anythin' t' do with it, which sho' is good t' hear." J J furrowed his forehead. "So who did it? Stuff like that's likely t' cause trouble."

"We haven't a clue," H'rhAtor said. "But we'll look into it, for sure."

"Yeah." J J rubbed his chin as he pondered. "That sho' is an *unfriendly* thing. You need t' figger out who did it an' stop 'em fo' bad things come of it."

"But who is it? What are they up to?"

J J gave him an amused grin. "You still don' got all the ins and outs of yo' powers, do you? Don' you worry; you'll catch on in time." He blinked one eye at him. "It's an *in*-verse cognitive function, don' ya know?" And with that, he vanished.

"Inverse cognitive function?" H'rhAtor turned to me in confusion. "What does that mean?"

"If I knew, I'd probably be able to vanish too."

"I hoped this was just a nightmare."

"It is," I said, grimly. "So what do we do now?"

"We find out who is responsible, and clip their ears!" H'rhAtor was outraged, and who can blame him? "Even Z'keBalf has to answer to the law!"

"We don't know it was Z'keBalf," I cautioned. "He has hundreds of Ancients in his anti-human faction, and common sense is not a requirement to be in the Chamber."

H'rhAtor turned to me. "That's the sad truth! Still, he's our best suspect."

"No doubt. But you might want to tread carefully with such accusations."

"There is that." He pondered for a bit as his ears sagged, then said, "We need to go at this systematically." He turned to U'tdaPagrn. "To start off, you need to alert the Arbiters for immediate damage control. I'll alert the Fleet Eldest. M'tinDegan, you get to Ancient Y'veNipbr, promptly!"

"Ah, perhaps we should consult with Fleet first, sir?" I'eiBida suggested. "They have more resources than we do, and we need to bring them up to a gallop in any case. No sense in pulling and hauling in different directions, especially if it means bringing charges against Z'keBalf."

H'rhAtor hesitated. "Perhaps so." He got on the telephone, and after running the usual interference, explained the situation to the

194

Fleet Eldest in person. His ears wilted as he listened, then he hung up. "The Fleet Eldest said they should find the guilty party before bringing Y'veNipbr or the Arbiters into it." He gave I'eiBida a disgusted ear twitch. "He'll start an investigation, so for now we're to keep our tails tucked up tight. He doesn't want us to look like we can't solve our own security problems."

"Withholding something this important doesn't seem wise," I said, doubtfully. "This is not the time to be covering tail with the Chamber."

"Maybe not, but that's the order."

"At least we can help from this end. Let's sniff around to see what we can find."

"Good idea, but we need to be discrete." H'rhAtor turned to C'traBenla. "In the mean time, please keep your temper in check, and don't work any more mayhem on L'datMparn! We don't want to draw attention to ourselves now."

Having gotten over her mad, C'traBenla was all contrition. "...I'm sorry...I can't seem to help it lately..."

§

...While we r'vebbe'd *over our own problems, the Fleet Eldest, duly alarmed, questioned everyone involved with operations. Unfortunately, the mission having been arranged by Z'keBalf through his 'informal' connections, and under Chamber seal, no one knew anything about it. Worse, before they started questioning the Eldests of the ships in orbit, ship 189 left on a deep space patrol, also arranged by Z'keBalf. Thus their canvas of the local forces came up blank as well, leaving the Eldest stymied. Frustrated, he passed it to Intelligence...*

§

...Later that morning, I went to see if W'kiLap and T'apiDien could help us in our investigation. The two were as busy as ever, lounging on plush seat cushions in surreal human splendor imbibing spiced *V'liz* and sour rolls. How they got anything done was beyond me, but their human interfacing software was making them rich. "So how fares your little social circle?" W'kiLap greeted me. "Have you all melted into a common mind yet?"

195

"Not yet, although it's starting to look that way at times. None of us are happy about it, I can assure you."

W'kiLap gave T'apiDien a sardonic ear twitch. "Just think: soon all of them will have M'tinDegan's intellect..."

"...and I'eiBida's martial zeal..."

"...and K'deiTai's charming disposition..."

"...as well as C'traBenla's temper!"

"Oy, such a frightful vision!" It was, come to think of it.

"So—whose Ancestors will come to claim whom, one wonders?..."

"...Or more than one..."

"...Or would that be just one...?"

"...One singular or plural...?"

"...Some things were not meant for mere mortals to know, I guess."

"Indeed," I sighed. "And that's on top of our other great mystery. One of our ships recently took a shot at the humans' 'Marco Polo'. We're trying to figure out what's going on."

That got their attention. "Did they survive?" W'kiLap asked.

"Apparently. But in a way, that makes it worse. We're not sure how the humans will react, but the possibilities are not comforting. We think Z'keBalf may be behind it. Have you had any luck tapping his phone?"

"It...ah...seems we're not the only ones doing security work for the Chamber," T'apiDien said. "Z'keBalf's phone lines are encrypted, and we haven't been able to break the code as yet."

"This *is* news," I muttered.

"What really matters is what it implies," W'kiLap said. "Why would Z'keBalf start encoding his calls all of a sudden?"

"Perhaps in response to the humans' hacking attempts you mentioned some time ago?"

"Not hardly!" W'kiLap snorted in contempt. "Two cans and a piece of string is *their* speed."

"He must be behind that attack," T'apiDien added. "It's the only answer which makes sense."

"No doubt." I excused myself and made for the door. "Please keep at it, will you? And let us know if you get anything."

"Certainly! Persistence is our middle name..."

"...*my* middle name..."

"...both of me..."

"...I'll work on it together day and night..."

"...One on each..."

"...and if that fails, we'll just read his mind...!"

§

...The mystery which landed on their desks alarmed Fleet Intelligence enough to startle them out of their usual procedural stupor. They turned out in force to question the same lot the Eldest grilled earlier, but Fleet's administration was so new and shaky that no one seemed to know their tails from their ears. Frustrated, the Eldest of Intelligence griped that Fleet's command and control needed a lot of improvement, not that theirs was any better at the time. And it didn't help that no one ever heard of a rogue combat mission before—an unlikely notion—so they didn't rightly know where *to start. After gyrating around for some time, they finally gave up and passed it back to Fleet...*

§

...I told H'rhAtor about Z'keBalf's encrypted phones when I returned to our grotto. "It certainly points to Z'keBalf as the guilty party."

"That's...not conclusive, by any means," H'rhAtor mused.

"Still, it's mighty suspicious, sir," I'eiBida said.

"There could be any number of reasons," K'deiTai said. "He might simply be reacting to the humans' wiretapping, for example."

"One would think so," I said. "But those two *'v'thorble* don't consider the humans to be a security threat."

"We should contact Pierre Roubidoux in any case," K'deiTai insisted. "We need to get a message to their Admiral to assure him this wasn't our idea before his superiors do something rash."

H'rhAtor agonized over that. "We can't; not until we can offer some explanation. We need to find out who and why or we'll simply shift the blame to the Chamber."

"Which would only make things worse," U'tdaPagrn added.

197

"Whatever we do, we can't let L'datMparn get the faintest taste of this!" I said. "If Z'keBalf is involved, he'll cover his trail."

"No doubt." H'rhAtor was not happy. "In the mean time, since we can't do anything, we'll have to hope Fleet can figure out what's going on..."

§

...Meanwhile, the Fleet Eldest reacted to Intelligence's failure by raking all and sundry over the coals seeking the faintest taste of a clue. The near-panic was enough to bring the paperwork *to a stand-still, which says a lot. He ordered a sweeping review of their recent operational records, which meant digging through truck-loads of files, but it did precious little good. In all the chaos and recriminations, the paperwork was hopelessly behind, and ship 189's movement order was buried somewhere under the growing backlog. The ship itself was long gone from both the local system and their memories, so all the tail biting came up empty. Still unable to find anything, The Eldest kicked it back to Intelligence with an urgent request for action...*

§

...Having wished the matter off on Fleet, our lives returned to normal, at least what was normal for us. Our new staff kept busy with hobbies or playing *V'wit'mo'nop* while we struggled through each day enduring our ever-growing psychic connection. But this was different; our normal burden of annoyance and frustration was overlaid with growing tension and a sense of near panic. It soon became such a distraction that none of us could think clearly, and our nerves were all on edge.

"What has everyone so upset?" I'eiBida wondered at one point. "It feels like near chaos!"

"It does," H'rhAtor grumbled. He closed his eyes and concentrated for a bit, then said, "It seems to be coming from Fleet. Perhaps they're getting worked up over the investigation into the attack."

"That must mean they're onto something," K'deiTai said. "No doubt they're sniffing Z'keBalf's trail and closing in on him fast."

"It can't come any too soon!" C'traBenla said, venomously. She was there on one of her infrequent visits after a physich's appointment so they could take advantage of the free cafeteria. Her pregnancy was well advanced by that point, and she spent less and less time in the grotto, to the boundless relief of the staff, who were finely tuned to the rumor circle, as always.

"Well that is good news, at any rate," I offered. "If they are this worked up about it, they must be uncovering all sorts of dirt. No doubt arrests will come shortly, and this crisis will be defused..."

§

...By then, Intelligence was thoroughly in a dither. This whole story was so bizarre and unlikely that even the hardened investigators had trouble believing it. Still, the possibilities were disturbing enough to turn them out for a maximum effort. Despite their skepticism, they laid waste to their operations security staff, turned over every rock and leaf between here and the spaceport, grilled scores of suspects, tapped hundreds of phones and intercepted thousands of e-mails searching for something—anything!

Nothing. They couldn't even come up with a plausible hint. After rocketing back and forth for several days, they gave up and threw it back to Fleet with ill-concealed and intemperate skepticism...

§

...What passed for our happy equilibrium was shattered a couple days later when we received an urgent phone call from Pierre Roubidoux. "There is trouble brewing, my friends," he said, somberly. "We must meet at once."

Needless to say, I'eiBida, K'deiTai and I headed promptly to the restaurant. Pierre was sitting at one of the outdoor tables in a remote corner when we arrived, and he didn't look happy.

"Our courier brought special instructions to the Ambassador," he told us. "He has not taken me into his confidence, but he told the defense attache to increase our security."

"But why wouldn't he tell you about it?" I'eiBida asked. "You're part of their intelligence network, and there's your special liaison role. Why cut you out of the herd?"

"A most troubling question. I can only presume it is because of my ties to you; the Ambassador may doubt my loyalty."

"That's nonsense! Is there anything we can do to help?"

"It is for me to resolve," he said, grimly. "For now, we must deal with this. My friend, the military attache, talked with the courier's captain, and he learned there has been an incident. He passed to me this *informal* communique, which I found most alarming." He took a hand-written note out of his pocket, unfolded it, and handed it to us.

> _Urgent_ *you shake the bushes for information about the recent attack on the 'Marco Polo'. Who is behind it? Why? What is the Ic'nichi Chamber policy? What is H'rhAtor's status? What does he know? Report _any_ findings by special courier run, priority 'Omega'.*
> *MacKenna*

"Not good," K'deiTai muttered. "I'm guessing priority 'Omega' is serious?"

"It is the highest level military imperative, overriding even the Ambassador's authority. Only I and the military attache may invoke it." We didn't need our psychic abilities to see Pierre was seriously perturbed. "What is this, my friends? Why have you attacked one of our ships?"

"I swear to you we don't know anything about it," I'eiBida said, grimly. "And none of us doubt your loyalty, Pierre."

"Thank you. But what about this attack? Relations were improving steadily!"

"We just learned about it ourselves, and we don't know who is responsible. It's certainly not authorized by the Chamber, and H'rhAtor would have protested loud and clear if they did."

"Then are you investigating this?"

"H'rhAtor kicked it up to Fleet, but we haven't learned anything about it because it's under Chamber seal."

"I urge you to pursue this with the greatest effort. And *please* have the Arbiters make some official disclaimer at once. If you learn anything, no matter how trivial, please let me know so I can get it on the courier." It was clear to us all how valuable Pierre's 'unofficial' connection was at a moment like this.

"I don't know what progress they've made," I'eiBida told him. "But I'm sure they are knotting tails left and right to find answers..."

§

...While that was going on, the Fleet Eldest was in fact on a rampage, knotting junior Elders' tails left and right with reckless abandon in his search for evidence. No ones' ears were safe in his present mood. The paperwork was completely broken down by then to a point where the fleet was hurting for supplies and even their pay. The administrative logjam being what it was, ship 189 wasn't missed, and despite their gyrating back and forth, none of them thought about the absent cruiser...

§

..."Ancestors!" H'rhAtor said when we showed him Pierre's message. "The humans are worked up. I was afraid this would happen."

"Do you think the humans will attack?" I asked. "There is that understanding between you and the Admiral."

"That will only go so far, and this may push him over the edge unless we can reveal the real culprit."

We all looked at each other in dismay as we absorbed that bit of news. "So what do we do, sir?" I'eiBida asked.

"This is too big for us. We need to send this note directly to the Eldest; he'll know what to do..."

§

...By that point, the complete lack of evidence had the Fleet Eldest doubting this wild tale of an attack on a human ship, and he was about to drop the investigation until Pierre's note galvanized him anew and rekindled panic throughout Fleet Circle. Normal operations collapsed as all and sundry pawed through the fleet records again, but ship 189's movement order, still backlogged, went unnoticed. Meanwhile, supplies piled up in spaceport warehouses, graduation of the senior class at the Academy

was held up, construction on new ships ground to a halt, and 'Dark Grays' everywhere were forced to tap their personal savings since the pay orders were still late. After several exhausting, nerve-wracking days, the now-frazzled Fleet Eldest kicked it back to Intelligence with a decidedly un*diplomatic request that* here *was proof the problem existed, and they should get their* hro'n'nad *tails in gear before the humans descended on us all...*

§

..."*Ancestors*, I *wish* we could get this psychic mess straightened out!" I'eiBida muttered as he paced back and forth in frustration. Ever since we passed the investigation up to Fleet, we had nothing to keep us occupied. Meanwhile, our psychic powers were growing faster than ever, and could be quite overwhelming. Our frustrations got the better of us at times.

"You should grumble," U'tdaPagrn grumbled. Both his wrists were bandaged, and he munched a steady diet of medication for his swollen, inflamed joints as he doggedly twisted his human hand game back and forth. "I hope we do go to war with the humans! It's no more than they deserve!"

"You need to get rid of that thing!" K'deiTai snapped at him. "You're driving us all *er'trxxda*."

U'tdaPagrn ignored him and kept on, polluting our psychic environment all the while with his sulfurous aura. In addition to the angst we received from Fleet, our own frustrations and worries were building up and feeding back on themselves, so the pressure became unbearable.

"I wonder how Fleet's doing with the investigation?" K'deiTai mused. "Do you think they found anything yet?"

"I'm sure they have," H'rhAtor said. "After all, look at how much we uncovered with a fraction of their resources. I'm sure they'll let us know when they're ready to make their move. In fact, I daresay they'll allow us the pleasure of arresting L'datMparn."

"Still, I can't help but wonder." For some reason, I wasn't entirely convinced Fleet's investigation would accomplish anything. "Perhaps I should check with our two computer *'v'thorbles* again, just to see what they've come up with."

H'rhAtor gave me an impatient ear twitch. "Go right ahead if you want to, not that it will matter..."

§

...Intelligence looked upon the return of their least favorite enigma with increasing frustration and no small amount of skepticism, but Pierre's accompanying note jolted them into action. For all their bureaucratic inertia, they knew their business, and reigned havoc over all and sundry in what was fast becoming the largest Intelligence investigation ever.

No one had the faintest taste of what they were talking about, and the gossip grew to such alarming and contradictory proportion that either the humans were about to wipe us out, or we were about to wipe them out, or both, depending on who you believed. There were no end of even more outlandish theories, too, including another alien invasion, a case of planet-wide mass er'trxxda, *and it all being a fiendish plot by the human Elvis Worshipers.*

Needless to say, every lead needed to be followed up and debated at length, and like all bureaucracies, they could never quite *bring themselves to discard even the most out-there notions.*

Despite their cherished tradition of secrecy (copied from human intelligence, since ours was so new) rumors soon started to spread in the news media. Intelligence bribed, pleaded and bullied to keep the story quiet, which bought them a little time since the media were skeptical, too. One prominent journalist even accused them of using this ridiculous story of a rogue combat mission as a coverup for something far more sinister. An Intelligence press rep, rather indiscreetly, told them to run with it if they chose, and they did. Despite their best efforts, they came up with nothing in turn, so the story pretty well killed itself.

Through it all, they were thoroughly stymied by the lack of even a hint about this rumored attack. There was nothing, not a blessed, Ancestorless thing to lend credence to the mystery. During all this, ship 189's movement order was accidentally thrown in the trash in a belated effort to clear away clogged aisles in Fleet Circle, and thus lost to history, not that it mattered in the event. Intelligence argued with themselves for several days until the panic wore off, and convinced themselves that the Fleet was full of ui'DmukNa, *and the humans (foolish aliens!) must have been taken in as well. They kicked it back to Fleet with a surly note about wasting their time...*

§

..."Sad to say we've had no luck," W'kiLap said when I went to see what progress they'd made. "Z'keBalf's encryption system is state of the art. We can't hack it."

"I know the fellow who designed it," T'apiDien grumbled. "He is *l'cc'vn* good and a devoted hard-liner. We won't have any joy with him around."

"Can you get to him somehow?"

"No. He won't bribe or bully. I doubt even C'traBenla could get him to talk."

"And we can't go any further," W'kiLap added. "We already tripped one intruder trap, and I don't doubt there are others."

T'apiDien nodded grimly. "I *think* we managed to avoid being traced, but Z'keBalf is alerted now. I'm afraid we can't help you."

"We're busted and wasted..."

"...used up and fed up..."

"...done and gone..."

"All right you two," I sighed...

§

...Meanwhile, several prominent Ancients, having heard of the logistics problems brought on by the gyrations at Fleet, began demanding answers. The Eldest did his best to calm them down, and despite having little confidence that Intelligence—or anyone, for that matter—could unravel this enigma, he sent the problem back once again with a brisk demand they get their tails straight and do their p'quas'tka *jobs before the Ancients started investigating...*

§

...On my way back, I stopped by the Institute for a long overdue check of my mail, and found a note from an old colleague:

Aboard Ship 189, 5th pv'rma'drg'de
My dear Tin,
I am so sorry I couldn't stop by to visit before leaving, but the most wondrous opportunity has come my way. A fleet cruiser is going to the Inner Sector for a sweep of the far edge outposts, and Learnéd N'detLeda arranged for me to go along, since he understood you weren't available, courtesy of no less than Ancient Z'keBalf. This will be a grand chance for me to do a comprehensive and comparative study of the sociological impact of frontier life! I understand we shall be gone for nearly a year, but it will be well worth it. I will, of course, ask you to vet the numerous papers—or perhaps I shall write a book?—which come of it. In any case, I wish you well in my absence. Until we meet again, my best to you,
Learnéd R'venBnen

I was surprised and pleased by that bit of news: R'venBnen and I were close friends and collaborators since our days at the Institute, and this would be a grand adventure for any sociologist. I could well imagine the wealth of data he would gather in the inward colonies, and it set me to daydreaming about collating and editing such a mass of knowledge...

...but then I realized the implications of this letter: it clearly tied ship 189 to Z'keBalf! I pocketed the note and *galloped* for the nearest trolley station, bemused all the while that N'detLeda, of all people, would be the breach in Z'keBalf's carefully laid schemes...

§

...Intelligence was alarmed by the implied threat of the Ancients digging into their problems. They still couldn't make tail or ears over this wild story, but no one wanted to look bad to an official investigation. So they turned to once more, going over the same ground, interrogating the same suspects, arguing the same rumors ad nauseam.

Not a blessed taste. They snarled at each other for several days, then admitted defeat and kicked it back to Fleet, complaining that it couldn't have happened, because they couldn't find a clue...

§

..."Ship 189 again?" H'rhAtor said when I showed him the letter. "Isn't *this* an interesting coincidence!"

"It sure waggles ears at Z'keBalf, sir," I'eiBida said. "I'd say there's little doubt he's behind the attack."

"It's inconclusive, but it makes more and more sense all the time. But why would he send them to the far edge?"

"To get the witnesses out of the way, of course."

"This also tastes like a covert move against you, M'tinDegan," U'tdaPagrn said. "Convenient, this *'opportunity'*! I wonder if he has similar plans for all of us?"

"It does seem odd," I said, morosely. "I suppose I should thank N'detLeda for unwittingly blocking Z'keBalf's move."

"No, don't do that!" H'rhAtor urged. "We don't want Z'keBalf to know we're on to his game."

"Z'keBalf should be arrested for treason!" K'deiTai said. "Here is the proof we need."

H'rhAtor wasn't thrilled. "You're talking about bringing charges against one of the strongest members of the Chamber of Ancients, and this is circumstantial at best. Unless we can deliver solid evidence, he'll skin us alive!"

"And, truth, we're not even sure it *was* him," U'tdaPagrn said.

"*Of course* it was him!" C'traBenla snapped. "This is *exactly* the sort of move that *un'tdar* would make!"

"She has a point, sir," I'eiBida said. "Remember how he kept interfering back during the war."

H'rhAtor was not pleased to be pinned down by the facts. "You're right, it's the only thing which makes sense. And he's certainly not afraid of provoking a war with the humans."

"He might even welcome it," K'deiTai said. "A war would increase his power in the Chamber."

"It would." H'rhAtor's aura was icy cold.

"So what do we do, sir?"

"Ancestors..." H'rhAtor brooded over it for some time. "I haven't the faintest taste. We have no solid proof, and if we brought it to Ancient Y'veNipbr, it could trigger a political crisis."

"And we'd all lose our ears in the process," U'tdaPagrn grumbled. "Even if Z'keBalf goes down, he could still crush us in passing."

"So you're just going to cover your tails, is that it?" C'traBenla demanded.

"There's nothing we can do, love," I'eiBida said.

"I'm sure Fleet knows all about it," H'rhAtor said at last. "They would have the movement orders, and all. Intelligence can sniff out the trail much better than we can, so we'll let them deal with it. No sense getting our tails knotted going up against him."

"All for the best, I suppose," I said. "No doubt the Inspectorate will deal with Z'keBalf while Fleet takes care of L'datMparn..."

§

...While we reassured ourselves with our sadly misplaced faith in common sense, little did we know how matters fared at the spaceport. The Fleet Eldest finally lost his temper, got on the phone, and accused Intelligence of being a herd of hro'n'nad n'bna'nmn *who couldn't find their tails with both hands and a road map; which evoked a countercharge that he was a* cc'v'renk t'pithm'ig *who spent too much time in Zero-G for his own good, and* x'mnnb' *on this wild story of his, too. And before you could say "This could only happen on earth!", they were practically at war with each other...*

*****

"The Best Defense"
(Extract of testimony)

'We're back to debacle again.'
'These screw-ups you can not defend.'
'At times like this you can be sure
you haven't got a friend.'
'We're back to debacle again!'

The mournful tenor of the Fleet Quartermaster was greeted by derisive cheers from a gaggle of junior officers celebrating the best news to hit Space Fleet in months: the downfall of Defense Minister Jacek Hogarthy. Word came down just that afternoon of Hogarthy's dismissal from the Cabinet in Geneva, and the mood in the base Officers' Club was festive.

Admiral MacKenna tried to be inconspicuous when he came in, and slipped quietly into the Senior Officers' alcove to avoid ruining the good mood. Ramon, the Philippine steward was there at once with a steaming mug of Navy coffee. MacKenna nodded unspoken thanks to him, and he bowed politely in turn before withdrawing without a word. It was a ritual acted out daily for seven long years: it comforted them both.

MacKenna settled in one of the recliners and savored his coffee while staring absently at the potted bamboo, heavy curtains, and subdued track lighting; 'early government issue' decor, like every O-club in the world. The familiar warmth of the Boiler Room Joe—thick and hot, with a pinch of salt—was a welcome diversion from the cares of his life. Such diversions were few enough.

Captain Rostokovich and Lieutenant Night Eagle turned up a few minutes later. "Good evening, Admiral," Rostokovich said. "I have report on fleet. All ships are as ready as they can be for tomorrow."

"And I have that detail you requested ready, sir," Night Eagle added.

MacKenna nodded morosely. Duty followed him even in here, disturbing what little peace he could find.

"They are happy Defense Minister is gone," Ivan muttered as the crowd in the main area burst into applause.

"They have reason to celebrate. Life will be a lot simpler from now on." He brooded over his coffee for a bit. "Any word from the latest courier run?"

"Nyet, sir. Pierre reports nothing. Ic'nichi must be keeping tighter security than usual."

"Or the courier is too slow for dealing with this crisis. I wish we had better communications! We need to know what they're up to!"

"He is friend of I'eiBida, sir, on their staff. He also knows Eldest H'rhAtor well, and has access to them both, as well as to Arbiters. He would hear something."

"Yeah, unless they've been cut out of the loop too." MacKenna sighed in frustration.

"Perhaps we should wait for the next courier run, sir," Night Eagle suggested. "He may turn up something yet."

"We can't. Hogarthy's replacement will likely put the brakes on us." MacKenna shook his head in frustration. "We'll just have to keep on with keeping on, I guess. That's the hell of being in command: you never have enough information to be sure you're making the right moves."

"Da, sir. Perhaps that is what J J Ballas meant by 'inverse cognitive function'?"

"Maybe. I don't know." MacKenna shook his head in frustration. "I wish they'd quit with the psychobabble and say what's on their minds."

"It's hard enough to understand our own people at times, sir," Night Eagle said. "They are too different; we may never really understand them."

"Yeah." MacKenna brooded for a bit, reflecting on how contact with now-several alien races had changed the already difficult task of comprehending friend and foe. "And it'll only get worse in the future. Thankfully it won't be my problem for much longer."

Ivan listened to the raucous singing with an annoyed look. "Is undignified, sir, even for Hogarthy."

MacKenna paused in his coffee, feeling their collective mood. They would depart for war in the morning: their good cheer at being rid of Hogarthy helped mask their anxiety from themselves. He knew the feeling all too well. "Let 'em celebrate. They won't have much to sing about tomorrow."

§

The sun was only peeking through the low clouds on the horizon, but the day was already sweltering. The cool sea breeze which normally provided some relief from the summer heat was dormant. Their sweat-soaked utilities clung to them like glue, and the humid air was thick as syrup.

'A taste of hell,' MacKenna thought as he struggled with *his field kit.* 'We're all headed there, likely; fair warning, I guess.'

"Allow me, sir." Leftenant Hythe-Morrison came *around to the passenger's side of the staff car, and took MacKenna's bag.*

"Thanks." MacKenna stretched to relieve the stiffness in his back, and looked around the tarmac.

Singapore Space Port was oddly silent: for the first time in years there was little movement other than the distant mob of ground staff gathered to watch their departure. One of the shuttles stood nearby, its cargo hatch open, pallets of rations and supplies unattended. A fork lift parked by it served as a temporary perch for its operator and the shuttle crew. Everyone was gathered to witness the solemn moment as Space Fleet departed for war against the Ic'nichi.

"This place is a freakin' ghost town."

"It is, sir," Hythe-Morrison muttered. "The ghosts of past wars have come to wish us off."

MacKenna sighed. "Truer than you know, Leftenant. Truer than you know." He looked around again at the

210

somber scene, and shook his head. They were all feeling the weight of this moment: the prospect Space Fleet lived with ever since its formation, he more than most of them. "I just hope we don't add much to that population."

"Speaking of the dead, sir..." Hythe-Morrison gestured to a staff car parked nearby, and to the short, rotund, forlorn figure of Jacek Hogarthy.

"Crap," MacKenna muttered. "I thought he'd gone home already."

"He is scheduled to leave this afternoon, sir."

"Well, let's be gracious, no matter how much it hurts."

Hogarthy watched as they approached. "Well, you got what you wanted, didn't you, Admiral?" he said bitterly.

"I got what I needed." Now that he thought about it, Hogarthy was so utterly unqualified for his former post that it was hard to hate him for his failings.

Hogarthy tried to put on a bold front. "I hear they chose Garibaldi for Defense. I guess things will be more to your liking now."

MacKenna nodded. They got word of that choice late last night. "He's a good man."

Hogarthy's bitterness overflowed at last. "Damn you, MacKenna, I regret the day you were assigned to this post!"

"You're not the only one."

"All the same, I wish you well in this." He wound down, and stared aimlessly at the nearby shuttle. Finally, he sighed. "I only hope you know what you're doing."

"You're not the only one there, either."

§

Captain Rostokovich was waiting at the shuttle hatch, dressed in utilities as they were, with a field bag at his feet. MacKenna eyed him curiously. "Something, Captain?"

"I go with you, Admiral." Before MacKenna could object, he added, "This is important battle. It will shape our future like battle at Dreamsingers' world. Ic'nichi are good people; many are friends. I stayed last time because I was needed here. This time honor demands I go."

211

MacKenna pondered the burly Ukrainian for a moment, then nodded. "All right, mister. You can bring my bag while you're at it."

Rostokovich took the Admiral's field kit from Hythe-Morrison, and followed him onto the shuttle.

§

The shuttle docked smoothly, and MacKenna slid through the narrow access hatch into the 'Marco Polo's central air lock, where Captain Morgan waited to meet him.

"Are you sure you're up to this, sir?" she asked as the elevator rose toward the habitat section.

MacKenna was silent for a time, staring at the wall of the hollow central column. What he saw filled him with misgivings: the ship showed her age; signs of metal fatigue and hasty repairs everywhere. 'God,' *he thought.* 'She belongs in a museum.' *He examined a section of obvious cracking braced up with crudely welded angle iron as they passed.* 'So do I,' *he added.*

"I have to be," he said to Morgan at last. "We've got to defuse this mess before it turns into an all-out shooting war." He was silent for a time, but once they reached the upper air lock, he turned to her again. "But I swear by all that's Holy this will be my last war."

Lieutenant Night Eagle was waiting when they arrived in the equipment bay at the top of the shaft, along with three of his Space Marines. MacKenna considered him in surprise as he returned their salutes. "You too, huh?"

"Yes, Admiral." Night Eagle gave him a grim, slightly smug look. "You asked for the best, and that's what you got."

MacKenna chuckled mirthlessly. "You are a piece of work, mister. In all my years, I've never heard of anyone deserting to the front."

"It's that whole 'bold new frontier' thing, sir," Night Eagle said, smugly.

§

The bridge of the 'Marco Polo' was crowded. All stations were manned, and he and Captain Morgan filled the cramped central section around the ladder which ran the length of the habitat section. The hatch to the navigation dome above was closed, since the original, damaged in the recent attack, hadn't been replaced yet. That was hardly unique; there were signs of hasty repairs everywhere.

The bridge crew sat in their crash couches, struggling against the confines of their bulky exposure suits and seat harnesses as they made final preparations. The main lighting was off; the dull red emergency lamps lit the bridge with a hellish gloom accented by the multicolored lights on the control panels and the view screens over their heads. The air was faintly stale, tinged with fear and hot electronics. There was a subdued chatter as the stations checked with their counterparts on the lower decks, the other ships, or Orbit Dock, making last minute preparations to get under way.

"Task force status?" MacKenna asked after taking in the scene.

"All ships report ready and standing by, sir."

The 'Conestoga' and the new 'Xanadu', their missile racks restored, drifted nearby, with the destroyers 'Comanche' and 'Tarter' flanking the formation as best as two ships could. The 'Henry Hudson' drifted ahead of them, already aligned on the course for d'enchia. They made a brave show, but it was a show which didn't bear close examination. It took a monumental effort over the last two months to patch the fleet together enough to function at even this minimal degree. The 'Conestoga' was barely spaceworthy, and the 'Tartar' only had part of her sensor suite back on line. They were all patched and hot-wired, and like the 'Marco Polo', the 'Hudson' was so rickety that MacKenna hated to send them out. The human fleet was about as 'unready' for battle as it could be and still be considered functional.

213

"Your opinion, Captain?" he muttered to Morgan.

"Unfit to print, sir." She stared straight ahead, her gray hair and waxy complexion turned ruddy by the emergency lights, her jaw muscles working like always. *"It reminds me of when we set out to aid New Patagonia."*

"Hmph. Yeah." They were as unready then, and faced the prospect of war against what was then an unknown alien threat of obviously superior strength. *"Fleet readiness?"* As if he wasn't aware of every broken part and rusted bolt in his entire command.

"Minimal, sir. If we didn't have to go out, I'd put most of these ships back in the dock."

So would he if he could. *"Morale?"*

"Zero."

The hands around them were quiet, focussed on their duties with the grimness of those facing a dreaded task which couldn't be put off any longer. There was no chatter over the general circuit, or the radios, either. Their collective angst was a mental haze of vague menace; threatening, brooding; it set their nerves on edge and affected their judgment. How far would this psychic thing go, he wondered, and what would be the consequences? The talking heads still couldn't provide an answer.

MacKenna fought that haze off, and focussed on the task at hand. *"The special ordinance?"*

"It's ready, sir."

"God, I hate this." He stared for a long moment at the view of earth filling one screen. So many years: a lifetime spent fighting to defend that beautiful blue and white sphere. Some of the scars showed from orbit, some only he could see. It would never end, although his part in that struggle would soon be over. It was all so futile somehow, although he couldn't see any other way his life might have played out. It all put him in a grim mood.

"Is your Ensign Ling ready?"

"Champing at the bit, sir. He claims he can practically drop us into orbit around d'enchia."

214

MacKenna gave her a sharp look. "Can he?"

"With a careful approach at just above C...and luck...yes."

That about summed up any battle. "Very well, Captain. Get the fleet under way."

§

They moved out one by one, taking up a widely spaced formation. The 'Hudson' was the first to jump into Hyper-C. They were normally assigned as the diplomatic courier for the human embassy on d'enchia: something the Admiral was depending on to make this work. The 'Hudson' was the only ship not bristling with missile tubes, although they carried something far nastier. The rest jumped on the Admiral's mark, and began the long, difficult task of maintaining some sort of formation through the eighteen day journey to d'enchia.

*****

"Panic, Wetness, And Running In Circles"
(Related by Learnéd K'deiTai)

It was several hands of days before we got over the hysteria about Z'keBalf's attack on the Marco Polo. What made things worse was our new staffers proved remarkably skittish. Gossip about the destruction of our former grotto had spread like wildfire, and every time C'traBenla came by, we lost a few more. H'rhAtor conceded to their fear, and reluctantly signed all their requests for transfer. The few survivors and a steady trickle of replacements were buried under the paperwork generated by the investigation, which at least kept everyone busy enough that they didn't have time to fret.

Mid-meal came, and the four of us were alone for the moment, as most of the ratings, aside from a lone watch stander, were off for another of their suspiciously long meal breaks. C'traBenla mostly remained at home since the Chamber physichs politely and discreetly advised her not to strain herself as her pregnancy neared its end, which was a relief. H'rhAtor was over at the spaceport taking care of fleet matters which *couldn't* be put off any longer, and the priceless L'datMparn was out somewhere.

It was another long, interminable session of the Chamber; I don't even recall what they were arguing over, not that it mattered. I was half asleep from boredom as we waited for our staff to return. U'tdaPagrn was fiddling with his human hand game, still trying to get the colored faces lined up on the little plastic cube while emitting a steady aura of frustration. M'tinDegan was dozing on his overstuffed seat cushion, and I'eiBida sat at a desk staring at the wall as he fretted over C'traBenla. She was due at any time; his agonizing over her and U'tdaPagrn's angst filled the grotto with a choking mental fog which depressed us all.

As much as I understood I'eiBida's concern, his constant anxiety was starting to get on my nerves. He'd been like this for days now. M'tinDegan made a point of calling her now and then, and she assured him she was doing well, not that I'eiBida was comforted by that reassurance. So we sat around the grotto day after day, fighting boredom and I'eiBida's fugue, waiting for the

Chamber to get their collective tails straight, or our Ancestors to drop in to claim us, or the Universe to implode.

'She will be all right,' I thought to him at last.

He jerked as if startled, and looked at me. "I know. I just can't help but worry."

"Well please try not to worry out loud," M'tinDegan grumbled.

"Sorry." M'tinDegan went back to sleep, and I'eiBida went back to fretting.

At least the pay was decent. Our role as 'civilian advisors to the Chamber' included some nice perks, but the endless waiting threatened to drive us *er'trxxda*. Our psychic angst fed back on itself as our frustrations reinforced each other until it was a wonder we hadn't all gone back to the egg. I, for one, wondered how much longer it would take for *that* to happen, which bolstered our collective fugue that much more...

"I DID IT!" U'tdaPagrn's hysterical outburst sent shivers through us all. "I...I...got it! Look! I did it!" He held up his little plastic hand game. "I solved it!"

I'eiBida took it from him and examined it closely. "Hmph! So you did." All six sides were solid-colored, for a miracle. "Congratulations." He set it on the desk, picked up a heavy office machine, and smashed it while U'tdaPagrn cried out in dismay.

"What are you doing!? My hand game!"

"Enough of this human *x'mnnb'!* It's a wonder it didn't drive you *er'trxxda.*" He took U'tdaPagrn gently by the arm and coaxed him out from behind his desk. "Now you go down to the Chamber physichs and get those wrists attended to. It's a wonder you didn't cripple yourself as well!"

"But...I solved it. You saw." U'tdaPagrn was shaken. "I really did solve it."

"Yes, you did. You defeated that fiendish human device; we're all proud of you. But now go get yourself looked at."

"But, I..."

My tail about fell off when the phone buzzed. I'eiBida grabbed it with a livid curse. "Special Liaison Grotto!" he snapped. There was a lengthy pause as we wondered what was going on, and why I'eiBida's mental aura was turning so agitated. "Yes, Ancient, we'll

217

be right there." He hung up and turned to us. "That was Ancient Y'veNipbr; we're to come to the Chamber *now*."

"Why? What is it?"

"She didn't say, but she said it was urgent, and she sounded worried."

That was all it took. We were out of there at a gallop.

§

Ancient Y'veNipbr's Aide intercepted us at the Chamber entrance. "Z'keBalf has placed a minute in the Chamber schedule to announce a 'strategic development involving the humans'," he told us. "He hasn't let anything leak, but knowing him, it can't be good."

"Wonderful," I'eiBida grumbled. "What's he up to now?"

"We better find out before it's too late," I said.

"If it isn't already," U'tdaPagrn added.

We were escorted directly into the Chamber without the usual screening of our appearances and the inevitable lecture on Chamber protocol, which was worrisome in itself. The dimly lit cavern was filled with a subdued rumble of voices seemingly like a distant surf. There must have been a major debate going on, since the little lights at each Ancient's dais glittered like a surreal starscape. I guessed about five hundred of those lights were yellow. Those must be Z'keBalf's anti-human hardliners. Of the rest, perhaps another five hundred were blue—showing their opposition. The rest were dark. Obviously whatever the issue was, it was hotly debated and far from settled. The subdued rumble of voices held a nervous edge. Ancient Z'keBalf was standing on the rostrum in the glare of spotlights, surrounded by the Inner Policy Circle, addressing the Chamber as we entered.

"Good, you're here," Y'veNipbr said when we arrived.

"What's happening, Ancient?" I'eiBida asked.

"I don't know, but from the rumbles I've been hearing, it won't be good." She gestured us to the row of visitor's seat cushions below her dais. "He's done something..."

"...scientific research has shown that contact with the Dreamsingers leads to mental alterations in those contacted," he said as we settled in. "These alterations include unusual mental

218

capabilities which I will now call upon my scientific advisor, Learnéd N'detLeda, to outline for you."

There was a pause as N'detLeda was summoned to the Rostrum. Ancient Y'veNipbr's dais was close enough that we could hear him clearly even without the amplifiers.

"The subjects show signs of precognition, heightened empathy, telepathy, and even telekinesis," N'detLeda said. "These powers have been growing steadily, and are now quite pronounced. While we haven't been able to determine the mechanism for this as yet, there is every reason to believe the process will continue until the subjects are fully linked as a common mind."

'Is that true?' I heard Ancient Y'veNipbr clearly behind me.

"Yes, Ancient."

I felt her surprise, and realized I had answered her unspoken thought. "He failed to tell us about *that* one!" she said, angrily.

"Ah...I thought C'traBenla would have mentioned it?"

"No, she didn't." Y'veNipbr was miffed. "She is a dear person, but somewhat *scattered*."

'Oy!' the four of us chorussed mentally.

Z'keBalf took over as N'detLeda returned to the shadows. "We recently learned the humans exposed to contact with this J J Ballas are showing identical symptoms. I used our intelligence assets to investigate, and they report that several humans are well advanced in these powers."

"I don't like this," I'eiBida muttered.

"It can't be good," U'tdaPagrn said.

"This explains a lot," Y'veNipbr added.

"The danger is clear," Z'keBalf went on. "The humans pose a terrible threat as is. If their military leaders are capable of reading our thoughts, or directing their fleet over stellar distances by telepathy, or even of striking directly at us with telekinetic powers, then the threat becomes unendurable."

I was out of my seat cushion without realizing it, horrified at the implications of what he was saying.

"The record shows we have argued this matter for years, ever since the humans were first contacted. The record also shows that despite my repeated urgings, this Chamber has proven *unable* to make a realistic policy concerning the human threat. With the emergence of this new danger, that threat can no longer be ignored."

"Great," I'eiBida muttered. "He's done something stupid..."

"As such, I have taken upon myself to authorize a covert military mission under Chamber seal. The greatest threat comes from the human Captain Morgan, who is the designated successor to Admiral MacKenna, and who has the most advanced powers among the humans, and who is known to be severely *er'trxxda*. I directed one of our cruisers to intercept and destroy Captain Morgan's ship, the 'Marco Polo'..."

"You...unspeakable...*N'BNA'NMN!*"

Z'keBalf spun in surprise; a moment later a spotlight hit me as a rumble went up from the gallery. "That was an act of war!" I cried. Ancient Z'keBalf huffed mightily, but I cut him off before he could reply. "Do you have any *idea* of how the humans will react to this?" I was getting hysterical, and at that point I really didn't care. "Haven't you read my reports? Didn't you learn anything from Pearl Harbor? Fort Sumpter? Singapore?" The Chamber Wardens were closing in to quell my disturbance, but Ancient Y'veNipbr waved them back. "You cannot treat the humans like this!"

"We have had enough of your impertinence..."

"This is exactly the sort of thing which will drive them into an *er'trxxda* frenzy!" The nightmares I lived with for the last four years were coming true right before my eyes.

"*If* they learn of it, which they won't!" Z'keBalf roared. "The 'Marco Polo' was a worn-out wreck, the attack was launched far from earth, and the wreckage impacted a planet. They will assume the ship suffered a catastrophic breakdown, and was lost by accident, so your hysteria is groundless."

"You're basing our survival on how you *presume* the humans will interpret what you did? You're the one who's *er'trxxda!*"

Z'keBalf gave me a contemptuous look. "Hear it for yourself, since you have so little faith in our fleet!" He turned and addressed the Chamber at large. "I call upon Second Degree defender L'datMparn!"

"Could they actually get away with this?" Y'veNipbr asked us.

"As much as I hate to say it, I wish they had," I'eiBida swore. "The consequences could be unthinkable."

"So you're telling me they failed?"

"Yes, Ancient."

"That's good—isn't it?"

"There are limits to what even Admiral MacKenna will accept," I said. "And we don't want to be on *his* bad side!"

L'datMparn appeared out of the shadows, and stepped up on the rostrum. "Did you lead the attack on the human ship?" Z'keBalf demanded.

"I did, Ancient. Per your instructions, I took command of Ship 189, one of our best warships, and used the intelligence data you provided to intercept the 'Marco Polo' at their New Patagonia colony."

"Did you fire on the 'Marco Polo'?"

"Yes, Ancient. I used one of the new mass polarizer-equipped missiles, which performed flawlessly. They never had a chance."

"And was the 'Marco Polo' destroyed?"

"I am certain of that, Ancient," L'datMparn said, proudly. "I ordered the warhead detonated myself." There was a long moment of stunned silence, and then I felt the chill descend over the room like a choking fog. N'detLeda caught it first, then Z'keBalf, then L'datMparn: our missiles don't have manual detonators.

"The...self destruct..." L'datMparn mumbled as his ears wilted.

"*hro'n'nad!* She tricked you!"

"That did it," U'tdaPagrn said. "Enough with the secrecy. I need to alert G'cetGian!" He took off at a trot.

I trotted up to the rostrum and called to the Most Ancient in a cold panic. "I must have *immediate* authority to go to earth and try to salvage what I can!"

The Most Ancient looked at me in confusion. "Surely you don't..."

"WE'RE AT WAR WITH THE HUMANS!"

"I endorse this call, Most Ancient!" Y'veNipbr cried over the rising pandemonium. The volume rose sharply as a bitter factional argument erupted. The pandemonium overflowed the gallery,

Ancients spilling out onto the floor in heated debate. Y'veNipbr joined a herd of Ancients lambasting Z'keBalf, who seemed disconcerted by this development. He finally left the rostrum, followed by N'detLeda and L'datMparn, and vanished in the general direction of the private exits. The Ancients *r'vebbe'd* at each other for a bit more, and Y'veNipbr returned to her dais. "How bad will this be?" she demanded of I'eiBida when she returned.

"That depends on how you define 'bad'." We hardly needed to be psychic to sense his alarm and dismay. From my knowledge of the humans and their wars, 'bad' would be bad indeed.

"I *swear* I will have his ears!" she muttered venomously. From what I knew of her, that would be bad as well. "Why didn't you tell me earlier?"

I'eiBida turned defensive under her tirade. "The fleet is investigating. They said to let them handle it, and we assumed they were dealing with it."

"I see we need to collect a *lot* of ears!" she snarled.

The near-riot went on for some time as the Ancients argued and debated and simply *r'vebbe'd* over the devastating news. Finally the Most Ancient managed to restore some semblance of order. "This is a most disturbing development," he said once he could be heard. "Most disturbing indeed. Something must be done."

"Then *do* something, you *hro'n'nad n'bna'nmn*," Y'veNipbr muttered. "Don't just stand there and dither, for once!"

The Most Ancient paused, and looked around the gallery. "I can tell from your reactions that you feel much the same as I do. This has to be the most unprecedented event ever reported in this great Chamber."

"Do *not* go back to the egg on us now!" Y'veNipbr's mental aura would have broken the old angst-o-meter right then.

"Action must be taken, of course, but what action?" The Most Ancient gazed around him at a Chamber reduced to near emotional collapse. "We shall have to create a special review circle to ponder the matter."

"*ui'DmukNa,*" Y'veNipbr grumbled.

"But..."

The Most Ancient avoided looking at us. "The Chamber will adjourn so that the Inner Policy Circle can select a review circle."

§

Needless to say, after the stunning revelations in the Chamber, we beat a hasty path to our liaison grotto to bring the world up to speed. As soon as we arrived, I'eiBida grabbed the nearest telephone and called the Herd Guide at the spaceport. "Hello? I'eiBida, sir, over at the Chamber liaison grotto. I need to speak with the Ki-Eldest, now! Yes, sir. This is a war emergency!"

H'rhAtor came in just as I'eiBida was talking, and halted in alarm. "What happened?"

I'eiBida covered the phone with one hand. "The secret is out: Z'keBalf and L'datMparn were the ones who tried to destroy Captain Morgan. It just broke in the Chamber."

"Those *hro'n'nad!*" H'rhAtor was appalled that they might have gotten us into a war with earth. "I was hoping that was just a nightmare."

"It is," I grumbled.

"What is the Chamber going to do?"

"They *adjourned* to refer the matter to a special review circle."

"Ancestors...if we ever needed the Chamber to move fast, now's the time. Where are those two?"

"Z'keBalf left the Chamber before we did," M'tinDegan said. "I don't know where he is now, but he's probably in his grotto."

H'rhAtor gave him a hard look. "What about L'datMparn?"

"Last I saw, he went with Z'keBalf."

H'rhAtor grabbed another phone. "I'll have their ears for this!"

"They're under the jurisdiction of the Chamber Wardens," I muttered.

"Take a number," I'eiBida said, bitterly. "Hello? Sir? I'eiBida. I have the proof we needed: Ancient Z'keBalf just admitted in the Chamber that he ordered L'datMparn and ship 189 to destroy the human ship 'Marco Polo'... Yes, sir, ship 189. What? I don't know where they are either! Yes, sir, he said it right out on the public record. Unless I badly misread the humans, we have a war on our hands." There was a lengthy silence as I'eiBida's aura of tension rose higher and higher. "Yes, sir..."

223

Then H'rhAtor snatched the phone from him. "Ki-Eldest? H'rhAtor. I've ordered L'datMparn arrested." There was another tense silence. "No, sir, I don't know where ship 189 is either. Yes, sir, we must assume the worst. I'm on my way back to the spaceport. Please have a shuttle waiting to take me into orbit." He listened a bit more then hung up. "The fleet is going to full mobilization," he told us. "Thankfully we're right in the midst of squadron rotations, so d'enchia is well protected, but the frontier colonies are naked."

"Ancestors, what a mess!" I'eiBida said.

"What more could *possibly* go wrong?" I groaned.

I should have expected my Ancestors to react to that one. No sooner did I speak than I felt an eerie, tense sensation in my abdomen. The way the others hesitated in confusion, I could tell they felt it too. And then it hit: a wracking spasm which started somewhere deep in my bowels and spread until my whole abdomen was tied in a knot. I had to lean against the wall to steady myself as I gasped in pain. I don't know how long it went on, but it seemed forever before the convulsion passed as quickly as it came. I sagged against the wall, holding myself up by main effort, and looked at the others, trying to comprehend what happened. I'eiBida flopped on the floor pallid and shaking, as did H'rhAtor. M'tindegan managed to squat rather than falling over and stared at me incredulously while the staff watched in alarm.

"What...?" H'rhAtor gasped. "What was that?"

"Nerves?" I muttered. "Stress?"

"It...can't be..." H'rhAtor staggered to his feet, and helped I'eiBida up. "Are you all right?"

"I...yes, sir. I guess." He was trembling and gasped for air. "Did we get some bad *bv'nunma* maybe?"

M'tinDegan struggled to his feet, and leaned unsteadily against the wall. "I didn't eat any *bv'nunma*, and most of us haven't had mid-meal yet."

Then I had a horrid flash of intuition. "We were poisoned! Z'keBalf poisoned us!"

H'rhAtor stared at me stupidly. "No... Even *he* wouldn't go that far. Would he?"

"It's...the only thing which makes sense," I'eiBida said. "It's the only thing which fits, and N'detLeda could provide him the drugs."

"Still, I find that hard to...ohhhhh...*l'cc'vn*...!" H'rhAtor curled up and fell over as another spasm came welling up out of my abdomen. Through my haze of pain and disorientation, I saw the others collapse in agony as well, and one of the staffers on the telephone calling for help.

§

Q'brnVen's Chamber Wardens and medical assistants were there in moments, with one of the attending Chamber physichs not far behind. That one was incredulous at the reports of whatever was wrong with us. "It seems unlikely," he said to H'rhAtor's claim of poisoning. "The symptoms don't match any toxin I'm familiar with, and even if you were poisoned, it wouldn't hit you all at once."

"Well then, what *is* it?"

He seemed vexed. "I'm not sure...the symptoms could mean anything..."

"Well do sssom...An...CESTORSssss!" H'rhAtor groaned as another collective spasm curled us all on the floor, again.

The physich did something: namely, he called for help. The first ambulance arrived just as a *fourth* spasm passed, and a stampede of Fire Wardens and rescue orderlies descended on us, only to be equally baffled by our enigma. The attending physich was dismayed at this mysterious outbreak, proclaiming loudly that he had never seen the like in all his medical experience. The orderlies, more pragmatic perhaps, ignored him and focussed on running field diagnoses. When all their tests came back negative, they started to get irate.

"There's nothing wrong with them!" the lead orderly complained.

"Then why does it *hurt?*" I whimpered.

He pondered me in confusion. "Perhaps it's a bit of gas?"

"It could be psychosomatic," one of his herd suggested.

"But all four of them at once?"

"Mass hysteria?"

"These are for the *l'cc'vn* brain mechanics," another grumbled.

"We don't know that," the attending physich said. "Let's stick to a medical cause; its familiar territory, at least." They gathered around and considered me like I was something unnatural which dropped out of the sky. "Any ideas?" he asked at last.

"Their vital signs are all normal," one said. "We're not even sure if they *are* sick."

"I am. Trust me."

"These are 'Dark Grays'," another one said with a gesture at I'eiBida. "Have any of them been to earth?"

"They were all stationed there," Q'brnVen told them. "This sort of thing goes on all the time around here. How I'm going to write *this* one up is beyond me."

"Some human infestation!?" one of the attendants asked.

"Perhaps..."

"But it surely would have shown up earlier," another objected.

"It would seem so..."

"I say it's a psychosomatic condition."

"Stress? Exhaustion?"

"Or some bad *bv'nunma*, perhaps?"

"It's gas. Just gas."

"Ancestors! Will you get your *p'quas'tka* tails straight and *do* something?"

"Irritable," another orderly noted. "Is that a symptom?"

"Hard to say," the physich said. "Patients are often out of sorts due to their discomfort."

"But we can't dismiss the possibility?"

"Hmmm...no, we can't."

"Trust me, I'm sick! We're all sick!"

The physich saw fit to notice me. "Well, yes, but with what?"

"It doesn't matter! We should be in the clinic!" I should have known this pompous *n'bna'nmn* was exactly the sort to be serving the Chamber.

He gave me an annoyed ear twitch. "Proper medical protocol..."

"Ooohhhh...never minnnnd!" I sobbed as we were wracked with another collective spasm.

The orderlies *finally* reacted: debate ended, I was loaded on a stretcher, carted to the nearest exit, shoved unceremoniously into their ambulance, and off we went to a nearby clinic which handled Chamber emergencies. Another ambulance was standing by as mine pulled out, with more coming on fast.

§

Soon we were in the clinic receiving, where we discovered two hands worth of others similarly afflicted, ambulances battling to get in and out of the entry way, gurneys stacked side by side, all of us heaving and groaning in unison as the spasms hit. The clinic staff were nonplussed as this stampede descended on them without warning, and before our fight-or-flight reflexes could kick in, we were hurting more than ever under a full barrage of medical tests.

"Ancestors! This stuff is horrible!" I tied to fight off the attendants who were trying to force a huge bottle of vile liquid down my throat. "Why do I need this?"

"The barium solution helps us image your digestive tract," the attendant said. "You want us to find a cure, don't you?"

"I'm not so sure about that!"

Another one came at me with an ugly-looking needle for yet *more* blood samples. "I've only got so much, and I need...OUCH!"

"There now, that wasn't so bad, was it?" On top of all their other indignities, they persisted in treating us like hatchlings. "We only need a few little samples to figure out what's wrong with you."

"Here, use this, then." I offered the jug of barium solution.

"You need to finish that so we can get X-rays." Another attendant was standing by with a sinister-looking portable X-ray machine.

"This is for your own good, you know," the receiving physich lectured me. "Unless we can figure out what's wrong with you, how can we cure you?" He was interrupted on that ominous note by the arrival of a new ambulance bearing Arbiter U'tdaPagrn. "What? *Another* one?"

U'tdaPagrn gave him an alarmed look. "What do you mean another one?" Then he saw us through the herd of medical staff and curious onlookers. *"Another one what?"*

227

He was answered when we all went into convulsions again as the physich looked on in dismay. No sooner did that pass, then the next ambulance delivered H'rhAtor's Worthy who looked even more wrung out than we did. That was followed in quick secession by more ambulances bearing any number of 'Dark Grays'.

"It's affecting the whole fleet!" H'rhAtor cried in dismay.

"Well...then it's probably not gas," the Receiving physich said, doubtfully.

§

The idea that a mass poisoning, or an outbreak of disease, or...something!...was going on in the inner corridors of the Chamber Of Ancients had alarm bells ringing all over the World Nest. It wasn't long before our little adventure was joined by the nest's health authorities, who took one look at us and quarantined the lot. The Chamber's public health officials arrived moments later, watched in wide-eyed dismay as we went through another round of convulsions, argued briefly over the symptoms, then issued a planetary medical advisory.

And it went downhill from there in a hurry: any number of hard-eyed investigators from the Chamber, Fleet Intelligence, the local Peace Wardens, and the Inspectorate descended on us wanting answers about what the *l'cc'vn* was going on in the Chamber and wanting them *now*. The commotion set off *another* stampede of network journalists who could be even more persistent than the official investigators, and before one could say, "This could only happen on earth!", we were headline celebrities around the world.

Have you ever been interrogated by the Chamber Wardens while enduring massive stomach cramps? I don't recommend it, *especially* when they perceive a threat to planetary security! Their job is to be paranoid, and we were Golden. They refused to accept our protestations of innocence, and grilled us relentlessly for answers we didn't have while we convulsed by the numbers.

"You're accusing a prominent member of the Chamber Of Ancients of attempted mass murder!" one lead Inspector said indignantly when the subject of Z'keBalf came up.

"We have no evidence of poisoning!" the Receiving physich insisted. "Toxicology thus far has come back negative, and all these other people couldn't have been poisoned as well."

The Inspector rounded on him. "So what is it, then?"

"We have no idea beyond the absence of any known toxins. It could be mass hysteria, or fatigue, or some earth disease..."

"The tests show no signs of infection," one of the other physichs objected.

"And why are they all convulsing at once?" someone else asked.

"Perhaps it is psychosomatic?"

"Mass hysteria; it's the only diagnosis which fits."

"Or gas?"

"*bv'nunma*. They must have eaten some bad *bv'nunma*."

"Enough of this yammer!" the Inspector shouted. "We have a crisis here, and I need answers, not speculation!"

The Receiving physich got his tail in a knot in turn. "*We* are the medical authorities, and *we* will determine what the problem is in due course!"

"Well then *what is wrong with them?*"

"Um...we're not sure." The physich pondered me uncertainly. "It *could* be poison...something new..."

"Or mass hysteria," someone offered.

"I still say it's gas."

"NONE of you are leaving here until we get an answer!"

"That is uncalled for! We're doing everything we can!"

"An earth disease is our best bet."

"I say mass hysteria."

"We'll have to autopsy them, of course."

"NOT until we get answers!" the Inspector roared. "Until then they belong to us!"

"Your Ancestors!" the lead Fleet Intelligence investigator snarled. "This is a matter of planetary security! *We're* in charge of them!"

"...proper medical protocol..."

"...*bv'nunma*..."

"...more tests..."

"...some sodium bicarbonate..."

"Can we *please* deal with a crisis without this endless quibbling, for once?" I cried.

C'traBenla came waddling in just then clutching a small carry-bag, and halted in surprise when she saw us. "I'ei? What are you doing here?"

"...hurting..."

She winced as another spasm hit which had us all whimpering in pain. "Oh, really, I'ei, this is not funny," she grumbled. "Quit these stupid games and mal up."

"...gladly...dearest..." he managed through gritted teeth as she trundled toward the admitting station. He lay on his side, panting for breath as the latest convulsion passed, then he mumbled, "Now we know."

"What?" I asked.

"What more could go wrong."

"What? What is it?"

"We're...in labor."

"Labor!? How?"

"We're telepathically linked to her."

"You had to ask, didn't you?" M'tinDegan grumbled.

§

"This is preposterous!" The Receiving physich was incredulous at I'eiBida's diagnosis. "You're mals; mals don't go into labor!"

"We're..." My reply was interrupted when we heaved simultaneously with another contraction. "We're telepathically linked to his bondmate," I gasped as I waved a feeble gesture at I'eiBida, who stared glassy-eyed at the wall and gasped for breath. "She was admitted a little while ago."

"But...mals aren't equipped to deliver eggs!"

"Tell me *all* about it!"

"They're pregnant?" The Chamber Inspector exchanged surprised looks with his Fleet Intelligence counterpart. "This is going to be a *really* strange report."

"Whatever," I sighed.

§

230

More ambulances. The clinic activated their disaster protocol, the off-duty staff were called in, and the stream of arrivals was herded into the clinic cafeteria. More ambulances. Soon we overflowed the receiving area, spilling into the halls, the cafeteria, and even unused office space—all and sundry heaving by the numbers with a precision which would put any Sliv review to shame. The physichs were at a loss to grasp what was going on while the staff scrambled aimlessly about trying to help and a growing herd of onlookers and curious patients clogged the halls.

"We don't have time for this," H'rhAtor muttered between contractions. "We're *supposed* to be dealing with a strategic crisis..." His complaint was cut off as we all heaved with yet another contraction. "An-*cestors!*" He gasped for air and vented a string of steaming curses.

"You won't be dealing with anything like this!" I griped at him.

"That reminds me..." M'tinDegan staggered to his feet and headed unsteadily for the lobby.

"Where are you going?" the Receiving physich demanded. "You're in no shape to leave!"

"I...just need to make a phone call." He gestured at the telephones in the lobby. The physich reluctantly let him go.

§

And our trials went on. At least the stream of ambulances died away after delivering several more hands of 'Dark Grays', which was good since the clinic was on the verge of shutting down. Not that we benefitted: our collective labor continued relentlessly, and I was appalled at how painful it was. Several of the staff physichs were gathered in a knot arguing among themselves over what to do while the attendants did what little they could for us.

Our fellow sufferers threatened to inundate the clinic by then, heaving by the numbers and feeling miserable. What was worse, we were now well into second stage labor, with short, sharp contractions coming in rapid fire succession.

"This is all your fault, I'eiBida!" U'tdaPagrn swore.

"*Me?* What did I do?"

Another contraction hit, curling us all up in pain. "...You...LIFE...*BONDED*...with her!"

231

"And you impregnated her!" I grumbled.

"Hey...she's my bondmate..." His protest was interrupted by another contraction.

"You keep it zipped from now on!" H'rhAtor snarled after it passed. "You two are a threat to planetary security! Until we get this telepathic thing straightened out, you keep it tucked away permanently! You hear me, mister?"

"Yes...Aaaaahhhhh!...sir..." We all heaved again.

"It will be just our luck if the humans attack right now," I said after it passed.

"Well I wish they'd get it over with," H'rhAtor sighed.

Our collective stupor was disturbed by a beeping telephone. The desk assistant took it, listened for a moment, then passed it to the senior physich. "Yes, Ki-Eldest, he's here." A brief pause. "We're not sure how, but he appears to be in labor." There was a lengthy pause as H'rhAtor watched morosely. "Ah...no, Ki-Eldest. *He* is in labor. I can't explain it, but the contractions are very close together now."

H'rhAtor sagged on his bed pad. "He had to tell them that?" He gave I'eiBida a chilly look. "We'll never live this down, you know."

"Oy. Sir."

The physich listened for a long moment as his ears and tail sagged in dismay. Then he covered the mouthpiece and said to the charge attendant, "Whatever's causing this is rampaging through the fleet! The spaceport clinic is overwhelmed with 'Dark Grays', and the ships in orbit are in desperate straits."

"There go our orbital defenses!" H'rhAtor gave I'eiBida a bitter ear twitch. "You two have a great sense of timing, mister!"

"His sense of timing is what got us into this fix!" I groaned.

§

And so it went. The rest of that afternoon was a painful, chaotic blur as we endured wave after wave of contractions alternating with wave after wave of specialists called in to offer suggestions, or simply there to stick their snouts into this bizarre medical mystery. They ran every test they could imagine and thought up new ones so our woes were punctuated by needles and

232

catheters and tubes and monitor cables, to no avail. No one had a clue, and the opinions soon degenerated into bitter arguments over the symptoms, causes, and possible treatments. Someone even suggested, out loud, that we had been cursed by the human Elvis Worshipers!

If any good came of it, the competing herds of security types were finally satisfied that nothing sinister was involved, and went their merry ways as bemused as the rest of us. The *media*, however, loved us: regular programming was suspended, and every moment of our collective debacle was reported, analyzed, and commented on with all the fervor befitting *the* news spectacle of the season.

We labored on—literally—as mid day advanced into evening and then to night. The physichs debated, the media vultures commented, the medical staff tended us as best they could, while we simply endured. Then came the moment we had all been dreading: as one, we felt the sudden rush as C'traBenla's egg exited her body. We all heaved in unison, and since our mal bodies weren't designed to pass eggs, our nervous systems improvised: we defecated...and vomited...by the numbers. The smell was nauseating, which sent the hospital staff scrambling to our aid while the herd of curious onlookers stampeded in the other direction, but we were so relieved that none of us cared.

§

The aftermath of our collective misadventure was a disaster in itself. All of us—including over fifty 'Dark Grays' cluttering up the place by then—were exhausted, aching, and thoroughly fouled. Some were semi-conscious, while others stared at nothing and trembled. All of us were gasping in the fetid atmosphere which large fans and the frantic efforts of the staff were only beginning to dissipate.

"Oy, war couldn't be any worse than this," H'rhAtor sighed at last. Then he confronted I'eiBida. "*You* had to go and life-bond with her!"

"I should have stood on my tongue," I'eiBida moaned. "Three more days and I was on my way home. Earth service will do this to you."

"That doesn't *begin* to excuse you. I've got the fitting punishment for you, mister!"

I'eiBida stirred and looked at him vaguely. "Sir?"

"*You* will write the official report!"

"That's not fair! I'm on medical release!"

"Imagine my sympathy," I grumbled.

We lay there silently trying to collect our wits while the clinic staff mopped up the mess and started rinsing our clothes out. Right then our collective psychic aura was too numb to care any more; we were simply glad *this* crisis was past.

"It *is* over, isn't it?" U'tdaPagrn asked plaintively at last.

"Ancestors...I hope so," I sighed.

"Unless..." It seemed M'tinDegan was struck by a bizarre notion.

H'rhAtor looked at him in alarm. "What?"

"...I was wondering...if we'll be telepathically linked to the hatchling, too." That stirred up all sorts of alarm at the thought of who-knows-what new horrors, but he was clearly fascinated by the idea. "Imagine: experiencing hatching all over again. We don't remember that far back since the brains are still forming. It would be a unique experience." He got all glassy-eyed as he contemplated the prospect. "I shall have to write a paper on it."

"Fine," I grumbled. "We'll use it for your first diaper."

§

After a while, I'eiBida staggered to his feet and made his way gingerly and none too steadily to the cubicle where C'traBenla was recovering. M'tinDegan staggered along behind him, no doubt out of scientific curiosity, although this hardly seemed like the time. H'rhAtor and I exchanged dubious looks, and went gimping after them; why was beyond understanding.

C'traBenla still straddled the laying bench while the lone attendant spared from the crisis outside tended to her. "Are you all right, love?" I'eiBida asked her.

"Oh, that wasn't so bad." She seemed a bit groggy. "They gave me a shot, so there wasn't much discomfort."

"Those *hro'n'nad p'quas'tka* could have thought to give *us* those shots!" H'rhAtor swore.

"That would be the sensible thing to do," I muttered. "Which is why they didn't think of it."

"Well, the worst is over, love." I'eiBida nibbled her ear tenderly. "They'll probably release you tomorrow."

"I'ei...what is that *smell?*" She looked around vaguely and wrinkled her snout. "I'eiBida, you didn't *mess yourself,* did you?"

"What? Who, me? Don't be ridiculous."

She gave him a curious look. "Why are you so pallid, love? Were you worried about me? This is my third, you know; pretty routine."

*****

"Sometimes There's No Sense In Giving Up"
(Related by Learnéd K'deiTai)

It was early the next morning before the physichs agreed that we could leave the clinic. By that point the Receiving staff had cleaned up the worst of the mess we created and rinsed out our clothes, but the fresh pre-dawn air was like a gift from the Ancestors.

"No one will ever believe this," H'rhAtor grumbled as we tottered to the trolley station leaving a trail of damp footprints.

"Proving it happened won't be the problem, sir," I'eiBida muttered. "*Explaining* it will be the real challenge."

"Explaining it? Ancestors, I was there, and *I* don't believe it!"

According to fragmentary reports we received, *hundreds* of fleet personnel were affected—everyone who had been in the battle at the Dreamsingers' world, and were subsequently drawn into their psychic realm as they tried to heal us afterward. It knocked every ship in orbit out of commission, and left ground operations staggering. A hastily organized attempt to evacuate the casualties groundside multiplied the confusion, reducing the fleet to chaos. They were still trying to figure out what happened, we were told, and it would likely take days to get it sorted out. If the humans attacked right then, our fleet couldn't find their collective tails with both hands.

"Oy, just *think* of the paperwork!" I'eiBida moaned.

"It's no more than you deserve! I'll give you credit, mister: you have a talent for knotted tails."

"Do I ever." I'eiBida sighed in dismay. "This is what comes from being assigned to earth, you know." By then even he accepted the notion that he was somehow responsible for our latest fiasco, as unreasonable as that was. One had to know C'traBenla and experience how *unpredictable* life with her could be to really appreciate our mood.

The cool breeze picked up, and the chill of our damp clothes had us all slightly overheated. I, for one, ached from snout to tail, and the grim aura around us said the others felt it too. Right then we were collectively wrung out and disgusted.

"Ancestors, I could have *sworn* we left this sort of thing back on earth."

"It does bring back memories, doesn't it?" M'tinDegan sighed.

"Which brings us to Z'keBalf and his latest *er'trxxda l'fru'ng*." None of us were thrilled to recall our *other* fiasco-in-progress. "That *M'mendoch* stirred up a potential disaster. Things will be lively in the Chamber, unless I miss my guess."

"No argument here." I'eiBida turned to H'rhAtor. "What now, sir?"

"We've got a Righteous First-Finger crisis on our hands, thanks to that *un'tdar*," he said, grimly. "I'm headed straight to the spaceport to salvage what I can. You three cover the Chamber and keep me in the circle on what happens." He was silent for a bit as the brooding tension grew around us. "I just hope Admiral MacKenna is more sensible than Z'keBalf," he added at last. "Or we could be in big trouble."

§

But, of course, politics shall not be stayed, not even by the prospect of war and the entire fleet going through collective false labor. No sooner did we arrive at our grotto that morning, much the worse for wear, than we were summoned by Ancient Y'veNipbr to the Chamber.

The Chamber Of Ancients was buzzing with tension; we hardly needed our arcane powers to feel it in the air. The floor around the rostrum was crowded with small knots of Ancients arguing among themselves while staffers scurried here and there and the Chamber Wardens tried to keep things flowing smoothly. Even so, it was some time after we arrived before they were able to escort us to Ancient Y'veNipbr's section. She was in a feverish discussion with several Ancients when we arrived, and greeted us with a curt, distracted tail wave. We held discreetly back until they finished and went their various ways, and she was able to turn her attention to us.

"I heard what happened. Are you alright?"

"No, we are *not* alright," I grumbled. "I *refuse* to be alright."

"We'll manage, Ancient," I'eiBida said. "What's the situation here?"

"You may have had it easy," she growled. "There's going to be ears collected today if I have anything to say about it."

"Do you think they'll arrest Z'keBalf, Ancient?" I asked.

She hesitated, and her ears drooped in an uncertain posture. "By rights they should, and I intend to give it a try, but you don't realize how powerful he is." Now that I thought about it, I could feel her weariness and frustration. "Things were galloping all night around here. Z'keBalf is politicking up a storm to build support for his war with the humans, and he's gained a lot of ground. We've argued just as persuasively to send you to earth to try to patch things up with them, but we're fighting a strong headwind with the immediate threat of war." Her weariness turned more toward anguish and despair. "That fiasco with the fleet didn't help, either." She gave I'eiBida a sharp look. "What's the current situation?"

"We're recovering, more or less, but I understand the fleet is a long way from operational. H'rhAtor is in orbit trying to straighten things out."

"What an *unbelievable* mess. It's enough to drive one *er'trxxda* just thinking about it." After a moment, she gave him a curious look. "How is your bondmate?"

"Ah...she's fine, Ancient. She's recovering."

"I only hope we can," I sighed.

"Good. When you get the chance, please send C'tra my congratulations." We were distracted by the ringing of the gong to call the Chamber to order. "But for the moment we have a crisis to deal with, so let's gallop."

Ancient Z'keBalf walked by as we were sorting ourselves out, followed by N'detLeda and T'virDoma who favored us with their usual smug superiority, but moved on without speaking. L'datMparn followed up a moment later, to our surprise.

"What are you doing here?" I'eiBida demanded. "Eldest H'rhAtor ordered you arrested."

L'datMparn paused and gave him a surly ear twitch. "*Eldest* H'rhAtor needs to learn his limitations."

I'eiBida snorted in contempt. "Z'keBalf saved your tail, eh? Enjoy it while it lasts."

"Z'keBalf wouldn't bother," I grumbled. "Not after this monumental tail knot."

"Actually he would," M'tinDegan added with an aura of malicious pleasure. "This one surely knows much which would be better kept quiet. Z'keBalf wouldn't want to risk him selling out to save his own tail, so no doubt he plans to deal with his failure *privately*."

L'datMparn shuddered. "He wouldn't..."

I'eiBida caught M'tinDegan's drift and gave L'datMparn an ominous ear twitch. "Are you so sure? If I were you, *I'd* worry, but then you know him better than we do, so you can decide for yourself." L'datMparn turned pale and wandered off, and I'eiBida glanced at M'tinDegan. "You've been reading those human spy thrillers again, haven't you?"

"Interstellar studies can be put to *some* good, you know."

"Still, it's not promising," I said as we settled on the guest seat cushions around Y'veNipbr's section. "If Z'keBalf's influence is strong enough to derail the justice system on something this huge, just how much power does he have?"

I'eiBida nodded. "His tail is long enough to defy the 'Dark Grays', too. Not good."

§

H'rhAtor snapped out of a weary haze when alarms started ringing aboard the flagship. "Incoming ship to ship message, sir," the Duty Elder said. "It's a human!"

As if to confirm that report, a prerecorded message came over the general communications band. "This is the Alliance ship 'Henry Hudson', on diplomatic service, requesting permission to enter orbit."

"I'cc'vn, their timing couldn't be any worse," H'rhAtor muttered.

The Duty Elder gave him an uneasy glance. "What do you think, sir?"

H'rhAtor stared glumly at the telescope monitor and cursed his luck. The sudden appearance of a human ship was the last *thing he needed. Despite his best efforts—and he gnawed tails without mercy all morning—the orbital*

239

defenses were practically useless. Half the ships' compliments were still groundside waiting for shuttles, and those in orbit were shaken and confused. His own flagship, one of their new cruisers, was about as close to operational as it could be in their present state, but he wouldn't want to try anything ambitious. If any good could be said of this development, at least it was their diplomatic courier, and not the human fleet.

"They sent one of the standard inter-lingual messages; that's a hopeful sign, at least. They must have come to try to resolve this mess." Or so he hoped. But they were waiting for an answer, and Fleet Traffic Control was still back in its egg, so he was it for the moment. "Ask them what they're doing."

"Yes, sir." The Duty Elder's aura was relieved as he punched up a standard query message.

§

It took some doing to get the Chamber settled down, and despite the best efforts of the Most Ancient and the Chamber Wardens, the rumble of voices never settled much below a muted undertone. It was mid morning before things quieted enough to proceed, and what finally got the Chamber focussed was Z'keBalf defying all tradition to take the rostrum without being summoned.

"Arrogant *un'tdar*." Ancient Y'veNipbr was fuming. "He must think he owns this place."

"He does," one of her associates said. "Unless we can discredit him and break his war momentum."

"I'm not sure we can," she said, grimly.

"One can never tell," M'tinDegan told them. "Let us see what develops."

"I hope you're right," she muttered, but her aura was not optimistic as she headed for the rostrum.

Z'keBalf reared up and held his arms out to gesture the herd to silence. The spotlights and cameras focussed on him, the rumble of voices died away to a muted hum. "Ancients! We stand now on the brink of an unprecedented crisis which calls for prompt and stern action..."

"Objection!" Ancient Y'veNipbr yelled as she came down the aisle. "The Ancient is not recognized! I request time to speak."

"Eh?" The Most Ancient stirred and looked at her in confusion. "Ah...quite so. Quite so. Ancient Z'keBalf is not recognized...so, um...I suppose Ancient Y'veNipbr has the rostrum."

"Not that it will do you any good," Z'keBalf grumbled.

"We'll see." She directed her attention to the Chamber. "Ancients! As was said, we stand on the brink of an unprecedented crisis which calls for prompt and stern action. Ancient Z'keBalf has exceeded his proper authorities beyond all reason, and thus brought down upon us the threat of war with the humans. In order to correct this misconduct, and hopefully restore the peace, I move that Z'keBalf be rebuked!"

There was a surge in volume as the Chamber echoed with stunned amazement. Z'keBalf gave Y'veNipbr a contemptuous ear. "Nice try, but you cannot rebuke without cause, and my actions are entirely legal." He turned to the Chamber and raised his voice. "An Ancient may authorize space operations on his own initiative in an emergency. What's more, an Ancient may take steps on his own initiative to protect the Nest he represents. The humans pose a dire threat to my Nest and to our race at large, thus my actions are beyond rebuke. Look it up if you choose!"

The Most Ancient seemed dismayed, or perhaps simply confused. "This is...most irregular," he said at last. "I, for one, am at a loss for any precedent to this...so, ah...I suppose we must refer to the Prefect for a ruling."

The Eldest Prefect, sitting behind and to his left, was already digging through his ornate copies of *The Laws And Wisdom* searching for something to guide their decision.

§

"This is the 'Henry Hudson' to d'enchia Control. We are here on a priority diplomatic mission," the intruder responded to their challenge. "Requesting clearance to enter orbit. Over?"

"I was right," H'rhAtor said. "They want to talk rather than fight."

"Oy, that's good news, sir," the Duty Elder said, fervently.

"Indeed. Very well, clear them into orbit."

"Yes, sir." The Duty Elder keyed his comm channel. *"d'enchia Orbital Control to human ship 'Henry Hudson', you are cleared into orbit."*

"This is the 'Hudson', acknowledge."

§

The silence stretched out as the Eldest Prefect pawed frantically through *The Laws And Wisdom*. He was reputed to know all forty volumes word for word, but this was so unexpected that he had to look it up. He kept flipping back and forth through several volumes, pausing to scribble notes on occasion.

"What do you think?" I'eiBida whispered to M'tinDegan.

"I'm not expert on *Laws And Wisdom*, but I suspect Z'keBalf is right. He would never leave himself open like that in any case."

"Wonderful." We were all dismayed by the realization that this was our last chance to avert disaster, and Y'veNipbr's ploy looked to be unsuccessful.

Finally, after endless digging, the Eldest Prefect sighed, and handed his notes to the Most Ancient, who stared at them blearily. "A-hem," he said at last. "The Eldest Prefect has handed me his findings." He considered the notes for a bit longer. "It seems Ancient Z'keBalf is correct. His actions are legal."

There was a collective psychic groan from our group, matching the upwelling of dismay from the Chamber.

"The motion to rebuke is refused."

§

H'rhAtor considered the distant human ship on his screen for some time, then recalled how quickly the combined fleets appeared at the Dreamsingers' world and launched their attack before the Black Sphere could respond. "All the same, send a general ears-up to the fleet. And the orbital defenses, too."

The Duty Elder gave him a nervous glance, but said nothing, and went to work on the comm channels.

§

"Now that we have these distractions cleared up," Z'keBalf said with a hostile glare at Ancient Y'veNipbr. "Let us get down to business." He turned his attention to the Chamber at large as Y'veNipbr trudged back to her dais. "No doubt you are all concerned with the news we received yesterday. Sadly, my intent to rid us of the menace posed by Captain Morgan went awry due to unforeseen complications. However, all is *not* lost, panicky tails notwithstanding. This misfortune poses us a great opportunity!"

"I tried," Y'veNipbr muttered when she reached her dais again.

"What happens now, Ancient?" I'eiBida asked.

"Now we go to war with the humans."

The television cameras closed in on Z'keBalf until his snout filled the overhead monitors. The graph displayed under his image showed his words were being heard by a huge audience all over the planet.

"I have long stressed the danger the humans pose to us, and this Chamber has long failed to act in its own best interest. Now we have no choice. Due to unforeseen failings, we now face the prospect of war with the humans. But this is *not* a time for panic! This is the time when we must act decisively..."

"If it please the Chamber," a voice rang out. "We exercise our right to speak and to be heard."

We all turned in confusion to the herd of newcomers who stood in the main entrance. The cameras and spotlights shifted to them, throwing their close-up image on the monitors. It took me a moment to recognize Eldest W'exMinin, and another to realize the intruders wore the medallions of the Esteemed Circle of *f'vem'bttri'ghim* Great Nest. "Where did *they* come from?" I wondered.

"Interesting," U'tdaPagrn said as he studied the scene. "We may have a whole new political equation here."

There was a rumble from the Chamber gallery as W'exMinin lead them to the central rostrum *without* the formal approval of the Most Ancient. Z'keBalf seemed caught off guard for once, and watched silently as the Esteemed Circle surrounded him on the rostrum.

"It's a remand!" I'eiBida muttered in amazement. "They're going to rebuke him!"

He was right: the act of circling an accused like that is long tradition. The circle closed; the Council members facing inward with their tails held high. W'exMinin stepped to the center of the rostrum, gave Z'keBalf a chilly look, then turned to the Most Ancient.

"I stand before the Ancients as the Most Esteemed of *f'vem'bttri'ghim* Great Nest, and speak in behalf of the Esteemed Circle and the people of our Nest." W'exMinin paused and gave Z'keBalf another chilly look. "It has come to our attention that our representative, Z'keBalf (we all noted the absence of the 'Ancient' honorific) has overstepped his authorities in a most alarming manner. Thus we come to petition the Chamber to correct this problem."

Then I remembered a certain phone call, and glanced suspiciously at M'tinDegan, who gave me a wholly innocent ear twitch although I could feel his duplicity as clearly as if he shouted it at me. *'You didn't...'* I thought. He offered a little smile and an air of guilty pleasure which should have been obvious to everyone.

§

H'rhAtor studied the human ship as it maneuvered to make another burn which would put them into orbit. As hopeful as he was that the crisis would be resolved, some unexplainable tension nagged at him. Something was not right, but what? The human courier's arrival seemed hopeful...but there was an undercurrent of angst...of worry and confusion. Something about this situation? Or something from the others down there in the World Nest? Whatever it was, he couldn't ignore it.

"Keep your ears up," he told the Duty Elder.

§

The rumble of voices, which welled up with the Esteemed Council's entrance, faded away again, and W'exMinin went on.

"Despite the contentions which plague this Chamber these days, The one thing we can agree on is that starting an interstellar war is far beyond the authority of any one Ancient. And yet, that

244

appears to be exactly what happened, as stated by his own admission just now."

"Remind me again about academic detachment," I'eiBida whispered to M'tindegan. "I seem to have overlooked something."

"Interstellar studies can be put to *some* good, you know."

"Z'keBalf has endangered our entire civilization, and yet I fear his power in this Chamber is great enough that he thinks himself above reproof." W'exMinin gave Z'keBalf another icy look. "He is mistaken. As Z'keBalf has ceased to represent the best interest of *f'vem'bttri'ghim* Great Nest, we, the Esteemed Circle, have voted to remove him as our representative...and to appoint Learnéd K'deiTai, sen V'ran, another distinguished member of our nest, to serve in his place."

M'tinDegan's ears shot up in a bemused expression. "Hmmm, *that's* interesting," he mumbled.

It took a moment to sink in, and when it did, I about wet myself in dismay. "B-b-but..."

"We are confident *Ancient* K'deiTai will serve the interest of his Great Nest with distinction," W'exMinin added.

§

The human ship's main engine fired, and as they watched, its position shifted slowly on their view screen. "I only hope our diplomats can satisfy them," H'rhAtor said. "They have every reason to be upset with us."

"They can give whoever did that to them with my blessing, sir," the Duty Elder said. "What they did was just plain hro'n'nad.*"*

*"*hro'n'nad *may be a crime when this is all over."*

"I hope so, sir. It would be a colossal waste of a crisis otherwise."

H'rhAtor couldn't help but agree. Obviously the changes wrought by their meeting the humans had some way to go yet, and this incident showed how much was left to do and how little time they had to do it. As much as he respected Admiral MacKenna, and believed they had an understanding on war and peace, he knew there was only so much the human could do to keep his leaders at bay.

For that matter, there was only so much he, MacKenna, could accept. Time was running out for all of them, after seven long years since the first contact. If anything positive came from this crisis, perhaps the Chamber would quit standing on their tails...

The Duty Elder was distracted by the image on his view screen. The human ship was still accelerating, their engine's heat bloom a bright shaft of light in the false color display. "Their burn is going on a long time..." he muttered. He fiddled with his controls, then turned to H'rhAtor. "They've exceeded burn time, sir. They'll be pushed back out..."

"This is the 'Hudson'! We've had a systems malfunction!"

"Ancestors..." The Duty Elder stared at the view screen in confusion, then keyed his comm circuit. "d'enchia Control to 'Henry Hudson', please repeat your message."

"We can't shut down our main engine! We have a computer malfunction! We're declaring an emergency! Do you copy, d'enchia control?"

"T'cc'vn," H'rhAtor said. "Plot their trajectory, fast!"

The Duty Elder punched the data into his console with lightning speed. "Ah...they're outbound, sir. They won't hit the atmosphere...and they don't seem to be on a collision course with anyone. I'll need more data for a firm trajectory."

That was some relief, at any rate. "Check the ready force. See if any of them can intercept them."

The comm system crackled with static. "d'enchia Control! This is the 'Hudson'! Do you copy our emergency?"

"d'enchia Control to 'Henry Hudson', we copy your emergency. We're working on it."

H'rhAtor studied the view screen unhappily. The last thing they needed was for the humans to lose a ship for any reason. *"I don't know what we can do. Hopefully one of our ships can reach them to render aid."*

"If they can get their drive shut down, sir." The Duty Elder was moving at a frantic pace to plot the human's trajectory while alerting various ships to see who could go after them.

§

"They can't do that!"   I was appalled by W'exMinin's announcement, and turned to the others in dismay thinking they might offer some help.

"Better you than Z'keBalf," Y'veNipbr snapped. It didn't take a telepath to see she was shaken by this turn of events.   "Most Ancient!" she cried over the hubbub. "*X'vem'ni'ngVnnn* Great Nest endorses this request!" There was a chorus of agreement over the general uproar, and hundreds of the blue lights came on all at once while many of Z'keBalf's faction doused their yellow lights.

"But...but...why me? What did I do to deserve this?"

Ancient Y'veNipbr gave me a sharp look.   "You're from *f'vem'bttri'ghim* Great Nest, aren't you?"

"W-well...yes...but..."

"No buts! We face the greatest crisis in our history, and this is no time for half measures. They need you, and you're perfect for the role, so stiffen your tail!"

"Thanks for nothing," I groaned.   Then I noticed M'tinDegan watching in obvious amusement. "You! You did this to me!"

"What? Me?"

"Don't deny it! I saw you go out to make that phone call. *How* could you bite my tail like this? I thought you were my friend!"

"Honestly, I didn't expect that part."

"Really, K'deiTai, why all this *r'vebbe*?" I'eiBida chided me.

"This is the opportunity of a lifetime, and a chance to make a lasting contribution to our people," M'tinDegan added.

"No thanks to you!" I flopped on my seat cushion in a total funk, disgusted with the lot of them.

§

"Sir?   What's that?"   The Duty Elder pointed at the screen. "I thought I saw something."

"What?"   H'rhAtor pondered the screen for a long moment, not sure what he was looking for. He was about to

turn away when he caught a faint flicker of light right where the Duty Elder pointed. "What is it?"

"...Unknown, sir," the Duty Elder said reluctantly. "But it's right where the human ship reported their emergency."

The faint light flickered again...like a missile's maneuvering jets... An ugly suspicion began growing in H'rhAtor's mind, fueled by the mental chaos around him, that Admiral MacKenna hadn't waited for explanations after all... "Focus in on that, whatever it is. Fast!"

§

The Most Ancient clambered to his feet and raised his arms to quiet the pandemonium. It took some doing, aided by the Chamber Wardens, to restore order. Finally, after the noise level dropped to a point where he could be heard, the Most Ancient spoke. "This is a most remarkable turn of events; most remarkable indeed. I for one cannot recall seeing the like in all my years in this Chamber."

"Brilliant," I grumbled. "With such a grasp of events, it's no wonder we're in such a fix."

"He's had worse days," Y'veNipbr said.

"While it appears Ancient Z'keBalf's actions may technically be legal, they are most irregular; I daresay extraordinary."

'Do you feel strangely agitated?' M'tinDegan thought.

'I'm not speaking to you!'

'Actually...yes, I do,' I'eiBida thought.

"To take an action which poses the prospect of war with the humans, despite the danger they may pose, treads on the tail of this revered Chamber. I cannot say it instills much confidence in me for Ancient Z'keBalf's sense of Chamber philosophy."

'What's happening? Why am I so upset?'

'If anything, its K'deiTai who should be upset.'

"If there is any one thing this Chamber and our people rely upon, it is our sense of the traditions and values which this body was founded on. Ancient Z'keBalf's act deviates from those traditions most alarmingly. Most alarmingly indeed."

'This is why they take forever to decide anything?' I'eiBida thought.

'Actually, they're galloping right along, for them,' M'tinDegan thought back.

"Get to it!" Y'veNipbr snarled.

The Most Ancient droned on. "And then we must take into consideration the appeal of the Esteemed Circle of *f'vem'bttri'ghim* Great Nest. Their wishes on representation cannot, in good conscience, be ignored."

'Oy.'

Ancient Z'keBalf stood motionless, his ears laid back in anger and dismay, as the Most Ancient said, "Some action must be taken, although I, for one, am at a loss for what that action might be."

"As if that's something new," Y'veNipbr said.

'I'm in no hurry.'

The Most Ancient looked around the vast Chamber, and for the life of me, I was certain he wondered where he was and how he got there. "The matter will be referred to the Inner Policy Circle in place," he said at last.

'Wonderful,' I'eiBida thought. *'He referred it to review circle again.'*

'With luck I'll die of old age before they make a decision,' I thought, bitterly.

The Inner Policy Circle left their seats, made their way through the crowd on the rostrum, and congregated in front of the Most Ancient. The microphones were cut off so we couldn't hear what they were saying, but from their gestures it was obviously a heated discussion.

'I have that feeling again...'

§

"What are they doing?" H'rhAtor muttered as he watched the view screen now at its maximum setting. The faint light came again, flickering fitfully against the blackness of space. He couldn't see what it was, but it certainly looked like a missile maneuvering for its attack run. The fleet comm channel in the background was buzzing as the ships and stations in orbit pulled themselves together. The wave of confusion and fear became overwhelming, drowning their focus in a sea of emotion.

249

"I don't like this, sir!" the Duty Elder said. "I recommend we go to Battle Quarters."

H'rhAtor studied the flickering light, trying to figure out what was going on, and trying to still his worse fears. But the tide of angst and fear was too great, made it too hard to think rationally. "Yes, go to Battle Quarters!" he snapped.

The Duty Elder hit the alarm buzzer; the rest of the command herd were already there, as fired up as H'rhAtor and the Duty Elder by the flood tide of emotions washing over them. The Weapons Elder didn't wait for instructions, but started a firing track as soon as his panel came on line.

§

"This is impossible!" I protested. "Didn't anyone think to ask me if I wanted this? What kind of society have we become if a hapless citizen can be dragged kicking and screaming into the government?"

"This is no time to *r'vebbe*!" Ancient Y'veNipbr lectured me in a hoarse whisper. "If anyone is qualified to represent *f'vem'bttri'ghim* Great Nest, its you; and right now your nest needs you! d'enchia needs you!"

"This will be the end of my Human Studies program! My Aide will never forgive me!"

"These are difficult times. Your Aide will have to bear up as the rest of us."

"This is *er'trxxda*!"

"What do you consider *er'trxxda* at a moment like this?"

"Ears up!" I'eiBida said. "They're breaking circle."

The Inner Policy Circle *was* breaking up and returning to their seats in fact. I cursed them bitterly for coming to such a prompt decision for once. They settled on their seat cushions, and the Most Ancient stood to address the Chamber as the spotlights and cameras focussed on him.

"After careful consideration, and taking into account the advice of several interested parties..." He paused to gaze vaguely around the cavernous chamber. "...The Inner Policy Circle concurs with the Esteemed Circle of *f'vem'bttri'ghim* Great Nest, and agrees Z'keBalf should be removed from his station."

Z'keBalf stood there for a long moment as if he couldn't believe what he heard while more of his faction's yellow lights went out one by one. Then he turned to W'exMinin, who gave him a dismissive ear twitch. Finally, he turned again, stepped off the rostrum, and vanished into the gloom.

"C'tra will love this," I'eiBida mumbled.

"So will a lot of people," Ancient Y'veNipbr said.

§

The faint light flickered again. "There is something there, sir!"

H'rhAtor was battered by a new wave of strong emotions pouring in from some unknown source; likely something going on down on the planet. His reaction was immediate and instinctive. "Alert the fleet! Lock onto whatever that is!" He turned and hit the button activating his command monitor: most of the ships and orbital defenses already showed Alert Quarters. The array started changing instantly as the fleet shifted to full battle status.

Weapons fiddled with his instruments, then turned to him. "What about the alien ship, sir? I have a firing solution, should we fire at them?"

"Forget them! They've done what they came for." The 'Hudson' was shrinking into the distance, careening in the general direction of the inner moon with their drive going full blast. "Get me a firing solution on whatever that is! Quickly!"

§

"Further," the Most Ancient went on, ponderously. "In view of his long record of service with the Arbiters, most especially with his success in negotiating the First Accord, and with his experience in general with the humans, we concur that K'deiTai, sen V'ran is eminently qualified to serve, and should be appointed as Ancient pro-tem for *f'vem'bttri'ghim* Great Nest, until such time as their Esteemed Circle can formally ratify his selection and present his credentials."

"I knew it!" I cried. "This is just my luck." I turned to the others in my anguish. "My Ancestors hate me! They must!"

251

"Stick your tail in it!" Ancient Y'veNipbr snapped. "This is a great honor. You should be proud they chose you."

"Think of it as the apex of your career," M'tinDegan said.

"Think of your duty to our people," Ancient Y'veNipbr said.

"Think of the prestige," I'eiBida said.

"*Think* of the paperwork! The politicking! The endless debates! What did I do to deserve this?"

"The Chamber summonses Learnéd K'deiTai, sen V'ran," the Prefect announced.

"There is no justice," I sobbed. There was nothing for it, so I turned and headed for the center of the Chamber. It was a long walk, and I could feel the entire gallery, thousands of people, watching my every step; no doubt snickering at my downfall and making snide remarks about me all the while. I probably would have been less troubled if I was going to my own execution. I reluctantly mounted the rostrum, passed through the Inner Circle, and stood in front of the Most Ancient waiting for doom to fall.

'I feel even more agitated,' M'tinDegan thought. *'Something's happening beyond this Chamber.'*

'H'rhAtor?'

"Learnéd K'deiTai, sen V'ran, the Esteemed Circle of *f'vem'bttri'ghim* Great Nest has put you forth to represent them as their Ancient," the Most Ancient intoned in that pompous, tedious ramble which made me want to scream. "The Inner Circle, having heard their petition and considered your qualifications, does concur with the Esteemed Circle. I ask you now, in behalf of the Chamber Of Ancients, if you will accept this charge and the duties and responsibilities which go with it?"

'Eldest? Can you hear me? Why doesn't he answer?'

'We better slip out and contact the spaceport.'

My friends were right, I reflected. This *was* a great honor and a rare recognition of everything I endured as our Arbiter to the humans. Few indeed are those chosen to govern our people, and it would guarantee me a place of honor in the histories. I *never* felt so miserable, but there was only one thing I could say.

"I...accept."

§

The ratings were still scrambling to activate the drive and defense systems. On his command monitor the position of the faint blip was starting to firm up as more and more ships homed in on it. H'rhAtor watched impassively, wondering what the humans were up to—they were clearly up to something—*and what he could do, if anything.*

"What are you planning, Brian?" he muttered. Despite all his training, despite the endless strategy sessions and practice drills, the reality was unnerving. He was about to do battle with the legendary Admiral MacKenna, who loomed large in their darkest fears.

More ships were coming on line, bringing their tactical sensors to bear on that faint, flickering light in the distance. Space was criss-crossed with laser beams as they sought to lock onto the target.

'It's one of their space mines' H'rhAtor thought. That was a dismaying revelation: those mines were equipped with stealth technology which their scans would have a hard time overcoming, and each mine was a target-seeking missile carrying a tactical nuclear weapon...

"Who are you targeting, Brian? Is it me?" The thought of dying, especially in so spectacular a manner didn't faze him so much as fill him with curiosity. What would it be like to witness such a fantastic weapon...

"The humans are using their capacitor, sir!" The human ship was accelerating rapidly, clearly drawing power from their mass polarizer.

"We have a firing solution, sir!" Weapons yelled...

...There was a brief, blinding flash on the viewscreens before they went blank, and the control circle erupted with sparks and smoke and loud arcing sounds...

§

And then, just as the Most Ancient was about to pronounce sentence on me, *just* when I thought things *couldn't* get any worse, the lights went out...

*****

253

"Short, Sweet, And To The Point"
(Related by Learnéd M'tinDegan)

We all hesitated in surprise when the lights went out. In one stroke, the vast Chamber was plunged into near darkness; only the faint light coming through the open entrance allowed us to see anything. Our surprise slowly turned to perplexity, then to rising fear as the power failed to come back. Then, after what seemed forever, the battery powered emergency lighting came on.

"Not good," I'eiBida muttered.

It certainly was ominous. The emergency lighting meant that the backup generators had also failed.

"Ancients!" Y'veNipbr called out in the gloom. "Since we seem to be having technical problems, I recommend we adjourn for the time being."

Parliamentary procedure was forgotten: no one bothered to endorse her motion as the stampede began. The Ancients left the stands, herded by the Chamber Wardens and staff, and made a hurried but orderly rush for the door. Thinking back on it later, I realize we were witnessing something monumental: for only the third time in it's two hundred and seventy-six year history, the Chamber Of Ancients was being evacuated. But then there were a number of history-making events that day. My nerves still haven't quite gotten over it.

§

We ran into the duty watch from our grotto outside as he was hurrying in, and managed to fight our way to him as we were swept along by the rush. "What's going on?" I asked. "What happened to the power?"

"I don't know, sir, but this was no accident," he shouted over the noise. "The telephones and teletypes in our grotto are out. So is the internet. Something big is happening."

The tension in the Chamber blossomed into full-blown fear as we were carried down the broad ceremonial corridor by a growing stampede. The main entrance isn't *nearly* as grand as it seems when ten thousand or more stumbled toward the subdued light from the art glass windows. How we managed to keep our feet was beyond me, but we didn't dare go down in the growing rush. Finally, somewhat the worse for wear, we spilled out onto the plaza.

"Ancestors! What is *wrong* with these people?" K'deiTai grumbled as he tried to straighten his suit. "We could have been trampled."

"The whole nest is without power!" I'eiBida was looking around at the urbanscape beyond the plaza. There were no traffic lights to be seen anywhere, the gaudy displays of the *v'vR gh'vadja* district were silent and dark, and a string of trolley cars was halted a few hundred paces distant, its passengers and operator milling around it in confusion.

"I don't understand," K'deiTai complained. "Aren't the trolleys on their own power supply?"

"They are," I'eiBida said, grimly. "So are the phones and teletypes, but everything is out."

L'datMparn came blundering up. "What's wrong with the power supply?"

"I..." I'eiBida paled. "...think I know. He turned to the Most Ancient, who happened to be passing nearby. "Sir! We need to get the Ancients to safety, fast!"

The Most Ancient faltered, and studied him in confusion. "Why? What's wrong?"

"Unless I miss my guess, this is some move by the humans!"

"The humans? Why do you think that?"

"It's the only explanation which makes sense, and..."

"Is that an airplane?" L'datMparn pointed to a distant speck descending toward us.

I'eiBida studied it uncertainly. "Its a shuttle!"

"Its not one of ours. The humans are invading us!"

"I'eiBida?"

"Don't be ridiculous. The logistics for that are impossible; I would know."

"Well...then it must be some sort of raid!" L'datMparn was in a near *r'vebbe*. "They must intend to capture the Ancients!"

I'eiBida gave him a contemptuous snort. "Good. Here's your chance to die heroically in the war you started!"

255

L'datMparn's protest was cut off as the shuttle flared and its engines roared as it touched down at the end of the plaza. Those human shuttle pilots were good: they managed to steer between the rows of ornate trees and avoid the fountains by the *narrowest* of margins as they descended on us in a rush.

"What do we do?" Chamber Warden Q'brnVen asked I'eiBida. "You're the defenders! We aren't equipped for fighting alien invasions!"

"Well here's your chance to broaden your job skills!" I'eiBida yelled. "Get them back inside, then get your Wardens to defensive positions! Fast!"

Q'brnVen shook his head in dismay. "You people lead weird lives."

"Weird? This is routine."

Nobody needed further instruction: the Ancients and their staffers scrambled back into the entrance, and we threw ourselves prone as the shuttle came to a shuddering halt at the last *possible* second. I suppose we all expected it to bristle with turrets and missile batteries, and for the plaza to erupt in gunfire, but once it came to a halt, there was no sound but for the fading whine of its engines. Finally that died out, and there was nothing but the popping of the shuttle's hull as it cooled.

"Now what?" I asked at last.

"No idea," I'eiBida said. "I'm new at this too." Despite his unsteady tone, he had taken charge and risen to the challenge without a moment's hesitation. That was strangely reassuring to all of us.

The silence stretched out as we lay there amid a rising aura of tension. At long last, there was a metallic 'clunk', and the shuttle's hatch opened slowly. Silence returned, and the only thing changed was the open hatch. The three of us finally collected our wits, and scuttled sideways to take shelter behind a planter. L'datMparn stared stupidly at us for a bit, then galvanized by our example, he crept toward the rear and vanished into the building.

We watched the shuttle for some time, but nothing happened except the occasional pop of cooling metal. "What are they waiting for?" K'deiTai muttered at last.

I'eiBida pondered the scene for a long while. "For us to make the next move, I guess."

"At least they have the sense not to take any unnecessary risks," I said.

I'eiBida glanced at me. "Yes, he would." I felt his confusion change to a rising sense of optimism as he clambered to his feet and headed for the hatch. Our herd instinct is strongest in moments of crisis: K'deiTai and I followed him without stopping to think about it.

Up close, the human shuttle was enormous, towering over us like a weathered gray wall. I'eiBida stopped a few paces from the hatch, then advanced and peered in cautiously.

"Admiral?"

"Good to see you, mister." Admiral MacKenna came to the hatch. "Hope you won't mind the grand entrance."

I'eiBida gave the swarm of Chamber Wardens around us a nervous glance. "With every respect, sir, I urge you not to make any sudden movements."

MacKenna looked over his head at the surrounding herd. "Yeah, I kind of figured on that."

"May I ask your intentions, sir?"

"I came here to have a little talk with your leaders. After that, we'll see what happens."

That left I'eiBida perplexed. "Um...yes, Admiral."

He backed out of the hatch to allow the Admiral to exit. MacKenna paused in the hatchway for a bit to look around, then stepped down onto the plaza, followed by Captain Rostokovich, Lieutenant Night Eagle, and three other Space Marines who formed a loose perimeter.

"Is H'rhAtor here?" MacKenna asked.

"No, sir. He's in orbit with the fleet."

"I'd hoped he was available. Glad you could be here at least, mister."

"Ah...welcome to d'enchia, Admiral," I said.

He turned and considered me for a long moment. "M'tinDegan, isn't it? The Sociologist?"

"Yes, Admiral."

He nodded. "Good. We may need you in the next few hours." Then he glanced at K'deiTai. "Arbiter K'deiTai, right?"

"Ah...yes, Admiral. For the time being, anyway."

"Excellent. We've got most of the 'A Team' here." He glanced at I'eiBida. "Which reminds me, is that wife of yours around?"

"Um...no, sir. She's...ah...recovering from labor." We all winced at being reminded of that misadventure.

"She is, huh? Good. And congratulations, by the way."

"Thank you. So...what happens now, sir?"

MacKenna gave the Chamber Wardens surrounding us an uneasy look. More of them were arriving by the moment, and a trickle of the nest's Peace Wardens and some defenders were starting to take positions around the plaza as well. We could all feel the tension and confusion in the air. One false move could set off a barrage of panicky shooting. "Lead the way, mister, and we'll find out."

§

Despite the Admiral's wishes, I'eiBida had him remain there while he cajoled the Chamber Wardens into herding the Ancients back into the Chamber. The news that the human Admiral wanted to address the Ancients after apparently neutralizing the planet's defenses left them confused and apprehensive. It was like herding hatchlings: many of them simply vanished into the distance, while the rest milled about in panicky disorder.

MacKenna and Ivan stood watching near the shuttle while Night Eagle and his Marines formed a loose perimeter around us. "Is hard to believe, sir," Ivan muttered. "You have complete initiative. We may pull this off yet."

"Yeah, taking the psychological high ground is half the battle."

"Something I will remember, sir." He turned his attention to us. "It is good to see you again, my friends. I wish it was in happier circumstances."

"If we all get through this with our tails, it will be happy indeed," I'eiBida grumbled.

"If so, then we must celebrate. You show us best restaurant, I will buy."

"Hell, I'll chip in for that," MacKenna added.

While they were talking, Ancient Y'veNipbr approached with a few of her faction in tow and hovered nearby, clearly wanting to meet the Admiral. I'eiBida noticed her, and gestured them forward. "Ah...sir, I have the honor to introduce you to Ancient Y'veNipbr, one of the leading advocates in the Chamber for good relations with you humans."

MacKenna gave her a small bow. "My pleasure, Ancient."

"This is big day, much to do, much talk," she said carefully. "My human language no perfect. Ancient K'deiTai answer you questions." K'deiTai sighed and shook his head in despair.

The Admiral gave K'deiTai a curious glance. "Your Swiss is quite good, madam. In any case, this is not the time for formal negotiations, so please feel free to speak your mind."

She looked him over carefully. "You name cause much *r'vebbe* in us. I hope we can...avoid fight."

"As do we. I intend to settle this peacefully if...ah...humanly possible."

W'exMinin and the Esteemed Circle came trotting over and confronted us. "What will happen now?" W'exMinin asked. He glanced nervously at the Admiral and Ivan, who were chatting with Y'veNipbr. "Are the humans going to attack?"

"He's here and wants to speak to the Ancients, so there's no immediate danger," K'deiTai told them. I didn't add that MacKenna's being here showed he felt *he* was in no immediate danger; they were unsettled enough.

"Then shouldn't you get going?" W'exMinin said, pointedly. "You're our Ancient; you need to be there."

"I never asked for this! Why pick on me?"

"Z'keBalf made a fine mess of things, and our Nest, *your* Nest, must have the best possible representation to handle this *p'quas'tka*. We need you."

"That's the story of my sad and sorry life." K'deiTai shook his head in despair. "I should have been an accountant."

§

Somehow it was done. Once everything was ready, a group of us including Ancient Y'veNipbr and her Aide led the Admiral and his escort to the Chamber...and ran into an unexpected check: the

259

Chamber Prefects, blocking the Ceremonial Entrance. "This is no time for heroics!" I'eiBida snapped at them. "The Admiral *must* speak to the Ancients!"

"He can't go in there looking like *that!*" The leading Prefect was scandalized. "He needs to change into a *proper* uniform!"

"I was right," Y'veNipbr's Aide sighed.

"What's wrong with my uniform?" MacKenna demanded when the situation was explained to him. He was wearing tan space utilities with his cap tilted belligerently down on his forehead.

"This simply won't do!" the leading Prefect said when I'eiBida translated the Admiral's challenge. "He needs to change into a dress uniform."

"*n'bna'nmn,*" Y'veNipbr grumbled. The Prefect bridled at that, but stood his ground.

"Tell him my nearest dress uniform is back on earth," MacKenna growled. "I came here to stop an interstellar war, but if he insists, I'll leave."

Faced with that daunting prospect, the leading Prefect wavered. "Well...have him button that button at least." He gestured at MacKenna's open collar. "And he needs to remove that...whatever that thing is on his head."

MacKenna buttoned his collar, and tucked his cap under his arm. "Happy?" he demanded. His tone needed no translation.

§

I swear our Ancestors should have given up on our entire race. We lead the Admiral into the chamber, he gawking at the sight all the while, and up on the raised rostrum. K'deiTai took over from there and mounted the rostrum along with him.

"Ah...if you please, Ancients, this is Admiral MacKenna, the leader of the human space fleet." He gave MacKenna a nervous glance, then added, "He wishes to address the Chamber, with your permission. I will translate."

There was an uneasy stir in the circle of Ancients around us, then the Most Ancient gestured to the Chamber Prefect, who took one of the small candles from their box and stuck it in the ornate holder bolted to the rostrum. He was about to light it when the Most Ancient halted him.

The Admiral eyed the candle curiously. "The tradition is that one may speak for as long as the candle burns," K'deiTai told him. "The unlit candle means you have unlimited time to speak."

"So?" MacKenna mused on the candle for a moment. "That's something our Parliament could use. Tell him to light it."

"But..."

"What I have to say won't take long."

K'deiTai gestured to the Prefect, who gave the Most Ancient a confused look, then reluctantly lit the candle. The small flame cast a warm glow on MacKenna's snout, highlighting him against the dim blue emergency lights.

"Ever since we first met, the big problem between us has been one of trust," he began. "We got off to a bad start when the 'Marco Polo' and your scout ship were wrecked by that natural phenomenon."

He paused for a moment as K'deiTai translated. At least the backup sound system was still in service. That, and the Chamber's flawless acoustics carried his words throughout the vast dome.

"Everyone assumed it was a deliberate act, and even after we learned the truth, despite best efforts all round, we've never been able to bridge the gap. This incident shows what will inevitably happen if we can't find it within ourselves to trust each other."

Further translation. There was a rising murmur from the assembly.

"I can't blame you for being afraid of us." MacKenna paused and surveyed the ranks of Ancients around him. "Our history doesn't inspire confidence in our good intentions, that's for damned sure. If we're to end this impasse, we all have to make a breakthrough in trusting each other, and the only way that will happen is to lay our cards down."

K'deiTai turned to him in confusion. "Lay your cards...?"

"We need to provide proof," MacKenna muttered to him.

"Oh." K'deiTai translated (loosely), and the Admiral went on.

"A little while ago, we detonated a high-yield thermonuclear device in low orbit. The electromagnetic pulse knocked out power and communications over much of this world...*and* (he paused for emphasis) it knocked out your orbital defenses."

261

That created an ominous rumble which echoed off the high domed ceiling. The Admiral had to raise his voice to be heard. "Right now we have your fleet under our sights." The herd rumble died abruptly, and he was able to continue. "By our count, most of your modern fleet are in orbit; their systems are down, as are those of your orbital defenses. We can blow the entire lot away at leisure, and then follow up by pounding this planet flat. After that, it will be a simple matter to wait until your ships return one by one, and pick them off. Within a few months, your entire fleet will be destroyed, after which we can do as we please with you."

The herd rumble swelled up again, with a panicky undertone to it. MacKenna was forced to hold his arms up in a gesture for silence, although it took some time before he could continue.

"We have you by your clappers; all we have to do is give a sharp yank, and its all over." (That took some doing to translate, and K'deiTai struggled to provide a version fit for public consumption.)

"But we won't," MacKenna went on after a bit, speaking to a tense silence. "The big problem has always been one of trust: well we have a saying, 'put up, or shut up'. That's exactly what we're doing. You stand defeated and defenseless...but we won't attack. Instead, we're going to withdraw and return to our space when we could crush you and end any threat you might pose to us forever. If this doesn't prove our good intentions, then there's no hope for any of us."

With that, he nodded to the Chamber Prefect, turned and walked out, leaving us standing there dumbfounded.

§

The Admiral ordered his shuttle to take off a short time later to retrieve Eldest H'rhAtor. Once it left, he settled on the lip of a planter and leaned against its small tree. "I'll be *so* damn glad when this is all over," he sighed.

"Unless I'm mistaken, sir, it pretty much is," I'eiBida said.

"Except for the histrionics," I added. "The Chamber Of Ancients is notable for their squabbling."

K'deiTai gave me a sour look. "You've seen the Alliance Parliament in action: how can you say that?"

262

He had a point, although it was hard to say which was worse. Since there was nothing much to do at the moment, we settled in around the planter to soothe our jangled nerves and await developments.

"Is beautiful city, sir," Ivan said as he examined the surroundings. "Is exotic. Ic'nichi have lovely architecture."

"They do." MacKenna looked around. "Sort of reminds me of the Taj Mahal. Did you ever see pictures of it?"

"*Nyet*, sir. Maybe I visit it some day."

"You can't." MacKenna turned somber at the memory. "It's not there any more."

"The Collapse, sir?"

"Yeah." He brooded for a bit. "I hope we don't see that horror repeated here. I'd hate to have that on my conscience."

"*Da*, sir."

There was a commotion on the perimeter, and I caught sight of a familiar human figure towering over the ranks of Chamber Wardens. "I'eiBida! It's Pierre Roubidoux."

I'eiBida reared up to scan where I pointed. "It is! What is *he* doing here?" He trotted away, and returned a bit later with Pierre in tow.

"Um...good day, Admiral..."

"I hope so, mister."

"...we saw your shuttle come down, so the Ambassador sent me to contact you if possible."

"Yeah, Bertrum is a good man, on the ball. How are things at the embassy?"

"Confused. Tense. The Ic'nichi seem disorganized, so there does not appear to be any danger for now."

"There won't be if we can keep ahead of the curve on this."

"I will help in any way I can, sir."

While they were talking, Ancient Y'veNipbr returned with a few of her faction in tow. Pierre noticed her, and gestured them forward. "Ah...sir, I have the honor to introduce you to Ancient Y'veNipbr, one of the leading advocates in the Chamber for good relations with us."

MacKenna clambered to his feet. "Yes, we've met."

263

"This is big day, much to do, much talk," she said carefully. "You cause much *r'vebbe*, Admiral, but I know it could be far worse."

"I hope it won't get any worse. I regret having to do this, but we had no choice."

"I give order Z'keBalf and L'datMparn arrest." She gave us a sardonic ear twitch. "This time they *stay* arrest."

"Good. What will you do with them?"

"Is our concern, Admiral, but be sure we make good any com...plaint of your Alliance." She offered a perplexed ear twitch. "You want mercy for what they do?"

"You can string 'em up by their plums for all I care," MacKenna said, harshly. "We've endured far too many of their sort over the years. Your best bet is to convince the Alliance their kind won't be a problem here."

Y'veNipbr nodded. "Indeed, we do no want their kind here."

"Then I'd say we're on course to settle this thing."

She pondered those words for a long time, then, "What we do now, Admiral?"

"We wait until H'rhAtor arrives, then we'll see."

§

Eldest H'rhAtor was thoroughly shaken when they landed early that afternoon. He climbed unsteadily out of the human shuttle, and took in the chaotic scene. The plaza was surrounded by a solid cordon of 'Grays' and Peace Wardens, with crews from the few television services who were back in commission scattered among a nervous throng of Ancients. Admiral MacKenna and our handful waited in a large open area near the entrance.

"Hello Brian," he said when they confronted each other. "Please forgive me, but under the circumstances I cannot say I am pleased to see you again."

"Understandable," MacKenna said, softly. "How are things up there?"

H'rhAtor sagged visibly, and his ears twitched in dismay. "Our intelligence was right about you: you have an uncanny gift for knotting your opponent's tail."

"Survive as long as I have, and it gets to be second nature."

264

"Your...weapon...burned out most of the systems on our ships, and most of the orbital defenses. I'm not sure how long it will take to get them working again, but I suspect your fleet will not allow that to happen."

"It had to be done. We needed to short-circuit this thing before it turned into a full-blown war."

"Thankfully you chose that course, even if you did take an appalling risk jumping in so close to the planet."

"You can thank a young ensign on the 'Marco Polo'. We'll be seeing more of him in the future."

"But how did you know it would work?"

"I figured this wasn't anything your government would do, so it had to be the act of a radical faction, and that you'd be appalled by it. I gambled you would ring the planet with your fleet, but that you would allow our courier in, so we used it to launch a surprise move."

H'rhAtor gave him a bleak ear twitch. "Actually, we didn't learn about the attack until a few days ago. You caught us just as part of our fleet rotated in to be relieved by the rest."

MacKenna was surprised. "How could you not know about something like this?"

H'rhAtor sighed. "It's a long-standing tradition: the Chamber can authorize space activities without the approval of the fleet. We're so new that the lines of authority haven't been cemented yet."

"One hopes that's a tradition you'll discard soon."

H'rhAtor glanced at Ancient Y'veNipbr, hovering nearby. "Indeed, we shall. But how could you be sure we weren't behind the attack?"

MacKenna looked him in the eye. "I trusted in your good intentions."

"So what are your intentions, Brian?" H'rhAtor asked hollowly. "We are defenseless. Is there a way we can avoid bloodshed?"

"There is." MacKenna gave him a grim look. "We can remember something we agreed to some time back during the late war. As you put it, we should 'remember that we serve our people'. There's no sense in our two races fighting a war now or at any other time. If we're to avoid it, we need to convince our respective governments to lighten up and trust each other."

"I only hope we can."

"In my experience, the true test of a military leader is to convince his superiors to end a needless fight."

"An interesting perspective."

"I made a little speech to your Ancients earlier, but it'll take more than that. They'll need to be sold on the idea, and as nervous as they are, that will take some selling. If anyone can, it'd be you. So where do we go from here?"

H'rhAtor gave him a searching look. "Since you have us at your mercy, that is for you to say."

"Our cards are on the table. Time for you to show your hand."

"Show my...? Oh." H'rhAtor sighed, and glanced at the anxious herd of Ancients hovering around them. "As you said, Brian, we serve our people." He extended his hand—the human gesture—as the television cameras focussed in. "We have a battle to fight, but not with each other."

MacKenna nodded, and took his hand in turn.

§

It was early evening before the near-panic in the Chamber was subdued. Small knots of Ancients were gathered on the plaza in a hundred lively debates, while others gawked at the shuttle, or watched the Admiral and H'rhAtor as they chatted about old times. The lights came on shortly before dusk, and we could see patches of lights reappearing across the nest as the utility crews worked to restore power.

"This is my kind of war," MacKenna grunted as he surveyed the scene. "Only two shots fired, and no real damage done on either side."

"How did you do it, Brian?" H'rhAtor asked. "If it wouldn't be revealing secrets."

MacKenna considered him somberly. "I figured you'd all be on edge after that attack, so we used it as the basis for a surprise move. I had our people wrap a high yield nuke with stealth camouflage, and added a strobe light to it. We hot-wired its arming circuitry to fire when it detected a certain signal strength of

266

your tracking lasers, so it would go off when most of your systems were trained on it. Your own paranoia assured you would use everything you had to try to knock it down: the EMP pulse did the rest."

"Clever: you turned our own anxiety against us. So it wasn't a new secret weapon after all?"

"Off-the-shelf hardware, all of it."

H'rhAtor reflected a time as we watched more street lights come on in the distance. The sky faded to a lovely orange and gray, and the breeze died down. The temperature was dropping, and we could tell it might rain later. For now at least the Universe was deceptively peaceful.

"You could just as easily have dropped it on the World Nest," he said, hollowly. "Thank you."

MacKenna gave him a hard look. "You've seen Singapore: you know I would never do that."

'I'eiBida?'

We all twitched in surprise at the unexpected mental contact. "What was that?" MacKenna asked as he glanced around.

"My bondmate, sir," I'eiBida said. *'I'm here, love. How are you?'*

"You can hear each other too?"

"Yes, Admiral," I said.

'I'm fine, love. You should see it: its the most beautiful egg!' We could all hear C'traBenla's thoughts clearly, and feel her ecstatic mood. *'The Egg Testers have finally cleared it, and they'll take it to the crèche soon. You need to hurry if you want to see it.'*

'I can't right now, love. We're in a bit of a crisis.'

'Was that why the power went out? What happened?'

I'eiBida gave the two leaders a harassed glance. *'Ah...we fought a war with the humans. It's over now.'*

We all felt her perplexity. *'We did?'*

'Thankfully the Admiral defeated us with one of his clever maneuvers. Its finished, and there was only minor damage which is mostly repaired by now.'

We could all tell it went right over her head. *'He did? Please give him my regards, and invite him over for dinner some time.'*

267

'Yes, love.'

'And what was all that in the Receiving ward earlier? Were you really in labor?'

I'eiBida gave MacKenna another embarrassed glance. *'Ah...we were were telepathically linked to you, love. We felt the labor contractions as you did.'*

MacKenna's eye ridges shot up, and he broke into a big grin. "You all went through labor *with* her?"

"Oy, did we ever," H'rhAtor groaned.

'It wasn't too painful, was it? You mals don't appreciate what we fems go through at times.'

'We're fine, love.'

'I saw Eldest H'rhAtor there, is he all right?'

'He's fine, love.'

MacKenna looked at H'rhAtor and laughed out loud. "I dare you to put *that* in your memoirs!"

"I'll *have* to get *that* classified as First Secret," H'rhAtor grumbled.

'Please be sure to invite him and M'tinDegan to celebrate, and K'deiTai too, I suppose.' K'deiTai offered a sour ear twitch, but managed to keep his thoughts to himself. *'And we must invite Pierre and Jeanette as well...'*

'This really isn't the time, love.'

'But we need to celebrate! I miss our egg already.'

"Great," I'eiBida said. "Her Possession Syndrome will be worse than ever."

'I can't help my maternal feelings!'

'I know, love,' he thought hastily. *'Look...things are really unsettled right now. I'll come to see you as soon as possible.'*

'Well, if you have to. But bring some bv'nunma *with you. The food here is terrible!'*

I'eiBida sighed. *'Of course, love.'*

"Un-friggin'-believable!" MacKenna said after her presence faded. "Nothing fazes her, does it?"

"She simply doesn't let little things like interstellar wars distract her," I told him.

MacKenna grinned and shook his head. "Gawd, I envy her."

But then he turned serious. "I see you folks are far more into this telepathy than we are. So how bad is it?"

"Its becoming a major problem," I said. Now that he mentioned it, I could sense the muted presence of the hundreds who were affected, like the low murmur of a crowd in the background. "Her labor pains crippled the fleet. Everyone who was at the Dreamsingers' world is affected."

"Yeah, us too. And my guess is it will get worse, soon. Any idea how far this will go?"

"Learnéd N'detLeda thinks we will eventually fuse into a common group mind. I can't imagine what it would be like, and I'm not anxious to find out." The aura around us was tinged with primal fear. Even the Admiral felt it.

"I don't see how we can function like this," H'rhAtor said. "At this rate, it will be a wonder if we don't all go *er'trxxda*."

"Yeah, a very real prospect." The Admiral was radiating his own unease: I wondered if we were seeing the start of the two races fusing together mentally.

"I wish we never heard of that J J Ballas! You humans can keep him, as far as I'm concerned."

"He meant well, I suppose. Still..." MacKenna hunched his shoulders in a forlorn gesture. "As we say, 'the road to hell is paved with good intentions'."

"It is that." H'rhAtor's ears sagged. "What can we do? I, for one, do not wish to go back to the egg from all the voices in my head, to say nothing of having to give up my duties at a time like this."

MacKenna shook his head. We could all feel his sense of despair and a rising hint of panic. "Damned if I know. Maybe the head-shrinkers can do something. But until we get some solid idea of how to cope with this, we all have to be considered unfit for duty."

H'rhAtor turned to him in surprise. "Head-shrinkers?" Then comprehension came. "Oh. One can but hope. You are right, Brian, none of us is fit for duty now."

"Yeah. Just when we're needed the most, too. I *hate* being the indispensable man."

"Indeed, galloping at the head of the herd is not a comfortable place. I don't see any answer to this dilemma. What can we do?"

"Has anyone thought to ask J J?" I wondered.

H'rhAtor and MacKenna both twitched in surprise. "I guess we have to," MacKenna said. "But it means another trip to their home world, and who knows *what* gyrations we'll have to go through to contact them."

"But...they gave us these powers to make it easier to communicate..." Acting on inspiration, I turned and addressed the area at large. "J J Ballas, are you there? We need to talk with you."

And there he was: a solid figure, as large as life, radiating a sense of amused pleasure. "Ah see you figurin' things out. Thas good. Thas mighty good."

There was a moment of awkward silence as we wondered what to say. I gradually realized the others were looking to me, as our race's sole xenosociologist, to deal with it. "Um...J J...we need to talk with you about these empathic powers. We appreciate the gesture, but we have to ask you to take them back."

"Well, that sho seems a might stand-offish." We could feel J J's perplexity. "Why wouldn't you want t' be connected?"

"Our species aren't equipped for telepathy. Both we and the humans evolved as we are over millions of years, and you can't just go and rewire our minds like that."

"Ah don' see why yo' wouldn't want t' have the ability. Don't seem natural, somehow."

"Not natural to you, certainly, but this is how we are."

"One thing I don't understand," MacKenna said. "From what I've seen, the Ic'nichi are far more along with this telepathy thing than we are. Why the difference?"

J J turned to him. "Thas' 'cause yo minds ain't quite the same as theirs; less flexible. It's harder fo' us t' change 'em."

MacKenna gave him a jaundiced look, then chuckled. "Yeah, we can be thick-headed at times."

"You say so, Boss!" J J chuckled.

"The problem, J J, is that changing us isn't working out," I said. "We have to ask you to put us back like we were."

"But youah so *alone!*" J J shook his head sadly, and we could feel his pity and mystification. "You-all lost in yo' own minds, ain't connected t' *nobody*. How can you live like that?"

"We are as ill-equipped for these powers as you would be if you didn't have them. I wonder if you can understand what it feels like to have something like this thrust upon you. It would be like you losing all your powers."

J J shuddered, and we felt a wave of primal fear and revulsion. "Lawd! That...sometimes happens t' one of us. Then they ain't nothin' we can do but put 'em out of they misery."

"You can see how we feel, then. This is more than just brain structure: our entire evolution, our histories, languages, cultures...they're all geared to non-telepathy. We really can't handle these abilities."

"You sho' 'bout that? Might be once you learn how, you'll think different."

"That's just it: we won't be us any more, even if it does work. That's something we're afraid of. It goes against every survival instinct of both races."

J J mused on that. "Might be. Honest, we don't rightly understand how you-all think, it bein' so strange to us."

"It's a matter of how we evolved, both physically and culturally. Please take a good, close look and see for yourself. I'll be your example."

J J focussed on me, and I could feel his presence in my mind, measuring my conscious being down to the last detail. It was an awesome, bizarre sensation, one which I can't put into words even now. "Hmph," he grunted at last. "Ah see what you mean. Ah guess we made a mistake tryin' t' change you."

"It's alright, J J," H'rhAtor said. "You meant well."

J J sighed. "Even so, it wasn't right. Ah guess th' only reason ah can give is we ain't never met folks like you befo'; folks that ain't connected."

"There are others who are connected?" I asked in surprise.

"Yeah, they's a few here an' there. Good folk, mostly."

I was momentarily bemused by the thought that there were other undiscovered empathic races in the Universe, not that I

271

should have been surprised. "Then you can see our situation. Please, J J, you have to take these powers away. Put us back like we were before."

J J gave me a skeptical look. "You sure you want this? It won't be easy fo' us to speak with you no more."

"I for one will regret it, J J, but it has to be done."

"Ah guess so." He gave us a winsome smile which filled us with an aura of regret. "Ah sho' gonna miss you-all. Its been an education, right enough, and weah deeply beholdin' to you fo' saving us. Its a shame its gotta be like this, but if that's what yo' want, then so be it."

MacKenna spoke up before he could do anything more. "One thing before you go, J J. What is an inverse cognitive function? You mentioned that when you visited us in my office."

J J gave him a quizzical look. "Well, thas' what we call it. Ah guess you would say if you don't know somethin', ask."

He gave us all a last gentle smile, and vanished. A moment later I felt the *oddest* sensation, as if the entire Universe was imploding in my mind. And then there was silence.

*****

"Epilogue"
(Related by Defender I'eiBida)

So we finally had our war with the humans, and unlike most wars everybody won, except for what the Admiral called 'the Bad Guys'. After Z'keBalf's hard-line faction was discredited, the Chamber Of Ancients shifted—stampeded is the better term—in its position toward earth. That, and the Admiral's stunning victory, undermined the Parliamentary hard-liners in turn. Improved relations between the races lowered tensions and expanded cultural and trade relations. Those little plush figurines became a hit here, too: at least they fixed the tail hem on C'tra's red sequin gown.

Z'keBalf was eventually tried for treason—an historic first—and will spend the rest of his life herding *NmFargs*. It takes one to know one, I suppose. The precious L'datMparn was broken to the ranks and *finally* got the transfer to Supply—records-keeping, no less—he so richly deserved. N'detLeda, of course, was and always will be N'detLeda. He managed to wiggle out from under Z'keBalf's debacle, but his professional reputation was ruined; not that I feel sorry for him. There may be hope for the psychiatric profession yet.

Most of us received fallout from these events, too. M'tinDegan's efforts at the embassy on earth and here on d'enchia were finally recognized when he was made Ki-Learnéd. He recently became Herd First of the vastly expanded Human Studies programs spreading throughout our society.

Poor K'deiTai wound up being confirmed in his appointment to the Chamber of Ancients, which dismayed him no end. I understand his Aide never did forgive him. U'tdaPagrn went back to earth, completed the Third Accord, and eventually became an instructor at the Arbiters' Institute, while H'rhAtor semi-retired, and is now an instructor at the Academy. I pity him.

And as for C'traBenla and me, well, as brief as the crisis was, it qualified me for hazard duty pay, which gave us enough extra for the crèche fees after all.

The End

"Appendix"

"Dramatis Personnae"

Ic'nichi

The Most Ancient retired due to his declining health shortly after the d'enchia Incident, and died a year later.

Ancient Y'veNipbr, che Ae'Kigin retired from the Chamber after the d'enchia Incident, and runs a garden supply shop specializing in earthly plants in her home Nest.

K'deiTai, sen V'ran, first Arbiter-To-Humans, continues to serve in the Chamber-Of-Ancients. He recently released a best-selling book on his experiences on earth, and plans to retire.

Ancient Z'keBalf, mar F'ragDi is now serving a life sentence at a *NmFarg* breeding station in the remote, arid *v'twii'inhhn* Great Nest penal community. He remains a staunch opponent of the humans, although his influence evaporated after his conviction for treason.

G'cetGian, chi B'nevd continued as head of the Arbiters' Service until he died in 277 Common.

U'tdaPagrn, dro Mev'menk served as the second Arbiter on earth Until the completion of the Third Accord. He is now an instructor at the Arbiters' Institute.

V'koBilen, p'chi eRadna, the first Arbiter-To-Humans, died in late 280 Common. His Aide/widow has retired.

M'tinDegan, cro V'menba is now Ki-Learnéd and serves the Chamber by directing the Interstellar Studies programs at major Institutes throughout d'enchia.

Learnéds W'kiLap and *T'apiDien* continue to run a small software business specializing in Ic'nichi-human interfacing products.

N'detLeda, tan E'triin was stripped of his credentials for 'unethical conduct', and ekes out a living as a 'political advisor'.

T'virDoma, ab Clas'nch recently completed her schooling in Human Studies. At last notice, her application to 'Dark Grays' intelligence has been rejected again.

H'rhAtor, tem dre Fradash, first Fleet Eldest of the 'Dark Grays' has retired, and serves as a part time instructor at the Academy. He and his Worthy wrote a book about the Contact Crisis which is due for release shortly.

I'eiBida, fan D'chr and his Worthy have been promoted to First Degree (equal to a naval Captain in human terms) and are assigned to the 'Home Defense' orbital defenses command. They are under consideration for promotion to Ki-.

L'datMparn, tii R'vebb is carried on the 'non-promotable' list, and holds a minor post in 'Dark Grays' logistics.

C'traBenla, rani D'enta authors a regular column on human cultural affairs, gives frequent lectures, and is a fem rights activist. She is still troubled by severe possession syndrome, and undergoes periodic therapy.

The Humans:

Jacek Hogarthy has *finally* retired from politics after first being removed from the cabinet, then not reelected.

Admiral Brian MacKenna, the humans' most experienced war leader, served as Flag, Space Fleet until after the d'enchia Incident. He then retired at age 92, after 75 years in uniform (most of it during the Collapse), and died shortly thereafter.

Captain Loraine Morgan was finally relieved of duty after the d'enchia Incident. She suffered post-traumatic stress from her childhood during the Collapse, and underwent extensive therapy. Her contact with the Dreamsingers had done much to heal her, and she eventually returned to Space Fleet as a staff officer, and retired a few years later.

Captain Ivan Rostokovich commands the Ic'nichi operations liaison office in Singapore. He is believed to be due for promotion to Commodore, and hopes to transfer to fleet duty.

Senior Leftenant Hythe-Morrison served as Admiral MacKenna's aide until the Admiral's retirement. He was promoted to Commander, and now serves on the Space Fleet planning staff.

Senior Lieutenant Night Eagle was promoted to Captain, and continued to command a company of the 5001st Peacekeepers (space marines) until he was killed in a training accident in the Aurora colony.

Agent Pierre Roubidoux, APA, was promoted to Inspector and now lives on d'enchia with his wife and their new daughter. He heads the security office at the human embassy.

J. J. Ballas, was an elderly Blues guitarist known by Captain Morgan when she was a child in the Champaign-Urbana refugee camps during the Collapse. Her memory of him provided the image used by the Dreamsingers to communicate with humans. Further contact with the Dreamsingers has been fleeting and rare.

"Addenda"

Human phrases:

Hash
Uniform insignia.

NINS
Now If Not Sooner.

Short-arm inspection
Military slang for a venereal exam.

Ic'nichi phrases:

An empty egg
A vulgar slang phase meaning to have nothing; comparable to the human term 'we don't have squat'.

Chasing Their Own Tails
Slang term for desertion, incompetence, cowardice.

Egg Testers
Crèche workers who test newly laid eggs for genetic defects, and break the defective eggs with a small hammer, the symbol of their office; referenced as a symbol of fear, similar to the human BoogeyMan.

First Finger
A common slang term among the Ic'nichi, which refers to their four mutually opposed fingers: the highest quality is 'first' (index) finger, followed by 'second', 'third', and finally 'fourth finger'; barely passing. The human equivalent are grades 'A', 'B', 'C', and 'D', respectively.

Go back to the egg
To become senile; to fall asleep from boredom; to become severely drunk.

I'll have his ears
  A euphemism for castration.

The set of his ears
  Refers to the movements of Ic'nichi ears, indicating their emotions; euphemism for secret thoughts.

Uttermost Darkness
  Ic'nichi belief that if their Ancestors judge them unworthy to join their bloodline, they will be cast out of the afterlife, dooming them to the formless void for eternity.

Ic'nichi words:

B'matapur —   A time period relating to an earthly month in the late spring on d'enchia.

b'Ven'gtt' —   A sport similar to team racquetball.

bv'nunma —   A popular light meal similar to tuna salad.

cc'v'renk —   Literally 'dishonored before ones' Ancestors'; acute embarrassment; disgraceful behavior; inability to make a decision; inability to see common sense; slang term for mental retardation.

er'trxxda —   Literally 'haunted by the Ancestors' voices'; obsession; insanity; delusion; raging temper; vulgar habits.

hro'n'nad —   Slang term meaning clueless or ignorant.

l'cc'vn —   A vulgar adjective.

l'fru'ng —   Brazen audacity; annoying habits; body odor.

l'ni'ddi —   A popular fast food similar to stew.

M'mendoch — Literally 'someone who thinks fast'; slang term for a hustler; trying to get out of a hopeless situation; avoiding being cited by the peace wardens for a minor violation.

n'bna'nmn — Slang term for an idiot; a vegetable pie; a bright color.

NmFargs — A food animal noted for their sexual prowess; a person whose sex drive is comically excessive.

p'quas'tka — A particularly vile obscenity.

riv'Agna — *A mythical spirit, similar to the earthly 'demon'.*

r'vebbe — Literally 'to feel one's Ancestors' disapproval'; slang term for being upset, shaken, or spooked by something strange.

'sti'eit — A popular brand of cheap liquor similar to ale, commonly served in service facilities.

TiHiuta — The juice of a small berry commonly used as a recreational drug, chemically similar to Vitamin C in earthly citrus fruit.

t'pithm'ig — A showoff; an immature dandy; a vain person.

tra'taj — A prostitute; a slut; a person lacking scruples.

uf'thoka — A popular vegetarian dish analogous to bean sprouts with a spicy garnish.

ui'DmukNa — Manure; slang term for anything stupidly offensive.

un'brapta — Cruel; heartless; self-centered; arrogant; the odor of unwashed linens.

un'tdar —   A crude, vulgar person; a pig-like animal; bad breath.

V'liz —   A popular beverage containing a mild stimulant, which can be prepared either like coffee or soup.

V'rima —   Bartering; black marketeering; a falsified invoice; con-artistry; seduction; to refuse to pay a debt.

'v'thorble —   Slang term roughly comparable to 'hot rock'.

v'vR gh'vadja —   A district in every major Ic'nichi circle devoted to social activities, shopping, and street carnivals.

V'wit'mo'nop —   A popular card game similar to poker.

x'mnnb' —   Literally 'dead fish'; slang for annoying, stupid behavior; comparable to the human term 'bullshit'.

znm'brVrv —   A month on d'enchia in mid-autumn.

*****

A Brief Note From The Author

Thank you for reading this novel, which is part of my favorite work of my writing. I hope it was a good read for you. I would love to hear from you, my readers, to let me know how I am doing as an author. Every bit of input helps me to make my next effort a better product for your enjoyment.

All my best,

Bob Boyd

You can learn more about me, and keep up to date on my efforts through our Blog:

Facebook.com/The Written Wyrd

*****

Titles from The Written Wyrd
2021-22

The Diplomacy Trilogy - Science fiction humor.
First contact from the aliens' perspective in a trio of lurid tell-all memoirs written by a team of alien diplomats sent to earth to open an embassy.

The MacKenna Trilogy - Science fiction military drama.
He was earth's greatest soldier; they needed his skills once more, but they didn't realize how wrong bringing him back from the dead was.

Nature's Way - Environmental disaster / apocalyptic horror.
This is the last day of our last stand against Nature out for revenge!

Trial - Science fiction political thriller.
The aliens demand justice for their murdered ambassador while right wing extremists plot revolution; which is the greater threat?

Overland - Period science fiction drama / romance.
He was trapped between a beautiful genetically enhanced revolutionary from the distant future and the inhuman monster sent to destroy her. Can he survive caught up in their titanic battle?

Playing God - Apocalyptic horror.
Brenda discovers she is the Dream Girl of a mad scientist capable of altering the past. Can she find a way to undo the disaster he wrought and prevent a nuclear holocaust?

The Big Snow - Environmental disaster / adventure.
A passenger train is wrecked at the top of Donner Pass in the worst storms in recorded history. Can the railroaders get the passengers to safety?

(continued)

Young Adult Demi-Novels:

Diplomacy's Children - YA humor / adventure.
A young alien space fleet recruit faces his greatest challenge in a self-centered, foul-tempered human youngling he is ordered to keep in check.

Star Flight - YA adventure.
She was an outcast, cursed with supernatural powers. She was offered a reprieve, a chance to start over, but could she survive the challenge?

Short Story Anthologies:

Deus Ex Machina - Humorous fantasy short story collection.
From bungling wizards to moronic barbarians to redneck elves, here are the old tales of epic adventure as we would love to see them told - just once.

Ghoulish Good Fun - Macabre short story collection.
Reality is a cruel practical joke. Laugh along with it if you dare!

*****

Available in print and Kindle from Amazon.
Visit our web site for details.

http://www.the-written-wyrd.org/shopping.shtml